Winter
in
Kandahar

STEVEN E. WILSON

HAILEY-GREY BOOKS

Dedicated to my loving wife Jennifer and my wonderful children.
Also dedicated to the innocents of Afghanistan,
may they someday find peace.

First impressions are rarely wrong.
The wise embrace them.

CHAPTER ONE

August 2001

It was an especially harsh day along the Taloqan front line. A biting wind whistled across the rock-strewn wasteland, thrashing everything in its path, as it whipped out of the plains of the Central Asian steppes. The blend of freezing temperature and icy drizzle chilled the bones.

Dwindling and dispirited Northern Alliance fighters were engaged in a desperate death struggle with advancing, extremist Taliban forces. The main line of conflict was a crucial high mountain pass to the west of the ancient city in the northeastern corner of Afghanistan. The majestic Hindu Kush mountain range dominated the barren landscape to the south and east of the narrow pass that was now the focus of a seesaw struggle between doggedly bitter enemies.

A haggard youth, with black curly hair and a close-cropped beard, crouched on his knees with the parts of a Kalashnikov AK-47 rifle disassembled before him on a worn blanket. He scraped at the breach with an oily rag impaled on the tip of a knife with hands covered by tattered, woolen gloves. A solitary teardrop cascaded from beneath a lock of hair that hung down over his drawn face.

An older man stepped up into the bunker and glanced toward the youth. Burhanuddin Jan set his cup of green tea on the wall and lifted the boyish fighter from the ground. He brushed the hair away from the youth's black eyes and clinched him hard against his chest. They spoke in the Persian-Dari language of the Tajiks.

"Ahmed, Allah will greatly bless those who suffer in his name."

The youth turned his head and wiped away the tears with his forearm. Burhanuddin grasped his chin and held his gaze.

"Ahmed, there's no shame in mourning. There's only disgrace for the man who does not honor his father's memory."

"Uncle, I feel death's heavy breath upon me. My heart cries out. There's no escape from this never-ending war. Once our family numbered more than the poppies in the meadow in springtime. Now we are but two. Is there no other purpose in life than to kill and be killed? Our home will never again see more than grief and pain and death."

Burhanuddin wrapped a brawny arm around his nephew's shoulders.

"This is not the purpose for our existence Ahmed."

Burhanuddin turned to scan the valley below. The hillside dropped off precipitously to a treeless gorge. The pass was littered with the rusting hulks of old tanks, personnel carriers, and other implements of battle. Many had lain unmoved for decades, forgotten vestiges of war long ended. Others were the spearhead of a desperate Taliban assault only the week before. One tank bore the charred body of a fighter who'd sacrificed his life fighting to wrest control of the pass from the Northern Alliance forces.

"Ahmed, our people lived and died in this place for a thousand years. The fathers of our fathers were farmers who cherished the land. They bore children on this land and their children bore children on this land. They worked the land and valued the words of the great prophet. *That* was the purpose for existence."

Burhanuddin paused and sipped tea from a cup. He peered down at his nephew.

"Then came the armies of the Great Alexander and the murdering hordes of Genghis Khan. One invader after another followed them. The savages raped our women, stole our land, and gave birth to the enemy Pashtun. Pashtun dogs have murdered our people and stolen Tajik land for more generations than the holy man can fathom. Your father was a warrior and his father was a warrior. We carry on the good fight to preserve the Tajik way of life."

Burhanuddin picked up a pair of binoculars. He scanned across the pass below and out to the horizon. He panned down to the men in an advance bunker positioned several kilometers to the southwest. All was quiet. He set down the binoculars and sipped from his cup.

"Many invaders have sought to steal our land. The Russians followed the British. These were only the latest. Many Tajik Mujaheddin died driving the infidels from this land."

Burhanuddin slid his hand into the inside pocket of his wool coat and retrieved a cigarette butt. He stuck the butt in the corner of his mouth, turned away from the wind, and struck a match between his cupped hands. He took a deep drag on the cigarette and blew out a cloud of smoke. The wind whipped out of the bunker in an instant.

"Now we fight the Taliban. They're nothing more than Pashtun dogs with a new name. We must always fight the Pashtun..." Burhanuddin took another drag from his cigarette. He gathered his coat and gazed toward the morning sun rising from behind the soaring peaks of the Hindu Kush. "Until the last one is dead."

Ahmed looked up at his uncle's leathery face. Burhanuddin's dark eyes were like hardened steel; his prominent aquiline nose a badge of family honor. Deep furrows ran across his face. They marked the years of struggle like the rings of a tree. His scraggly beard was black with a sprinkling of gray, as was the hair beneath his woolen hat.

Ahmed checked the action on his rifle and finally shoved in a full magazine. He looked up at his uncle.

"I long for the day that we—"

Burhanuddin raised his hand and peered out toward the mouth of the pass. For several seconds there was only quiet. Suddenly, the silence was pierced by the whoosh of jet engines. A dozen Taliban SU-22 and MIG jets were upon them in an instant.

Burhanuddin dove across the bunker to a heavy machine-gun emplacement. He crouched to his knees and sprayed a line of tracer fire into the path of the strafing jets. A chorus of Alliance machine guns joined in. Together, they threw up a barrage of steel. Ahmed knelt behind the bunker wall and balanced his AK-47 within a firing breach.

A five hundred-pound bomb whistled toward the ground. It made a direct hit on an artillery piece positioned just up the hillside. The gun and six men disappeared in a thunderous blast that scattered debris for a hundred meters. The concussion threw Ahmed to the ground and triggered a rockslide far up the embankment. Ahmed struggled to his feet just in time to duck beneath a mammoth boulder that pulverized the bunker wall. The rock rumbled down the incline and crashed into a command center far below. The roof caved in under the force of the impact. Muffled screams echoed above the din of battle.

Ahmed jumped behind the heavy machine gun. A line of tracers erupted from the muzzle, as yet another formation of jets streaked across the Alliance positions. They strafed the hillside with cannon fire and vanished into the east.

A telltale cloud of dust, accompanied by the grinding treads of tanks, appeared on the western horizon. Burhanuddin stumbled to his feet and peered toward the attacking forces through his binoculars.

A Mujaheddin fighter jogged to the entrance of the bunker. He bent over to catch his wind and breathlessly called out to Burhanuddin.

"Commander Jan, the radio's been knocked out. What are your orders, sir?"

"Haji, tell the men to hold their positions and fight. A red flare will signal my order to retreat to the east. Tell the men to concentrate fire on the tank commanders. Hurry!"

The messenger disappeared as quickly as he came.

Four Russian-era helicopters swooped down over the hilltop behind the Tajik positions. One helicopter, machine guns blazing, turned in a tight circle above the rocky hillside and launched two missiles. The rockets exploded into a line of artillery, launching debris high into the air. A trail of bullets from another helicopter climbed the hill to the base of the wall directly in front of Ahmed and tracked through the adjoining bunker. Half a dozen Tajik fighters died in the blink of an eye.

One helicopter banked to the right, away from the bunker-covered hillside. A handheld missile streaked across the early-morning sky and detonated into the fuselage. The aircraft exploded into pieces and fiery remnants cascaded to the valley floor below.

Ahmed rushed headlong to the other side of the bunker. He crouched behind the wall with the gun barrel protruding through a breach. Burhanuddin swiveled the barrel of the heavy machine gun toward the mouth of the canyon where more than fifty tanks and armored vehicles were advancing up the pass.

Ahmed grabbed the binoculars and pressed them to his eyes. Hundreds of foot soldiers carrying Kalashnikov rifles and rocket-propelled grenades were tailing behind the first line of tanks. A round of Alliance artillery landed amongst the Taliban. The explosion blew a hole in the disorganized formation. The ranks closed within moments and the army pressed forward.

The first Taliban tanks were within five hundred meters of the forward Tajik position. As if on cue, the hillside erupted in a conflagration let loose from the Northern Alliance bunkers. Bullets and grenades shredded through the Taliban lines. Still, the dust-shrouded throng of men and machines pushed onward up the pass.

The advancing tanks began to rain shells on the Alliance bunkers. One shell exploded directly below Ahmed in a pocket of Alliance fighters on the valley floor. An Alliance battery unleashed a concentrated salvo of artillery. One shell made a direct hit on a Taliban tank. The explosion sent the turret and gun spinning into the air.

A sense of calm enveloped Ahmed. He peered across the valley at the swarming Taliban hordes. He set the binoculars on the wall and crouched to take aim. He trained his gun sight on a sprinting Taliban foot soldier, but the man ducked behind a boulder along the side of the road. Ahmed waited, finger on the trigger, for the man to move. He squeezed off a burst from the rifle the instant the Taliban warrior leapt from behind the rock. The bullets ripped through the fighter's chest, and he crumbled to the ground. Ahmed lined up another black-turbaned fighter and fired again.

Another formation of Taliban jets emerged from behind the cliffs on the opposite side of the valley. The planes streaked across the gorge toward the Northern Alliance positions on the southern wall. A cluster of bombs dropped among the hillside bunkers to the south with characteristic dull, thudding concussions.

Another missile streaked skyward. It tore the wing off one of the tailing jets and set the plane spinning out of control. The stricken aircraft burst into flames and thundered into the hillside.

The tanks at the front of the Taliban line hastened their advance up the barren valley, weaving in and out of the hulks of other vehicles destroyed in countless prior attacks. The first tank emerged through the maze of obstacles. It raced forward with its gun turned toward the hillside, firing one shell after another at the Alliance bunkers. A thunderous mine explosion launched the tank into the air. It fell on its side in a smoldering heap, blocking the progress of the trailing tanks.

A squad of Tajik Mujaheddin jumped up from behind a rock formation in the midst of the tanks. Several were cut down in a hail of machine-gun fire. Three of the Tajiks launched their rockets — two more tanks exploded into balls of fire.

A tailing tank rammed into the underside of the wreck attempting to clear the flaming hulk from the road. Ahmed took aim at the commander with his Kalashnikov. At that instant, a shell made a direct hit on the wall of the bunker. The blast hurled Ahmed to the ground. He rolled over and pushed himself to his knees.

"Uncle!" he gasped.

Burhanuddin was lying on his back peering skyward behind the heavy machine gun. Blood poured from a wound in his side. He managed a weak groan.

Ahmed turned just in time to glimpse a Taliban warrior scrambling around a rock outside the bunker. The young warrior raised the barrel of his rifle and pulled the trigger. It jammed. Ahmed leapt toward his own weapon and aimed to fire. The Taliban fighter raised his arms. He gawked in disbelief.

"Ahmed," the man uttered.

"Khan!" Ahmed whispered, as he held his weapon on the lone figure.

It seemed like time stood still, as the two young men stared at each other and the battle raged in the pass below.

A burst of heavy machine gun fire tore through the young man's chest. Ahmed whirled to his right. Burhanuddin was crouched behind the machine gun. He pumped round after round into the young man, as he tumbled backward down the hillside. Burhanuddin grimaced.

"No Pashtun prisoners!"

Burhanuddin slumped toward the ground. Ahmed leapt to his uncle's side and cradled his head in his lap.

"Uncle, this was Khan from Taloqan."

"He dressed as Pashtun. He fought as Pashtun. He was Pashtun. No Pashtun prisoners."

Burhanuddin stared into Ahmed's eyes. The old man managed a weak smile.

"Ahmed, bring honor to your father's name."

Burhanuddin grasped Ahmed's arm and slumped in death. Ahmed pulled his uncle against his chest and cried out with grief.

A tank shell exploded just outside the bunker with a thunderous clap. Ahmed rose to his knees and peered out over the wall to the pass below. The lead Taliban tank was still trapped behind the flaming hulk. It crashed into the underside and sent the smoking carcass tumbling over an embankment, clearing the road up the pass.

Ahmed picked up his AK-47 and leaped over the bunker wall. He charged headlong down the rugged hillside, screaming in a blind rage.

The leader of a group of Taliban fighters spotted Ahmed streaking down the hill. He pointed his gun and fired. Bullets ricocheted off the rocks around Ahmed's feet. An Alliance machine gun opened fire and cut the Taliban fighter down.

Ahmed sprinted to the road fifty meters from the first cluster of Taliban tanks. The commander of the lead tank spotted Ahmed and turned his machine gun to fire. A burst from Ahmed's rifle struck the man down.

Ahmed tossed his AK-47 to the ground and snatched an anti-tank rocket launcher from the hands of a fallen comrade. He sprinted toward the lead tank, knelt to one knee behind a rock, and trained the sight on the charging behemoth. He fired. The rocked streaked across the pass and exploded into the turret of the lead tank, just as a burst of machine gun fire ripped through Ahmed's shoulder.

Another squad of Alliance fighters carrying anti-tank rockets fanned out from behind a formation of rocks at the bottom of the pass. They trained their sights on the Taliban formation. Three more tanks exploded into flames and billowed black smoke.

The surviving Taliban armor began a headlong retreat down the pass. Hundreds of foot soldiers fled after them in confused disarray. Some of the black-turbaned fighters cast their weapons to the ground, as they ran away in terror.

Alliance Mujaheddin in the hillside bunkers stood in unison and shouted in mocking derision. They trained their guns on the fleeing Taliban fighters and unleashed a withering fire that cut the Taliban to pieces. A succession of explosions marked the destruction of one enemy tank after another.

The Taliban retreat lasted for more than an hour. Finally, the valley floor grew silent.

CHAPTER TWO

Two weeks later, September 9, 2001

A hmed, his arm in a sling, trotted up to the guard station at the Khoje Bahauddin base along the Amu Dar'ya River and dismounted his horse. It was the third checkpoint he'd approached in the last kilometer of his journey through the heart of the Northern Alliance stronghold. One of the guards approached, as the other stood behind a wall with his Kalashnikov rifle at the ready.

"What is your purpose?" the sentry barked gruffly.

"I'm ordered to report to commander Massoud."

"Identification."

Ahmed handed the man his papers, including the letter from Ahmed Shah Massoud himself. He scanned across the single-story brick and earth buildings that made up the Northern Alliance headquarters while the guard sorted through them.

The small northern province garrison was buzzing with activity. Dozens of men were resting on benches in front of what appeared to be a field hospital at one end of the square. Some wore bandages on their heads. Others were using crutches to get around. Alliance Mujaheddin sentries with Kalashnikov rifles were posted throughout the headquarters complex. Dozens of men crisscrossed the street in every direction.

The guard looked up from the papers.

"You're Ahmed Jan? Commander Jan's son?"

"Yes."

The guard's attitude changed immediately.

"It is an honor to meet you Ahmed Jan. I never imagined the hero of Taloqan would be so young."

The guard handed Ahmed back his identification.

"I must examine your belongings, sir. Get them down from the horse."

"Of course. Where do you want them?"

"Here, let me help you."

The guard untied Ahmed's backpack and blanket from the horse's back and set them on the table. He opened each of the pockets in the backpack in turn. Then he sifted through Ahmed's clothing and supplies before unrolling the blanket. Once the guard was satisfied, he pushed the backpack and blanket across the table and stepped around the end.

"I must examine your bandage and sling, sir."

"Okay, that's fine with me."

Ahmed held up his arm, while the guard searched the sling and pressed on the bandage from his elbow to his shoulder.

"Okay, you can go, sir. Leave your rifle here. It will be returned when you leave. That's Commander Massoud's office there behind the Northern Alliance flag. Do you need help putting these back on the horse?"

"No. I'm fine."

Ahmed pulled his Kalashnikov down from his horse and set it on the table. He rolled the blanket with one hand and began securing it on his horse. As he was fumbling with the rope, a pickup truck rumbled up behind him on the dirt road and screeched to a stop at the checkpoint. A man jumped out of the cab on the passenger side and strode toward the guard.

"Mohammed, how goes it?"

"Shah, my friend. What are you doing here?"

"I brought the Islamic Information Center reporters to interview Commander Massoud. Here's the paperwork and their passports."

The guard looked through the paperwork and peered toward the truck. There were two dark-skinned men with white turbans sitting in the cab.

"Belgian passports? Why are they traveling on Belgian passports?"

"I don't know. I was told the commander's interpreter had arranged this interview. I just brought them here."

"Have them bring their belongings and put them on the table."

"What about the television camera?"

"I need to see everything. Have them put it all on the table. Open up the hood of your truck."

Shah ambled back to the truck. The sentry turned toward the guard shack and spotted Ahmed Jan sitting on his horse in front of the gate. He inserted a key and turned a switch. The barrier opened just wide enough for Ahmed's horse to pass. It clanged closed behind him, as the sentry called after him.

"May Allah bless you, Ahmed Jan!"

Ahmed rode into the square and tied his horse to a post in front of the command building. He walked up the dirt path and through the open door. There were two men with Kalashnikov rifles standing on either side of an inner door in the back of the room. Another man wearing a white turban was sitting at the desk. He looked up from his work.

"Yes?"

"My name is Ahmed Jan. I was ordered to report to Commander Massoud."

The man practically leapt out of his seat. He rushed around the desk and gave Ahmed a bear hug.

"Of course! He's been expecting you, Ahmed Jan. My name is Asem. Let me express my personal sorrow over the death of your uncle Burhanuddin. He was a good friend and a great commander."

The inner door burst open behind them.

A wiry man in a tan tunic wearing a jaunty pakool hat pushed back on his head stepped out of the room. He had dark expressive eyes with vertical creases above his nose and crow's-feet at the temples. His black hair and beard were peppered with gray. He grinned broadly and wrapped his arm around Ahmed.

"Ahmed Jan! Let me look at you. You were just a boy the last time I saw you. You look just like your father!"

Ahmed smiled.

"He had the greatest respect for you, Commander."

"Ahh, he was a great friend. I think of him often. And now we've lost Burhanuddin."

Massoud shook his head mournfully, as he grasped Ahmed by the shoulders.

"That's why I sent for you, Ahmed. I want to give you my personal condolences and express our appreciation for the great sacrifice your family has made for the Tajik people."

"Thank you, Commander. It means a lot to hear it from you."

Massoud motioned toward the sling.

"I have heard of your courage in the battle for Taloqan. It is already legend among our men. How's the arm coming?"

"It's getting better. The doctor told me to wear this sling for three weeks. I've just about had enough of it."

"I'm happy to see you getting around so well. Your father and uncle were both master chess players. Do you play?"

"I haven't played for several years, but we played all the time when I was a boy."

"I know a chess player when I see one. How about a quick game?"

Massoud showed Ahmed into his office. The windowless walls were lined with maps of Afghanistan with labels indicating forces. A small wooden desk sat near the back. To one side there was a small table with a chessboard and pieces of carved black and white stone. Massoud motioned to one of the chairs and sat down in the other.

"You move first."

Ahmed advanced his white queen's pawn two squares. Massoud smiled. He advanced his black pawn to match and the game was on. It didn't take long for Massoud to get the upper hand. Ahmed found himself in checkmate ten minutes later. Massoud clasped his hands and chuckled with glee.

"You even play the Russian style of your father."

There was a light knock on the door.

"Yes!"

The door creaked opened. It was Asem.

"Commander, the Moroccan reporters are here to film the documentary."

"Tell them I'll be with them in just a minute, Asem."

"Yes, sir."

Asem closed the door. Commander Massoud stood up behind the chess-board and walked to a bookshelf on one side of the room. He pulled a black-covered book down from the top shelf.

"Ahmed, I wish I had more time to chat, but it's important to keep the outside world informed about our struggle against the Taliban. I also asked you to come today to tell you myself about your promotion. You will assume command of your uncle's forces immediately."

Ahmed flinched with surprise.

"It's is a great honor, Commander. But I'm a young man. Surely there are others in our clan who are better prepared to lead."

"Nonsense, you are ready, Ahmed Jan. Many of my best commanders are young men. Young men take chances and are not paralyzed by the uncertainties of the old. You have the support of Mullah Habid and the men. You are my choice."

"Thank you, Commander. I hope I'm worthy of your faith in me."
Massoud handed Ahmed the book.

"I want you to have this, Ahmed. Do you know the great fourteenth-century Iranian poet Shamsoddin Khaja Mohammad Hafez?"

"No, Commander. I've had no time for poetry."

"No poetry! A man must always find time for poetry, Ahmed Jan. Even when the battle rages all around you, there must be time for poetry. Without poetry, there can be no love."

"There hasn't been time for love either, Commander."

Massoud expression became forlorn. He shook his head.

"I pray that will change one day, Ahmed. Hafez wrote 'When you have met your desired one, bid farewell to the world and let it go.' Always remember this, Ahmed Jan. Mark my words. You will find your desired one somewhere along your journey."

"Thank you, Commander. That is truly a day I look forward to."

Massoud patted Ahmed on the back and walked him to the door. He opened it.

"Take care my friend. Let me know if there is anything I can do to help you. You will be in my prayers."

Ahmed strode into the foyer. Two Afghani men were standing talking to Asem. One of them held a small video camera. Two Arabic men sat in chairs next to Asem. They both looked up as Ahmed exited the office. One of them had deep-set black eyes with bushy eyebrows. He was wearing an Islamic cap. There was a large television camera sitting on the floor beside him. Something about the man made Ahmed uneasy. He looked away and headed for the door. Asem called out after him.

"Ahmed Jan, may Allah bless you greatly!"

"Thank you, Asem. Take care of our dear boss."

Ahmed strode down the walk to his horse. He opened one of the pockets on his backpack and stuffed the book of poetry the commander gave him inside. He mounted the horse and turned toward the entrance to the compound.

A tremendous explosion erupted from within Commander Massoud's office building. A cloud of debris billowed from the front door. Hundreds of papers fluttered in the air across the complex grounds.

Ahmed's horse reared and threw him to the ground. In an instant, dozens of men came running toward the building from all across the complex. One of the Moroccan men sprinted through the door from Massoud's office and into the yard. A bodyguard ran out the door a few steps behind him. The guard stopped, raised his Kalashnikov, and cut the fleeing man down with a burst of rifle fire.

Ahmed sprinted for the door. The outer office was totally demolished. The other guard and Asem lay on the floor against the outside wall. Both of them were dead.

There was a gaping hole in the wall that once stood between Massoud's inner office and the reception area. Ahmed rushed through the void with two other fighters. Commander Massoud's body was lying in a pool of blood in the back of the room. His face, chest, and legs were riddled with shrapnel. Both of the Afghani men who'd been waiting in the office were lying against the sidewall. One lay motionless. He was bleeding from his legs and face. The other was sitting up and had burns across his arms and neck. Ahmed glanced around for the other Arabic reporter. He spotted what appeared to be a pair of mangled legs lying across the room beneath the bookshelf. Dozens of books were scattered across the floor around the limbs. There was no sign of the rest of the body.

One of the fighters knelt beside the commander and pressed his fingers against his neck. He turned toward the others with a look of anguish.

"The Lion of Panjshir is dead. We are lost."

CHAPTER THREE

Kabul three months later, December 7, 2001

It was a quiet late afternoon in Kabul. From time-to-time one heard the screech of American fighter planes arcing high above the city or the thudding concussion of the bombs they dropped on Taliban targets. These sounds of war had become more and more distant over the previous weeks, as the Taliban fled to the south.

Two men in traditional Afghani dress sat waiting in a darkened room lit by a single flickering kerosene lantern. A small fire crackled in the back corner. The air was smoky, with an odor that smelled of mildew. The accommodations were simple; there was a lantern and a teapot on a wooden crate. An assortment of tattered rugs and quilts lay on the dirt floor. Several rocket-propelled grenade launchers and rifles were stacked against the wall in one corner of the room.

"Tea, Mullah?"

The old cleric nodded and Osman filled his cup.

The mullah was sitting on the floor next to the crate. Short in stature, he had earned his position through fierce determination and loyalty to his people. His face was heavily furrowed with the lines of the seventy-one years he had endured this merciless land. His left arm, long ago twisted by polio, hung limply at his side.

"Osman, is there news from Kandahar?"

"No, nothing, Mullah. There is fighting between United Forces and scattered groups of Taliban in the mountains above the city. There are rumors Mullah Omar is among them. No one has news of bin Laden. There's a report he crossed into Pakistan, but I heard another rumor he's fled to Yemen. Two Arabs were discovered in the back of a truck attempting to cross over to

Pakistan on the road to Islamabad. Habeel interrogated both of them yesterday. He is bringing the report with him. Perhaps he knows something more."

"Omar must be found. Afghanistan will never find peace as long as the one-eyed jackal lives."

"We will find him, Mullah. There are many caves in the mountains where he can hide. But we will find him. It is only a matter of time."

The drape over the door opened and two men dressed in wool coats ducked into the room. They brushed the snow from their gloves and woolen over-garments.

"Welcome my sons," the mullah called out. "Warm yourselves near the fire. Only young men are fit for travel in such weather. Osman, pour our guests tea."

"Allah's blessing, Mullah Habid. The snow has come early to the North this year. But the roads are still passable. It is good to be here with you in Kabul."

The mullah nodded.

"Hopefully, it is only a brief storm and we will enjoy a spell of mild weather before the winter arrives for good. It's too early for the bitter cold to endure. At least that is my prayer."

The visitor put his arm around the younger man and shuffled him forward.

"Mullah Habid, I have brought Ahmed Jan."

Mullah Habid laughed with a toothless smile. He embraced the young man with his good arm.

"Ahmed Jan. You are the image of your father. I knew your father and uncle well, my son. They were great men. They will long be remembered as men of honor and dedication to their people. I owe my very life to your father. He surely has a place of highest honor in paradise."

Ahmed bowed his head.

"My father spoke of you many times, Mullah Habid. I am your servant."

"I heard about your heroism in the battle for Taloqan, my son."

"I did only what any man would've done. It was only a fleeting victory. The Talaban forces overran our positions three weeks later."

"But the Mujaheddin will long remember your valor, Ahmed. Please, make yourself comfortable. I'm afraid we only have naan and a little dried meat to eat."

Ahmed sat on a carpet in front of the mullah. Osman set a cup in front of him and filled it with black tea.

"Habeel," the mullah began, "Osman told me of the Arabs captured near Kandahar."

"I finished their interrogation yesterday. They were al-Qaida. Mullah Omar and other Taliban leaders are among those hiding in the mountains north of Kandahar. There is no word of bin Laden or other al-Qaida leaders. The strength of the remaining Taliban forces is estimated to be ten thousand. These include Arabs, Chechens, and Pakistanis. Most of the others have escaped to the northern Pakistani tribal territories."

"What happened to these Arabs?"

"They are dead."

Mullah Habid nodded. "The Americans have already begun to lose interest. Now Tajik, Uzbek, Hazara, and Pashtun sit together in the new Council of Afghanistan. But it is only a matter of time before ancient rivalries that have plagued this country re-emerge. We must find the instigators and punish them, along with the Arabs and Pakistanis who supported the Taliban murderers."

"Mullah Habid, killing Taliban is ever our goal."

"Ahmed Jan, have you now joined Habeel and the southern forces of the United Front?"

Ahmed glanced at Habeel. Habeel nodded.

"Mullah, Ahmed Jan has uncovered evidence of a new threat to our people."

The mullah's expression did not change. He leaned forward and picked up his teacup. He took a sip and set the cup back down. He picked up his useless left arm and returned it to his lap. Finally, he stroked his beard with his right hand.

"Tell me, Ahmed Jan, what is this new threat?"

Ahmed bowed his head.

"Mullah Habid, I will tell you all I know. I was taken prisoner by the Taliban two months ago when our positions near Taloqan were overrun. I was transported to a Taliban camp south of Kabul with several other Tajik prisoners. We were beaten and starved for weeks. One of the men broke under torture. He told them I was the son of Commander Jan. The Taliban interrogators held my hand over fire for sport."

Ahmed held out his left arm. The hand was white with contracted scars that webbed his fingers together. All of the fingernails were gone. Three of the fingers were amputated at the tips.

The mullah reached out and gently touched Ahmed's scarred hand.

"Savages," he seethed.

"I told them about the American agents who came to Taloqan. I told them about the new Russian weapons."

Ahmed bowed his head in shame.

"I would have told them anything."

The mullah reached out and rested his hand on Ahmed's arm.

"So would any man, my son. So would any man."

"They brought in a young Arab during my interrogation. He was captured on the road outside of Kabul in a car filled with al-Qaida documents. The Taliban fighters were enraged at al-Qaida for bringing the wrath of the Americans against them. They tortured the Arab and hung him from a hook in the ceiling. American soldiers attacked the Taliban outpost a week later. They slaughtered more than fifty Taliban fighters. They probably would have killed me too, but the American soldiers had a Tajik translator with them. He knew my name. The Americans took everything from the headquarters. They boxed up documents, computers — everything. They let me go just before they blew up the compound. I had only the clothes on my back and a coat I took from the compound."

"What is this threat to our people?"

"Two weeks ago a seam on this coat began to unravel. Right here," he said, pointing to a front panel. "I found these papers hidden in the lining."

Ahmed unfolded two manila pages and handed them to the mullah. The mullah looked at them and shook his head.

"It's Arabic."

"Yes, the coat must have belonged to the young Arab. I attended school for four years in Saudi Arabia when I was younger. The document is difficult to grasp. It is filled with propaganda."

He pointed to the middle of one of the pages.

"Here it speaks of a new weapon. In this paragraph it says the weapon will be transported to Venice during Carnevale."

"What is this weapon?"

"There is no specific information. But the letter contains the Arabic word for pestilence in several places."

"Does it say where the weapon will come from?"

"No, there's no mention of anything except the Hotel Danielli in Venice."

"Could it be the pox?"

"It doesn't say. But it is this second page that deeply troubles me."

He leaned over and pointed to the middle of the second page.

"It outlines plans to spread the pestilence in Panjshir."

The mullah stared into Ahmed's dark, intense eyes. He took the papers and held them up.

"Who else knows of this?"

"I brought this to Habeel yesterday. He was my father's friend. I trust him alone. I have not shown them to anyone else."

"Mention this to no man, Ahmed Jan. Leave me now, I must pray. Remain here among us. We will speak again before the sun sets."

With that Ahmed and Habeel stood. They bowed and ducked through the drape into the courtyard.

The compound was little more than a pile of rocks and mud-walled huts. Most of the structures had been blasted apart by one thousand and two thousand-pound bombs dropped by the Americans shortly before the Northern Alliance returned to Kabul. Habeel guided Ahmed to an area of the compound where a single hut remained standing. The door was a blanket held up by splinters of wood from one of the bombed-out structures. There were embers in a fire ring on the floor. Habeel picked up two blankets and handed them to Ahmed.

"Sleep here where it is warm. I will wake you when Mullah Habid calls."

"Thank you, Habeel."

"Get some sleep, Ahmed Jan. I will have my men take you home to Panjshir tomorrow. Your family will be overjoyed to see you."

Ahmed bowed his head and sighed.

"I have no family left, Habeel. I'm the only one now."

Habeel's face contorted in disbelief.

"Allah forgive me. I did not know. Allah's blessing upon you, Ahmed Jan."

Habeel turned and ducked beneath the blanket. Ahmed cleared a spot on the ground near the fire, covered himself with the blankets, and fell into a deep sleep.

Ahmed was startled awake by a shake of his forearm. It was Habeel. Ahmed glanced at his watch. It was nearly five in the afternoon.

"Mullah Habid will see you now, Ahmed."

It was dusk outside and the snow had nearly stopped. There was only a dusting of white on the ground, but the whirling wind blew stinging flakes against Ahmed's face. His skin was red and chafed from the cold.

Ahmed followed Habeel back to the single-room mud hut. They ducked through the door. Mullah Habid was sitting in the same spot. A dozen Afghani men were scattered around the room. The mullah motioned Ahmed to a spot on the ground in front of him.

"Ahmed Jan, we must follow the guidance of Allah. His hand brought this message to you. You are the chosen one."

"What would you have me do, Mullah Habid?"

"The Taliban will stop at nothing to destroy the Tajik people, my son. We must seize this pestilence and use it to teach the enemy a lesson they will not soon forget."

The mullah stood. He paced back and forth across the small room several times, while the men around him sat in silence. He finally spoke out to the group.

"Our options are limited. We will not put our faith in the Americans. They're consumed with their own concerns. We will send Ahmed Jan to snatch this weapon from the hands of the enemy. We will give him whatever support he needs to accomplish it."

The mullah scanned slowly around the darkened room. Each man nodded in turn.

"We know only a time and a place. We cannot risk diversion and arrival by some other route. Ahmed, you will seize the weapon in Venice."

The mullah continued to pace the room for several moments. He was deep in thought. Finally, he stopped and turned toward Ahmed.

"Ahmed Jan, you studied medicine in Saudi Arabia. Am I right?"

"Yes, Mullah. I studied at the King Khalid National Guard Hospital in Jeddah."

"You know smallpox? You know anthrax?"

"Yes. I know these diseases. But I am not an expert."

"You are an expert among the Tajik people, Ahmed Jan. Allah prepared you to serve your people."

"I am Allah's servant, Mullah."

Mullah Habid placed his hand on Ahmed's head.

"Our men will deliver you through the Khyber Pass to Islamabad. The other routes are choked with snow."

The mullah shook his index finger.

"And the enemy will not expect you in Khyber."

The mullah handed Ahmed several papers and a passport.

"These documents will identify you as a diplomat of the Afghani Council assigned to the Netherlands. Your Afghani passport is also there. Amsterdam will be your base. Many of our countrymen have lived there since the Russian invasion. This paper has the name and phone number of your contact in Amsterdam. Hide it carefully."

Mullah Habid turned and pointed toward the corner of the room.

"This is Mustafa and this is Mohammajon."

The two men nodded without speaking. They were both wearing heavy wool Afghani jackets. Mustafa had black hair and black eyes with a prominent mustache, but no beard. He wore a bandoleer of ammunition diagonally across his chest. Ahmed guessed his age at thirty. Mohammajon was much older. Salt and pepper hair tumbled from beneath his pakool cap. His long, gray beard only partially hid a pockmarked face.

"Mustafa and Mohammajon will accompany you to Amsterdam. Mohammajon is a member of the Panjshir council and will advise you on my behalf. If at any point you encounter the Americans, identify yourself as Alliance fighters and use the phrase 'It may be a long wait for the springtime.' Do you understand?"

He paused for a moment to assess the impact of his words on the young Tajik. Ahmed's expression did not change.

"I will do my best, Mullah Habid."

"Our communications cannot be trusted, Ahmed Jan. You will decide among you about what course to take until you arrive in Amsterdam. I expect you to confer on any decision before proceeding, but Ahmed Jan will have the final say. Is that understood?"

He stared at Mustafa and Mohammajon. They both nodded their heads.

"I pray Allah gives you the wisdom to make the right choices. If the contraband does not arrive in Venice at the expected time, or the enemy eludes you, then my standing order is for you to inform the Americans immediately. If that happens, tell them everything."

The old man stroked his long beard and then reached out and tapped Ahmed on the shoulder.

"Mustafa will lead the men until you get to Islamabad. Mustafa and Mohammajon will help you in every way they can to carry out your mission. The other men will return to Kabul once you reach Islamabad. Do you understand, my son?"

"Yes, I understand, Mullah."

"One more thing. Mustafa has the funds you need for bribes, supplies, and horses to get you to Islamabad. There should also be sufficient money to travel from Islamabad to Amsterdam. If not, or if anything unexpected happens, you are to use this credit card."

Ahmed took the card and turned it over. His name was embossed on the front. Ahmed slipped the card into his pocket.

"How did you obtain this so quickly?"

"We have our ways. Hide the card in a safe place."

"I will, Mullah."

"Go now, Ahmed Jan. There is no time to waste. May Allah be with you."

Chapter Four

Heavy snow was falling. At another time and place the flurry would have been beautiful. But the wind and cold would only serve to make the journey to Islamabad even more treacherous. Ahmed wrapped a tattered woolen scarf around his neck.

He crouched in the courtyard and began to gather his belongings. He didn't have much. His only possessions were the clothes on his back, the Kalashnikov AK-47 rifle, and a backpack with half a loaf of naan, a rusty old knife, a few photographs, a spare pair of worn boots, and a book of poetry.

Ahmed slipped his arms out of his old black coat. He fetched the papers he'd shown the mullah and the papers the holy man had given him. He meticulously folded each paper into a small square. There were five in total. Ahmed took the paper squares and the Visa card and slipped them back through the separated seam and deep into the wool fibers that lined the coat.

Ahmed unfastened the main flap on his backpack. He sorted through the inside compartment until he found a small tin. He opened the tin and carefully withdrew a needle from a piece of cloth. The tin also contained a rectangle of cardboard wrapped with strands of black, green, white, and blue thread. He threaded the needle with the black thread and carefully mended the coat seam.

Ahmed lifted the coat and carefully inspected the seam. The repair was nearly undetectable. Satisfied, he put the needle and thread back in the tin and slipped it into his backpack.

Ahmed looked up at the sound of footsteps crunching on the snow. It was Mustafa. He was carrying a metal container about the size of a shoebox. He tossed the box down on the ground next to Ahmed.

"We rest now and leave after midnight. There are enemy eyes and ears everywhere in Kabul. We travel only under cover of darkness. Store as much ammunition as you can in your pack. You will have only what you can carry."

Ahmed looked up from his backpack at the Mujaheddin. Mustafa had a youthful look, but the piercing dark eyes and humorless face betrayed a lifetime of hardship. The struggle had robbed him of his childhood. He'd learned to stalk the enemy when most boys concerned themselves with hide and seek, soccer, and other innocent pursuits of youth.

"How will we travel?"

"We will ride by truck from Kabul to Jalalabad. The road is now in Northern Alliance hands and patrolled by the American jets. We have an identification beacon from the Americans. Its signal will identify us as Northern Alliance. Most of the mines were removed by British troops, but there is still great risk."

He squatted in front of Ahmed.

"From Jalalabad we will travel to the east of Peshawar. This will be the most dangerous part of our journey. There are many pockets of Taliban and al-Qaida scattered along the Khyber Pass. They hide there from the Americans and British. We will try to buy horses in Jalalabad, if there are any available. If not, we will carry what we can on our backs. We should reach Islamabad in just over a week."

"You have taken this route to Islamabad before?"

"I traveled this way only once when I was a young man. But Mohammajon has made this journey many times."

A group of fighter jets screeched above the compound. Both men glanced toward the black sky. Within a few moments, the drone of the engines faded into the distance. Less than a minute passed before the concussion of bombs resounded in the distance. Then there was silence.

"That was close," Mustafa muttered, as he peered toward the horizon. "We must take care along the road."

Ahmed opened his backpack and stuffed a few of the smaller ammunition boxes into his pack. He tied the pack closed with a frayed rope.

"Mustafa, where are you from?"

Mustafa looked down at him with a quizzical expression.

"I'm Tajik."

"Yes, but what province of Afghanistan are you from? Are you from the North?"

"I was born in Badakhshan near the border with Tajikistan. My father was Tajik and my mother was Uzbek. My mother took us to Mazar-e-Sharif when I was young. The Russians killed her. One day our village was there on the hill outside the city. The next day it was rubble."

Mustafa tossed a rock against the base of the wall.

"A bomb hit the house in the middle of the night. My younger brothers and sisters were also slaughtered. My older brother and I were in training in Panjshir Valley or we too would have been killed. Since that time, I live where the holy man tells me to live. Mullah says we live in Kabul now. That is where I live."

"I know Mazar-e-Sharif. My father was commander of the forces there for two years before he was killed. There have been many battles in Mazar-e-Sharif the past five years. Did you fight there?"

"Yes, I served under Commander Jan for more than a year. The Taliban forces attacked the city time and again. They finally overran our positions when we ran short of ammunition. Most of the Alliance warriors were killed or captured. My brother and I were captured by a group of Uzbeks who were allied with the Taliban. Commander Jan led the counterattack that set us free."

The temperature was dropping. Mustafa tied his coat around him.

"Your father was a great leader, Ahmed Jan. Some commanders fight for personal profit or glory. Commander Jan fought out of love for the Tajik people. This earned him the undying respect of all Mujaheddin."

Mustafa held his fist to his chest.

"I, Mustafa, am honored to have fought with him."

Ahmed mindlessly traced patterns in the dirt at his feet. He looked up to the sky. Flakes of snow pelted against his face and accumulated on his heavy brows. He stared off in the distance without speaking for a moment, as if he'd been transported to another time and another place. He looked at Mustafa.

"When I turned fifteen he gave me this Kalashnikov."

Ahmed chuckled.

"I could barely lift it. He taught me to brace it against my hip to fire. I could shoot rocks off a fence from fifty meters by the time I was sixteen. I fought with him in battle when I was seventeen. I never thought about what life would be without him."

Ahmed tossed another stone against the battered wall.

"His memory is always with me. It will never fade."

Mustafa squatted and tore a twig from a fallen tree. He placed it in the corner of his mouth and chewed as he spoke.

"You are like him, Ahmed Jan. You have the same intensity in your eyes. You have his determination."

"I *am* determined, Mustafa. I'm determined that one day our people will live in peace and cultivate this land. I will raise chickens, goats, and horses. I'll marry and have ten children. I want my children to live happy lives and die of old age. That is why I fight."

"I once heard this dream from another man," Mustafa sighed. He took the twig from his mouth and flipped it away. "Commander Massoud, the Lion of Panjshir. He often spoke of family. He also longed for these things. Then the Arabs killed him."

Ahmed studied the face of the young Tajik warrior. His eyes were cold.

"Mustafa, did you know Commander Massoud?"

"Not well, but I knew him. I served as an aid to Mohammad Akbar, one of the Jamiat commanders. I returned to the fight in Taloqan when the Hezbi Mujaheddin killed Commander Akbar. I only talked to Commander Massoud one time. But I heard him speak many times."

Ahmed tossed the stick away and blotted out the drawing he had made in the dirt with his heels. He looked toward Mustafa.

"Why do you fight, Mustafa?"

"Me?"

"Yes, every man needs a dream."

"I am a soldier. I've always been a soldier. There is no other reason."

Ahmed stared into Mustafa's eyes.

"There must be a reason. Do you fight for your country?"

"I have no country, Ahmed Jan. The Taliban and the Arabs destroyed my country."

Ahmed gazed up at him without speaking for a few moments, trying to gauge his sincerity.

"Mohammajon? He also feels this way?"

"No, Mohammajon is a true believer. He fights in the name of Allah. I am loyal only to Mullah Habid. He's been like a father to me since I began to walk."

"So you fight for Mullah Habid?"

"I fight because I'm a soldier and there is a battle to be fought. It does not matter if the battle ends in Afghanistan. There will always be another."

Ahmed picked up a stone and hurled it against the low wall surrounding the enclosure.

"I pray I will never love battle for its own sake. Someday peace will come to Afghanistan. That will be a day to celebrate."

"I hope you find your dream one day, Ahmed."

Mustafa stood up from his crouch.

"Get some sleep, Ahmed Jan. I will wake you when it is time to go."

Mustafa turned and strode away. Ahmed watched him disappear around the wall surrounding the enclosure. He took a deep breath and leaned back against his backpack. He spread the blankets across his legs and closed his eyes.

CHAPTER FIVE

A hmed was awakened by a gentle shake of his arm. It was Mustafa.
"Let's go, Ahmed. The truck is ready."
Ahmed rolled over and pushed himself to his feet. He arched his back
to stretch and glanced at his watch. It was a little after midnight. He pulled his
coat on and threw the backpack across his shoulder. He leaned over, picked up
his Kalashnikov, and followed Mustafa out of the courtyard.

The snowstorm had nearly passed. Only an occasional flake drifted to the
ground. The sky was clear and a quarter moon was visible just over the top of
the wall surrounding the compound.

The two men tracked down the snow-covered path to the gate. A Russian
Tatra 138 six-by-six diesel truck sat idling just outside the gate. Behind it was
an early model Chevrolet pickup truck. The larger of the two trucks belched
black smoke from its stacks. The air smelled of diesel.

The Tatra 138 was more rust than metal. One of the front fenders was
missing and empty holes were all that remained of the headlights. The cabin
was built to hold four men, but several others could ride in the bed. A 50-mm
machine gun was mounted in the bed. The gunner operated the killing
machine from the standing position. Thick metal shields protected the gunner's
sides, as he swiveled the gun for a full 360 degrees.

The bed of the Tatra was packed with tents, ammunition, supplies, two large
diesel barrels, and one medium-sized gasoline barrel. Several rocket-propelled
grenades were stacked in the bed.

The pickup truck was in even worse shape. Faded, red paint was peeling
from its hood. A large crack meandered across the windshield from one side to
the other. The tires were completely bald.

Mohammajon was supervising the loading of the last of the supplies. He looked up as Mustafa and Ahmed approached.

"The trucks are loaded, Mustafa. We have less than four hours of darkness. We must leave now."

Mustafa peered into the back of the Tatra 138.

"Only two barrels of diesel?"

Mohammajon nodded his head.

"It's all they could spare. It should be enough to reach Jalalabad. We must find more so the men can bring the truck back to Kabul."

Mustafa jumped into the bed of the Tatra.

"Okay. Let's go. Ahmed, you ride in the cab with Mohammajon."

The driver was named Shah. He greeted Ahmed with a toothless grin and nod of his head. Ahmed climbed into the back seat of the truck. The fabric on the seats had disintegrated to expose the metal springs. The springs were partially covered with a hodge-podge of dirty old blankets. Ahmed took care not to impale himself on one of the sharp metal cables. Mohammajon slid into the back seat beside him.

"Haji!" Mustafa called out. "Get in the front seat."

Three of the Mujaheddin leapt onto the tailgate and crawled into the bed of the Tatra. Two Mujaheddin jumped into the pickup truck, and it pulled forward into the street. Mustafa pounded on the cab of the Tatra and the truck lurched forward away from the compound. Shah tailed the pickup truck through the darkened streets of Kabul.

Ahmed peered through the window, as they passed block after block of bombed out buildings. It was close to one in the morning. The swath of destruction extended for several kilometers. As they moved away from the center of the city, there were areas of destruction intermingled with zones that were untouched. Some buildings appeared to have been bombed in the recent past. Other rubble was left over from the Russian invasion or the civil war that followed. The fresh layer of snow lent a false impression of purity.

The streets and alleys were deserted. Few ordinary people had returned after the fall of Kabul to the Northern Alliance. Most feared the reprisals that invariably followed when an Afghani city changed hands. Most still recalled the killing that ensued after the fall of Kabul to the Mujaheddin at the end of the Russian war. Many of the Pashtun citizens of Kabul had become refugees in squalid camps along the Pakistani boarder. Bands of hungry dogs scavenging for food seemed to be the only inhabitants of the darkened city.

Mohammajon pointed out the window as the truck approached a major intersection.

"Taliban police headquarters."

Ahmed pressed his face to the window to get a better view of the destruction. Bombs had decimated the compound. Several charred automobiles sat next to the complex. A Pashtu banner was draped across the wreckage. It read "Death to America."

Mohammajon pointed out the window once again a few blocks later, as they sped past a cluster of demolished buildings.

"Rishkore barracks. That post on the corner is where they hung Abdul Haq."

Ahmed recalled the story. The Taliban executed Abdul Haq, the legendary Pashtun guerilla fighter, when they caught him cajoling Pashtun chiefs to turn against Taliban rule at the beginning of the American bombing.

The trucks approached the outskirts of Kabul. Mohammajon pointed out the window once again.

"The football stadium."

Ahmed could scarcely make out the unlit façade of the stadium. The Taliban used the stadium for the public execution of citizens who violated their decrees. Even women were shot for crimes such as adultery and blasphemy.

Ahmed shook his head.

"Stupid morons."

The abrupt end of the pavement was signaled by a series of bone-jarring jolts. The Tatra 138 hurdled over ridges and potholes that dotted the muddy road. Even though the truck slowed to less than a third of its former speed, the ride became a jarring jump from one water-filled rut to the next. Ahmed braced himself against the jostling by grasping a leather loop next to the window with both hands. He peered over the driver's shoulder and tried to anticipate the jolts. It was a useless exercise.

The truck pounded through an especially deep rut that threw the men in the cabin against the ceiling. Mustafa pounded on the cabin roof.

"Stop, stop!"

Shah hit the brakes and the truck skid to a stop.

Ahmed looked through the back window. Mustafa hoisted one of the fighters back into the truck by the arm. He pounded on the roof again and the truck lurched forward.

The truck bumped and wove on toward Jalalabad for more than two hours. Ahmed pressed his hand against his side to ease the ache from being thrown repeatedly against the side panel. Suddenly, Haji pointed up the road.

"Fire! Stop, fire!"

Shah jammed on the brakes. The Tatra 138 skidded to a stop in the middle of the road. The pickup truck rumbled into the trench alongside them. A fire was burning a short distance down the road.

Mustafa barked out orders in Dari. Haji leaped from the truck with his rifle and sprinted into the cover along the side of the dirt road.

Mustafa leapt down from the bed. He signaled the driver to pull the truck off the road. He motioned again and three of the Mujaheddin ran off along the edge of the road in the direction of the fire, ducking from cover to cover, keeping their Kalashnikovs pointed toward the fire ahead.

Ahmed and Mohammajon leapt from the truck. Mustafa motioned them across the road, before disappearing into the ground cover.

The night was still, except for the distant crackling of flames. Ahmed positioned himself behind a rock and balanced the barrel of his Kalashnikov on the edge. He peered down the road through the sight of the rifle.

Two short bursts of machine gun fire echoed from the distance.

"Should I go back them up?" Ahmed whispered to Mohammajon.

"No, stay here with the truck. I'm moving to the other side of the road."

Mohammajon ran across the muddy road. He stumbled in a tire rut, but managed to keep his footing. He stacked several rocks in the trench and lay on the ground with his rifle atop them.

Ahmed stayed prone on the wet ground. All was quiet, except for the intermittent crackle of the dying flames up the road.

A short time later, two figures came trotting down the road toward them. The men's guns were silhouetted in the light of the fire.

Mustafa reemerged from the cover on the side of the road just in front of Ahmed. He knelt behind a rock with his rifle pointed toward the approaching figures.

"Hold your fire," he said in a barely audible voice.

"Commander," one of the men called out, "it's a bombed-out Taliban truck. We killed two survivors."

Mustafa stepped into the road

"Ahmed and Mohammajon, get back into the truck. You two get in the pickup. The rest of you get into the Tatra."

A rap on the cabin prompted the driver to edge the military transport truck back onto the road. Shah edged forward in first gear toward the burning vehicle.

Ahmed caught his breath as they pulled alongside the carnage. The rear end of the truck had been pulverized beyond recognition. Several bodies were scattered on the ground around the vehicle. They'd been blown clear of the vehicle by the bomb's destructive force.

Ahmed's eyes were drawn to the driver. Spared the direct impact of the bomb, he'd been engulfed in the resulting inferno. Charred to the bone, his arms were extended into the air in a macabre salute. The sickening smell of burning human flesh permeated the air. Ahmed never got used to it. He turned away as the truck rumbled on.

Mohammajon kept to himself during the first few hours of the journey. Seemingly deep in thought, he occasionally mumbled to himself in the Dari language of the Tajiks. At one point, Ahmed asked Mohammajon a question about Mullah Habid. He abandoned further attempts at conversation after Mohammajon's curt reply.

The truck bounced and ground along the road toward Jalalabad. At one point, Ahmed tensed as a jet whooshed over in the dark sky above. He glanced at the transmitter fixed to the dash. The flash of the red light on the face of the device provided only limited reassurance.

The unremitting revving of the engine and grinding of gears were deafening. Sleep was impossible. As the truck wove through the twisting turns, Ahmed stared out the window at the darkness that surrounded them.

Mohammajon finally spoke up two hours into the journey. When he did, it was as though the old Tajik had been reading Ahmed's mind.

"Allah is great, my son. Put your faith in Him. If you are worthy, He will protect you."

The old Tajik pointed out the window.

"The morning is approaching. We will stop soon."

Ahmed sensed it was lighter outside, but the walls of the cliff surrounding them were still shrouded in darkness.

"In Jalalabad?"

"No, my son, Jalalabad is still two days journey. We will stop along the road today and rest. We'll go on again after dark."

"I've never been to Jalalabad."

"We'll not enter Jalalabad. It's too dangerous. Some areas are still controlled by the Taliban. There's a road to the east that bypasses the city."

Mohammajon paused for a few moments and then resumed the conversation.

"Have you ever been through Khyber Pass, Ahmed Jan?"

"No, this is the first time I've been south of Kabul."

Mohammajon chuckled and jabbed Shah with his elbow.

"Allah picked a worldly man to save our people."

All of the men had a hearty laugh. Ahmed waited for them to stop.

"I've traveled to many countries. We always flew out of Kabul or Mazar-e-Sharif. There was never any reason to travel to the south."

Mohammajon nodded.

"Where have these journeys taken you, my son?"

"My father served as a diplomat before the Russian invasion. He took me on many of his trips. I've been to Cairo, Baghdad, Istanbul, Rome, London, and many other cities. I studied in Saudi Arabia for four years."

"Have you traveled in America?"

"We traveled to Vancouver many times. That's the closest I got to America."

"Have you traveled to Mecca?"

"Yes, my family went on Hajj when I was a boy."

Mohammajon nodded his head.

"You have been most fortunate, Ahmed Jan. I've only visited Pakistan. Tell me of the holy cities. Are they as beautiful as the mullah says?"

"I don't remember that much. I was only a small boy."

Mohammajon leaned back and stared at the ceiling.

"My dream is to one day make the Hajj. Allah willing, I will pray in the Kaaba and see the sacred Masjid before my time is through."

The truck abruptly decelerated and made a sharp turn to the right. Ahmed grasped the leather strap to maintain his balance, but still thumped his head against the window. The truck eased to a stop.

"We will rest here today," Mustafa shouted.

He leaped to the ground from the bed of the truck and sprinted ahead carrying his Kalashnikov. Two other men followed him up the dead-end canyon.

Haji shuffled out of the cabin. He began unloading supplies with the other Mujaheddin. Ahmed was the last one out. He patted the driver on the back.

"Good job, Shah."

The driver beamed with self-satisfaction.

"I drove taxis in Kabul for twenty years. It was good preparation."

Ahmed chuckled.

"I imagine it would be. Hopefully the roads were a little better."

"The roads to Jalalabad are good this time of year. The springtime is bad."

Ahmed shook his head and laughed.

"I'll remember never to journey with you in the spring."

The clouds cleared a short time later. The sun lingered behind the mountains to the east, but the sky lightened to the point that the clearing was bathed in morning light. It was the beginning of a beautiful winter day.

The camp was surrounded on three sides by rocky cliffs. A waterfall tumbled into a clear pool at the back of the box canyon.

Two of the Mujaheddin took up positions behind large boulders near the entrance to the canyon. The rutted, grassy road was the only route in or out. The lookouts would detect anyone who tried to enter the secluded gorge.

Haji and Adib worked together setting up three old tents near a large fire pit in the middle of the clearing. Mohammajon gathered kindling from a box in the back of the pickup truck and started the fire. Within a few minutes it was crackling.

Mustafa and Ahmed walked toward the tents together. Mustafa sat down next to the fire. He removed his gloves and held out his palms to warm them. Ahmed was content to stand with his back to the fire. He turned to look, as the truck engine roared back to life. The driver slowly backed the Tatra 138 truck into the grass beside the tents. When he was satisfied with the position, he set the brake and turned off the engine.

Mustafa slipped his gloves back on and motioned to Haji.

"You and Adib take the first watch. Stay alert, Haji. I'll leave you behind if I catch you sleeping."

Haji pulled himself up into the bed of the truck and sat on a crate positioned behind the machine gun. Abid sprinted off to take up a position with the other men near the entrance to the canyon. Mustafa turned to the remaining Mujaheddin.

"Aman and Sandir, you sleep for three hours. Haji will wake you when it's your watch."

"I will take the watch after Aman," Ahmed offered.

"Not today, Ahmed. Take some food and get some sleep."

"I will take my turn, Mustafa."

"No, Ahmed. Haji and Abid slept on the trip. They will alternate watch with Aman and Sandir."

Ahmed shook his head and leaned back against a rock.

Mohammajon began passing out bread with bowls of stew a short time later. Ahmed took a bowl and sat down on the ground next to the fire. He grasped the bowl in both hands and took a sip. He gagged.

The broth tasted of spoiled meat mixed with a few vegetables. His initial impulse was to spit it out, but he managed to suppress the urge and swallow. He braced himself and gulped down the rest. It was the only food he'd get for some time. He set the bowl down on the ground beside him.

Mustafa was sitting on the ground cleaning his Kalashnikov.

"Ahmed, you sleep with Mohammajon in the tent closest to the fire. I'll be in the tent near the truck."

"Mustafa, I want to take my turn at watch."

"Ahmed!" Mustafa exclaimed, as he turned. "Why do you torment me? These men don't know you. They will not even trust a Jan to stand watch. *They* won't sleep and *you* won't sleep. What good can come of this?"

Ahmed shook his head with resignation.

Mohammajon reappeared and began to gather the empty bowls. He filled one of them with stew, handed it to Mustafa, and meandered away toward the truck.

Mustafa downed the stew in two large gulps. He tossed the bowl into a box lying near the fire.

"That's the worst I've tasted yet. I've seen flies die in Mohammajon's stew."

Mustafa stood up and fetched his rifle.

"Get some sleep, Ahmed."

Ahmed watched Mustafa wander back toward the truck and duck into his tent.

"Stubborn goat," he muttered beneath his breath.

Ahmed rose to his feet, slung his pack over his shoulder, and picked up his rifle. He walked to the nearest tent and stepped inside. The tent was completely empty. Ahmed set his pack down in the back corner and laid the gun down along one side. He lay down next to the gun and covered himself with a wool blanket.

Ahmed stared up at the roof of the tent. The early morning light penetrated through dozens of holes in the canvas. A soft drumming on the fabric signaled the onset of a light rain. Ahmed listened as the rain became louder. He closed his eyes and took a deep breath.

"Allah, give me strength."

CHAPTER SIX

A hmed started awake at the sound of a long, loud grunt. There was a prolonged silence and then the fitful resonating snore began anew. Ahmed turned his head. Mohammajon was lying on the other side of the tent pole. He was on his back with his mouth wide open.

The pinpoints of light were no longer visible in the canvas roof. Ahmed glanced at his watch. It was 5:30 P.M.

He rose to his feet and stepped through the canvas door. He could barely make out the silhouette of a man sitting in the tail of the truck manning the machine gun in the fading light. Glowing embers were the only remnants of the fire. Two Mujaheddin were reloading supplies in the bed of the truck. Mustafa was sitting in the front seat of the truck looking over a map. He spotted Ahmed.

"We'll be leaving as soon as it's dark. Get your things ready."

Ahmed stepped back into the tent. Mohammajon was stirring. The old fighter rolled over and arched his back toward the ceiling.

"I hope my snoring didn't disturb you, Ahmed Jan."

"I had no trouble sleeping. It was the first undisturbed sleep I've had in weeks."

"You will need it tonight, my son."

Mohammajon strode from the tent with a pile of blankets and his Kalashnikov. Ahmed gathered his pack and rifle. He pulled the center pole down as he emerged through the front flap. The tent collapsed behind him. Two Mujaheddin fighters pulled the stakes, folded the canvas, and loaded the tent into the truck.

The truck was fully loaded fifteen minutes later. Ahmed ducked into the back seat and Abid joined him. Mohammajon sat in the front passenger seat. Mustafa climbed into the bed of the Tatra.

The pickup truck pulled away in front of them. Mustafa pounded on the cab and Shah fought with both hands to force the gearshift into first gear. He let the clutch out and the truck lurched forward. The bone-jarring journey began anew.

The fighters in the trucks crouched with guns at the ready while the vehicles retraced the short dirt road from the canyon back to the old caravan road. The vegetation lining the road was barely visible in the darkness. It was impossible to make out the canyon walls on either side of the box canyon. The light of the full moon was nearly obscured by a dense cloud cover.

"This is a perfect spot for an ambush," Mohammajon uttered. "I used it myself once. Keep your hand on the gun."

The truck slowed to a crawl at the junction with the main road. Shah made the right turn and gradually accelerated. The poor visibility and jostling of the men limited the speed. The truck bounced through several ruts and bottomed out on a deep hole that stretched across the road.

"What did you do before the war, Mohammajon?"

"I taught history at Kabul University for twenty-one years."

"You were a history professor? What kind of history?"

"Afghani history was my specialty area. I mainly taught freshman courses, but I also had graduate students from time to time."

"I always loved history. I took several courses during the time I studied medicine in Saudi. It was mainly the history of Islam and Saudi Arabia. My uncle taught me the little Afghani history I know. I remember him thrilling me with grand stories about Alexander the Great when I was just a small boy."

"We are in the midst of history. Many great armies have invaded our land along this route."

"Is this the Khyber Pass?"

"Not yet, but we'll soon enter the fabled corridor to southern Asia. *Khyber* is a Hebrew word. It means 'fort.' You will soon see why it was given this name. This ancient highway has been a part of the fiber of this land for centuries. The armies of Timur, Babur, Mahmud of Ghazna, Nadir Shah, and Alexander the Great marched this way in search of conquest. They all had their day. The Khyber was the principal invasion route for thousands of years."

"Why is this road so empty?"

"We're on the old caravan road. The asphalt highway runs a mile to the east, but we're safer here."

"Pakistan controls the pass now?"

"That's right. The Pakistani ISI security forces oversee everything that happens here. The main road is dotted with Pakistani checkpoints. Many Taliban and Arabs are hiding from the Americans farther down the Khyber Pass. The ISI supports them. From there they can reach the southern Pakistani tribal provinces."

"How long is the pass?"

"It's about fifty kilometers. It winds and twists through the Sefid Koh mountain range. The mountain cliffs on either side of the pass can only be climbed in a few places. You'll see one of these spots when we stop to rest during the day."

Ahmed strained to make out the walls of the nearby cliffs. It was no use. There was only darkness surrounding them.

"If stones could talk," he mumbled. "The stories they could tell."

Shah slammed on the brakes. The pickup truck in front of them skidded to a stop in a pool of water. Mustafa leaped from the bed of the military truck and splashed past them with several of the other Mujaheddin right behind him. The other fighters filed out of the cabin. Mustafa strode back a few moments later. He was shaking his head.

"The road is completely washed out. We'll need to repair it to go on. Grab the shovels."

Several of the men grabbed shovels from the back of the truck. Mustafa directed Shah to ease the Tatra 138 forward to the edge of the water.

"Stop!" he yelled out.

Shah put the truck in neutral and set the emergency brake.

Mustafa grabbed a shovel. He carried a shovel of soil from the embankment on the side of the road and tossed it into the water in front of the truck. He walked back to the embankment.

Ahmed joined a line of men working to fill the pit from the other side of the road. He filled a shovel with wet dirt, carried it to the front of the pickup, and tossed it into the water. The fill disappeared into the slow moving water. Haji stepped up behind him and heaved another shovelful of earth into the void. One after the other, the men carried shovel after shovel of soil and pitched them into the water. Another Mujaheddin jumped into the pit and packed the mud with his bare feet. It was nearly an hour before the washed-out span was reduced to a shallow puddle.

"Okay," Mustafa called out, as he tossed the shovel in the bed of the truck, "let's try it with the pickup."

Several of the men got behind the truck. The driver put the transmission into gear and began to ease forward.

"Everyone push! Don't let it stop!"

The pickup truck rolled into the water and pulled onto the road on the other side.

"Okay, now the Tatra," Mustafa called out.

The men lined up behind the military truck and pushed against the tailgate. Shah let out the clutch and eased the heavy truck forward into the water. The truck's front wheels passed across the mud-filled pit. But the rear wheels bogged down, as the tail end of the truck rolled into the muddy bed. The wheels spun in place and spewed water and sludge over the fighters struggling to keep it moving.

"Push harder!"

The men strained against the rear end of the truck. The truck inched through the gully, as Shah gunned the engine to keep it from stalling. Suddenly, the wheels gripped the bank on the opposite side of the mud-filled pit and the truck lumbered forward onto the dirt road.

Mustafa stumbled to the embankment next to the road and collapsed on his backside. He used his hands to clear the mud from his hair and face.

"Damn it!"

Ahmed collapsed on a rock by the side of the road. His fingers and toes were numb. He struggled to pull off his right boot. He poured the water onto the ground and slid the boot back on. He repeated the effort with the left boot. Ahmed crossed his arms across his chest and tucked his fingers into his armpits to warm them.

"There's a well about an hour away," Mustafa called out. "We'll stop there for the night. Ahmed, get back into the cabin of the Tatra with Mohammajon and Haji. Abid, you and Zahr get into the pickup."

Ahmed climbed back into the cabin of the truck with Haji. Mohammajon rifled through the supplies in the bed until he found the blankets. He passed one to each man in the bed, jumped into the front seat of the Tatra next to Shah, and slammed the door.

Mustafa climbed back into the bed of the truck, crouched behind the machine gun, and wrapped the blanket around his shoulders. He pounded on the cabin.

"Okay, let's go."

The pickup pulled out first. Shah ground the transmission into first gear and inched forward along the road behind them. Within minutes, they were weaving through narrow curves that took them higher and higher into the mountains.

The pickup forged ahead and disappeared. Shah double-clutched and shifted between the two lowest gears to keep the lumbering Tatra moving through the never-ending switchbacks.

The blankets were little comfort against the wet and cold. The heater wasn't much help either. It generated little more than a chilly draft. Shah finally turned it off.

No one in the Tatra said a word. Each man was content to suffer in silence. Ahmed had just begun to feel a little warmer when Mohammajon spoke up.

"Shah, stop the truck. Mustafa's going to freeze to death back there."

Shah pulled the truck to the side of the road. Mohammajon climbed down to the ground.

Ahmed, still shivering, stepped out behind him and gathered his coat. The temperature was close to freezing. It would have been barely tolerable when he was dry, but it was agonizing now that he was soaked to the skin.

Mustafa was nearly unconscious. Several of the Tajiks hoisted him down to the ground. He raised his hand, as if to speak, but could only mutter incoherently.

"Put him in the back seat," Mohammajon whispered in quivering voice.

Ahmed helped several of the men lift Mustafa into the back corner of the Tatra. He threw one of the blankets over Mustafa and got out of the truck. Mohammajon stepped toward him.

"Ahmed, stay in the cabin."

"No, Mohammajon. I will take my turn in the bed."

Ahmed climbed up on the tailgate and sat down behind the machine gun before anyone could block him.

"Ahmed, get into the truck," Mohammajon ordered once again.

Ahmed ignored him and leaned over the machine gun. He pulled one of the damp blankets across his back. Mohammajon, too cold to argue, waved his hand and climbed back into the front seat of the truck.

The truck bumped and ground, as it wound ever higher in the pass. Ahmed began to shiver uncontrollably as the wind whipped beneath the soggy blanket that covered him. Little by little, he drifted into a dazed stupor.

CHAPTER SEVEN

Ahmed gradually became aware of the crackling of a fire. He was naked and lying on the ground wrapped in blankets. He raised a hand to shield his eyes against the bright sunlight and lifted up just enough to catch sight of several of the men sitting on the other side of the fire.

Mustafa saw Ahmed stir. He walked around the pit, knelt beside him, and raised his head to a cup.

"Ahmed, sip this soup. We bought it from a family on the road. It'll warm you and give you strength."

Ahmed sipped the broth. It was aromatic and delicious. He took another sip and laid his head back on the ground.

Mustafa gripped his arm.

"Ahmed, I want you to have this."

Mustafa held a photograph close so Ahmed could see. It was a picture of Ahmed's father. He and Commander Massoud were sitting at a table playing chess. Both men were wearing pakool caps.

Ahmed managed a slight smile, before he laid his head back down. Mustafa patted him on the arm and slid the photo into his hand.

"Sleep well, my friend."

The day passed quickly and without incident. Ahmed gradually regained his strength. By mid-afternoon he was sitting next to the fire. His face and neck were red with windburn and his scarred hand was throbbing. His lips were cracked and bleeding. But he was alive.

The men loaded up the trucks shortly after dark. Ahmed took his seat in the back of the cabin of the Tatra 138 with Haji beside him. Mohammajon sat in the front. Mustafa jumped into the bed and manned the machine gun.

"Abid," Mustafa called out, "you take the point with Zahr."

The Tajik Mujaheddin ran ahead and jumped into the pickup truck. The truck screeched out of the camp toward the dirt road. The transport truck pulled out a few seconds later.

Ahmed could still make out the walls of the pass on both sides of the road, but the sky was darkening. He bobbed and weaved, as the truck ground through the turns. The jarring seemed to get worse, the nearer they got to Jalalabad.

Ahmed spoke up an hour out of camp.

"Mohammajon, what year did Alexander the Great bring his army to Afghanistan?"

Mohammajon turned in the front seat.

"He marched through the Khyber Pass to India in 325 B.C."

"Over two thousand years ago. That's incredible. How many armies have conquered the Khyber Pass?"

"Too many to count, my son."

Mohammajon leaned forward in the seat and snatched a map from the dash.

"In the tenth century alone the Persian, Mongol, and Tartar armies fought their way through the pass. These conquerors brought Islamic truth to India. The Greeks also came this way. Then there were the Scythians, White Huns, Seljuks, Sassanians, Turks, Mughals, and Durranis. How many is that?"

Mohammajon rubbed at his beard while he surveyed the map with a small penlight. Ahmed leaned forward and peered at the map over his shoulder.

"It's amazing. We are retracing the steps of ancient history."

"Without a doubt, Ahmed. The legend of this pass is one of agonizing tragedy and unrivaled glory. Let your imagination run, my son. The armies of Ghenghis Khan are high above us on the cliffs. Imagine his hordes raining arrows down on the road."

Ahmed stared out the window at the darkness surrounding them.

"General Pollock used the Khyber Pass on his way to Afghanistan in 1839 during the First Afghan War."

"I have heard of this war," Ahmed replied.

"Yes, it's an important part of our history. The most famous battle was fought in January 1842. Afghani Mujaheddin slaughtered more than sixteen thousand British and Indian troops. The only survivor was a doctor. Legend has it he rode into Jalalabad on a stumbling pony."

There was a tremendous flash and explosion ahead of the truck. Shah jammed on the brakes and the Tatra skidded to a stop. The rapid deceleration threw Ahmed and Haji against the back of the seat.

Mustafa jumped down from the bed and ran along the side of the road in the direction of the blast. Three of the other Mujaheddin disappeared into the darkness behind him. The remaining Mujaheddin scrambled into the surrounding brush.

The darkness was eerily quiet. Ahmed knelt behind a boulder on the side of the road. Mustafa called out from the shadows a short time later.

"All clear. Hold your fire!"

He jogged up to the truck with two of the fighters.

"The pickup hit a mine. Abid and Zahr are dead. Haji, take the point. We will follow in the truck."

Haji ran up the road with his Kalashnikov in hand. Ahmed and the other Mujaheddin loaded back into the truck. Shah put the truck in gear and eased ahead.

The pickup truck was almost unrecognizable. Several Mujaheddin helped Mustafa pull the mangled bodies from the smoldering wreckage. They laid the two corpses along the side of the road and covered them with a blanket. Many supplies were thrown clear of the pickup truck by the explosion. Mustafa sorted through them and salvaged everything that was usable. It took nearly an hour to bury the two men along the side of the road.

The remaining men piled into the military truck. Haji was once again on the point. He jogged ahead on foot. The truck followed him through the curves at slow speed.

"Now there are only eight," Ahmed sighed. "Will that be enough men?"

Mohammajon didn't respond for a few moments, as if pondering the question. Finally he answered.

"It will be critical to find horses or donkeys in Jalalabad. We cannot carry the supplies without them now. I pray Allah will provide for our needs."

"Who set the mine on the road?"

"It's hard to say. Most likely the Taliban placed it to cover their retreat. But it could have been the local tribes."

"Where are we now? Are we getting close to Jalalabad?"

"We're nearing the turnoff that will take us east of Jalalabad toward the Torkham border station. Torkham is the last checkpoint in Afghanistan before we cross into Pakistan. It's been in the hands of Yunus Khalis since the Taliban fled Jalalabad in November."

"I've heard this name."

"Yunus Khalis is bad man," Shah blurted out abruptly.

Mohammajon paused for a moment.

"Yunus Khalis is a Pashtun mullah. He lived in Jalalabad most of his life. At one time, he and his supporters dominated Jalalabad and a wide area around it. The Taliban suppressed him for many years. He reasserted control over the area once the Taliban fled. It is rumored he befriended the Arab militants."

"It sounds like we should avoid him."

"Unfortunately, we cannot avoid Yunus Khalis. He has the horses. But he can be bought. Mullah Habid has good relations with him. He will expect a handsome bribe, but he will recognize it's in his best interest to cooperate. He has a well-known history of opposing the Americans and courting the Arabs. Mustafa will use this to our advantage."

"What if he doesn't cooperate?" Ahmed queried.

Mohammajon did not answer. The question hung in the air like smoke. Suddenly, the truck veered to the left onto an even smaller road.

"This is the turnoff to the Torkham border station."

The truck continued on along the rutted and winding path for nearly an hour. Shah kept a safe distance behind Haji. The fighter jogged on foot with a flashlight, ever vigilant for signs of a disturbance of the soil that could indicate a freshly laid mine. The truck rocked and weaved, as it made slow progress.

Mohammajon jumped down from the cab of the Tatra. He directed Shah up a gentle slope and into a clump of trees about five hundred meters from the trail. Shah pulled the truck to a stop in a small, protected clearing.

"Okay," Mustafa called out, "we will camp here. Hide the truck with foliage. No fires or tents. There are undoubtedly Taliban in the area. They would attack us for supplies if they stumble on us. Even the local tribal people are dangerous."

The Mujaheddin set about cutting branches to hide the truck. Ahmed wandered away from the clearing to the nearby tree line. He squatted where he could watch the sunrise beneath the clouds. The grassy knoll below him gradually transformed to a light shade of purple. He sat there alone a few minutes, until the branches rustled behind him. He jerked his head around. It was Mustafa.

Mustafa held out a small leather pouch.

"Here."

Ahmed took the pouch and looked at Mustafa with a puzzled expression. "What's this?"

"It's the rest of the money. Some of it is in American dollars. The rest is in diamonds. I took what I'll need to buy horses. I'll meet with Yunus Khalis to arrange the purchase. Come, you should hear what I have to say to the other men."

Ahmed followed Mustafa back to the clearing. Several of the Mujaheddin were gathered near the shrouded truck. Mustafa walked up to Mohammajon, took a loaf of naan from his hand, and spoke just loud enough to be heard.

"I will take Gul Kabulin with me. Haji, you stay here with the other men."

Haji clearly did not like being left behind. He turned, kicked at the dirt, and swore under his breath. Gul Kabulin took offense.

"Haji, you're a pig. You've always been a pig and you'll always be a pig. Just like all Jamiat."

Haji was upon him in an instant. He bullrushed Gul to the ground and pummeled him with his fists, before the other men could react. Mustafa caught Haji's arm and pulled him off of Gul. Gul struggled to his feet and tried to break away from two of the other Mujaheddin.

Mustafa shook Haji to get his attention.

"Listen to me! We will have none of this. Do you understand me? Haji, I want you to stay here because you and Mohammajon are the only ones who have traveled the route from Jalalabad to Islamabad. You will help Mohammajon lead Ahmed Jan to Islamabad if I do not return. Do you understand me?"

Haji shook his head and looked toward the ground. Mustafa whirled around.

"Gul Kabulin, I'll slit your throat myself if you insult Haji again. Do you understand me?"

Gul did not respond. He stood in the grasp of Ahmed, fuming with his face contorted in anger. Mustafa grabbed Gul by the chin.

"Do you understand me, Gul?"

Gul Kabulin stared at the ground.

"Yes, I understand, Commander. But it is he who insulted the Hezbi."
Mustafa jerked his chin up and glared into his eyes.

"I don't want to hear anything more. You can cut each other's guts out
once we get to Islamabad. I really don't give a donkey's butt. But this fight is
over until we get there. I'll kill you both myself if there's another outburst before
then. I mean it. Now Haji, get over there and unload the supplies from the
truck."

Haji turned away dejectedly and walked toward the truck. Mustafa
watched him for a moment and then turned back toward Ahmed Jan and the
others in the group.

"I'll be on my way now. If I'm not back by sundown tomorrow, leave the
truck here and go on by foot to Islamabad. Haji knows the route around the
Torkham border station. Avoid everyone until you reach Islamabad. Any
Pakistanis you encounter in the Khyber Pass are likely ISI. They are Pashtun
and they sympathize with the Taliban. Do not trust them."

Ahmed Jan stepped forward and hugged the stoic warrior.

"Good luck, Mustafa. I pray Allah will protect you."

"It's you who needs Allah's protection," Mustafa teased with a broad smile.
"I'll see you tomorrow before the sun has set. If I'm not back, it more than likely
means I found a bar girl in Jalalabad who was to my liking. Come on, Gul, let's
go."

The two men walked away with their Kalashnikov rifles hung on their
shoulders. Ahmed watched as they disappeared into the trees surrounding the
clearing.

"Now comes the hardest part of our journey," Mohammajon muttered, as
he turned and began to walk away toward the truck.

"The journey through the Khyber?" Ahmed called after him.

"No, the wait to see if we have horses or we must walk all the way to
Islamabad."

CHAPTER EIGHT

December 11, 2001

The rest of the day was uneventful. The evening was surprisingly mild for December in Afghanistan and the sun rose to reveal a beautiful cloudless day. Mohammajon prepared green tea and naan for the morning meal using a can of fuel gel salvaged from the pickup truck.

The sun reached its high point above the pass just after noon. Ahmed was sitting at the edge of the cluster of trees surrounding the truck when the sound of approaching vehicles reverberated from the south. He crouched in the grass behind a rock.

The sound grew nearer and dust rose above the trees about one kilometer away. Mohammajon scrambled to Ahmed's position with a heavy machine gun and two rocket-propelled grenade launchers. Two of the other Mujaheddin trailed behind. They all lay on their bellies. The clatter of the vehicles and the cloud of dust grew closer and closer.

"It sounds like a convoy of trucks," Ahmed Jan whispered.

"No," Mohammajon replied, "they're tanks. Several of them."

Mohammajon rolled over on his side and began setting up the base of the machine gun. He whispered loud enough for all of the men to hear.

"No firing unless they leave the road and come toward us. If I open up with the gun, fire at will. Otherwise, keep your stinking heads down and don't make a sound."

At that moment, a pickup truck with a machine gun in the bed came over the rise on the trail below. There were three men in the bed. Directly behind the truck came an old Soviet tank with its treads clattering distinctively. A man with goggles, a long beard, and a black turban was riding on the turret.

"Taliban," Mohammajon whispered.

In succession, two more tanks and a military transport truck came over the rise and followed along the road headed toward the south. The convoy sud-denly ground to a stop when it reached the point on the road closest to the clump of trees that hid the Tajik Mujaheddin.

The soldier riding on the lead tank appeared to be in charge. He barked out orders in Pashtu, jumped off the tank with a rifle, and headed on foot directly for the cluster of trees where Ahmed and Mohammajon lay concealed in the brush.

"He's coming right at us," Ahmed whispered.

Mohammajon turned his head and whispered.

"Hold your fire. Keep your heads down!"

Ahmed buried his face in the brush. He peered through the blades of grass and watched as the Taliban commander strode nonchalantly toward the tree line less than twenty meters from their position. A rifle was draped over the man's shoulder.

The man stopped when he reached the trees. He glanced into the clearing where their truck was hidden by tree branches. He leaned his Kalashnikov rifle against a boulder and pulled his pants down to expose his naked buttocks to the six Northern Alliance soldiers. He squatted to relieve himself while they watched in silence.

When he'd finished, he wiped with a cloth and discarded it on the ground. Finally, he urinated at the base of the tree in front of him.

The soldier pulled up his pants and picked up his rifle. He headed back down the open embankment toward the convoy.

Haji sneezed just as he reached the midpoint between the trees and the tanks. He partially muffled the sound with a hand pressed against his mouth, but it seemed like a canon shot to the six Tajiks crouched together in the brush.

The Taliban commander stopped and turned back toward the tree line. He stood in the same spot for several moments scanning the hilltop. He looked directly at them. Ahmed felt his adrenaline-driven heart accelerate. It pounded with such force, he felt as if it would leap from his chest.

Ahmed clutched his Kalashnikov rifle and slid it forward in the grass. He took dead aim at the commander and slid his sweaty index finger firmly against the trigger.

Suddenly, the Taliban commander turned and resumed walking back to the tanks. When he reached the lead tank, he pulled himself up on the turret and barked out another order. The lead pickup pulled away along the trail. The rest of the convoy filed out of the clearing behind him. Ahmed watched in silence until the last truck disappeared over the southward rise.

Ahmed sighed loudly and rolled over on his back.

"Allah is great," he muttered with relief.

"It was the will of Allah," replied Mohammajon.

One by one, the Alliance fighters pushed themselves up to their feet and strode back to the truck. Haji took a drink of water from a canteen and knelt just inside the tree line with his Kalashnikov in hand.

The day passed slowly. Every couple of hours the watch changed and another of the Mujaheddin would take up a position in the stand of trees nearest the road.

Ahmed was sitting near the edge of a cluster of trees reading the book of poetry by Hafez Commander Massoud had given him. As he read, the last rays of the sun disappeared behind the steep walls of the pass. He glanced at his watch. It was a few minutes before three in the afternoon.

"Commander."

Ahmed turned.

"Yes, Haji, what is it?"

"It's your watch, Commander."

Ahmed closed his book. He sat for a moment staring at Haji without speaking. Bushy black eyebrows framed the young man's deep-set dark eyes. They were kind eyes.

Ahmed smiled and got to his feet. He patted the Tajik fighter on the shoulder.

"Yes, it is my turn. Thank you, Haji."

Haji grinned back at him. It was the first time Ahmed had seen him smile. Several of his upper front teeth were missing from the right side. He grasped Ahmed's arm with a strong grip, before he turned and walked away toward the truck.

Ahmed took up a position at the tree line. He watched and waited, as the afternoon light faded and the temperature slowly dropped. The trail below was deserted.

The grass rustled behind Ahmed and he turned to look. It was Mohammajon. He was carrying a steaming cup and a portion of bread.

"Ahmed, my son, here is a bit of naan and a cup of green tea."

He handed Ahmed the bread and set the cup of tea on the ground next to him. He crouched down on a rock beside Ahmed. Ahmed took a bite from the bread. He spoke as he chewed.

"Where's Mustafa? I expected him by now."

"It is in Allah's hands, Ahmed Jan. If it is Allah's will, he will return. If it is not, he will surely not return. You must learn to place your trust in Allah. When you do, these worldly events will no longer trouble you."

Ahmed took a sip of his tea and studied the leathery and sunburned face of the old Mujaheddin. His gray beard was matted and several crumbs of bread were nested in it. His cap rode low on his forehead. Deep-set dark brown eyes portrayed a perpetual sadness.

"Mohammajon, what's your dream for Afghanistan?"

The old man turned to gaze out toward the road. He seemed to ignore the question, as he stared in silence toward the unseen cliffs on the opposite side of the pass. Finally, he cleared his throat.

"I have no dream for Afghanistan. My only wish is that Allah's will be done."

Ahmed stared at the old fighter with puzzlement.

"Don't you want peace, Mohammajon? How about prosperity for our people? What about enough food for every man, woman, and child to eat? Don't you pray for these things?"

"If these things are Allah's will, then they will come to pass."

Ahmed shook his head.

"How can you be so cold to the suffering of our people, Mohammajon? Don't you believe men can influence the events surrounding them? Why are we here? Why did our maker give us brains to think? We must strive to bring peace to this land. If we don't do this for our people, then who will?"

The old man grinned at the rising aggravation in the young Tajik's voice. He placed his hand on Ahmed's knee.

"My son, once I had this fire. The Russian invasion stirred our people. Tajiks, Pashtun, Uzbeks, Turkmen, and Hazaras — we all set aside our ancient differences to fight together and drive the infidel from our lands. I was a commander in Massoud's army. There was no end to our dreams. We were idealists who prayed that this unity would lead our country to a new golden age."

Mohammajon sighed loudly and forced a few errant strands of his salt and pepper hair back beneath his Chitrali cap.

"But alas, it was not to be. No sooner had the infidel been driven from our land, than the old rivalries rose to reveal their ugly heads. Pashtun and Uzbek fought against Tajik. Tajik fought against Tajik and Pashtun fought against Pashtun. The inferno of hatred that followed was far worse than the Russians. It consumed my brothers, my wife, and both of my sons. A gang of Pashtun bandits lined them up against the wall that surrounded our home in Taloqan and mowed them down with machine guns. Starving dogs were eating the flesh off their bones when I found them the next morning."

Mohammajon turned his head and stared into Ahmed's eyes. His expression bore no witness to the pain inside.

"That is when I learned to accept the will of Allah."

"Then why are you on this mission? Why did you volunteer?

Mohammajon glared with defiance.

"I did not volunteer. The mullah ordered me to help you with the mission."

There was a prolonged silence. Ahmed pondered the words of the old man. The parallel between their lives was palpable. Yet their views were diametrically opposed.

Mohammajon stood and strode a few paces toward the truck. Ahmed called out after him.

"But this is a new day. The Taliban have been destroyed and the United Nations will help us to forge a new nation. There can be peace in Afghanistan if the Tajiks all work together to achieve it. I too lost my family. If I can accept the past as the past and work toward a new future for Afghanistan, then so can you. We must maintain hope that one day this will come to pass."

Mohammajon turned and walked back toward Ahmed.

"You are a foolish dreamer, Ahmed Jan, just like your father. The British and Americans will pack up and leave when they have killed or captured all of the Taliban and al-Qaida leaders they can find. The Pakistanis, the Iranians, and the Russians will meddle in our affairs to suit their purposes. Tribe will turn against tribe and people against people. Mark my words, within two years war will rage throughout Afghanistan. It has been so for centuries. It will always be so."

Mohammajon turned and walked off. Ahmed shook his head and watched as the old man limped away toward the truck.

Haji came to relieve Ahmed from the watch an hour later. Ahmed chatted with the Mujaheddin for a while and then headed into the clearing. Mohammajon was sitting on the running board of the truck putting supplies into his pack.

"It's five fifteen and there's still no sign of Mustafa. What are we going to do?"

Mohammajon didn't look up. He spoke as he sorted through the supplies.

"Fill your backpack with as many loaves of naan and boxes of ammunition as it will hold. We will wait one more hour. Then we will go on. We must make our own way into Pakistan tonight."

Ahmed fetched his pack from the truck and began organizing it. He crammed in several boxes of ammunition and a few loaves of naan. He finished packing and sat down with the other Mujaheddin.

Ahmed looked toward the tree line when the conversation lagged. The walls of the cliff were no longer visible beyond the silhouettes of the treetops. He glanced at his watch. It was nearly thirty minutes past six. Mohammajon called out from behind him.

"Okay. Let's go!"

The Mujaheddin stood up and fetched their rifles and packs. Several of them picked up rocket-propelled grenade launchers. Mohammajon addressed the group.

"We're going to travel parallel to the old dirt road to the Torkham border station. Stay off the trail itself. There will be absolutely no talking. Pockets of Taliban and Arab collaborators are undoubtedly hiding along the trail. It'll be worse once we cross into Pakistan. Stay alert and do not fire your weapon unless I give the order. Our only hope is to slip through undetected. Haji, you will scout the way. Mark your route with these."

Mohammajon handed Haji several strips of cloth. Haji stuck them in a pocket and strode away toward the tree line. The others followed a few seconds later. They were a hundred meters beyond the trees when the faint sound of voices echoed across the clearing. The men hit the ground and aimed their rifles to the south. The voice was almost imperceptible at first. It slowly became louder and louder. Ahmed suddenly realized it was Mustafa. He was singing.

"If I were a rich man. Yabba dabba dabba, do-oo-oo. All day long I'd willey willey wonk, if I were a wealthy man."

The whinny of a horse echoed across the clearing. A pack of horses trotted from a cluster of trees on the opposite side of the road. There was a man riding one of the horses. It was Mustafa.

Ahmed spotted another man draped across the back of one of the horses. Mustafa trotted across the road and stopped abreast of the Mujaheddin. Gul Kabulin moaned as he tried to dismount. He slid off the horse to the ground. He reeked of alcohol.

Mustafa was only slightly more graceful. He threw his leg over the horse's back and caught his balance, as he stumbled off the mount. He laughed and then threw his head back to sing.

"If I were a rich man, Yabba—"

Mohammajon cut him off in mid sentence.

"Shut up, Mustafa! You'll get us all killed."

"Okay, okay, Mohammajon. Allah's will be done."

Mustafa swiveled around awkwardly and pointed a quivering index finger into the air.

"Mustafa has brought you ten of Yunus Khalis' finest horses."

"You're drunk," Mohammajon called out incredulously. "What a pig you are."

Mustafa's face became stern. He glared at Mohammajon for a few moments. Then he broke into a big grin and laughed boisterously.

"I am a pig. But I'm a gracious pig. Commander Amin, the leader of Yunus Khalis' forces, offered to share his finest whiskey. What was I supposed to do, offend him?"

Mustafa continued to grin uncontrollably, as he stumbled and turned toward his fellow Mujaheddin. Several of them snickered. This only encouraged him. He grinned and raised his arms wide into the air.

"If I were a rich man. Yabba dabba dabba, doo-oo-oo. All day long I'd—"

Mohammajon stepped forward and battered Mustafa in the back of the head with the butt of his rifle. Mustafa crumbled to the ground facedown. Mohammajon rolled him over with his foot.

"Damn fool. Strap him onto a horse."

Several of the men lifted Mustafa by the shoulders and legs. They draped him across the back of the horse on his stomach. Haji tied Mustafa to the mount with a length of rope he fetched from his pack. He did the same with Gul Kabulin.

"We must be on our way in thirty minutes," Mohammajon bellowed. "Load the supplies on the horses."

Each Mujaheddin took a horse by the reins. Aman held the reins of the horses carrying the fallen comrades. Haji reached out to take reins of the horse bearing Mustafa."

"No," Aman called out gruffly, as he turned away toward the truck, "I will take care of Mustafa."

It took close to half an hour to load the remaining supplies from the truck on the backs of the horses. As soon as the job was finished, the men remounted the horses and retraced their steps down the embankment toward the road. Mohammajon led the way. He turned on his horse and called out to the men.

"We will ride to the east of the road. Stay well clear of the trail."

The platoon of horsemen trotted down the gently sloping hillside to the road and crossed to the clearing on the other side. They turned to the south and rode toward the Torkham border station.

Haji headed off ahead of the others. The group made good progress toward the border. They held the horses to a leisurely pace. At one point, Mustafa, still strapped to his horse, lifted his head and moaned. He retched loudly and vomited across the ground beneath the horse's feet. His body bobbed up and down as the horse trotted along behind the others.

After an hour of riding Mohammajon spotted one of the cloth strips hanging on a tree branch at a junction in the trail. He pulled the rag down, dismounted, and motioned for the other riders to halt.

"We're less than a kilometer from the Torkham border station. Dismount here. Total silence! We will take this trail to the east of the station."

Each man dismounted and took his horse by the reins. They proceeded single file onto a narrow and winding path that snaked downward along a crevice near the east wall of the pass. At times, it was nearly impossible to make out the path, much less the canyon wall. They were immersed in darkness.

The group passed two junctions where paths diverged in opposite directions. Each time Mohammajon indicated the correct route and the other men followed. In one stretch, the path narrowed until it was no more than two feet wide. The trail descended deep into the crevasse. On the right was the crevasse wall. On the left was a sheer drop off into blackness. Ahmed hugged the wall and gently guided his horse down the path. The winding trail finally bottomed out next to a meandering stream. After a short stretch along the bank of the stream, the path ambled upwards toward the top of the ridge.

Mohammajon led his chestnut mare at the front of the scattered line of Mujaheddin. Just as the group neared the ridge, the horse suddenly spooked.

The animal whinnied, lost her balance, and stumbled against the canyon wall.

Mohammajon tugged on the reins to steady the horse and comforted him with a pat on the neck. He led the animal upwards along the narrow path.

The convoy rounded a blind turn at the top of the ridge. Haji was huddled against the wall of a small cove. He placed his fingers to his lips and motioned toward the path ahead.

With Haji and his horse leading the way, the group proceeded onward along the twisting path. The trail widened to nearly three times its previous breadth less than on hundred meters out of the crevasse. Haji stopped and pressed his finger against his lips once again. Ahmed stopped to listen. Distant voices seemed to echo from the trail ahead. Haji motioned for Ahmed to follow.

The trail turned due south. Ahmed steadied his horse and patted the animal's flank, as the voices of the unseen men became louder and louder. The Tajik Mujaheddin walked through a sweeping turn. As they pressed onward, they heard the loud ramblings of a man speaking Pashtu. His discourse was peppered with the laughter of other men.

Ahmed led his horse forward a few more steps. Through the brush along the trail, he suddenly spotted a group of more than twenty Mujaheddin sitting around a campfire. It seemed to be a meeting of sorts. One man wearing a white turban was standing. He was engaged in a heated exchange with a man wearing a maroon turban who was sitting by the fire.

"I say we kill them all," the man in the maroon turban bellowed. "We have no food to share with prisoners, especially Tajik pigs."

"Mohammad, you are a goat. I gave my word. You'll receive your share of the toll. This is the way it will be. It is my decision."

"The toll is only a fraction of the value of the supplies and money they are carrying. Yunus did not even bargain for more. The horses alone are worth three thousand U.S. dollars."

"I've bargained with Mullah Habid's men many times before. He's been a good customer for many years. The price is always the same. One hundred dollars for each man, two hundred fifty dollars for each horse."

Ahmed had nearly passed the partial clearing when he spied the bodies of three men dangling from the ends of ropes tied to the branches of a nearby tree. The bodies bore the characteristic black turbans and tunics of the Taliban.

"Where are they?" the man in the maroon turban bellowed. "I would never trust a Tajik. They cheat you blind."

"Mustafa will come. He gave me his word."

The conversation faded as the caravan pressed along the trail. The route wound through a seemingly endless series of switchbacks. Finally, they reached a junction with a much larger dirt road. At Mohammajon's command, the men remounted their horses and continued on for almost two hours in the darkness.

Mohammajon dismounted and pulled his horse into the surrounding brush. The others quickly followed. Within moments, the approaching rumble of truck engines became a deafening roar.

The motor convoy was led by a pickup truck with several Mujaheddin in the bed. One fighter was manning a heavy machine gun. Two sports utility vehicles followed close behind and another pickup truck full of men brought up the rear. Two of the men in the bed of last pickup truck looked European. They seemed strangely out of place in the middle of the Khyber Pass.

Ahmed surmised they were reporters from one of the many services striving to bring news from the war in Afghanistan to their readers. Hundreds of reporters and cameramen had invaded from Pakistan since the collapse of the Taliban. The rough countryside was dangerous for natives. For foreigners, it was frequently deadly. Another convoy passed the Tajiks about an hour later. This one was far more ominous. Two vintage Russian military transport trucks led the line of vehicles. Both trucks were filled with men toting rifles and rocket-propelled grenade launchers. Three pickup trucks teeming with fighters brought up the rear. They were heading north toward Afghanistan.

Ahmed was uncertain of the identities of the men in the second convoy. He imagined they were possibly Pakistani Jihadists, stirred up by local mullahs, heading for Kandahar to fight for the Taliban. But they could just as easily have been Arabs on their way to the Qaida stronghold of Tora Bora in the southeast of Afghanistan or tribal warriors returning home at long last after being driven into exile by the Taliban. Such was the confused state of Afghanistan. It was rarely possible to determine the allegiance of a particular group of men from their appearance. It had always been so.

After another hour of riding, Mohammajon pulled up and signaled for the group to stop. He pointed toward a rusty old sign on the edge of the trail.

"Welcome to the Khyber Pass. We are now in Pakistan."

He pointed west. The tops of the mountain peaks were beginning to come into view.

"It will be sunrise soon. There's a cave up there among the rocks. We will stay here today and go on toward Peshawar tonight. We are still two or three days travel from Islamabad."

Ahmed glanced back down the trail.

"Wouldn't it be better to press on a little farther? I'd like to put those Pashtun fighters as far behind us as possible. The farther we go, the better I'll feel."

"That was Yunus Khalis speaking to his tribal council. Khalis is a liar and a cheat. Mustafa was a fool to deal with him. He won't follow us into Pakistan. He has many enemies here in the Pakistani tribal areas."

He pointed toward a gap in the range to the south.

"Peshawar is twenty kilometers south of that pass. There are many Pashtun refugee camps along the route we will follow. The ISI patrols this road and many of their officers collaborate with the Taliban. It is safer to stay here until tomorrow night. We have been fortunate so far. We can't afford to have those drunks wake up while we are hiding from a Pakistani patrol."

Ahmed glanced at the two inert figures slung across the horses. Gul was intermittently snoring in short rapid-fire puffs. Mustafa was fast asleep. Ahmed turned his horse around.

"You're right, Mohammajon. We should sober these two up, rest the horses, and continue on after sundown."

Ahmed guided his horse in behind Mohammajon's mount and followed him through a series of short switchbacks toward the wall of the pass. The other men on horseback trailed close behind. The trail ended in a small clearing. A fire pit full of ash was surrounded with rocks. There were no other signs of life.

Ahmed gathered his coat against the stiff wind. He followed Mohammajon's horse across the rough and rocky terrain toward the canyon wall. The other riders trailed behind.

The morning sky began to lighten and the vistas beyond the walls of the pass soon flooded into view. Ahmed gazed with awe at the raw beauty surrounding them. Purple, snow-capped peaks soared behind the rolling hills within the pass. Two kilometers below the trail there was a narrow strip of green surrounding a lazy river. The river meandered through the rock-strewn oasis and into the distance. The richness of the green stood in stark contrast to the shades of brown they'd left behind.

Mohammajon turned and motioned for quiet, as he dismounted from his horse. He handed the reins to Ahmed and signaled for Haji to follow. The two men ran up a trail with their Kalashnikov rifles and disappeared behind a massive rock formation. Haji reappeared a moment later and waved for the others to follow.

Ahmed dismounted and guided his horse along the side of the rocks. A steep incline led up the backside of the formation. The mouth of a cave sprung into view halfway up the slope. The entrance was completely hidden by the rocks in front of it.

Ahmed walked his horse into the cave behind Haji. The short passage inside the mouth opened up into a huge cavern with a span of over a hundred meters. The horse's hooves echoed between the walls. A pool of sparkling water was set against the back wall of the cave. A trickle flowed down the face of the rocks and dribbled into the crystal clear water. Concentric ripples spread out from the tiny waterfall across the surface of the pool.

Mohammajon had already fetched a bucket of water for his horse. He was squatting next to the pool drinking from a cup.

Ahmed dropped the reins of his horse. He turned in place with arms extended and his gaze directed upwards. Dozens of carvings were dug into the solid rock in ceiling of the cavern.

"This is magnificent!"

His voice echoed through the cavern.

"How did you know this place?"

"I traveled this road with my father when I was a boy. He learned it from his father. We stopped here many times to rest."

"Who owns this cave?"

"Travelers have sought refuge in this cave for a thousand years. No man can live here. All who pass this way understand this. It is an oasis where one may dwell for a day or two. Then it's time to move on or endure the wrath of the local tribes. The locals are Pashtun people who've kept to themselves for centuries. This is their holiest place."

"Many must know of this place. Others could stop here."

"It's possible, but unlikely. I've been here over fifty times the past forty years. Not once has another caravan come at the same time. Many are afraid of the ancient tribe of warriors who live nearby. My father and my father's father led vast caravans with spice and silks from China through this valley. They paid tributes of silks and fine horses to the leader of this tribe. I have known him since I was a boy. If he comes, he will welcome me."

Mustafa and Gul were still unconscious. Several of the men lifted them down from their horses. They laid them out on blankets on the ground.

All of the Mujaheddin fed and watered their horses. They unloaded the supplies and stacked them against the wall of the cavern. Although the cave was wet and cold, it was clearly a cut above the open terrain outside where they would've been exposed to wind, rain, and the ever-present danger of attack.

Mohammajon ordered Haji to stand the first watch. The young Mujaheddin took up a position in the rocks where he could detect any movement toward the cave from the trail below. Ahmed settled down with the other Tajik fighters to wait for darkness to fall.

CHAPTER NINE

Mustafa began to stir several hours later. He sat up and pressed his head between his knees while rubbing his forehead with both hands. After a while, he lifted his head and glanced around with bleary eyes. Gul was still sprawled out on a nearby blanket.

Ahmed Jan noticed Mustafa stirring. He brewed a cup of green tea and tore off a piece of naan.

"Here Mustafa, drink this tea. It'll make you feel better."

"What happened?"

"You drank too much whiskey. You passed out."

Mustafa rubbed at the back of his head.

"I've got a knot the size of a hen's egg on the back of my head."

"You fell backwards against a rock. It knocked you unconscious."

Mustafa moaned and struggled to his feet. He walked to the pool, splashed water over his face, and peered up at the ceiling.

"What is this place?"

"We're in a cave in the Khyber Pass," Mohammajon replied. "Peshawar is a little over twenty kilometers to the south. We'll rest here until darkness falls."

Mustafa took a drink from the pool. He rolled his head around on his shoulders to easy the tightness in his neck and rubbed his temples with both hands.

"What happened with Yunus Khalis? What was the charge at the Torkham border station?"

The old Mujaheddin turned a page in the Quran without lifting his head.

"We didn't pay. We bypassed the border station on the crevasse trail."

Mustafa whirled around, his black eyes flashing anger like bolts of lightening.

"You old fool! I promised Khalis bakshish of five thousand dollars. What have you done?"

Mohammajon ignored the insult. He looked up from the Quran.

"We passed his camp undetected in the night. They were plotting to kill us and take the horses and money."

"Yunus Khalis gave me his word. He would not break his agreement with Mullah Habid."

"It does not matter. We're a long way from Afghanistan. We saved five thousand dollars."

"Damn it. It doesn't matter how far we are from the border. He will seek revenge. You can be sure of that."

"Allah's will be done," Mohammajon uttered, as he returned to the Quran.

Mustafa whirled around and glared toward Ahmed Jan with a look of disgust. He picked up a cup and filled it with water. Striding across the cave, he tossed the cup of water in Gul's face.

"Ahh!" the Mujaheddin screamed, as he bolted upright.

"Get up!" Mustafa yelled. "We must double the watch. Yunus Khalis will be looking for us."

Gul Kabulin scrambled to his feet blurry-eyed. He fetched his Kalashnikov from the back of one of the horses and stumbled off toward the mouth of the cave.

Mustafa bent down and washed his face and hands in the pool. He fetched a blanket and another loaf of naan before retreating to a rocky ledge in an isolated corner of the cave.

Ahmed Jan waited for nearly an hour before he dared to approach the fuming Mujaheddin. Mustafa was sitting with his legs dangling over a boulder. He was starring at the ground, absorbed with his thoughts. Ahmed sat down and waited for him to speak. Mustafa finally raised his head and pounded his hand on the rock.

"It's my fault. Whiskey steals my mind."

"We've traveled far from the Afghani border. Yunus Khalis will not search this far. We are a drop of water in the Arabian Sea."

"It does not matter if we ride to China. We snubbed his honor and brought ridicule upon him. He is a proud man. Remember my words: Yunus Khalis will come after us."

"We have ten fine horses and Mohammajon knows this country well. If it is Allah's will, we will make it to Islamabad."

"You're beginning to sound like the imbecile. Take care lest you go the way of the fool."

Mustafa took a bite from the loaf of naan. He chewed exuberantly with his mouth open, as he peered toward the ceiling. He swallowed and took a drink of water from his cup.

"Perhaps Mohammajon's right. This is a good place to hide. The Taliban and al-Qaida are in disarray."

"What did you find out in Jalalabad?"

"Yunus Khalis told me the Taliban disintegrated over the past week. The American bombings devastated the Taliban and al-Qaida forces. Thousands of the enemy soldiers were killed. The Taliban abandoned Jalalabad just a few days after the fall of Mazar-e-Sharif and Kabul. Now there is fighting in the streets of Kandahar and Mullah Omar has fled to Pakistan."

"It's hard to believe that it could happen so quickly after all these years."

"Dostrum has twenty thousand Taliban and al-Qaida soldiers surrounded in Kunduz. The American planes bomb them night and day. There are said to be more than three thousand Arab, Pakistani, Chechen, and Chinese al-Qaida trapped in the city. Al-Qaida slaughtered many Taliban soldiers who tried to surrender to the Alliance. Dostrum will not spare them. He will kill them all."

"What word is there of bin Laden?"

"Yunus Khalis thinks he's in the mountains in southeastern Afghanistan in Tora Bora. His close associate Mohammed Atef was killed just outside of Kabul a few days ago. An American bomb landed on his head. Anti-Taliban tribesmen supported by American Special Forces are closing in on the southern-most areas of the country. Pakistani forces guard the routes from Tora Bora into Pakistan. Even sympathetic Pashtun are abandoning the Taliban. Mullah Naqibullah and Haji Basher, two Pashtun tribal leaders who fought the Russians, took control of Kandahar. The war could be over in days."

"I never imagined it could change so quickly. The Taliban seemed invincible."

Mustafa spit on the ground.

"Bin Laden and al-Qaida, they are stupid. They could have controlled the Taliban and Afghanistan forever. Who would care if they bombed a few embassies in Africa? So what if they bombed an American warship in some port now and then? There would have been a few months of saber rattling by the

Americans. Maybe the U.S. would've launched a few missiles. Then al-Qaida could have gone about their business. But what do these idiots do? They kill three thousand people and attack the American homeland. What did they expect would happen? It's good for our people they are so stupid."

"Who will rule Afghanistan?"

"Burhanuddin Rabbani returned to Kabul and claimed his previous position as president of Afghanistan. But he doesn't have the support of the people. The Americans and British are planning to form a coalition of Tajiks, Uzbeks, Turkmen, Hazaras, and moderate Pashtun. The Taliban will be excluded."

"Mohammajon thinks there will be a new civil war within two years."

"For once he's right about something."

Ahmed reached out his hand. He held the small leather pouch of diamonds and money Mustafa had given him. Mustafa grinned and shoved it into his pocket.

Ahmed picked up a stone from the ground and tossed it high into the air. He caught it and tossed it even higher. He caught it once again and tossed it away.

"There can be peace in Afghanistan. But first there must be a reason for people to want peace. There must be food. There must be good jobs. Every man needs a home where he can shelter his family. Only when these necessities are restored to the people of Afghanistan will there be hope of lasting peace between the Tajiks and the Pashtun."

"You are a dreamer, Ahmed Jan. These things cannot come to all people of Afghanistan. Perhaps for the Tajiks or for the Tajiks and Uzbeks, but not for all."

Suddenly, loud shouts resonated from outside of the cave. A burst of rifle fire echoed through the chamber. The Mujaheddin raced toward the entrance. They ran from the cavern to discover Haji writhing on the ground with blood soaking through the back of his shalwar kamese. Gul was dead. Blood flowed from a tight cluster of bullet holes in the middle of his chest.

"He stabbed me!" Haji screamed. "He stabbed me in the back! Stupid Hezbi!"

Saaed Zaki took offense to the insult and raised his rifle. He pointed it at Haji. Mustafa seized the Kalashnikov from Saaed's hand.

"Listen to me. If there is anymore fighting, I will kill you both."

Mustafa turned toward Ahmed.

"Even Tajiks kill each other over nothing. What hope is there for peace?"

Mustafa handed the rifle to Ahmed and crouched over Haji. He turned the wounded man on his side and lifted up the top of his tunic. There was a deep slice across his lower back. It was oozing blood. Mustafa pressed his hand against the wound to stem the bleeding.

"Get me a rag!"

Mohammajon trotted into the cave. He ran out a few moments later with a bundle of sterile gauze.

"Here, I got this from the Americans. It's clean."

Mustafa pulled Haji's top over his shoulders. He pressed a wad of the gauze against the wound."

"Hold this!"

Mohammajon pressed on the wad of gauze, as Mustafa wound several layers around Haji's waist and tied it in place. The bandage immediately soaked through with blood. Mustafa turned and stared up into Mohammajon's eyes.

"Carry him inside the cave," Mohammajon ordered.

Ahmed and Sandir picked Haji up by the legs and shoulders. They carried him through the mouth of the cave and into the center of the cavern. Mohammajon spread a wool blanket on the ground.

"Put him here. Saaed, go gather some wood for a fire."

Saaed jogged out the cave entrance. He reappeared a few minutes later with kindling and a dead tree branch. Mohammajon broke the branch into several pieces and stacked them in a depression next to Haji. He surrounded the branches with kindling.

Mohammajon got up and fetched a small plastic box from his pocket. He opened the container and pulled out a matchbook. He tore a match from the book, struck it, and knelt down to light the kindling.

"Water," Haji pleaded, with a quivering voice.

Ahmed grabbed a cup, filled it with water, and knelt beside the wounded Mujaheddin. He lifted Haji's head with his twisted left hand and held the cup with his right. Haji drank from the cup until it was empty. Exhausted, he laid his head back on the ground, breathing heavily.

"Please, I'm cold."

Ahmed fetched several blankets and covered the wounded warrior. Haji grasped his arm.

"Don't let me die here, Commander. Please don't let me die here."

"You're not going to die, Haji. Be quiet. Save your strength."

"Promise you won't leave me. Promise me."

"I won't leave you, Haji. I'll take you from this place. I promise."

Ahmed rearranged the blankets and stood up. He glanced first at Mustafa and then at Mohammajon. They both stared back without speaking.

Ahmed peered out of the mouth of the cave to the valley below. Dark foreboding clouds were accumulating in the southeast. The towering distant peaks had vanished. A flurry of wind-whipped snow stung against his face. He glanced at his watch. It was a little after three in the afternoon.

He ducked back into the cave and poured a ladle of soup into a cup. He walked across to where Haji was lying and picked up one edge of the blanket. The bandage on Haji's back was already tinged with blood. Haji opened his eyes.

"How do you feel, Haji?"

"I'm better, Commander."

"You need to eat this soup. Here, let me help you up."

Ahmed helped Haji sit up. He pressed the cup to the man's lips. Haji took two gulps of the broth and then pushed the cup away.

"The cave is spinning. Let me lie back down."

Ahmed helped him lay back on the ground and rearranged the blankets. Haji began to shiver uncontrollably. He opened his eyes and pleaded with Ahmed with a weak and shuddering voice.

"Please, I'm cold."

Ahmed jogged across to the supplies. He lifted a canvas cover and pulled out a stack of blankets. He turned and caught sight of Mustafa speaking with Mohammajon on the other side of the cave. Mustafa thrust his arms in the air and turned away from Mohammajon. Mohammajon strode away toward the cave entrance and disappeared outside.

Ahmed carried the blankets over to Haji's pallet. The Tajik fighter had stopped shivering. Even so, Ahmed knelt and spread three more of the heavy wool blankets across his body. Ahmed shook his head and turned around on his knees. Mustafa was standing behind him. He beckoned with his hand.

Ahmed stood up and walked to the horses with Mustafa.

"What is it, Mustafa?"

"Haji's not going to make it. We must leave him here."

Ahmed's expression turned first to shock and then to outrage.

"No! I'm not leaving him in this place!"

"Ahmed," Mustafa pleaded.

Ahmed shook his head determinedly.

"No! I'm not leaving Haji here. I gave him my word. I will not break my promise."

"Ahmed, listen to me. Haji's dying and we can't do anything about it. It's a long and dangerous ride to Islamabad. He'll only slow us down."

"You go ahead with the others. Just leave me two horses and I'll take him to the hospital in Peshawar. I'll meet you in Islamabad in three days."

"We cannot leave you, Ahmed. Mullah ordered us to stay with you."

Ahmed turned his head to look toward Haji. Mohammajon was kneeling beside the wounded man with a large knife in his hand.

"No!" Ahmed yelled.

He bolted across the cave and grasped Mohammajon's arm. Ahmed twisted Mohammajon's arm behind his back and forced him to drop the knife.

"Ahmed," Mohammajon replied in a calm voice, "I must sterilize the wound. He will die of infection."

Ahmed stared into the tired old man's eyes. He released Mohammajon's arm. Mohammajon retrieved the knife off the ground and wiped it with a rag. He knelt and heated the blade over the fire until it was red hot.

"Hold his arms, Ahmed. Mustafa, you grab his legs."

The two men grabbed hold of Haji's limbs. Mohammajon pulled the bandage down to reveal the angry, gaping wound. He handed Ahmed a small rag he'd rolled into a cylinder.

"Put this in his mouth."

Ahmed slid the roll between Haji's teeth. Mohammajon pressed the hot blade against one side of the laceration. The blade sizzled against the exposed muscle.

"Ahh!" Haji screamed with wild-eyed delirium, as he flailed his arms and legs.

Mohammajon held the blade over the flames until it glowed red-hot once again.

"One more time."

He pressed the blade against the wound once again. Haji convulsed involuntarily and let out a guttural scream, before slumping into unconsciousness.

Mohammajon applied ointment from a tube into the wound and redressed it with a fresh bandage. He stood up and turned to Ahmed.

"Ahmed, we must leave now. Haji's only chance to survive is here in the cave. We will set a fire among the rocks outside to attract the local tribe."

"No, Mohammajon, I will not leave him here."

Ahmed turned and strode from the cave. He reappeared a few minutes later dragging two large tree branches. Ahmed sat down on the ground next to Haji. He took the knife and began trimming away the smaller branches. Mustafa squatted beside him.

"Ahmed, Peshawar is a nest for Pashtun fighters. We can't take Haji there. They will kill us all."

Ahmed trimmed away the foliage from the two branches until he'd fashioned two large staffs. He selected the stoutest of the horses, a gray mare, and fashioned a rope harness that suspended the staffs on opposite sides of the mount. He wove a rope back and forth between the two staffs to form a sling that hung behind the horse. Finally, he covered the sling with a pair of blankets.

It took almost an hour to build the travois. Once he was done, Ahmed stood up and turned around. All of the men were standing in silence behind him.

"Come on. Let's go. Load up the supplies."

Mustafa shook his head and turned away. He strode across the cave and sat on a rock at the edge of the pool of water.

Mohammajon directed the other Mujaheddin to reload the supplies on the horses. One item at a time, they replaced the tents, blankets, food, and ammunition on the horses. Mohammajon stamped out the fire with his shoe when they were done. He grabbed the reins of a fully loaded mare and led her toward the mouth of the cave. Ahmed watched him disappear outside, before he turned toward the other men.

"Sandir, take Haji's feet."

The two of them lifted Haji off the ground and positioned him on the travois. Haji's body hung low between the staffs. His backside nearly touched the ground.

"That's not going to work," Mustafa bellowed.

He dismounted his horse.

"Put him back on the blanket."

Ahmed took Haji's torso and Sandir took his legs. They lifted Haji back onto the ground.

Mustafa retied several of the lines extending between the tree limbs. He retrieved another length of rope from his pack and used it to fashion several taunt extensions beneath the sling. Finally, he spread the blankets back across the travois and tucked the ends beneath the rope lines.

"That should work better."

Ahmed helped Sandir lift Haji off the ground again. They positioned him back near the top of the travois. The wounded Tajik's body hung nearly a half-meter higher above the ground.

Mustafa took the reins of the horse bearing the travois and knotted them together with a rope extension. He handed the end of the rope to Ahmed.

"Let's go."

Mustafa remounted his horse and trotted out of the entrance to the cave. Ahmed mounted his own horse and followed behind with the mare in tow. The ends of the travois clattered down the rocky incline to the trail below. Ahmed glanced at his watch. It was straight up 9 P.M.

CHAPTER TEN

J ust as Mustafa predicted, the group's progress slowed to a snail's pace. The bitterly cold southeasterly wind bustled in their faces. It took all of the effort each man could muster to just stay on the trail. Ahmed stopped every few minutes to readjust the travois to keep Haji from falling off, as they wove through tight switchbacks and steep inclines.

Haji regained consciousness several times along the way. Each time he awoke, Ahmed forced him to drink water from the flask he kept slung across the bottom of the travois. The Tajik's pulse grew more faint as the group traveled on.

Twice during the night the rev of heavy vehicles groaned above the punishing wind. The Tajiks sought cover by the side of the trail each time. Both vehicles were pickup trucks. One headed south and the other north. The northbound vehicle had ten men piled into the bed. They were wearing black turbans.

Travel became more perilous as the night wore on. The cloudy sky cleared to reveal a nearly full moon. It seemed to hang above the wall of the pass like a beacon, before rising over the mountaintop. The moon's reflection shimmered in the river that meandered along the side of the trail. The beauty of the nighttime panorama belied the danger. The watchful eyes of an unseen enemy could have easily spotted them from a distant ridge.

They rode in silence across rolling hill after rolling hill, and from one valley to the next. From time to time, the whistling of the wind rose above the pounding of the horse's hooves and the grating of the wooden supports of the travois against the ruts that marred the winding path. They made only a few kilometers per hour.

Mohammajon led the group onward. Six hours into the night's journey, as they crested yet another ridge, he suddenly whirled his steed in place. He pointed into the distance, as the others ascended the crest beside him.

There in the distance in the sprawling valley below them were the glimmers of more than a thousand campfires. Like fireflies, they flickered in the stiff breeze and stretched out toward the horizon as far as the eye could see. In the center of the fires was a dark area that was sprinkled with lights. The trail wound down the slope of the hill toward the far away beacons.

"That's Peshawar," Mohammajon called out above the whistle of the wind. "The campfires are the refugee camps."

"It's incredible," Ahmed hollered above the din. "There must be a million people."

"They're mostly Pashtun," he yelled. "We are not welcome there."

Mohammajon jabbed his feet gently into his horses flanks. His mare whinnied in protest, but trotted on down the trail. The others followed close behind with the travois bearing Haji's body clattering along the rocks to the rear.

They came upon a junction about a kilometer down the trail. Mohammajon led them down the fork that snaked east away from Peshawar. The Tajiks traveled on for nearly an hour, as the trail took them along a series of ridges that paralleled the ancient city. The trail broke sharply to the east when the flickering fires were nearly behind them. The city disappeared from view behind the crest, as they walked the horses down a steep grade.

"Look!" Sandir shouted.

He pointed toward a gathering of lights behind them. Mohammajon turned to look.

"Calm yourself. They are fires of the refugee camps at Peshawar."

The Mujaheddin held their horses steady and peered behind them. Mustafa suddenly whirled his horse around. He shouted above the howl of the wind.

"They're moving! They're men with torches!"

Mustafa jabbed his heels into the flanks of his horse.

"Ha!"

The horse jumped beneath him. In an instant, the Tajik band was galloping headlong from one switchback to the next down the treacherous trail. The thunder of hooves echoed between the rocks around them. The reins of the horse pulling the travois were ripped from Ahmed's hands and the frightened animal bolted past Mustafa's mount to the lead. The travois careened from one rock to the next and smashed against the wall of the cliff. Still the horse continued its frenzied dash.

A single shot from a rifle echoed above the wind. It seemed to come out of the ground cover in front of them. Sandir cartwheeled off the back of his horse with blood pouring from a gaping wound in the side of his head.

Ahmed leapt off his mount and dove for cover among the rocks and brush surrounding them. He crawled on his belly to Sandir's side. He was dead.

Ahmed slithered away through heavy brush to Mustafa's position behind a rock.

"Who are they?"

"I don't know. They could be bandits or possibly ISI. We're trapped between this group and the one behind us."

A man bellowed above the wind from the distance.

"Mustafa, you swine, did you think you could drink my whiskey and then cheat me blind?"

"It's Yunus Khalis," Mustafa whispered. "Pray for Allah's mercy."

Mustafa glared toward Mohammajon. He cupped his hands around his mouth and hollered above the wind.

"Yunus, it was not my intention to cheat you. I am a cheap drunk. I passed out and my comrades took the crevasse trail. They didn't know of our deal. I planned to pay you on our return."

"You lying dog!" Yunus called from the distance.

"I am not lying. You and me, we have been friends since Taloqan. I always keep my word. I am a stupid goat. I'll pay you ten thousand U.S. dollars for my drunken mindlessness, double the fee we agreed to."

The whistle of the wind was the only sound for a few seconds. Then Khalis yelled again.

"Okay. Stand up with your hands in the air and walk toward me. All of you! We'll kill you all if you try anything stupid."

Mustafa stood up without his rifle and thrust his hands into the air. He called out to the Tajiks.

"Okay, all the rest of you stand up!"

Each Tajik dropped his rifle, stood up, and thrust his hands into the air. There was a rustling in the bushes and a dozen men in white turbans emerged from the brush. They fanned out and surrounded the Alliance fighters. More than forty fighters on horseback trotted down the hill behind them. A huge man with a long beard was in front. He swung a leg over his horse's back and stretched down to the ground.

Khalis strode up to Mustafa and slashed him across his face with a long knife. Mustafa fell backward across the ground. Blood spurted from a deep gash that ran across his chin and down his neck.

Khalis spit on Mustafa.

"You Tajik pig! Do you not know the ways of the Pashtun? I took my revenge after a hundred years and I took it quickly. You are lower than a snake. Where's the money?"

Mustafa reached into his coat and pulled a wad of bills from an inside pocket. He started counting through the bills.

"All of it!" the angry Pashtun yelled.

He shoved his rifle barrel into Mustafa's belly. Mustafa held out the money. Khalis snatched the bills from his hand.

"What else?"

Mustafa held up the leather pouch containing the diamonds. Khalis snatched it out of his hand.

"What else?"

"Nothing," Mustafa muttered, as he pressed the arm of his jacket against his face to slow the flow of blood. "That's it."

Khalis motioned to one of his men.

"Search him! Slit his throat if you find anything of value! The same with the rest of you. Give me all your money and valuables."

The other four Tajiks emptied their pockets and removed their watches. One by one, the Pashtun searched them. Their packs were emptied out onto the ground. Khalis sifted through the booty first. He stuffed what he wanted into his pack and left the rest for the others.

Khalis strode to the travois where Haji was lying motionless. He searched Haji's pockets and found a few bills and a wallet. He stuffed them into his pack. Khalis lifted his Kalashnikov and fired a burst into Haji's chest. He pulled his knife from a sheath and cut the travois from the mare's back. Haji's body fell to the ground. Khalis took the reins of the mare and strode back toward the Tajiks.

He barked out orders to the fighters in Pashtu. Several men fetched rope from their horses and bound the Tajiks' hands behind their backs. Finally, they fashioned crude nooses and slipped them over the heads of the Tajiks.

Khalis mounted his horse and yelled in Dari.

"Okay pigs, on your horses!"

The Pashtun tribesmen helped the five Tajiks mount their horses. Each Alliance fighter was tethered to a Pashtun rider by the noose around his neck. Other Pashtun fighters took the reins of the riderless horses.

"Let's go. If one of them falls from his horse, drag him by the neck."

Winding back up the trail to the crest of the hill, they made their way back to the ridge where the refugee camps surrounding Peshawar flooded back into view. Once they reached the main highway, the riders retraced their previous route at a slow gallop. They pulled the Tajiks from one switchback to the next by the nooses around their necks.

The snow began to fall again, slowly at first, and then harder. It accumulated in Ahmed's hair and beard. It built up in his eyebrows. It melted against his skin and dripped from the tip of his aquiline nose. It took all the effort he could muster to just stay on the horse.

The riders pulled up at a junction after a little more than a half hour of riding. Khalis directed the group to a road that took a direct line along the east wall of the pass. On his command, the riders stopped a few hundred meters from the canyon wall. Khalis trotted on toward the cliff with another rider. He rode back a few minutes later and waved the riders forward.

They rode past a series of bunkers dug into the ground and built up with boulders. Each bunker was outfitted with a heavy machine gun manned by three or four men with black turbans. The fighters kept their guns trained on the riders as they passed. Two larger bunkers sported light artillery pieces.

They rode over a rise and a small compound came into view. It was partially hidden beneath an overhang in the wall of the pass. The complex had three small mud-brick huts and a much larger structure that was part mud-brick and part wood. Two of the windows in the larger building were boarded over. The roof was blanketed with a three-inch accumulation of snow.

The group rode on toward the main building. As they drew closer, Ahmed spotted a pile of human corpses on the ground in front of the main building. Three more bodies hung from poles next to the heap. The stench of death was in the air.

Several fighters in Afghan dress were milling around the compound with Kalashnikov rifles. Some wore black turbans, while others wore white. One of the men called out in Arabic, as the group rode into the large open courtyard in front of the building. Khalis trotted his horse toward the large building. He pulled up just short of the front door. The other riders eased the prisoners' horses to a stop.

Another Arab in a white turban stepped out of the building. He parlayed with Khalis for a few moments, before reaching out to hand him a cloth bag. Khalis opened the bag and looked inside. Satisfied, he wheeled his horse around and galloped back to the group.

The Arab shouted above the whistle of the wind. Several of the black turbaned fighters ran to the horses and pulled the Tajiks off their mounts. One man wrenched Ahmed toward the door of the large building by the noose around his neck. Mustafa struggled to turn his head back toward Khalis and his men.

"Khalis, you swine! Don't forget to tell your men about the diamonds and fifty thousand dollars you stole from me!"

Khalis spun his horse around. He dug his heels into the horse's flanks and galloped back to Mustafa. He pulled up at the last moment and laughed boisterously.

"Don't worry, Tajik, I'll tell them. None of them care about the money. Every one of them would pay me for the pleasure of slitting your Tajik throat."

The Arab pulled Mustafa off balance with the noose around his neck. Khalis surged forward and swung his rifle. The butt cracked against the back of Mustafa's head with a sickening thud. He crashed to the ground. Khalis turned his horse and trotted away.

Two of the black-turbaned fighters picked Mustafa up and carried him through the door. They shoved other Alliance fighters in behind them.

A line of men was standing next to the door inspecting the Tajik prisoners, as they stumbled into the room. Most of them wore Afghani dress. Ahmed raised his head, as he was yanked through the crowd by the rope around his neck. His eyes locked with a dark-skinned man with neatly trimmed black hair. The man was wearing smart military attire. Ahmed recognized the uniform. It was the standard issue of the Pakistani ISI security forces. The man smirked at Ahmed, as the Arab jerked him into the room.

The inside of the building was illuminated with electric lights. A generator was humming in the adjoining room. Two tables in the middle of the room were strewn with maps and other papers. Communication equipment was stacked on a desk along the sidewall. Boxes of weapons were piled to the ceiling in the back of the room.

There was a huge map of Afghanistan on the other sidewall. Dozens of different colored pushpins dotted the topographic map. There were black pins concentrated around Kandahar, Kunduz, and tribal areas along the Pakistani border. Several other black pins were clustered across the border near Peshawar. Yellow pins covered most of the rest of Afghanistan. There were blue pins concentrated near the northern border with Tajikistan. Two blue pins labeled an area outside of Islamabad.

A large metal desk was positioned in the exact center of the room. There was an Arabic-looking man sitting in the chair. He had a long bushy beard and wore a black turban adorned with gold.

The fighters shoved the Northern Alliance soldiers directly in front of the sinister-looking figure. Mustafa, still unconscious, was laid out on the floor behind the Tajiks. The man behind the desk sat and regarded them for a few moments. Then he slowly rose to his feet and walked around the desk to the front of the line of men. He spoke in English.

"My name is Ayman Al-Zawahiri of al-Qaida. Who's your leader?"

Al-Zawahiri stared down the line of men for a few seconds and then walked over to Mohammajon.

"Are you the leader?"

He stared at the old Tajik for a few seconds and then proceeded on to Ahmed.

"Are you the leader?"

None of the Mujaheddin responded. They stared straight ahead. He walked over to Saaed and glared into his eyes with a wild-eyed smirk. There were beads of sweat on Saaed's forehead and terror in his eyes. His breathing was labored.

Al-Zawahiri, without breaking his stare, slid a long curved knife from a sheath that hung from his pants. He held it up in front of Saeed's eyes. The Tajik recoiled with a whimper. Two of the black-turbaned fighters grabbed him by the arms and shoved him forward. Al-Zawahiri pressed the knife against his throat.

"I am only going to ask you once, Tajik. Who's your leader?"

Saaed broke. He pointed toward Ahmed.

"He is!" he cried out.

Al-Zawahiri turned his head toward Ahmed and grinned. He flicked the knife without looking away. A stream of blood spurted from Saaed's neck. The Tajik dropped to the ground like a lead weight. He gurgled for a few seconds and then fell silent.

"Get the Tajik pig out of here. He's soiling my floor."

Two soldiers lifted Saaed's body from the floor and carted it to the door.

They disappeared for only a moment and returned wiping the blood from their hands with rags.

Al-Zawahiri took a few steps to his right. He turned in place and stood face-to-face with Ahmed.

"So, you are the leader of this band of Tajik pigs."

Al-Zawahiri turned toward his men.

"They scrape the barrel, these Tajiks."

He turned back and scowled at Ahmed. Al-Zawahiri held the knife at his side, as he interrogated Ahmed in a hushed voice.

"What is your mission, Tajik?"

"We have no mission," Ahmed replied calmly. "We travel from Kabul to Islamabad to escape the fighting. We are deserters."

The Arab, toe-to-toe with Ahmed, stared into his eyes.

"You will tell me your mission Tajik pig. You think you are a tough man. I see it in your eyes. You don't think you'll tell me. But rest assured, you will beg to tell me. What is your name?"

"Ahmed Jan."

The Arab turned toward his comrades with a look of surprise. He nodded.

"Jan. That is a famous name in the North. Where are you from?"

"My family lived in Taloqan."

"Taloqan. Are you related to the Commander Jan who was killed by Taliban forces?"

"He was my father."

Al-Zawahiri whirled toward the group of men standing in the corner of the room.

"We've captured a Jan. Hafizullah, weren't both your sons killed last year in the battle for Taloqan?"

A scowling fighter wearing a green turban answered from the back of the room.

"The Tajiks hung my oldest son from a lamppost in the square."

Al-Zawahiri leaned forward until his face was little more than a centimeter from Ahmed's.

"You thought you'd destroyed us, didn't you? We are stronger than ever. We have over two hundred Taliban fighters and more than fifty al-Qaida in this post alone. We are only toying with the Americans. We will soon be ready to spring our trap."

He traced the tip of his blade across Ahmed's cheek. A drop of blood trickled from a cut beneath Ahmed's right eye.

"Come here, Hafizullah," Al-Zawahiri ordered. "You and I are going to have a little chat with Commander Jan. Take him to the interrogation room."

"Praise Allah!" Hafizullah bellowed. "I've prayed these past months for the chance to avenge my sons. Allah is indeed great!"

Two of the Qaida fighters held Ahmed's arms. Hafizullah jerked him backward by the noose around his neck. Ahmed stumbled to the floor and Hafizullah kicked him in the crotch. As Ahmed writhed on the floor, Hafizullah used the noose to drag him across the floor to the back door. Hafizullah slammed the door shut behind them. A terrifying scream echoed from the next room. This was followed by shouts in Pashtu and three loud thumps. Then there was silence.

"Lackey pigs," al-Zawahiri seethed. "It is our pleasure to reward you for Mazar-e-Sharif, Kabul, and Jalalabad. Many holy al-Qaida and Taliban warriors died in the American bombing. You are nothing but women."

He strutted down the line and pushed the point of the knife against Mohammajon's cheek.

"Did you celebrate your victory? Perhaps you had a little pussy. Did you have a little koos, Tajik? Maybe a young Pashtun girl?"

Al-Zawahiri sneered wickedly.

"Kamaluddin, I think this is the one who spoiled your daughter."

Mohammajon stared straight ahead without responding.

"Answer me!" Al-Zawahiri bellowed.

Then his voice faded to almost a whisper.

"Have it your way, you greasy dog."

Al-Zawahiri jerked his knee up into Mohammajon's crotch. Mohammajon fell backwards across Mustafa's body. Moaning in pain, he rolled into the fetal position and clutched his legs to his chest.

"You stinking pigs. Take them out to the road and hang them from poles at the junction," al-Zawahiri commanded. "Let them be a warning to all Tajik dogs who dare come to the Khyber Pass."

Several al-Qaida and Taliban fighters grabbed Aman and Mohammajon and dragged them toward the door. Mustafa was beginning to rouse. A Taliban fighter jerked him to his feet by the noose around his neck and pushed him toward the main door. The fighter kicked Mustafa in the side and jerked him backward with the noose. He shoved Mustafa out the door.

Al-Zawahiri called after them.

"Castrate the bastards before you hang them. Stick their organs in their mouths."

A gauntlet of Taliban and al-Qaida fighters pummeled the three Alliance Mujaheddin, as they dragged and kicked them down the snowy trail to the main road. One of the Arabs knocked Mohammajon unconscious with a stone. Kamaluddin used the noose to drag him to the road.

Two Taliban fighters dug holes next to the road and mounted three tall wooden posts. They dragged Mustafa across the dirt to the base of the first pole and began to hoist him into the air.

Two thunderous explosions boomed from the compound. The concussion threw the Qaida and Pashtun fighters to the ground. Dazed by the impact, several of them struggled to their feet, only to be blown to the ground again by an even larger explosion.

Mustafa raised his head off the ground. The smaller buildings were in flames. The main building had vanished. Mustafa lowered his head back to the ground. He heard the whoosh of attack helicopters and, a few moments later, men shouting in English.

Some of the Qaida and Pashtun fighters stumbled to their feet, only to be cut down in a hail of machine gun fire. A soldier in a white uniform and helmet leaned down over Mustafa. He had white paint on his face and a pair of night binoculars at the rim of his helmet. He raised his machine gun.

Mustafa managed to stammer the code the mullah had given them.

"It may be a long wait for the springtime."

The soldier lowered his barrel.

"Dog ears. Get over here!" he bellowed above the howling wind.

Another soldier in white sprinted toward them from the main compound. The second fighter sprayed a cluster of Taliban and al-Qaida fighters with the machine gun as he ran. The clatter of machine guns echoed all around them.

"What's up?" the second soldier puffed, as he jogged toward them.

"This one has the Alliance code, sir."

The second soldier was a bear of a man. He was carrying a machine gun and had a string of grenades across his chest. He stooped beside Mustafa.

"How many are you?"

"Four. One's still in the compound."

"Ain't no one alive in there. The compound is a shit heap. Where are the others?"

Mustafa lifted his head and pointed toward Mohammajon and Aman. They were both sprawled motionless across the road. The soldier turned and yelled into a communicator attached to his collar. A helicopter swooped to the ground beside them a moment later.

The three Alliance soldiers were put on stretchers and hoisted into the helicopter. Two medical attendants knelt beside them treating their wounds.

"What's the destination, Lieutenant?" the co-pilot yelled back to the burly American soldier, as the helicopter rose off the ground.

"The base in Jalalabad. That's the closest medical facility."

Mustafa grabbed his arm and pleaded with his eyes.

"No! Please! Take us to Islamabad."

"That's an hour away, buddy. You've lost a lot of blood. Jalalabad is closer."

Mustafa raised his head off the stretcher and squeezed the soldier's arm.

"No, please. Islamabad."

The lieutenant pursed his lips and stared at Mustafa for a few moments. Finally he called out.

"He wants to go to Islamabad. He's got the Alliance code. Take him there."

"You got it, buddy," the pilot called out.

The helicopter banked into a sweeping turn as the pilot radioed ahead.

"We aren't cleared for Islamabad," he yelled a moment later. "The closest we can get is Rawalpindi. It's ten kilometers from Islamabad. We'll land at Chaklala Air Force Base in fifty minutes."

Mustafa lowered his head back into the pillow on the stretcher.

"Who are you?"

"Lieutenant Miller. U.S. Army Rangers," the soldier barked.

Mustafa closed his eyes.

"Allah bless America."

The last sound he heard was the beating of the main rotor. He drifted into unconsciousness.

CHAPTER ELEVEN

December 15, 2001

Mustafa opened his eyes. He was lying on his back in a brightly lit room. A ceiling fan was slowly rotating above him. The room was white and lined with cabinets. The paint was peeling off the wall in several places and some of the ceiling tiles were missing. There were no windows. An IV in his arm was connected to a bag of saline.

Mustafa's head throbbed with a pulsating pain that radiated from the back of his head and down his neck. He rubbed his hand across his brow and lifted his head.

Mohammajon was lying in the bed next to him with a bandage wrapped around his head. He was sipping from a cup filled with orange juice. A plate of rolls was sitting on the bedside tray. Aman was lying in the third bed. He was on a respirator and his leg was lifted into the air in a traction device. His head had been wrapped in bandages and one eye was patched shut. Aman's chest rose and fell rhythmically, as the bellows on the respirator expanded and contracted.

"What is this place, Mohammajon?"

Mohammajon set his cup down.

"We're in the Pakistani military hospital in Rawalpindi. It's good to see you awake."

Mohammajon blotted his mouth with a napkin.

"How long?"

"We've been here two days. How do you feel?"

"Like I got clubbed with a rock. My head feels like it's going to explode."

"The doctor says you have a concussion. Aman isn't doing well. He had emergency surgery after the helicopter arrived here at the hospital. He has a crushed rib cage and a collapsed lung. I have no idea what happened to Ahmed."

"He died in the bombing."

"The bombing? What bombing?"

"American planes bombed the main building at the Qaida compound. The Americans saved our lives. Taliban fighters were about to hang me from a post when the bombs hit. I remember a helicopter. They put us inside and took off. That's the last I remember. Are you hurt?"

"Every muscle in my body aches. I'm fine other than that. I got knocked out, but I got away with a mild concussion, a bruise in my groin, and an ankle sprain."

Mustafa lifted a glass off the tray next to his bed and took a drink. He tore a piece of bread from a loaf and stuffed it into his mouth. Leaning his head back into his pillow, he exhaled loudly.

"What'll we do now?"

Mohammajon didn't answer. Mustafa turned his head. Mohammajon was staring at him with a finger pressed to his lips.

Suddenly, the door swung open. In walked a nurse dressed in a clean white uniform with a scarf covering her head. She was a striking dark-skinned woman with high cheekbones who looked to be about twenty-five years old.

"Well, look who's awake."

She slid a thermometer into Mustafa's mouth and took his wrist. Looking at her watch, she waited a few seconds and then dropped his arm. She picked up the clipboard and began to write.

"I'm Fatima, your day nurse. How are you feeling?"

"I'm a little groggy. My head is throbbing."

"That's not surprising. You have a subdural hematoma."

"What's a hematoma? Sounds like some kind of cancer."

"It's a big blood clot sitting on your brain."

She glanced at her watch.

"There's a follow-up CT scan scheduled at three. You still might need surgery to drain the clot."

"No one's cutting my head open."

She set the clipboard back on a hook at the end of the bed and looked up at Mustafa. He'd picked up a magazine and was thumbing through it.

"You'd rather die?"

"I'm too mean to die."

Fatima smirked and walked to Mohammajon's bed. She inserted a thermometer into his mouth and took an arm to check his pulse.

"You won't be so mean if that hematoma gets any bigger; it's hard for a drooling vegetable to be mean."

Fatima picked up the clipboard at the foot of Mohammajon's bead and made a few entries.

"You weren't so mean during your bath yesterday."

Mustafa looked up from his magazine.

"You gave me a bath?"

"Shahla and I did. You were encrusted in dirt when they wheeled you in here. That's what nurses do. How did you think you got clean?"

Mustafa grinned.

"Were you impressed?"

Fatima snickered, "With what?"

"Anything?"

Fatima didn't answer. She partially closed the curtain separating Mohammajon's bed from Aman's. The sheets rustled and Aman moaned. There was a long silence before she pulled the curtain back against the wall.

Fatima walked toward the exit. She started to open the door, but stopped and turned around. She placed an index finger to her lip.

"No, I wouldn't say I was impressed with anything. Except for the size of the bruise on your rear end. See you at three."

Mustafa stared in silence at the closed door for a few moments, before glancing back down at the magazine.

Two men in green military uniforms sat at a console monitoring a bank of TV screens. A cloud of cigarette smoke drifted in the air. The door opened. Both men shot to attention and saluted.

"Good afternoon, Colonel," they blurted out in unison.

Colonel Mohammad Ali Khan was tall for a Pakistani. He had neatly trimmed black hair that was slicked back and a thin, trim mustache. Black-rimmed glasses only partially covered his bushy eyebrows. There was a pistol in the holster fixed to his belt.

"Good afternoon, Lieutenant."

Khan glanced up at the screen. He stared at the monitor for a few moments and listened as the two Afghanis continued their conversation.

"When did the man named Mustafa wake up?"

"About an hour ago, Colonel."

"What did they say when the younger one first woke up?"

"The old fighter asked about a man named Ahmed. The younger one told him the man Ahmed was killed in an American air strike. Mustafa asked Mohammajon what they should do now? Mohammajon didn't answer."

"I want to personally review the tape this afternoon. Keep monitoring them. They're hiding something. Even a Tajik has enough brains to stay out of the Khyber Pass. I want one of you two listening to them twenty-four hours a day. Do you understand?"

"Yes sir."

"These men are only to leave the room one at a time, and only for medical reasons. Tell the staff to feed them in the room."

"Yes, sir."

Colonel Khan closed the door and walked a few steps down the hall. He opened the door to the Tajik's room and walked in.

"Good afternoon. I'm Colonel Khan. I'm glad to see you're feeling better."

Mustafa glanced up from his magazine.

"We're grateful for the care and the hospitality of the Pakistani government."

"You are most welcome. It's my job to see that you receive everything you need while you're our guests here. I understand the Americans saved you from a band of renegade Taliban and al-Qaida camping near Peshawar. How did you get there?"

"Al-Qaida weren't camping there. They had a permanent facility."

"That's impossible, Mr. Mustafa. The ISI controls everything in the pass. We would not allow Taliban or al-Qaida operatives to set up an installation in our country. That must have been a nasty knock on the head. What were you doing in Khyber Pass?"

Mustafa looked toward Mohammajon. Mohammajon wrinkled his brows, but did not speak. Mustafa continued the conversation.

"Colonel, I'm sorry to say we're deserters. Once the Taliban lost control of Jalalabad, we decided it was time to flee Afghanistan. We've had enough of the constant fighting."

"That's understandable. It surprises me you didn't head north. The war is nearly over in northern Afghanistan."

"But the war isn't over in the South. None of us were willing to die liberating Kandahar."

"How many men escaped with you?"

"We were originally ten. Now it's just us three."

Colonel Khan smiled.

"You might have done better in Kandahar after all."

"It looks that way."

Colonel Khan pointed toward Aman.

"Your friend is not so well. He had a terrible blow to the head. His ribs were crushed and his lung collapsed. He also has injuries to his liver and kidneys. His foot was amputated. Dr. Zafar thinks he'll survive. But it will be a long time before he recovers."

"Pashtun bastards!" Mustafa fumed.

The colonel went rigid. He frowned.

"Many Pashtun live here in Pakistan. It would be best if you remember that. Our president lent support to the American war against the Taliban under threat of annihilation. The Taliban made the mistake of allowing al-Qaida into Afghanistan. They have paid dearly. But your anti-Pashtun sentiments are not shared here in Pakistan."

Mustafa didn't respond. He laid his head back on the pillow. Colonel Khan stepped back into the hall and closed the door behind him.

"Especially in the ISI," Mustafa muttered under his breath.

Mohammajon waved his arm and frowned toward Mustafa without speaking. He pointed toward his ear and then to the ceiling.

It only fueled Mustafa's fury.

"Who gives a damn? It was the ISI pigs that supported the Taliban from the beginning. They killed Commander Massoud."

He looked up toward the ceiling and shouted.

"Do you hear me, you pigs?"

Mustafa clinched his fists and slammed them into the mattress. He leapt from the bed and walked to Aman's side.

Suddenly the door swung open. It was Fatima.

"Hey, what's going on in here?"

Mohammajon nodded toward Mustafa.

"My comrade is a hot head."

"Aman's like a son to me. The Taliban murdered his father when he was a boy. I myself taught him to ride a horse when he was eleven and to shoot a gun when he was fourteen. He's been with me since the early days in Mazar-e-Sharif. He's a brave and loyal Tajik fighter. Look at what the Pashtun did to him."

Fatima walked to Aman's bedside. She stood next to Mustafa.

"Take a deep breath and calm down. You're going to break the clot loose in your brain. Mr. Aman is getting a little better. His high fever broke. I want you to lie down. It's time to check your wound."

Mustafa strode across the room and sat back on the bed. Fatima pulled the tape back from his chin and neck. There were more than fifty stitches extending down the middle of his chin to his neck.

"It looks good. No sign of infection."

Fatima cleaned the area with warm water from a stainless steel basin using a washcloth. She applied antibiotic ointment from a tube. Mustafa glanced up at her high cheekbones and velvety skin. He looked down at her left hand holding the basin. There was no ring. He grinned.

"I hope the Taliban didn't ruin my handsome face."

Fatima held another gauze bandage over the wound and began to tape it down.

"Some women like a man with a scar on his face."

Mustafa smiled and grasped her hand.

"How about you?"

She playfully slapped his hand down.

"You were easier to take care of when you were unconscious. It's time for your CT scan."

Fatima took the IV bag down from the pole, clamped the line, and tossed it on the bed. She pulled the bed away from the wall. She shoved the door open with her backside, pulled the bed into the hall, and let the door close behind her.

She pushed the bed down a long hall and made a left turn around a corner. It was just a few steps to the elevator. She pushed the button. Mustafa propped himself up on his elbows.

"Where are we going?"

"Radiology. It's on the first floor."

The door of the elevator slid open. The car was empty. Fatima pushed the bed through and the door closed behind them. The elevator jerked downward.

"Are we going past the cafeteria?"

"You can't eat until the surgeons decide whether to do surgery."

"I don't need surgery. I need some lamb stew."

"No stew. Doctor's orders."

The door opened and a fat older nurse with a wrinkled uniform stood up from behind an old metal desk. She helped Fatima move the bed into an adjoining room. A large sign above a door read "Radiology Department" in several languages.

"What's he here for?"

Fatima handed the chart to the woman.

"Mustafa, ward 2-E, room 23. CT of the head."

Fatima smiled at Mustafa and stepped back onto the elevator.

"Have a good time. See you later."

She waved as the door began to close. The old nurse wheeled Mustafa's bed toward the back of the room and through a set of double swinging doors.

Chapter Twelve

T he door swung open. In walked a short stocky Pakistani man dressed in a dark suit and wearing a white coat. He had a stethoscope around his neck and a hospital ID pinned to the lapel of his coat.

Mohammajon was kneeling on the floor chanting morning prayers. The doctor walked around his makeshift prayer rug and strode across the room to the bed where Mustafa was lying. He pulled the vitals clipboard from its hook. After reviewing it for a few moments, he peered over his half-eyed glasses.

"Mr. Mustafa, my name is Dr. Zafar. I'm the chief of surgery here at Chaklala Military Hospital. How do you feel today?"

"I've been better, Doctor. The pain medication the nurse gave me chased away my headache, but I'm seeing squiggly lines."

"That's not surprising. The subdural hematoma is localized over the occipital lobe of your brain. That's in the back of your head. There was good news from the CT scan yesterday. The hematoma was stable compared to the CT you had when you first arrived. It's still a major concern. Any more bleeding could blind you. A major re-bleed could kill you."

"My left hand is numb."

"When did you first notice that?"

"It was that way when I woke up this morning."

The doctor pulled a penlight and reflex hammer from his coat pocket.

"Look at the door," he ordered.

The doctor illuminated each of Mustafa's pupils and then swung the penlight back and forth between the two sides.

"Follow this light."

Zafar moved the penlight to the left and right, then up and down, while following Mustafa's eye movements. He lifted Mustafa's arm and began testing his reflexes. Each time the hammer fell, Mustafa's arm jerked. Zafar placed his hand against Mustafa's shoulder.

"Push my hand away from your chest."

Mustafa complied and easily pushed his arm out against the resistance from the doctor. The doctor grasped his wrist.

"Okay, flex your arm."

Mustafa flexed his elbow against the resistance until his wrist lay near his shoulder.

"Now extend your elbow. Okay, flex your wrist. Now extend your wrist. Your strength is good. Now close your eyes."

Mustafa closed his eyes and the doctor took a straight pin from a holder in his pocket.

"Tell me if you feel this."

He poked the pin into Mustafa's forearm.

"I feel that."

The doctor poked from Mustafa's elbow down to his fingertips. Then he turned the arm over and repeated this sequence down the back of his arm and hand. Mustafa felt each of the sticks.

"Okay. Now tell me, does this feel the same as this?"

He first poked the left forearm and then the right forearm.

"No, it hurts a little more on the right."

Dr. Zafar repeated this comparison for Mustafa's arms and hands. He delineated an area on the left forearm and hand where there was diminished sensation. Zafar marked the boundaries of this area with a purple marking pen. When he was finished with the arms, he repeated the same maneuver on each of Mustafa's legs. Finally, he took the sharp end of the hammer and raked it across the bottom of Mustafa's foot from his heel to his toes. Satisfied, the doctor slid his tools back into his coat pocket.

"We need to watch that numbness. It likely means there is some compression of the brain opposite the hematoma. Let me know immediately if there's any change in the numbness or if you notice any weakness."

Zafar opened the chart he was carrying and made a note.

"I'll see you tonight. Try not to lose your temper again. Any rapid increase in your blood pressure could be very dangerous. Do you understand?"

"Yes, I understand. Can you keep that ISI pig out of our room?"

"I'll see what I can do."

Mohammajon rose from his prayer rug. He rolled it up and set it on the counter, before sitting down on the side of his bed.

The doctor strode to Mohammajon's bed and checked his vital signs on the clipboard.

"How are you feeling, Mr. Mohammajon?"

"Better! I'm ready for a walk."

The doctor repeated the same eye examination and tested the reflexes in each of Mohammajon's extremities. He spoke while he was testing.

"You seem to have gotten off light."

"Praise be to Allah."

"Yes, Allah must be watching out for you. That was a nasty blow to the head. But there are no signs of internal damage."

"I always told Mullah Habid you had a hard head." Mustafa called out.

"It's a fresh-baked loaf of naan compared to yours," Mohammajon shot back.

The doctor chuckled.

"Unfortunately, I can't let you go out for a walk just yet. The colonel ordered us to keep you in the room except when you have a CT scan. There's a guard at the door."

"That's a shame. I could use some fresh air."

"It's raining outside anyway. I'll try to talk them into letting you take a walk down the hall later today. Try to keep your friend quiet."

Zafar made a brief note in Mohammajon's chart. He walked over to Aman's bed and retrieved the clipboard. He frowned and shook his head as he surveyed the vital signs.

Zafar put the clipboard down on the counter. He leaned over the bed and examined Aman's pupils with the penlight. He tested the Tajik's reflexes with the hammer. He stroked the sharp end of the hammer against the bottom of Aman's right foot. Aman's toes spread widely and the big toe stretched upwards. Zafar pulled his stethoscope out of his coat pocket and listened to Aman's chest and abdomen. He opened Aman's chart and wrote a detailed note.

Mohammajon waited for Dr. Zafar to stop writing.

"How is he?"

Zafar looked up from the chart.

"Maybe a little better. His pulse is still erratic and he has signs of serious central nervous system damage. I think he's paralyzed below the waist. But his vital signs have stabilized compared to yesterday."

Mohammajon shook his head and looked at Mustafa. Mustafa stared straight ahead at the wall.

Dr. Zafar closed Aman's chart and tucked it beneath his arm.

"I'll see you later this afternoon. Mr. Mustafa, remember to let the nurse know if there's any change in the numbness in your hand or you notice any weakness."

Mustafa didn't answer. He stared straight ahead at the wall. The doctor opened the door and started to step out into the hall. He paused, stepped back into the room, and pressed his back against the door.

"Mr. Mustafa."

Mustafa did not acknowledge him. He continued to stare blankly ahead.

"Mr. Mustafa, I'm speaking to you!"

Mustafa looked at Dr. Zafar.

"I am Pashtun, Mr. Mustafa."

Mustafa regarded him for a moment before responding.

"So what?"

"I just thought you should know."

Zafar turned and stepped into the hall. The door closed behind him.

Fatima was in and out of the room every hour to check vital signs and administer medication. She checked Aman's respirator and recorded the volume in his urine bag. If he was soiled, she cleaned and changed him.

Mustafa's mood brightened each time Fatima entered the room. He watched her every move and smiled each time she looked his way. Fatima pretended not to notice. She maintained a pleasant, yet professional, manner.

Occasionally Mustafa or Mohammajon rang the bell to use the toilet. Fatima dutifully unlocked the door to the bathroom and waited patiently by the door to escort her patient back to bed.

Fatima entered through the door just before two in the afternoon and fetched the clipboard from Mustafa's bed.

"Open up!"

She inserted the thermometer into his mouth. Mustafa grinned and stared into her eyes, as she wrapped the blood pressure cuff around his arm and pumped the bulb. Fatima pretended not to notice. She placed the stethoscope against his arm and monitored the gauge. After a few moments, she pulled out the thermometer and raised it into the air.

"Your eyes are beautiful jewels," he whispered. "There could be none more lovely in all of Pakistan."

Fatima tried to ignore him. She looked down and wrote on the clipboard. But she became flustered as he continued to stare. He leaned forward and whispered again.

"How is it one so beautiful isn't married?"

At this, she lost her grip on the clipboard. It slipped from her hand and clattered to the ground. She picked it up and glared at him.

"I was married, Mr. Mustafa. My husband was killed in a gas attack during the Iraq-Iran war."

Mustafa looked down toward the blanket.

"I'm sorry, I—"

Fatima wasn't ready to let him off that easy.

"If you don't behave yourself, I'm going to ask my supervisor to assign another nurse to this room."

A Pakistani soldier pushed the door open. He glanced inside to see what was causing the commotion. Fatima slammed the clipboard back on its hook and brushed past the soldier. The soldier glowered at Mustafa for a moment and closed the door.

Mustafa looked at Mohammajon. Mohammajon stared at him in disapproving silence.

"What?"

"Why don't you leave her alone?"

Mustafa tossed his magazine on the bed.

"I just told her she was beautiful. What's wrong with that?"

"She's not interested. Can't you see that?"

"She's beautiful. She's the most beautiful woman I've ever seen."

"Mustafa, how many beautiful women have you seen?"

Mustafa nodded.

"You have a point."

Mustafa sighed.

"I used to watch American movies at the theatre in Mazar-e-Sharif before the Taliban invaded the North. The women were goddesses."

Mustafa leaned his head back on the bead and smiled. He turned to look at Mohammajon.

"*Cleopatra*, did you see it?"

"No, I missed that one."

"Ahh, it was my favorite. You should see it. Elizabeth Taylor must be the most beautiful woman in the world."

"That's an old movie, Mustafa. She's a very old woman now."

Mustafa waved his hand.

"Shhh, I don't want to know."

He picked up the magazine once again and began thumbing through the pages.

"I fought at the front for five years and four months. I haven't seen a young woman's face since the Taliban attacked the North."

"You've missed much in life, Mustafa. Perhaps it's Allah's will that you leave Afghanistan. Maybe you will find a wife and have many children."

Mustafa sat up in his bed with his legs hanging over the side facing Mohammajon.

"Have you ever married?"

There was a long pause. Mustafa thought he might have misunderstood.

"Have you married, Mohammajon?"

Mohammajon looked up. There was a hint of a tear in his eyes. The Tajik brushed the sleeve of his gown across his eyes.

"I was married once. My family arranged a marriage to a young Tajik woman from a wealthy family in Kunduz. She was only thirteen when we married. I was twenty-one. She was not beautiful, but her heart was gold."

Mohammajon smiled for a moment, as if remembering a happier time. The smile disappeared just as quickly as it came. He clenched his teeth.

"What happened to her?" Mustafa asked.

Mohammajon picked up the glass of water from the tray. He took a sip and set the glass down.

"The Pashtun killed her. She died when the Taliban invaded the North in 1995. They killed my sons too."

"Pashtun swine," Mustafa seethed.

Mohammajon pulled his feet up on the bed and reclined against the elevated head of the bed.

"It was the will of Allah."

CHAPTER THIRTEEN

Mustafa glanced at his watch. It was nearly 3 P.M. He slid the magazine beneath his sheet and leaned back into the mattress.

"Ugh," he called out in a guttural yelp.

He reached across and grabbed his left arm.

Mohammajon bolted upright from a deep sleep.

"What's wrong?"

"My arm — I can't lift my arm!"

Mohammajon punched the emergency call button. A loud horn went off in the hall outside the room. Within moments, Fatima came through the door with another nurse.

"What is it?" Fatima yelled above the screech of the alarm.

"It's Mustafa. He can't lift his arm."

Fatima ran to the bed and deactivated the alarm. She placed her stethoscope against Mustafa's chest for a few moments. Then she checked his pulse and blood pressure.

"How long has it been this way?"

"I just woke up. I couldn't move my left arm."

Fatima turned to the other nurse.

"Get the doctor!"

The woman ran out through the door. Fatima took the saline bag down from its pole and released the brakes on the bed. Dr. Zafar hustled through the door to the bedside with the nurse right behind him. He checked Mustafa's pupils with a penlight. Then he held Mustafa's arm with both hands.

"Flex your elbow."

Mustafa couldn't overcome his resistance. The doctor turned from the bed.

"Fatima, call radiology. Tell Dr. Shakir we're bringing Mr. Mustafa down for an emergency head scan with contrast. Then call the OR and tell them to get room six ready. Come on, let's go."

Fatima helped the doctor push Mustafa's bed through the door and down the hall. The Pakistani soldier followed close behind. They shoved the bed into the open elevator and pressed the button for the first floor. The elevator lurched downward.

A doctor in a white coat was waiting on the first floor when the door opened. They pushed the bed through the door in the rear of the room and down a short hall into a back room. A large instrument with a hole in the center occupied the entire room. The two nurses left the room and joined the guard in the hall. The radiologist turned to Zafar.

"Dr. Zafar, stay and help me read the scan. Okay, Mr. Mustafa, please scoot over to the transport."

Mustafa held his left arm against his body and used his right to move over from the bed to the transporter.

"How do you feel, Mr. Mustafa?"

"A little better. I think my arm is getting its strength back."

"We still need to do the scan. Lie completely still."

The radiologist walked to the console and pushed a button. The instrument began to whirl. The transporter started moving. Mustafa's head passed through the opening in the instrument. Dr. Zafar and the radiologist watched the console as one frame after another appeared on the screen. Once Mustafa's head passed completely through the ring, the transporter retracted to its original position.

"Okay, now we need to do it again with contrast."

Dr. Shakir crimped the intravenous tube, cleaned the injection port with an alcohol swab, and inserted a needle. He injected clear liquid into the port until the syringe was empty. He returned to the console and pushed another button.

"Lie still, Mr. Mustafa."

The instrument whirled back to life and Mustafa's head passed through the hollow core. A series of new images appeared on the monitor.

The CT transporter shifted back to its original position. The radiologist pushed a series of buttons on the console. Several brain sections enlarged on the monitor. The radiologist pointed out important details to Dr. Zafar.

Mustafa moaned.

"This is uncomfortable, can I move back to the bed?"

Dr. Shakir turned away from the console.

"I'm sorry."

He strode over and pushed the bed against the CT scanner.

"Okay, Mr. Mustafa. Scoot over."

Mustafa slid across to the bed and leaned his head back on the pillow.

"We're almost done, Mr. Mustafa."

The doctor returned to the console. Both of the physicians leaned across the counter to get a better view. The monitor clicked from one cross-sectional image to the next.

Mustafa glanced back over his shoulder toward the console. The two doctors were completely preoccupied with the images. He leaned over and grabbed a ballpoint pen off the counter next to the bed. He turned the magazine to page thirty and quickly jotted down a note. Mustafa slipped the pen inside his gown and the magazine beneath the sheet.

Dr. Zafar strode over to the bed.

"Mr. Mustafa, if anything the subdural hematoma looks *smaller*. It's becoming more consolidated. But your new symptoms mean the blood is still compressing your brain. We need to drain the hematoma."

Mustafa began alternately flexing and extending his elbow.

"I'm feeling a lot better now. I don't need surgery."

"Mr. Mustafa, you *do* need the surgery. You could be paralyzed."

"No, I'm feeling better. I don't want any surgery."

Dr. Zafar turned toward Dr. Shakir and raised his hands in surrender.

"Have it your way. But it's against medical advice."

Zafar opened the door.

"Nurse, take him back to his room. He refuses surgery."

The two nurses moved the bed to the elevator. They pushed him into the car and the door slid shut. The car opened on the second floor and the two women pushed him back down the hall to his room. Fatima shoved the bed back against the wall. She glanced at Mohammajon's bed. He was asleep.

"You're a stubborn man. Why do you refuse surgery?"

Mustafa looked down toward his arm, as he flexed it several times.

"I'm feeling better."

"But the hematoma is unstable. You could be paralyzed."

He looked up to her almond-shaped eyes. He looked at her lips. They were full and red.

"I'm fine. I don't need surgery."

"You're afraid, aren't you? You shouldn't be afraid. Dr. Zafar is a great surgeon. One of the best in all of Pakistan."

Fatima pulled up Mustafa's sleeve and wrapped the blood pressure cuff around his arm. She pumped it up and held the stethoscope against the inside of his arm.

"Lie back. I'm going to change your bandage."

Mustafa laid his head back against the bed. She gently lifted the edges of the tape, pulled the bandage to one side, and examined the sutures with a penlight. As she leaned to look at his wound, a golden medallion on a chain tumbled out from the top of her uniform. It hung directly in front of Mustafa's face. Mustafa took it in his fingers. It was a delicate and detailed golden bird.

"This is magnificent. What is it?"

"It's a falcon. My father gave it to me when I was a little girl."

Fatima took the medallion and dropped it back inside her collar. She shined the penlight back on his chin.

"It's healing up nicely."

Fatima put the penlight in her pocket and walked to the sink. She opened a sterilization bag and retrieved a small metal basin. She poured water into the basin from a bottle. Then she squirted soap from a plastic bottle into the water and opened a package of sterile gauze.

Fatima walked back to the bed, sat on the edge, and began to gently clean his wound. Mustafa gazed at her face.

"I'm sorry I upset you this morning. Please forgive my forwardness. I've not seen a woman's face for five years."

She smiled. "I overreacted. You embarrassed me."

She opened a tube of antibiotic and applied a small amount to the suture line.

"Can I kiss your cheek?"

"No," she mouthed inaudibly with a hint of a smile.

Fatima gazed into his piercing dark eyes. She looked apprehensively toward the door. It was closed. She glanced at Mohammajon. He was still asleep. She spread the ointment over the sutures with the tip of a gauze pad.

Mustafa raised his hand to her face. Her skin was soft as silk.

"Just one little kiss?"

Fatima lingered for just a moment, allowing his fingertips to caress her cheek. She turned her head ever so slightly, so her ear brushed against his rough hand. Suddenly, she turned her head and stood up.

Fatima walked to the counter and opened a new packet of sterile gauze. She shuffled back to the bed, leaned over Mustafa, and taped the gauze into place with several strips of tape.

"I can't," she whispered. "They're watching."

Fatima stood up. She walked to the door and into the hall without looking back.

It was nearly six in the evening before the door opened again. Another nurse carried dinner trays through the doorway. She was a middle-aged Pakistani woman with a scarf covering her head. Only her eyes were visible.

"Dinner!" she called out cheerfully.

The nurse set one tray in front of Mustafa and slid the other onto Mohammajon's table. Mohammajon stood up from his evening prayers and rolled up his prayer rug.

"Praise be to Allah. I'm starving. I must be getting better."

"My name is Shahla. I'm your nurse tonight. Wait just a minute. I need to check your temperature."

She put a thermometer in each man's mouth and checked Mustafa's pulse and blood pressure. She recorded the vital signs on the clipboards. Finally, she pulled the covers from the plates.

"We have lamb tonight. It's not bad. I ate some myself."

Mustafa fetched his magazine from beneath the sheets and handed it to the nurse.

"Could you give this magazine to my friend? Mohammajon, there's a story on page thirty about Commander Massoud. It has pictures of his funeral."

Shahla handed the magazine to Mohammajon. She walked over to Aman's bed and closed the curtain.

Mohammajon took a spoonful of vegetables and stuffed them into his mouth. He set the spoon down on the tray, put on his reading glasses, and turned the magazine to page thirty. It was an article about Massoud. His eyes were drawn to the handwriting in the upper margin.

There was a printed message in Dari. It read, "I'm all right. We must leave soon."

Mohammajon glanced up from the page. Mustafa was staring at him. He gave a hint of a nod. Mohammajon quickly tore away the corner of the page. He rolled the scrape of paper into a ball between his fingers and slipped it into his mouth. He picked up a slice of lamb and took a bite. He chewed for a few moments and swallowed.

CHAPTER FOURTEEN

Around eight the next morning a nurse they'd never seen before pushed the breakfast cart through the door. She was a thin Pakistani woman who appeared much too old to be working. Her white uniform was yellowed and fit loosely, extending from her neck to her shoes. A white scarf covered her hair and draped over the back of her dress. She nodded at Mustafa and pushed the cart next to the bed. The old woman was missing most of her teeth. Only a few brown and decaying remnants were visible on one side of her mouth. She set the plate on Mustafa's tray.

"My name is Maasi. I'll be your nurse today."

"Where's Fatima?"

"It's Monday. This is her day off. She'll be back Wednesday. Don't worry. I'll take good care of you. I found this English newspaper in the cafeteria. It's a couple of days old, but I thought you might like to look at it."

She set the copy of *USA Today* down on Mustafa's tray.

Maasi took Mustafa's vital signs and recorded them on the clipboard. She checked Mohammajon's temperature, blood pressure, and pulse. Finally, she drew the curtain next to Aman's bed. The bang of a pan was followed by the sound of running water. Then the rustling of sheets echoed from behind the curtain. Finally, the old woman pushed the curtain back against the wall.

"Your friend is moving a little. He's still unconscious, but that's a good sign."

Mustafa got up from his bed and walked across the room. He stared down at Aman's ashen face for a few moments. Aman's left eyelid fluttered open.

"He *is* moving. I saw his eyelid move."

Mustafa reached his hand out and patted his friend on the arm.

"Aman, can you hear me?"

The young man did not respond. The only sound was his chest rising and falling with the respirator.

"Aman, Mohammajon and Mustafa are with you. You're getting better. We'll stay with you until you recover. Do you hear me?"

Mustafa raised Aman's eyelid with his finger. His eye was rolled up into his head. He let the lid close and took a deep breath.

The nurse walked out past the guard standing in the hall. Mustafa lingered at the bedside for a few minutes and watched his young friend. He didn't see any other movements.

"My friend. Keep fighting! When you recover we will take you to rest at the fountains in Taloqan."

Mustafa walked back to the table stand next to his bed. He lifted the cover on of his plate. The nurse had brought some kind of cereal. He let the cover fall back down with a clank.

"I can't take anymore of this constant boredom. I'm going mad."

Mustafa picked up the newspaper and sat on the edge of the bed. He glanced at the pictures on the first page for a few moments and then turned to the second. He jumped up from the bed and walked around to Mohammajon's bed.

"Mohammajon, what does it say on the front page next to these pictures of bodies lying on the ground?"

Mohammajon took the paper from him and read for a few moments.

"Kunduz fell to the Northern Alliance. Several thousand Taliban soldiers were killed there. The Alliance let hundreds of Pashtun go free. Several Qaida fighters surrendered. They were being held in the old fortress. There was a fight and they managed to overcome the guards and break into the armory. An American was killed at the beginning of the uprising. This story says he was a CIA operative. After three days of battle, the Alliance and American's killed all of the foreign Qaida troops. Just a few survived. This second story says the Taliban is barely holding on in Kandahar. The Americans have flown in more than a thousand troops and they're preparing to attack."

He turned the page and read silently for a few minutes before looking up.

"There's a rumor Mullah Omar was wounded trying to flee to Pakistan in a convoy leaving Kandahar. Al-Swahili's wife and children were killed. It says al-Zawahiri may have been killed."

He looked down at the paper.

"We already knew that, didn't we?"

"Bastard, I hope they slit his lying Arab throat."

Mohammajon frowned to quiet Mustafa and continued reading.

"This story says American planes and helicopters destroyed ten trucks in the convoy just outside of Jalalabad two days ago. Bin Laden may be hiding in caves in Tora Bora. American B-52 planes are bombing there twenty-four hours a day. Several thousand tribal soldiers are moving into the area to join the American Special Forces. They're preparing to attack the caves where he may be hiding. The tribal leaders want the twenty-five million dollar reward."

Mustafa slapped his hand against his hip.

"Damn!"

Mohammajon looked up from the paper over the tops of his reading glasses.

"What's the matter?"

"I spent the last five years in dirty, stinking trenches at the front lines. I was surrounded by death and defeat the entire time. My best friends got blown to pieces by grenades in battle. We escaped from Afghanistan and the Taliban were routed. I have missed the final battle."

He turned away from the bed and slammed his fist into his palm.

Mustafa turned around and glanced toward Mohammajon. Mohammajon folded the paper and tossed it on the bed. Mustafa shook his head and grabbed the newspaper again. He sat on the edge of the bed and began to scan through the rest of the pages.

Suddenly the door flew open. Colonel Khan strode across the room to the foot of Mustafa's bed.

"Good morning, Mr. Mustafa. You seem to be feeling better."

Mustafa didn't look up. He turned to the next page.

"Yes, we are ready to leave."

Colonel Khan chuckled.

"So soon? Unfortunately Dr. Zafar is of the opinion you must stay as our guest for another week. I'll put you on the first helicopter back to Kabul next Monday."

Mustafa threw the paper down on the bed and looked up at the colonel.

"I told you before, we can't go back to Kabul. We're deserters. They'll hang us."

Khan smirked.

"Mr. Mustafa, that is not my concern. We cannot release you here in Pakistan. My Pashtun countrymen hate the Tajik. They would hang you before you reached the highway."

Mustafa scowled at the colonel. He picked up the newspaper and continued looking through the pages.

Colonel Khan stood silently for a few moments. Then he spoke again.

"There is no point in continuing this charade, Mr. Mustafa. I know you're not deserters. You came to Pakistan on a mission. Tell me what this mission is and I will consider helping you. We are on the same side now."

Mustafa continued to stare at the newspaper. Finally, he looked over the top of the page.

"I don't know what you are talking about."

Colonel Khan frowned. He turned toward Mohammajon.

"How about you? Do you also say you are only a deserter?"

Mohammajon didn't speak for a moment. He looked at Mustafa and then shrugged his shoulders.

"It's no use, Mustafa. We might as well tell him the truth."

Mustafa threw the newspaper down on the bed.

"Shut up, you old fool!"

The door swung open and two other men in ISI uniforms strode into the room with pistols drawn. Colonel Khan raised his hand to stop them and then turned back toward Mohammajon.

"What is your mission?"

Mohammajon glanced sheepishly at Mustafa and then at the colonel.

"We aimed to kidnap bin Laden. There are reports he fled to the tribal territories in Pakistan. We were out for the twenty-five million dollar reward."

Colonel Khan rolled his eyes and turned his back to the Tajiks. After a few moments, he turned and fixed his stare on Mohammajon.

"You think I'm a fool, Mr. Mohammajon. I don't know what your objective was, but I do know it wasn't to kill bin Laden. You were sent from Afghanistan at this moment for a very specific mission. But you will not succeed. You will return to Kabul."

"Where are our passports?" Mustafa queried.

Colonel Khan smiled.

"They are in a safe place. I'll return them when you arrive in Kabul. I will consider helping you if you decide to tell me your mission. If not, your mission is over."

"What about our comrade?" Mohammajon asked, as he shrugged toward Aman.

Colonel Khan turned and marched to Aman's bedside. He looked down at the frail figure lying on the bed. Khan reached down and picked up the clipboard. He slapped it against Aman's elevated leg. There was no response.

"I am afraid your friend is paralyzed. That's Dr. Zafar's opinion. He's usually right, but we'll know for sure after he performs some tests."

He grasped the breathing tube in Aman's mouth.

"It would be better for him if I pulled this tube."

Mustafa jumped from the bed. He attempted to shove past the two guards, but they restrained him. His face was distorted in rage.

"Leave him alone."

"Mr. Mustafa, this man would already be dead if we hadn't saved his life."

The colonel placed the clipboard back on the hook at the end of Mustafa's bed.

"Let my men know if you want to speak with me again."

Khan turned and walked from the room with his men trailing behind him. The door swung closed. Mohammajon and Mustafa looked at each other. Neither spoke.

CHAPTER FIFTEEN

CIA headquarters in Langley, Virginia

Stone Waverly sat quietly among a dozen men and women in the CIA situation room. They were gathered around a mahogany table lined with high-back leather chairs. Several small groups were sitting around the table laughing and talking. Waverly didn't recognize anyone in the room. He sat in silence, doodling on a notepad.

Waverly wasn't quite sure why he'd been invited to the foreign intelligence 9/11 task force meeting. The committee was formed three months earlier in the wake of three jetliners piloted by terrorists slamming into buildings that stood as icons to American prestige and power. It was true he was an operative of relatively senior rank in the CIA counter-terrorism group and he had an intimate knowledge of Afghanistan and the surrounding countries. But agents of his rank were rarely included in such high-level discussions. He was accustomed to preparing reports to pass on to his seniors.

These compilations were based on information gleaned from a variety of sources. It was his job to sift through mountains of information derived from electronic surveillance technologies, agents in the field, security agencies of other countries, and many other sources. He was charged with separating the wheat from the chaff. Rarely was there any indication that these reports were read, much less that they somehow influenced important decisions made by his superiors within the CIA or in the U.S. government as a whole.

The double doors swung open. Robert Richards, the deputy director of the CIA, strode into the room, tailed by two aides. Instantly, the atmosphere in the room became more formal and all conversation abruptly stopped. Those in attendance scooted their chairs up to the table in anticipation of the start of the meeting.

Richards was a short, stocky man with bifocal glasses. He had a scruffy gray beard and mustache. The ever-present, half-chewed stogie bobbed in the corner of his mouth. He was dressed in a faded tan corduroy jacket with olive slacks and a wrinkled white shirt. His green tie was loosely tied around his neck with the knot twisted toward the left. No one was certain of his age, but he appeared to be pushing seventy.

Richards was a career agent who had risen through the ranks of "The Company" to assume one of its highest posts. Despite this, the crusty scrapper still felt a measure of resentment that he hadn't been tapped to assume the directorship of the CIA. That honor went to another with more established political connections.

Richards walked to the head of the table and sat down. One aide placed a stack of papers in front of him, while the other opened a panel along the sidewall. The screen behind the panel had a detailed topographic map of Afghanistan and all adjoining countries.

Richards looked up from the agenda and nodded. The unlit stogie bobbed up and down in the corner of his mouth as he spoke.

"Good afternoon. Before we start in on the agenda I'd like to introduce Stone Waverly and welcome him to our task force."

All eyes in the room turned toward Waverly. Stone felt self-conscious, as he turned and nodded to those around him. He felt his cheeks blush, as they always did when he was the focus of attention.

"Mr. Waverly, we try to be informal here. Can I call you Stone?"

"Yes, of course, sir."

"Good. Then would you take about five minutes and tell the members of the committee a little bit about yourself? Everyone in this room has top-secret clearance, so you can speak freely. Start with college. You were a Razorback, weren't you?"

"That's right, sir. I graduated from the University of Arkansas. My major was history with a minor in U.S. military history. I spent six months of my sophomore year as a foreign exchange student studying military history at Humboldt University in Berlin. Late in my sophomore year I joined the ROTC. I wanted to be a pilot, but my eyesight wasn't good enough. That was before laser eye surgery. I became a lieutenant in the army assigned to the Rangers when I graduated in 1975. There wasn't much going on in the army around that time. The Vietnam War had just ended."

Stone cleared his throat and took a sip of water from a glass on the table.

"Out of boredom, I joined a clandestine surveillance contingent of the Rangers in 1973. There weren't too many opportunities for promotion in the army. I planned on quitting to join my brother in a family furniture manufacturing business once I served my time.

"A CIA recruiter approached me just as my four years were ending. He offered me the opportunity to join a new unit being formed to serve as a sort of paramilitary surveillance and enforcement arm of the CIA. One charge of this group was to mount clandestine operations against terrorist organizations that were perceived to be a threat to the United States."

"Was that the so-called Abbot unit?" Richards asked.

"Yes, that was the original name. Later it became known as the Scorpion Corps. My group had several assignments during those early years. We focused on eliminating members of terrorist organizations based in the Middle East and Asia. For the most part we concentrated on the leaders of these organizations. But we also eliminated a couple of Soviet agents that infiltrated the units to manipulate the terrorists."

"Did that include Joseph al-Badir?" asked one of the men at the table.

Waverly glanced questioningly at Richards. Richards nodded his approval.

"Yes, we eliminated al-Badir and several other members of the Islamic Jihad who were thought to be Soviet operatives. I didn't personally carry out these sanctions, but I helped plan the operations. After that, the number of missions diminished as political assassination fell out of favor with Congress and the country at large."

Stone took a drink of water from a glass.

"Then the Soviets invaded Afghanistan. That changed everything. I was shipped off to Afghanistan as an advisor to the Mujaheddin. I provided them with intelligence about the Soviet forces and with weapons like the Stinger missile. I also helped with the design and construction of some of the cave complexes in Tora Bora, Kandahar, and several other locations."

"You did a great job in Tora Bora," one of the women quipped.

"Yeah, too good!" Richards chimed in.

His laugh sounded like a series of loud snorts. This provoked laughter around the table. It was impossible to be sure if the attendees were laughing at the conversation or Richards' characteristic laugh. Waverly recalled a rumor that went around the Company. It seems President Bush banned Richards from Security Council meetings because of his irritation with Richards' laugh.

Richards pulled a pack of wooden matches from his shirt pocket. He struck one of the matches and twirled the cigar until the end was lit. He took a puff and blew the smoke across the table.

"Stone, I think you knew I was the field chief in Afghanistan for two years before the invasion. We abandoned the embassy in Kabul when the Soviets invaded."

"Yes, I did know that. I remember reading a report you prepared about the leadership of the various factions in the country. It was very helpful."

"I almost got myself killed doing the field work for that report," Richards replied.

"The Soviets withdrew from Afghanistan in 1989. I was reassigned to New Delhi a few months later. I worked there for six months and then in Islamabad for almost a year. I worked on improving coordination between the CIA and the security services in India and Pakistan. Then in 1991 I was assigned to be a liaison to the Kurds in northern Iraq. I worked there until the agency called me home in 1994. I've served as a team leader in the counter-terrorism group here in Langley since 1994."

"Stone," Richards continued, "if I'm not mistaken you're fluent in Arabic, Dari, Pashtu, and one of the Kurdish language dialects. Is that right?"

"That's right, sir. I am also conversant in the Surani dialect of the Kurds."

An older man in a blue suit with a bow tie cleared his throat and smiled.

"So Stone, was it your group that caught flack for the lack of warning about al-Qaida's intentions for 9/11?"

Waverly chuckled.

"Yeah, we've taken quite a bit of heat since 9/11."

"Stone isn't sticking up for himself," Richards interjected, as he took another puff from his cigar. "I saw the report you submitted in July. You concluded, based on conversations between an al-Qaida lieutenant and a known operative in Germany, that there was likely to be a major al-Qaida operation. Unfortunately, that report went to the director's office. No one on his staff read it until the week after the attack."

"I wasn't very specific about the threat. The report was based on information provided to us by the Jordanian intelligence service indicating an impending al-Qaida operation. I concluded that likely targets would be our embassy in Egypt or Saudi Arabia. I also mentioned the possibility of an attack on the congressional delegation that was planning to visit several countries in the Middle East in October. I went back and looked at the information we had in the year prior to the New York and Washington attacks. I don't think there was anything that would have given us advanced warning. I guess I should say nothing except Mohamed Atta."

"Tell us what you know about him."

Mohamed Atta made contact with an Iraqi intelligence officer named Ahmad al-Ani on April 22, 2001, in the Czech Republic. Al-Ani was expelled from the Czech Republic a short time later for conduct inconsistent with his diplomatic status. He got caught photographing the Radio Free Europe building. We believe he was providing information for an attack on that facility. Atta also met several Islamic extremists in a hotel at a beach resort near Barcelona in July of 2001. The Syrians alerted us to the meeting with the Iraqi intelligence operative. If we'd kept a closer watch on Atta, we might have come up with clues about the ultimate plan. We thought Atta was a relatively low-level al-Qaida operative. There are hundreds of these al-Qaida agents throughout the world. We just didn't have the resources to keep tabs on them all."

"So, Stone, do you think Sadaam Hussein was involved in the 9/11 attacks?" asked the woman sitting next to Richards.

She was a pleasant looking, middle-aged woman in a conservative charcoal suit. She peered at him over a pair of half-eye reading glasses.

"Absolutely. So far I don't have any hard evidence. It's all based on circumstantial information. I doubt we'll find anything that directly links him to 9/11. He's one damned cunning psychopath. But if he didn't at least know about it, then the information we've developed represents an incredible series of coincidences."

"Thank you, Stone," Richards interjected. "Let's move on."

Richards rested his hand on the arm of the woman sitting to his left.

"This is Marilyn Harrison, Stone. Marilyn is intelligence chief for Central and Southern Asia. Marilyn, could you update the committee on the latest information on the situation in Afghanistan and the hunt for the leadership of the Taliban and al-Qaida."

"Yes, thank you, could we please see the map?"

One of the aides turned the projector on. A map appeared on the side wall next to the conference table. Harrison pushed her chair away from the table and strode to the map. She picked up a long wooden pointer from a tray beneath the map.

"We're concentrating almost all of our resources on trying to accomplish three things. First, we're looking for bin Laden and other major al-Qaida lieutenants. Our best information, based on Afghani agents in the South, Special

Forces observers, and information obtained from surveillance photos from satellites and aircraft, is that bin Laden is in Tora Bora with close to twelve hundred al-Qaida fighters."

Harrison pushed a couple of buttons on the console beneath the sideboard and the map disappeared. In its place, a photograph was projected from the rear. It showed a man on a horse surrounded by several riders carrying Kalashnikov rifles.

"This photo was taken by a CIA satellite we moved over Afghanistan just two days ago. We believe this man is bin Laden. This is an area high up in the White Mountains near the largest of the underground command bunkers. He has been known to use doubles, so we're also searching for him in far eastern Afghanistan, in this area around Kandahar, and even in the northern tribal areas of Pakistan. But we think he's most likely in Tora Bora. This is the best evidence we have."

The picture changed. The new photo showed a young woman dressed in a long parka and a scarf. Several children were playing in the snow around her. The kids appeared to be building a snowman. Two men with rifles were standing nearby.

Stone shook his head at the clarity of the photograph.

"We're certain this is bin Laden's wife and several of his children. Local Pashtun tribesmen also spotted his older son in the area. We don't believe bin Laden would leave them behind. His movements have been severely restricted by the fall of the Taliban. Our troops are closing in around him and there is continuous bombing in this area. We don't think he'd take the chance that his wife and children would be captured while he's somewhere else."

"How many anti-Taliban tribesmen are within striking distance of the Tora Bora cave complex?"

"Just over two thousand, with more on the way. We've paid three Pashtun leaders to move more fighters into the area. They're also influenced by the twenty-five million dollar reward they'll get if they capture or kill bin Laden. They aren't a very cohesive fighting unit. In fact, I would say they're completely disorganized and just as likely to kill each other as they are the remaining Qaida fighters. There are about three thousand more anti-Taliban troops on the way, and by the end of the week there should be more than four hundred U.S. and British Special Forces in the area. We hope an air strike will take out bin Laden. But it may be necessary to go in with troops and root them out of the caves. We'd obviously like to avoid that. There's some concern that bin Laden might have a dirty nuclear bomb hidden up there. If he does, he might blow it up if we trap him and he felt there was no way out. He'd probably like to take out as many of our men as he could and go out with a bang."

Richards took the cigar out of his mouth.

"Stone, didn't I read somewhere that you met bin Laden?"

"Yes, I met him twice during the seventies in Afghanistan. In retrospect, I'm amazed that the quiet man I knew is creating all this havoc. He was dedicated to Islam and the jihad against the Soviets, but he treated me well."

"Do you think he would leave his family in Tora Bora and move into Pakistan?"

Stone answered without hesitation.

"No, not if there was a real danger of their being killed or captured. I think he'd try to take them out with him."

"Go on, Marilyn," Richards called out with the wave of his hand.

Marilyn pushed a button on the console and the map of Afghanistan reappeared.

"Okay. The second thing we're trying to do is locate other al-Qaida leaders and Mullah Omar and his Taliban associates. We're certain that Mohammed Atef was killed in an air strike south of Kabul with several other al-Qaida leaders. Atef's daughter is married to bin Laden's son. He was considered al-Qaida's military chief and bin Laden's likely successor. Ayman al-Zawahiri's family was also killed. He's also one of the top three in al-Qaida and is widely considered the real brains in the organization. Al-Zawahiri himself may have also been seriously hurt or even killed in the Khyber Pass. We have a body. We're trying to confirm that it's him. Mullah Omar is thought to be hiding in this area just outside of Kandahar. There's a covert operation underway to find him and kill him."

Richards cleared his throat and leaned over the table for emphasis.

"What I'm about to say doesn't leave this room. Make sure they don't arrest the son-of-a-bitch. Even if he tries to surrender, he should be shot trying to escape. That goes for bin Laden and any other al-Qaida or Taliban leaders."

"I'll make sure our operatives are prepared to act, sir. Finally, we're looking for remaining pockets of al-Qaida and Taliban forces that have dispersed throughout the country. There's a group of about two thousand Taliban troops in this area outside of Kabul. We are monitoring their movements and calling in air strikes. We also think between five and fifteen thousand Taliban and al-Qaida troops are in this area north of Kandahar. We directed air strikes into that area yesterday. We aim to wipe out all of these fighters, and we certainly don't want them joining up again to overthrow the new government once the American forces pull out of Afghanistan."

Richards glanced at his watch.

"Okay, Marilyn, it sounds as if everything is going well. I'm meeting with the director in ten minutes. Don't want to be late for that," he muttered sarcastically under his breath. "Any comments?"

Richards looked around the room. No one else spoke up.

"Okay. Let's meet next week at the same time. Stone, I want you to participate in future meetings. You know the players in Afghanistan as well as anyone. I want you to speak up if you think we're about to mess anything up. With the endless tribes and alliances in this God-forsaken country, we could step into it at any time. You also have intimate knowledge of the caves in Tora Bora. That may come in handy."

Richards stood up from the table. He walked toward the door followed by his aides. He was about to open the door, when he stopped and turned around.

"Oh, I almost forgot. Stone, an old friend of mine got in touch with me from Afghanistan yesterday. He asked if I could find out about a group of Tajiks who left Kabul about six weeks ago. They were trying to make it to Islamabad through the Khyber Pass. From there they planned to go on to Amsterdam to join a Northern Alliance diplomatic mission. I told him I'd look into it. I remember seeing a report about a group of Tajik Mujaheddin being rescued from al-Qaida forces by U.S. Rangers in northern Pakistan. It was the same raid where we got al-Zawahiri. At least we think we got him. Several of the Tajiks had life-threatening injuries. The Rangers took them to the Rawalpindi military hospital for treatment. Could you try to find out what's going on with them?"

"Sure, I'll look into it today, sir."

"Let me know what you find out so I can get back to my friend."

"I'll look into it right away."

Richards nodded and disappeared into the hall outside the meeting room.

CHAPTER SIXTEEN

Fatima opened the door slightly and slipped into the room. Mustafa opened his eyes and grinned. She smiled broadly and walked to Aman's bedside. Fatima pulled the clipboard from its hook. She scanned the vital signs and shuffled through the reports from the last few days.

Fatima looked up and smiled shyly at Mustafa, as she put the clipboard back on the hook. She checked the tape holding the tube in Aman's throat and the line to the respirator.

Mohammajon rolled his legs off the bed and sat up on the edge.

"Where've you been Fatima? We missed you."

"I'm off on Monday and Tuesdays. I enjoyed a Ramadan feast at my neighbor's on Tuesday. I spent the rest of the time sewing. It's good to be back."

"I hope you had good weather. We don't know if the sun is shining or snow is falling inside this room."

"It was a little cold on Monday. But the sun was out for a few hours yesterday."

Mohammajon smiled.

"You changed your hair."

Fatima looked up from Aman's bed and smiled sheepishly. She lifted her hand to the new curls that fell from beneath the white scarf covering her head.

"My neighbor's wife helped me style it a little differently."

"It's lovely on you."

"It's difficult to improve on perfection," Mustafa called out.

She blushed.

"Thank you. When did Dr. Zafar take out your stitches?"

"Yesterday. The scar makes me look dangerous. Don't you think?"

She smiled, looked down, and busied herself removing bubbles from the intravenous line. She stepped to the side of the bed and inserted a thermometer into Aman's mouth. She glanced up at Mustafa and looked down again when their eyes met.

Fatima retrieved the clipboard at the end of the bed. She carefully recorded the vital signs.

"I think he's getting better."

She walked to the head of the bed.

"Mr. Aman, can you hear me? Blink your eyes if you can hear me. Blink your eyes."

There was no response.

Fatima stepped to Mohammajon's bed and checked his vital signs. When she was done, she recorded them and poured a glass of water from a pitcher. She moved to Mustafa's bed and inserted a thermometer into his mouth. She took his arm and pressed her fingertips against his wrist. Mustafa stared at her, as she looked at her watch and pretended not to notice. The tension between them was electric.

Fatima finished taking his pulse. She took the thermometer from Mustafa's mouth and raised it up to her eyes.

"I missed you," he whispered.

Fatima giggled nervously.

"You say that to all the nurses."

She wrapped a blood pressure cuff around his arm.

"You look more beautiful every time I see you."

Fatima pumped the blood pressure cuff. She looked at Mustafa and smiled before placing the head of the stethoscope below the cuff. Mustafa began to speak again. She shook her head to silence him. She smiled.

"You have a follow-up CT scan scheduled this morning. I'll be back to get you in about thirty minutes. I brought you this."

She retrieved a copy of the *London Times* from beneath the apron on her uniform and handed it to him.

"I missed you, too," she whispered.

Fatima walked to the door. She glanced back with a smile, as she opened the door and disappeared into the hall.

Mustafa jumped off the bed. He walked to Mohammajon's bedside while scanning the photos on the first page. He handed the newspaper to Mohammajon.

"What's happening?"

Mohammajon scanned the front page.

"Tora Bora has fallen. Several hundred al-Qaida were killed in intensive bombing, but more than a thousand fighters escaped along the trails through the White Mountains to Pakistan with assistance from some of the Pashtun troops who were brought to Tora Bora to attack al-Qaida positions."

"Pashtun scoundrels," Mustafa fumed. "When will the Americans learn? They cannot be trusted."

"A few al-Qaida surrendered. They're being moved to the American prison in Cuba."

"What of bin Laden?"

"There's no sign of him. The Americans thought they heard his voice giving orders on a radio in Tora Bora a few days ago. They're still searching for him among the dead and in some of the remote caves. They're also looking for him in areas around Kandahar. There are many rumors he already escaped to Somalia, Yemen, or even Chechnya."

"They'll never find him. Bin Laden would order his men to kill him and hide his body if his capture was imminent. He would not give the Americans the pleasure of his capture."

"There are reports he's being hidden by Pashtun tribes just across the border in Pakistan."

"That's where I'd look. Maybe one of the chiefs will betray him for the twenty-five million dollar reward."

"Why would they do that? Bin Laden would give them thirty million dollars to hide him."

"You're probably right. I'll bet the ISI was involved in leading him to safety. They play the Americans for fools."

Mohammajon frowned and rolled his eyes.

"The ISI wouldn't want bin Laden in Pakistan. He'd only stir up trouble among the conservative Islamics in the tribal territories."

"I guess so. What will you do when we return to Afghanistan?"

"I plan to return to the North and reclaim the land that belonged to my family. I want to establish a school to teach Islam and history there. There's a great need among our people for education. What will you do, Mustafa?"

Mustafa smirked.

"You mean if the Northern Alliance doesn't execute us for deserting? I don't know. I'm a soldier. I know no other trade."

"Our country will still need soldiers."

Mustafa sat back on the edge of the bed with his feet dangling.

"For what?"

"To maintain peace among the Tajik and Pashtun. Perhaps peace is Allah's will for the future of Afghanistan."

"I don't believe this will ever come to pass. The hatred is too strong. The country will explode again as soon as the Americans leave."

"If this is our future, then you will have no trouble finding work."

"Perhaps it is you who will be right. Someday even the people of Afghanistan will tire of endless war."

Mustafa scooted down off the bed and walked over to Aman's bed. He watched as his chest rose and fell to the rhythm of the bellows on the respirator.

"I hope I never end up like Aman. Only the machine keeps him alive."

Mustafa lifted Aman's hand and flexed it repeatedly at the elbow. Then he moved the young man's shoulder in a wide circle.

He glanced at Mohammajon.

"Did you ever see the American movie *Patton?*"

"I've never seen a movie."

"You've never seen a movie?" Mustafa asked incredulously. "When I lived in Mazar-e-Sharif before the Taliban, I'd go to the movie theater at least once a week. They showed American movies with Dari subtitles. It was a chance to practice English and learn new words."

Mustafa moved to the other side of the bed. He began working on Aman's left side.

"I loved the war movies. My favorite was *Patton*. I saw it more than ten times. It was about the American general, George Patton."

"I've heard of him. He fought in the second war between the United States and Germany."

"He was a great leader of men, but with many personal shortcomings. Patton believed men lived many lives. He was convinced he'd fought with the Carthaginians and served as Napoleon's field marshal in his previous lives. He loved the sting of battle. Patton said the only proper way for a soldier to die was to be killed by the last bullet, in the last battle, of the last war."

Mustafa set Aman's arm down on the bed and looked toward Mohammajon.

"I too feel this way. There will be no place for me in this new Afghanistan. I will search for the last battle of the last war."

The two men stared at each other. Mohammajon laid his head back against the pillow and stared at the ceiling for a few moments.

"Do not search too hard, Mustafa. You are still a young man. The last battle will find you soon enough, my friend. I pray you will find fulfillment before that day comes to pass."

Suddenly the door flew open. Fatima pushed a wheelchair into the room.

"Let's go. It's time for your CT scan, Mustafa."

She pushed the wheelchair around behind him and set the brakes.

"I'm fine, Fatima. Let me walk."

"No, it's against hospital rules. We must use the wheelchair."

Mustafa smiled and threw his arms up in surrender. He sat back into the chair. Fatima released the brakes and wheeled him toward the door.

"Mohammajon," Mustafa called out over his shoulder. "Read the paper. The next battle is already brewing somewhere. I must rely on you to tell me where."

A guard in an ISI uniform held the door open, as Fatima pushed the wheelchair into the hall. He stepped in front of the chair.

"Where is he going?"

"Mr. Mustafa is scheduled for a CT scan of the head. We're going to radiology."

The guard glanced at a paper on his desk.

"So he is. How long will it take?"

"About an hour. I'll bring him back."

"Don't let him out of your sight."

Fatima smiled.

"Don't worry, I won't."

Fatima pushed the wheelchair down the hall and rounded the corner. Fatima glanced behind them, just as they came abreast of the elevators. The hall was empty. She jerked the chair to the right and pushed it through the door into the supply room. Mustafa looked up in shock.

Fatima reached down to pull Mustafa into her arms. She kissed him longingly on the lips and then kissed him several times on the forehead. He wrapped his arms around her and kissed her lips with growing passion.

"I missed you," she whispered, as she kissed his ear and held him against her. "I was so afraid you'd be gone. I couldn't sleep. I couldn't eat. I thought only of you."

"I missed you too," he sighed as he ran his fingers through her hair and down her slender body.

Her breathy kisses on his ear sent a tingle down his back. Fatima pressed against him. She grasped his hands and brought them to her breasts. Mustafa caressed her through the uniform, as he pushed her back against the counter and pressed his body against her. A wave of splendid rapture overcame him.

Mustafa began to lift Fatima's dress. She slipped her hands into his and pulled his arms around her.

"We only have a short time. They're waiting for us in radiology."

"Fatima," Mustafa whispered. "I need your help. They're planning to send us back to Kabul in a few days. I can't go back there. Can you help me?"

"I'll do what I can."

"We need to find our passports. Do you know where they might be?"

"I don't know. They could be in the ISI office."

"Where's the office?"

"It's on the second floor, two doors down the hall from your room. They rarely leave. I think they watch your room with a TV. They also could be in Colonel Khan's office down the hall beyond the elevators. Be careful, many men have disappeared in the night."

"We only have five days before the colonel sends us back to Kabul. Is there any way you can arrange to work nights for a few days? It's very quiet at night. You could help us find the passports and prepare our escape."

"I will do all I can, my love."

She kissed him tenderly on the lips and ran her fingertips across the scar on his chin. She smiled and gazed into his darkly mysterious eyes.

"We must be careful. Khan will arrest us both if he suspects."

"I'll take care."

Mustafa pushed the curls back from her face and kissed her tenderly on the lips.

"Leave with me."

Fatima pressed her body against him and whispered into his ear.

"Mustafa, I can't leave with you."

He held her away from him.

"Why? What's to keep you here?"

Fatima didn't answer. She pressed her body against him and relished the sensation of loving warmth. Finally, she whispered.

"I have a little boy. My little Nadir."

Mustafa held her away again. He stared into her dark almond-shaped eyes. He smiled.

"Bring him with us. We'll find a better place. Where would you like to live?"

Fatima thought for a moment. A far away look came to her eyes.

"Santa Fe," she muttered.

Mustafa looked down at her with bewilderment.

"Santa Fe. Where's that?

"It's in the United States."

"Why there?"

"I saw a story on television once. Santa Fe is full of shops and studios that sell the work of painters, sculptors, and other artists. It seemed like a magical place to live."

Mustafa stared at her for a few moments. He nodded.

"All right, we'll go to Santa Fe."

Fatima stared up at him and slowly shook her head. There was sadness in her eyes. She threw her arms around him and began to sob uncontrollably.

"I can't leave with you, Mustafa, but I'll do all I can to help."

Fatima kissed Mustafa again. She guided him back into the wheelchair. She grabbed a bundle of towels from the shelf, placed them into his lap, and pushed the wheelchair against the door.

Shahala was waiting for the elevator in the hall. She looked up with surprise.

"There you are. Dr. Shakir sent me to look for you."

Fatima's hand quivered, as she pointed to the bundle in Mustafa's lap.

"We needed more towels."

The elevator door ground open. Colonel Khan was standing inside the car with another soldier. He held a pistol in his hand.

"Where did you find them?"

"They were here in the storeroom getting towels, Colonel Khan."

Khan looked down at the towels. Then he looked at Mustafa. He looked at Fatima. He barked at the ISI soldier.

"Stay with him, Sayyid. Don't let him out of your sight. From now on one of the guards must go along every time he leaves the room. It'll be your skin if he escapes. Do you understand?"

The soldier snapped to attention.

"Yes, Colonel!"

"Nurse, take him to radiology."

Fatima began to push the wheelchair onto the elevator. Khan grabbed her arm.

"No, not you. I want to speak with you."

The second nurse stepped behind the wheelchair and pushed it into the elevator. The ISI guard stepped in behind them. Mustafa glanced up at Fatima. Their eyes met, as the door closed between them.

"Come with me," Colonel Khan ordered.

Khan guided Fatima away from the elevator. He made a left turn down the hall away from the nurse's station gripping Fatima's arm. He stopped in front of an unmarked door.

Khan retrieved a ring of keys from his pocket. He sorted through and inserted a key into the doorknob. He opened the door, shoved Fatima into the room, and shut the door behind them.

The room was a stark windowless office with an old wooden desk and several chairs. A framed picture of Mohammed Ali Jinnah, the first leader of Pakistan, hung on the wall. There were stacks of files scattered across the top of the desk and along the back wall.

Colonel Khan flipped on the desk light. He turned Fatima by the arm.

"You look very beautiful, my dear. I like the way you wear your hair these days."

He reached out to touch her hair. Fatima turned her head.

"So," he bristled, "you no longer welcome my touch? Perhaps you grow fond of the young Tajik?"

"He is my patient. That is all."

"I see the way that he looks at you and you at him. I've seen the whispered conversations. Do you think I am a fool?"

"You are a fool, Ali. There have been no whispered conversations."

Colonel Khan reached out to stroke Fatima's cheek. She turned her head away from him.

"There was a time when you longed for my touch."

Fatima jerked her head around. Her eyes burned with fury.

"That was long ago, Ali. You promised to marry me. You abandoned me to a life of shame when I was with child."

A crooked grin emerged on his face. Khan reached out toward her.

"I've missed your charms. I want you back, my dear."

She pushed his arms down from her waist and pulled away.

"Never, Ali. Little Nadir was born a bastard."

Fatima spit on the ground.

"I'd rather be with a goat!"

Colonel Khan swung his arm and slapped her flush on the cheek. Fatima crashed against the desk. She began to sob.

Khan jerked Fatima to her feet by her hair. He reached behind, yanked the zipper on her dress down, and jerked her dress around her waist to expose her breasts.

Her cheek flushed bright red from the blow. A trickle of blood ran from her nostril and down to the corner of her mouth.

Fatima stood defiantly before him. She continued to glower without speaking, as her exposed breasts rose and fell with each labored breath.

"Your son would be proud of you."

He stood silently regarding her.

Fatima turned and gathered the top of her dress up to cover her bosom. She turned back and walked around the colonel to the door. He didn't try to stop her. She opened the door, stepped into the hall, and closed the door quietly behind her.

Colonel Khan stood staring at the picture on the wall before him. He reached up with both hands to straighten his cap. He ran his hands down his uniform to smooth out the material. Finally, he opened the door and walked out of the office.

CHAPTER SEVENTEEN

M ullah Habid, kneeling on a multicolored prayer rug, was just finishing his afternoon prayers. The mullah stood up from the floor and rolled the rug. Osman crouched into the room of the mud-walled hut with his arms full of wood. He placed the logs in a rack in the corner.

"Good morning Osman. Is there word yet from your Mr. Richards?"

"No Mullah, nothing yet. He promised to contact me as soon as there was news. Mr. Richards has always kept his word. He will call. Would you like tea?"

"Yes, thank you. What am I to do, Osman? I've heard rumors the men were captured by al-Qaida forces. How long should I wait to organize another mission? Time grows short. The delivery is scheduled to arrive in Venice with the next full moon."

Osman handed the Mullah a cup of tea. He took a few sips and set the teacup down on the table.

"Perhaps we should inform the Americans."

"This is your decision, Mullah. Do you want me to notify Mr. Richards?"

The Mullah didn't respond for a few moments. Finally, he sighed loudly.

"No, Osman, not yet. We will wait a few more days. I've seen documents that were captured here in Kabul after the fall of the Taliban. These records point to spies at high levels in the CIA. The worst possible outcome would be for the pestilence to be diverted. We cannot risk it."

Mullah Habid took a bite from a loaf of naan and sipped his tea.

"I want to know about this pestilence. We may never know the truth if the Americans intercept it. They're trying to encourage the tribes of Afghanistan to live together. The coalition would surely crumble if a plot to release some terrible scourge were revealed."

"The coalition will also fall apart if this Arab plan is successful, Mullah. Tajiks will die, but so will Pashtun and Uzbeks. The Arabs could gain total control of Afghanistan."

The mullah turned and placed his cup on the table.

"We'll wait a few more days. But I want you to have Commander Shah provide me with the names of twenty fighters. He will lead a new mission. He must stay here in Kabul and be prepared to leave through Turkmenistan at a moments notice. Don't tell him anything about Ahmed Jan or the plot until I decide it is necessary."

"As you wish, Mullah."

"Let me know immediately when you hear from Richards."

"I am ever your servant."

Richards sat at the desk in his office in CIA headquarters watching the snow accumulate on the ledge outside the window. The phone rang. He lifted the receiver.

"Richards."

"Hello, Stone," Richards bellowed, as the chewed cigar bobbed in the corner of his mouth. "Thank you for getting back to me. What did you find out about our Afghani friends?"

Richards listened attentively for nearly a minute before speaking.

"It was al-Zawahiri himself, huh. Damned bastard got better than he deserved. Don't issue a statement. It's better that he just disappears. No sense creating a martyr."

Richards listened for a few more moments.

"Provide whatever assistance is necessary to get the two healthy ones out of Pakistan. Find a way to spirit them out of the hospital and fly them to the Indian airbase outside of Delhi. They can go on to Amsterdam from there. Give Tom Nethers in the South Asia Section a call. He'll put you in touch with company operatives in Pakistan. Let me know the minute they're out."

Richards hung up the phone and stared out the window. The snow was still falling. He put his hands on the desk and used them to push himself to his feet. He walked to the window and took the cigar from his mouth. He looked out over the main entry gate. There was a black sedan idling at the checkpoint.

Two men with extension mirrors examined the vehicles undercarriage from front to rear. Another man peered into the engine compartment, as still another inspected the interior of the car. They finished and the driver stepped back into the car. The barrier in the road retracted and the car pulled into the compound.

"Goddamn Arab bastards," Richards muttered.

The deputy director turned from the window and walked toward the door.

CHAPTER EIGHTEEN

C olonel Khan was waiting for Mustafa when the nurse wheeled him out of the CT scanning room.

"Lieutenant Sayyid," he ordered, "take the wheelchair."

The nurse stepped aside, as the uniformed ISI soldier shuffled behind the wheelchair and pushed Mustafa toward the elevator. Khan pushed the button and the door opened. Sayyid rolled the wheelchair to the back of the elevator. Colonel Khan depressed the button and the door rattled closed.

The elevator lurched upward. It paused for a moment during its assent and then continued upward. The door opened on the second floor.

Khan marched to the main hall and rounded the corner to the left. Sayyid followed with Mustafa in the wheelchair. Khan opened the door to his office. Two men in ISI uniforms were already sitting on the side of the desk. They snapped to attention as Colonel Khan stood aside to allow the wheelchair into the room. He slammed the door shut.

"Get him out of the chair!"

Two of the soldiers grabbed Mustafa by the arms and lifted him to his feet. They held Mustafa as Khan stepped in front of him.

"Mr. Mustafa, I'm done fooling around. You're going to tell me your mission. I don't want any more nonsense about bin Laden. Do you hear me?"

Mustafa didn't respond. He stood erect, his eyes staring forward, with his jaws clenched together.

Colonel Khan strode to the desk and opened one of the side drawers.

"Have it your way, Tajik!"

Khan pulled a length of pipe wrapped in black tape from the drawer. Without warning, he stepped back across the room and swung the weapon in a wide sweeping arc. The end of the pipe struck Mustafa just above the left eyebrow with a resounding thud. Mustafa careened backward onto the floor from the force of the blow.

The two soldiers pulled him back up.

"What is your mission?" Khan demanded.

Mustafa stood in defiant silence. A dark blue welt began to swell above his left eye.

Khan swung the weapon again and bashed the side of Mustafa's head. A stream of blood erupted from his ear. Mustafa groaned.

"Tell me!"

As the two soldiers held the Tajik up, Khan hammered Mustafa with one blow after another. Each time he refused to respond, the ensuing blow became more vicious. Khan finally raised the pipe with both hands above his head and swung it down on the crown of Mustafa's head. Mustafa slumped unconscious into the wheelchair.

"Tajik trash! Take him back to his room!"

The two soldiers put Mustafa's feet on the footrests and wheeled him out of the office. They pushed him down the hall to the Tajik room. One guard held the door open, while the other pushed the chair into the room.

Fatima was dressing Aman's head wound, while Mohammajon knelt near the center of the room reciting his prayers. Mohammajon bolted to his feet. Fatima gasped and rushed toward the wheelchair.

"Who did this?" she demanded.

"Step back!" the soldier ordered.

The two ISI soldiers grabbed Mustafa's arms and pulled him up in the chair. Each man took hold of a shoulder. They lugged him across the room and dropped his upper torso on the bed. One of them lifted Mustafa's legs and rolled him to the center of the bed. The soldiers strode from the room.

Fatima jabbed at the emergency alarm switch. She pressed her fingertips against Mustafa's neck. The door sprung open and Maasi rushed into the room.

She gasped at the sight of Mustafa's battered and swollen face.

"Maasi, get Dr. Zafar!"

Maasi ran back out the door. Within moments, Dr. Zafar jogged into the room out of breath. He took one look at Mustafa and pulled a pen light from his pocket. Zafar struggled to lift both of Mustafa's grotesquely swollen and blackened eyelids. He checked each pupil.

Colonel Khan stepped inside the room and stood next to the door in silence. Mohammajon lingered behind the doctor.

"Who did this?"

Dr. Zafar ignored Mohammajon.

"What are his vitals, nurse?"

"His pulse is 125 and his blood pressure is 97 over 58. His respirations are 25 and shallow."

"Call radiology. Tell them we're bringing him down for an emergency scan."

Colonel Khan stepped forward.

"That won't be necessary, Doctor."

Dr. Zafar stood up from the bed and turned toward the colonel.

"This man had a subdural hematoma. His vital signs are unstable. He may need emergency surgery."

"The Tajik will stay in this room. He's a security risk to the country. I am taking charge of these men."

Khan turned to the guard standing behind him.

"The Tajik doesn't leave this room for any reason. That's an order."

"Yes, sir," the soldier barked out.

"Tell me when he wakes up. I have some more questions. Perhaps he'll be more cooperative."

"I will let you know, sir."

Khan looked down at Mustafa and then turned his piercing glare on the doctor.

"That was a nasty fall. I told him to wait for the elevator, but he insisted on taking the stairs."

Khan turned and walked from the room.

"Stupid Tajik," he muttered, as he disappeared around the corner.

Doctor Zafar turned toward the guard.

"He needs a CT scan."

"You heard the colonel. He stays here."

The guard pushed the wheelchair out the exit and closed the door behind him.

Fatima was already sitting on the edge of the bed cleaning the cuts and bruises on Mustafa's face. She looked up at the doctor. There were tears in her eyes.

"Is he going to be okay, Dr. Zafar?"

"I don't know Fatima. Keep his head elevated and put in an IV. I'm going to give him prophylactic hyperosmotics to counteract any brain swelling. How much does he weigh?"

"Sixty-two kilograms."

"Run in a hundred grams of mannitol."

Dr. Zafar turned to Mohammajon and shrugged.

"I wish I could do more for your friend. I'm not in charge at this hospital. If you are on some mission, you might consider discussing it with Colonel Khan. That's the only way your friend is going to get proper medical attention. He may die without it. He may die anyway."

"It is the will of Allah," Mohammajon muttered in a barely audible voice.

Mustafa regained consciousness early the following morning. The room was dark. Mohammajon's irregular snore reverberated throughout the room. Fatima bathed Mustafa's forehead with cold alcohol. He groaned and managed to partially open his right eye.

"Don't talk," Fatima whispered.

She dipped the washcloth in the basin and wrung it out, before once again applying it to his forehead.

Mustafa slid his hand across the bed and touched Fatima's arm.

"Thank you."

She grasped his hand and squeezed it.

"I love you," she mouthed.

The door cracked open and Shahla slipped quietly into the room.

"Go on home now, Fatima. I'll take care of him."

"No, I want to stay. Could you get me another dose of mannitol and a bag of normal saline with five percent glucose? Dr. Zafar ordered a second dose at 2 A.M."

"Sure, princess, but you must rest when I return. You've been here for over twenty hours."

"I'll take a break after I run in the mannitol. Will you stay with him?"

"Sure, honey, I'll take care of him."

Shahla returned ten minutes later with two IV bags. She closed the valve on the tubing, pulled down the old IV bag, and disconnected it from the tubing. She picked up the smaller bag and inserted its connector into the tubing. Finally, she elevated the pole and opened the valve on the tubing. Drops began to fall in the clear window in the IV tubing.

"Okay, Fatima. I'll stay with him. Go take a nap now."

"Thank you, Shahla. You're such a good friend. Is there anything I can do for you?"

Shahla smiled.

"Bring me flowers from your garden in the spring."

Fatima smiled and nodded. She stepped into the hall. The ISI surveillance station door creaked as she passed. She turned her head and caught a glimpse of an eye peering out of the darkened room. The door clicked closed.

All was quiet at the 2-E nurses' station. Fatima sat in a chair with a clear view down the corridor. She rested her head in her arms on the countertop and closed her eyes.

The door to the ISI surveillance room creaked open. Fatima did not stir. She watched through her arms as a soldier in ISI uniform stepped from the room. He stood and peered down the hall toward her for a moment. Fatima didn't recognize him. He eased the door closed and hustled away from the nurses' station. He turned left toward the elevators.

Fatima waited a few seconds before scurrying down the hall. She knocked on the surveillance room door. There was no response. She knocked once more. Again there was no response.

Fatima twisted the doorknob and opened the door. There was nobody inside. She darted into the room.

Two televisions were mounted over a desk on one side of the room. Fatima looked up at the monitors. Shahla was sitting on the edge of the bed sponging Mustafa's forehead. The other monitor was output from a camera directed at Mohammajon. He was sound asleep. Two video recorders were sitting on the desk. A red light was illuminated on each one.

A cabinet next to the desk drew her eye. Each shelf was packed with a neat line of video boxes labeled with dates and times. Fatima ran her finger across one row. There was a pair of tapes for each eight-hour interval extending for two weeks.

Fatima rifled through the drawers in the desk. The top drawer contained a few pens and a ring of keys. She picked up the keys. They looked similar to her keys to the supply room at the nurse's station. Fatima slipped the keys into her pocket and closed the drawer. The two remaining drawers were jammed full with videotapes, video cables, and an assortment of electronic gear.

Fatima closed the drawers and scurried out the door into the empty hall. She eased the door closed and walked briskly down the corridor past the Tajik's room.

She knocked on Colonel Khan's office door. There was no answer. She knocked louder. There was still no response.

Her heart raced, as she fumbled in her pocket for the key ring. Her hand shook as she tried the first key. It didn't fit. She tried two more keys. Neither fit. The fourth key slipped into the lock. Fatima opened the door and scooted inside.

The office was pitch black. Fatima turned on the lights and rushed to the desk. The top drawer of the desk was locked. She pulled as hard as she could, but to no avail. The three lower drawers were unlocked. They were overflowing with papers and notebooks.

Fatima glanced at her watch. Six minutes had passed since the guard left. There was a file cabinet against the wall behind the desk. She rushed over and began pulling out the drawers. Every one was filled with old files. She closed the last drawer and scurried toward the office door.

Fatima grasped the knob and pulled the door ajar. She stopped and fetched the key ring out of her pocket once again. A smaller key caught her eye. She ran back to the desk and tried the small key on the top drawer. It slipped into the lock.

Fatima opened the drawer. There was a clipboard filled with papers on top. She pulled it out. Four green booklets were lying in the bottom of the drawer. She picked up the first booklet and opened it. She caught her breath. It was Mohammajon's passport. She opened the second booklet. It was Mustafa's passport. The third was Aman's. She didn't recognize the name on the fourth passport.

Fatima's thoughts raced with indecision. She started to slip the passports in her pocket. Finally, she stuffed them back in the bottom of the drawer, covered them with the clipboard, and locked the drawer.

She ran back to the door and cracked it open just far enough to peer down the hall in both directions. The corridor was empty. She darted out of the room and closed the door behind her.

Fatima's heart was pounding in her chest. She raced past the elevator cove to the ISI surveillance room. She knocked. There was no answer. She opened the door, rushed to the desk, and opened the drawer. She tossed the keys inside and slammed the drawer shut.

Fatima was out the door in a heartbeat. She ran to the nurses' station, sat down in the chair, and rested her head in her arms. She dripped with perspiration.

Less than a minute later the ISI soldier sauntered out of the cove from the elevator. He had a cup in his hand. She watched surreptitiously, as he strode toward her. He walked past the surveillance room door and into the station.

"Nurse," he called out.

She ignored him.

"Nurse!"

Fatima lifted her head and peered at him with bleary eyes.

"What is it?"

The soldier held out his cup.

"Do you have any ice? The ice machine in the cafeteria is broken."

Fatima stood up and took the cup. She walked to the ice machine in the hall outside the supply room and filled it with ice. She handed the cup to the soldier.

He smiled.

"Thank you. You're sweating. Are you all right?"

"I'm not feeling well. I'm running a fever."

"Doctors and nurses," he replied sarcastically with a shake of his head. "They take care of everyone but themselves. How many hours have you worked today?"

Fatima glanced at her watch.

"Almost twenty-one hours."

He shook his head.

"You need to go home. The other nurse can take care of the Tajik patient. Go home."

Fatima peered up at the soldier. He had a pleasant face with prominent laugh lines at his temples.

"I can't. Colonel Khan may come and beat him again."

The soldier's expression changed to a frown.

"No one beat the Tajik. He fell down the stairs. This wouldn't have happened if the Tajik hadn't been so stubborn about using the wheelchair."

"When do you expect Colonel Khan? Dr. Zafar wanted me to tell him that Mr. Mustafa must stay in the hospital beyond Monday. We need to monitor him closely for a few days."

"Colonel Khan won't be back until Friday. He had to go to Karachi. Captain Motah will be in charge today. I'll let him know about the Tajik. You go home and get some rest."

"Thank you. That's very kind of you. I'll just tell the other nurse I'm leaving."

Fatima walked down the hall to the Tajik's room. Shahla was standing next to Mustafa's bed shaking the thermometer.

"He's asleep," she whispered. "Go home and get some rest, Fatima. You won't be of any use to him or anyone else. I called the nursing supervisor. Maasi is taking your shift today. I'll take her shift this afternoon. You can take my shift tonight. So go home now!"

"Thank you, Shahla. Allah will bless you."

"See you tomorrow. Don't worry about the Tajik. I'll ask Maasi to take care of him."

CHAPTER NINETEEN

Fatima slept until nearly three in the afternoon. She could have dozed even longer, but the babysitter had to tend to business of her own. Fatima asked her to come back to the house around 10:30 P.M.

Fatima opened the oven, pulled out the baking tray, and placed it on a hot pad on the counter. The smell of fresh bread drifted through the small two-room apartment. She opened a canister on the oven, scooped up a spoonful of powdered sugar, and sprinkled it over both loaves of bread.

She glanced across the room at the crib. Nadir was lying on his back peering up at a string of plastic beads that dangled above his head. He raised his hand and tried to grasp the colorful toy.

Fatima smiled and walked to the crib. She handed the cherub a bright red ball. He grinned and raised it to his mouth.

"Nadir is such a good boy. Your mommy loves you. Are you hungry?"

Fatima picked up the infant and clutched him to her bosom. She headed back into the kitchen and fetched his bottle from a pan on the stove. She sprinkled milk onto her forearm. It was lukewarm. She stuck the nipple in Nadir's mouth and returned him to his crib. He sucked at the nipple and gazed up contentedly.

Fatima picked up one of the loaves of bread and slid it into a waxed bag. There was a knock at the door.

"Just a minute!"

Fatima checked on Nadir and strode to the door. She leaned against the jamb and called out from behind the closed door.

"Who is it?"

"Ardeshir Advani from the Bareq-Shaf Mosque. I'm looking for Fatima Asefi."

"What do you want?"

"I want to speak with her about an Afghani believer. His name is Mustafa."

A bolt of fear surged through Fatima's body like an electric arc. She pressed her body against the door, paralyzed by panic.

"Mrs. Asefi, are you there?"

"I don't know anyone named Mustafa. Please, go away."

"Mrs. Asefi, please speak with me for a moment. The nurse Shahla told me you would help. I mean you no harm."

Fatima took a deep breath. She grabbed a scarf from the back of a chair and covered her head. She unbolted the door and opened it just wide enough to scrutinize the man standing outside. He was a Pakistani of average build with a neatly trimmed mustache. She guessed he was in his late fifties. He smiled and — palms up — signaled his benevolence.

"I'm Fatima Asefi. What do you want?"

"May I come in? I'd like to speak with you for a few minutes."

Fatima opened the door.

"I'm sorry. Can I get you anything? A cup of tea?"

"Thank you. A cup of tea would be nice."

Fatima held out her hand toward a chair.

"Please sit here."

"You are very kind."

Fatima rushed to the stove and poured two small cups of tea. She returned to the sitting area, handed Mr. Advani a cup, and sat down across from him. He took a sip of the tea and set the cup down on the coffee table.

"Mrs. Asefi, I'm going to be very direct. My associates are very concerned about Mr. Mustafa and Mr. Mohammajon. I can't tell you who sent me. Let me just say they're friends of the Pakistani people. The ISI is not sympathetic to people of Tajik descent. They are planning to send Mr. Mustafa and Mr. Mohammajon to prison here in Rawalpindi. They're likely to be killed there."

"If Colonel Khan doesn't kill them first," Fatima snapped.

"What do you mean?"

"Colonel Khan is the ISI officer in charge at the hospital. He beat Mr. Mustafa unconscious yesterday. He claimed Mr. Mustafa fell down the stairs. But, believe me, he was beaten."

Mr. Advani shook his head.

"Mrs. Asefi, we need your help to get the Afghanis out of the hospital. We'll take care of them from there. All you need to do is take a message to them.

We'll do the rest. Will you help us?"

Tears began to well in Fatima's eyes. She sobbed and lifted her apron to blot the moisture from her cheeks.

"Please don't be afraid, Mrs. Asefi. We will protect your identity. No one will know you helped the Tajiks."

"I'm not afraid for myself. I'm terrified the Afghanis will be killed."

"Fatima," a frail woman called out from the adjoining room, "who's there? Fatima?"

Mr. Advani turned and looked across the room. Fatima set her teacup down and stood up.

"It's my mother. I'll be right back."

Fatima walked to the door on the other side of the room. She opened the door, walked into the room, and closed the door behind her.

Two large chests were set against the wall. Stacks of neatly folded clothing were arranged in one corner. There was a single bed in the center of the room and a crib in the corner. A frail old woman was lying in the bed. She peered up at Fatima with confusion in her eyes.

"Mother, there's a visitor here from work. He'll leave in a few minutes. Can I get you anything?"

"Send him away, Fatima. You must not be in the presence of a man without an escort. It will bring disgrace to the family. I need to go to the bathroom."

"Okay, let me help you. Then I'll send him away."

Fatima helped her mother to her feet and guided her to a corner in the room. She held her arm, as she stooped over a basin and urinated.

Fatima handed her mother a washcloth. She pulled her mother to her feet, rearranged her robe around her, and guided the old woman back to the bed.

"Thank you, my Fatima. What would I do without you?"

"I love you, Mother."

"I'm so much trouble for you. I pray Allah's hand will take me."

"Mother, don't talk this way. Nadir and I love you. We'd be lonely without you."

Fatima stepped over several pieces of clothing scattered on the floor and picked up the urine basin. She poured the urine into a large bottle, screwed on the cap, and set it back on the floor.

"Mother, I'll be back in a few minutes. I'm just going to send the visitor away."

Fatima stepped from the room, closed the door, and returned to the sitting area in the living room.

"I'm sorry."

"Will you help us get a message to the Afghanis, Mrs. Asefi?"

"Yes, I can take a message to them this evening when I return to work. I've been trying to help them. I found their passports in Colonel Khan's office."

"Don't take unnecessary risks, Mrs. Asefi. We can provide them new documents. This is what we need you to do."

The two conversed for more than an hour. When they finished, Mr. Advani stood up to leave. He walked to the door and opened it.

"Thank you, Mrs. Asefi. We'll do all we can to protect you, but you must understand, there is some risk."

"I understand, Mr. Advani. It's a chance I must take."

Advani regarded Fatima for a moment. He leaned forward on the couch.

"Mrs. Asefi, are you involved with one of the Afghanis?"

Fatima didn't respond. She stared into Advani's eyes without answering.

"Mrs. Asefi, once these men leave Pakistan they can never return."

He waited for a few moments for a response. Fatima nodded without speaking.

"You are a brave woman, Mrs. Asefi."

Advani opened the door and stepped outside. Fatima shut the door behind him and peeked out through the shade. Advani limped across the street to a black van, unlocked the door, and stepped inside. He drove away a moment later.

Fatima scanned the street in front of her house. There was a food vendor with an old horse-drawn cart selling an assortment of bread and vegetables on the corner. She watched as he bargained with the neighbor who lived across the street. The woman paid the old man and he handed her a loaf of bread. The vendor climbed up on the seat of the cart and tugged the reins. The horse resisted at first, but the old man whipped the animal and he finally began to walk. The cart disappeared down the road.

Fatima's mother called from the adjoining room. She turned and let the shade fall.

"Fatima, are you there?"

"I'll be right there, Mother."

Fatima's eyes welled with tears. She blotted her eyes with her sleeve, as she checked the crib. Nadir was sound asleep with the bottle clutched in his arms. Fatima walked to the bedroom, took a deep breath, and opened the door.

CHAPTER TWENTY

December 31, 2001

Maasi stood beside Aman's bed charting vital signs. Fatima opened the door and walked into the Tajik's room. It was just a little after 11 P.M.

Mustafa was lying in the bed with his head elevated. His eyes were closed. A half-empty food tray sat on the stand next to his bed. Mohammajon was lying on the edge of his own bed with his head propped on his arm reading the Quran by the dim light of a candle.

"Hello, Fatima," Mohammajon whispered. "I hope you're feeling better tonight."

"I'm feeling much better, thank you. I got a little sleep."

Fatima motioned toward Mustafa.

"Maasi, how's he doing?"

Maasi put Aman's clipboard on the hook at the end of the bed and shuffled toward them favoring her left leg.

"He's a little better. He ate a little tikkas before he fell asleep. He's not seeing well out of his left eye."

"What happened to your leg?"

"Oh, it's nothing. I slipped and turned my ankle a bit."

"Maasi, I am so grateful. Thank you for switching shifts."

"Anytime, Fatima. It's not often I get a chance to spend the night with my husband."

"How about if we work each other's schedule until Monday? Then neither of us will need to work a double shift."

Maasi smiled.

"It's fine with me. Will you make sure it's okay with Janisa?"

"I'm sure she won't mind. Plan on taking my shift until Sunday unless you hear from me in the morning."

Maasi winked.

"I've only been home two nights a week in the two months since Hassan and I married. He's teasing me about needing to take a second wife. Would you like to make a permanent trade?"

Fatima laughed.

"No, thank you, just this week. I'll lose my babysitter."

"Okay, see you in the morning. Good night, Mr. Mohammajon."

"Good night, Maasi," Mohammajon muttered, as he looked up from the Quran. "May Allah bless you."

Maasi walked to the door and stepped into the hall.

Fatima strode to Mustafa's bed. She took the thermometer from its tube and inserted it into his mouth. Mustafa stirred and opened his swollen eyes. He smiled weakly. Fatima pursed her lips.

"Shhh."

Fatima placed her fingertips against his wrist and looked at her watch. She dropped his wrist and wrapped the blood pressure cuff around his arm. As the cuff deflated, she lifted the gauge and turned to search for enough light to read the dial. Her gaze fell upon a lamp hanging from a hook in the corner of the room. Several cords wound down the chain to the lamp. Fatima looked away and removed the cuff from his arm.

"You're getting better, Mr. Mustafa."

She recorded the vital signs on the clipboard and then moved to the other side of the bed. She positioned herself between the hanging lamp and Mustafa.

"Get some sleep," she winked. "I'll be back when it's time for your medication."

Fatima glanced toward Mohammajon. He was deeply engrossed in the Quran. She patted Mustafa on the arm and walked to the door. Fatima stepped out of the room and strode down the hall toward the abandoned nursing station. She glanced at her watch. It was close to midnight.

Fatima spent nearly an hour going from room to room checking vital signs and dispensing medication to the other patients on the ward. She sat down at the counter in the nurses' station when she finished.

The time passed slowly. Several patients called her with their attendant buzzers over the next two hours. Fatima rushed to respond, before returning to the counter at the nurses' station to monitor the door to the surveillance room.

The surveillance room door opened shortly after 2 A.M. Fatima buried her head in her arms and feigned sleep. She peeked through her arms, as the ISI soldier stepped from the room. He glanced toward her. When she didn't stir, he marched down the hall, rounded the corner, and headed toward the elevator.

Fatima counted to ten, got up from the counter, and rushed to the Tajik's room. Both men were asleep. Fatima positioned herself between Mustafa and the lamp in the corner. She shook him.

"Mustafa, wake up. It's time to take your medication."

Mustafa sat up with a start, but relaxed when he realized it was Fatima.

"Here, take your medicine."

She handed him two aspirin tablets and a glass of water. He tossed the pills in his mouth and swallowed them with a drink of the water. She took the glass and set it on the nightstand.

She winked.

"Let me help you to the bathroom. I'll be handing out medication to the other patients for the next hour. I won't hear the buzzer."

Mustafa shifted his legs over the side of the bed. Fatima helped him to his feet and supported him, as he shuffled to the bathroom. She shut the door behind them and leapt into his arms.

He kissed her lips and hugged her against him.

"I love you," he whispered.

"Oh Mustafa, I love you too."

She hugged him once more and whispered into his ear.

"We only have a short time. Listen to me. The video cameras are in the hanging lamp in the corner. Watch out for them. Mustafa, a man came to my house today. He's going to help you and Mohammajon get out of Pakistan."

Mustafa peered at her suspiciously.

"What man?"

"His name was Advani. I've never seen him before. But he told me to tell you that it may be a long wait for the springtime."

Mustafa's expression changed to relief.

"Praise Allah, he's sent by the mullah. What else did this man tell you?"

"There'll be a car waiting outside the hospital on Saturday night at 2 A.M. The driver will take you to safety."

"How are we going to get out of the room? The guards watch us all the time."

"The guard takes a break every night around 2 A.M. They record everything that happens in this room. But we have a plan to fool them long enough for you and Mohammajon to slip away."

Mustafa smiled and hugged her to his chest.

"What about our passports?"

"They're in Colonel Khan's desk. But Mr. Advani told me to leave them. He'll provide you with a new identity and documents for your escape."

Mustafa took Fatima's head in both of his hands.

"How can I ever thank you?"

"You don't need to thank me, Mustafa. I love you."

He hugged her and kissed her tenderly on the lips. She returned his kiss and then pulled back, keeping her hands on his still swollen face. She rubbed gently at the black bruise around his eye.

"Mustafa, there were four Afghani passports in Colonel Khan's desk."

Mustafa frowned.

"Four?"

"Yes. I found your passport, Mohammajon's, Aman's, and another man's."

"What was this other man's name?"

"I don't remember. It was a short name. I think his last name was naan or something like that. I don't remember his first name. He's a young man."

Mustafa peered down at her.

"Naan, Naan, I don't know anyone named Naan."

Suddenly, he jerked his arms up and held her by the shoulders.

"Fatima, was the name Jan? Ahmed Jan?"

"Yes, that's it Mustafa. Ahmed Jan."

Mustafa's mouth dropped open.

"Ahmed Jan is our Tajik commander. He was with us in the Khyber Pass."

He grabbed Fatima's hands with a look of excitement.

"He must be alive!"

Fatima pressed her finger to his lips to quiet him.

"Fatima, he must be somewhere in the hospital. Where could they be keeping him?"

"I don't know Mustafa. I guess he could be on one of the other wards. But I think I would've heard if there was another Tajik here in the hospital."

"Maybe they hid him for some reason. Fatima, I have a secret. You must not whisper a word about this to anyone. We're on an urgent mission for my people. Many people could die unless we succeed. Do you understand?"

She nodded without speaking.

"Ahmed Jan is critical to the mission. We can't leave without him."

Fatima thought for a moment. She whispered.

"The nursing supervisor is an old friend. I'll ask her if she knows anything about Ahmed Jan."

Mustafa took her by the hands.

"Be very careful, my love. Don't ask unless you're certain you can trust her. Above all else, don't even hint about our mission."

"I can trust her. She was my teacher. She'll help me if she can."

Mustafa wrapped his arms around Fatima's back and hugged her tightly.

"Fatima," he whispered. "I want you to come with us."

Fatima pulled back and smiled lovingly. She furrowed her brow with sadness.

"Oh Mustafa, if only it were that simple. I want to come with you. I do with all my heart. But I can't."

"Why not Fatima? We'll start a new life together. We can live in Santa Fe or anywhere you like."

Fatima shook her head.

"No, Mustafa. I can't. We live with my mother. She's very old. I can't leave her here alone."

Mustafa sighed deeply. He took her hands.

"Fatima, bring her too."

She smiled sadly and shook her head again. "Now I know you really love me." She hugged him tightly and whispered, "I can't, my darling. Mother isn't well enough to travel."

Fatima kissed him on the cheek. "I must get back to the nursing station. The guard will be back soon. Happy New Year, darling."

He smiled.

"It's New Year's?"

She nodded, embraced him once more, and turned to open the door. He grasped her arm.

"Wait, Fatima!" he whispered. "We must tell Mohammajon."

"I'll tell him tomorrow night. Don't try before then. They'll realize something's up. Quiet now, let me help you to the bed."

She opened the door and supported Mustafa by the arm, as he shuffled to the bed. She covered him with the blanket.

"Thank you," he stammered weakly.

"You're welcome, Mr. Mustafa. I'm glad to see you're feeling better."

Fatima walked to the door. She stepped into the hall and nearly bumped into the ISI soldier. It was the same guard she'd seen the night before.

"There you are! I've been looking for you. I brought you a pastry from the cafeteria."

Fatima beamed.

"That's very thoughtful of you. I didn't catch your name."

"Mohammed Qazi. I'm glad to see you're working nights. It's boring being here alone all night long. If you need to talk to someone, just knock on that second door on the left. My watch ends at 6 A.M."

She smiled sweetly.

"Thank you, Captain. I'm by myself on the ward. I won't have much chance for conversation."

He smiled.

"I'm a lieutenant. How about talking over breakfast in the morning?"

She frowned and smiled sweetly.

"Oh, I wish I could. I really do. But I must get home right after work to relieve my babysitter."

Qazi looked down at her hand.

"Babysitter. I didn't know you were married."

"I'm a widow, Lieutenant. I have an eighteen month-old son."

He smiled.

"I see. Well that doesn't bother me. I love children. Maybe you can have the babysitter stay late sometime so we can have breakfast. How about tomorrow night?"

Fatima sauntered toward the 2-E nurses' station. She looked back over her shoulder and smiled.

"She can't do it tomorrow, Lieutenant, but I'll ask her about Sunday."

The soldier watched Fatima walk to the end of the hall and disappear around the corner.

Fatima lifted the receiver on the phone in the supply room. She dialed a few numbers and put the receiver to her ear.

"Hi Janisa, this is Fatima. I'm sorry to wake you."

She listened for a moment.

"I traded shifts with Maasi. What time are you coming to work in the morning?"

Fatima held the phone against her shoulder while she listened.

"That's perfect. Could you come by when you get to the hospital? I need to talk with you about coverage for the rest of the week."

She listened again.

"Okay. I'll see you then."

Fatima hung up the phone. She took a deep breath and headed back out to the station. A call light was flashing. She cancelled the signal, walked down the hall, and stepped into the room.

CHAPTER TWENTY-ONE

January 1, 2002

Janisa arrived at the 2-E nurses' station a little after 6 A.M. She was a stocky woman about forty years old. Her graying fuzzy hair was covered with a dark blue scarf. She wore a loosely fitting dress that covered her white tennis shoes.

Fatima had just finished refilling the prescription cart. She turned at the sound of footsteps behind her.

"Hi, Janisa. Happy New Year."

"Happy New Year to you, Fatima. How's little Nadir?"

"He's getting big! Last week he said 'ball' for the first time."

"How's your mother?"

"She gets worse every day, Janisa. Some days she doesn't even know who I am."

"I pray Allah will give you strength. Let me know if I can help. I don't know what I'd have done without you when my mother was dying."

"Thank you, Janisa. I'm okay right now. Mother sleeps all day long. She only gets up to eat and to use the bathroom. Half the time she doesn't even get up for that."

Janisa sat down on the edge of the desk.

"Bring Nadir over to my house sometime. My little Fatima would love to play with him. It'd give us a chance to catch up on gossip. I really miss seeing you. By the way, did you hear Dr. Khorram left? He moved back to Tehran."

"No, I hadn't heard that. Why'd he leave?"

"I don't know for sure. I guess he finally gave up on you. He wanted to find a wife. There aren't too many marriageable Persian women here in Islamabad."

"He was a nice man, Janisa. But there was never a spark. Do you know what I mean?"

Janisa's smile melted to bewildered dismay. She sighed.

"No, Fatima, I don't know what you mean. You're a working widow with a young son and a sick mother. The passion fades soon enough. This isn't the time for a schoolgirl's infatuation. You need a man to provide stability."

Janisa glanced at her watch.

"I have a meeting in ten minutes. What do you want to talk about?"

"I worked a double shift to take care of a sick patient. Maasi and I switched. Can we switch shifts until Monday and go back on schedule after our days off?"

"It's fine with me. Just make sure the shifts are covered. Is that it?"

"No, let me show you something in the supply room."

Both women meandered around to the back of the station and through an open door. The adjoining room was lined with several rows of shelves full of boxes with bags of saline, tubing, catheters, and other medical supplies. Fatima removed the wedge that held the door open and pushed it closed. She locked the door.

"Janisa, did you hear about the three Afghanis on 2-E?"

"Yes, of course. Your old friend Colonel Khan asked me to place them on this ward when they first arrived."

Fatima winced at the mention of Khan's name.

"He beat one of the Tajik patients. Did you know that?"

Janisa frowned.

"Are you sure?"

"I'm certain. The man named Mustafa was beaten senseless two days ago. Colonel Khan claimed he fell down the stairs, but his eyes are nearly swollen shut."

"So what can I do? Do you want me to call up Colonel Khan and tell him to stop beating the Tajik patients? Did you know Colonel Khan sometimes comes to the hospital looking for nurses late at night? He's always drunk. He's raped two nurses right here in the hospital. One of them filed a complaint with the hospital director. She disappeared the next day."

Fatima did not speak. She stared with shame toward the floor.

"I'm sorry, Fatima. I didn't mean to insult you."

Janisa lifted Fatima's chin.

"What do you want me to do, Fatima: report Colonel Khan?"

"No, it would be a death sentence. Have you heard anything about another Afghani named Ahmed Jan?"

"No, I haven't heard this name. There are two Pashtun on ward two-south. They're old men. I'd guess they're probably sixty or sixty-five."

"No, this is a young Tajik man. He's in his late twenties or early thirties."

Janisa shrugged.

"I don't know about any other Afghanis. You know, now that I think about it, there's been something going on at the 3-E satellite ward. That's the high security ward where they occasionally treat Pakistani military officers and government leaders."

"So that's what that is. I've seen guards by the doors in the corridor when I rotated to 3-E. But I didn't know what went on in there."

"They have two operating rooms and two private patient suites. It's basically a self-contained clinic and operating suite that's staffed with high-security military doctors and nurses."

"Have you ever been in there?"

"I've only been in that unit twice. The first time was just before it became operational. They asked me to help set up the operating rooms. The other time was just three weeks ago. They called me with a staffing problem. I helped out at the nursing station for a few hours. Both operating rooms must have been running. There were a bunch of doctors and nurses coming and going from the unit. One doctor was American. A nurse at the station mentioned they were treating a man who had three surgeries in two days. That's all I know."

"Is there any way to find out if the man named Ahmed Jan is a patient there?"

Janisa frowned.

"Fatima, I've learned not to ask questions. I just do as I'm told."

Fatima stared at her friend in silence. She took Janisa's hand.

"Janisa, the Tajik who got beat up is my patient. His name is Mr. Mustafa. There's a rumor his friend Ahmed Jan is in the hospital. Mr. Mustafa asked me if I could find out."

Janisa stared at her friend in disbelief.

"Fatima, are you crazy? Why are you taking such risks?"

Fatima looked down without answering. Janisa lifted Fatima's chin with her hand.

"Fatima, are you involved with this man Mustafa?"

Fatima stared at her friend without speaking. Janisa shook her head with dismay.

"Fatima, why can't you find some nice doctor to marry? Why would you fall in love with some soldier from who knows where? Why do you put yourself in danger?"

Fatima lowered her head.

"Why, Fatima?"

"I don't know, Janisa. Why does any woman fall in love?"

"How about security, stability, and a good family? That's what's good for little Nadir. What are you going to do, run off with some Mujaheddin fighter? How can you be so selfish? You're a mother, Fatima. That is where your duty lies."

Fatima didn't answer. She gazed at the floor.

"Fatima, I'm switching you to another ward. It's for your own good."

Fatima gripped Janisa's hand. She looked up with pleading eyes brimming with tears.

"No, please don't do this, Janisa. Please, just forget I asked. I know I ask too much, but there was no one else I could trust."

Janisa took both of Fatima's hands in hers. She sighed.

"Fatima, you've been a true friend. I'll see what I can find out."

"Thank you, Janisa. I wouldn't ask if there was any other way."

"Be careful, for Nadir's sake, if not for your own. I'll come by your house after work. Okay?"

There was a knock on the door.

"Be very careful," Janisa whispered again.

She opened the door.

It was Maasi. She looked at Janisa with surprise.

"Hi, Janisa. I thought I heard someone talking in there. Fatima, are you ready for report?"

"I'm ready. I didn't get a chance to finish dispensing medication. I was talking with Janisa about our switch. She approved our change until Monday."

Maasi beamed.

"Thank you, Janisa. My husband will be so happy. I'll finish the medication rounds when Chasi gets here. Let's do report."

The two nurses reviewed the status of the patients on the ward for nearly thirty minutes. Fatima had a list of the expected tests, procedures, and other particulars about the twelve patients on the ward. Maasi set about dispensing medications when they were done.

Fatima had seen the ISI lieutenant hanging around in the hall. She suppressed her yearning to check on Mustafa. She donned her scarf and veil, gathered her belongings, and ducked into the stairwell. She walked down the stairs and slipped out the side of the hospital. The bus stop was just outside the door.

Ten minutes passed before the bus arrived. The dirty green vehicle belched diesel as it screeched to a stop in a turnout near the hospital side entrance. The doors opened and Fatima stepped on along with several other hospital employees.

It was a blustery day in Rawalpindi. The drafty bus was even more chilly than usual. Fatima crossed her arms and leaned against the side panel.

The bus made the turn out of the hospital complex and bumped along the pot-holed streets. It stopped and started at frequent intervals, as it wove through heavy traffic.

Fatima was lucky to find a window seat. It isolated her from the hustle and bustle of swarms of people getting on and off the bus at each stop. She peered out the window at the throngs of men dressed in tunics and turbans who strode purposefully along the streets lined with shops, cafés, and bazaars.

At one stop, a group of ten to fifteen men was clustered around a fire pit. Fatima's attention was drawn to two older men. Their faces contorted in rage, as they carried on a heated discussion punctuated by vigorous hand waving. Fatima was left to guess the topic. Were they debating recent events in Afghanistan? Perhaps they were sorting out the discord surrounding the terrorist attack on the Indian parliament? Would there be war with India or would there be peace? Fatima shook her head and the bus lurched away from the curb.

The bus squealed to a halt at the top of a hill just outside the city. Several people scurried off the bus before a group of local men dressed in the garments of a strict Islamic sect stepped on. One man in the group stared disapprovingly at Fatima and the unaccompanied woman beside her. Fatima looked away. She noticed a wooden bench a few meters back from the curb where a woman in a tattered, blue burqa was sitting next to a little old Pakistani man. The woman sat motionless and stared straight ahead through the silk mesh covering her eyes, as her husband perused a newspaper. The bus eased away from the curb, bounced over two large potholes, and merged into traffic.

The bus jerked to a stop a few blocks later.

"Excuse me," Fatima said to the woman sitting next to her.

The woman stood up without reply. Fatima slipped out of her seat and hurried down the steps to the weedy dirt path that lined the road. The doors hissed closed behind her. The bus revved its engine and pulled away.

Fatima tucked her hair beneath her scarf. She wove her way up the path past several muddy puddles along the side of the road. She heard footsteps following her. Her heart jumped, as she whirled to look behind. It was Mr. Advani.

"Don't turn around, Mrs. Asefi. Keep walking. Nod if you can hear me."

Fatima nodded.

"It's imperative that we go ahead tonight. An informant let us know the Tajiks will be moved to a secret ISI installation on Sunday. Nod if you're willing to help."

Fatima nodded her head again.

"The details haven't changed. I know you're working tonight. Take the ten o'clock bus. Do you have a burqa?"

Fatima nodded.

"Good. Wear it tonight on the way to work. I don't want anyone to recognize you and sit down for a chat. There are likely to be just a few people on the bus. I'll sit alone near the rear. There'll be a canvas bag beneath the seat in front of me. Sit there and take the bag when you get off. It'll contain everything you need. You'll find two gas-driven injection syringes in the bag. Each one is designed to deliver ten injections. Just remove the cap and jam the tip against an arm or a leg. You can even inject through clothing, as long as the target isn't wearing a heavy coat. One injection will incapacitate for one to two hours. Three injections will kill. Do you understand?"

Fatima nodded.

"A white Suburban will be parked on the east side of the hospital at 3 A.M. Get the men to the turnout and we'll take care of the rest. Any questions?"

She shook her head.

"Good luck then; see you tonight."

Fatima turned the corner onto her street without looking back. Mr. Advani continued up the main road. Fatima crossed the street to her apartment complex. Her porch was the first one along a narrow path that passed between two buildings.

Fatima treaded softly along the walk. She sensed a slight movement of the curtains in the apartment on the other side of the path. She fumbled for the keys in the bottom of her bag and mounted the steps to her apartment. Fatima inserted the key in the lock, opened the door, and stepped inside. She shut the door and sighed with relief.

The babysitter was sitting holding Nadir with her back to the door. He was sucking hungrily on a bottle. Rahima turned and smiled wearily.

"How was your night, Rahima?"

"It was a long night. Your mother stayed awake most of the time. She tried to wander out of the apartment at three in the morning. Fortunately, I heard the door slam. I caught up with her just before she reached Kashmir Road."

Fatima stooped over and lifted Nadir out of the young woman's arms. She smiled.

"I'm sorry, Rahima. I really appreciate your help. Can you come back at 10:45 tonight? It's only temporary. They asked me to work the night shift until Monday. We'll be back on the normal schedule after that."

"Sure, I'll be here. I'll stop by the store and buy some milk. You're almost out. Your mother used the bathroom a few minutes ago. I fed her just before that. Maybe she'll let you sleep."

"Thank you, Rahima. I really need it."

The young woman picked up her purse and opened the front door.

"Get some rest, Fatima. I'll see you later."

"Bye Rahima."

Fatima locked the door. She carried Nadir to the bedroom and opened the door. Her mother was lying on her side sound asleep in the middle of the bed. Fatima eased the door closed.

She carried Nadir to the stove. There was a half eaten loaf of naan on a plate on the top of the counter. Fatima broke off a small portion and took a bite before wandering to the front of the apartment to a stack of blankets. She pulled the top blanket down onto the floor and set Nadir in the middle. She curled up behind him and pulled a second blanket over them. She was sound asleep within minutes.

CHAPTER TWENTY-TWO

Mohammajon was kneeling on his makeshift prayer rug with his face to the floor. He chanted a prayer and pushed himself up off the floor.

Mustafa turned the page of the newspaper and glanced at the photos. One series caught his eye. It was a morbid death scene outside the Indian Parliament following an attack carried out by Islamic extremists on December 13. The gruesome photos showed a line of six dead men who'd carried out the attack.

The door opened. Dr. Zafar walked in accompanied by the nurse named Shahla.

"Good morning, Mr. Mohammajon. How are you feeling today?"

"Praise Allah, my head feels clear for the first time in several weeks."

"That is a good sign, sir. It is common for the cobwebs to linger for several weeks after a severe concussion."

"And you, Mr. Mustafa? How are you?"

"I feel much better today."

Mustafa pointed to his still-swollen eyelid.

"I can't see much out of this eye."

The doctor strode to the side of the bed and shined a penlight on Mustafa's face.

"That's quite a shiner you have there. I'm going to lift your eyelid. You tell me how well you can see."

Mustafa winced, as the doctor raised his eyelid with a cotton tip applicator.

"It's bad, Doctor. I can just make out Mohammajon's shape. I can't see his face."

The doctor frowned and released the eyelid.

"I'm going to ask an ophthalmologist to come by and see you later today. I don't see any blood in the front of the eye. That sometimes happens after a blow like this. But you may have damage to the retina or lens."

He glanced at the clipboard.

"Your vital signs are stable. I wish I could do one more CT scan. I'll see if I can get permission to have that done."

Dr. Zafar strode over to Aman's bed and examined the vital signs on the clipboard. He pursed his lips and nodded his head, as though pleased with the values.

The doctor retrieved a hammer from the pocket of his white coat and tested the reflexes on one side and then the other. Aman's chest rose and fell with the rhythm of the respirator.

"Mr. Aman," Zafar called out. "Squeeze my hand if you hear me."

The doctor placed his right hand down on the bed and leaned over to raise Aman's eyelids with his thumb and index finger.

"Mr. Aman, move your eyes if you can hear me."

He waited for a moment and then released Aman's eyelids. He turned toward Mohammajon and Mustafa.

"He's still unconscious. His vital signs are stable now and the reflexes have normalized on the left side. He could remain this way forever or he might wake up this afternoon. No one can tell."

The door suddenly swung open and Colonel Khan walked in trailed by three ISI soldiers. The colonel walked to the foot of Mohammajon's bed and peered down with malevolence.

"Nurse, will you excuse us please?" he barked without looking away.

Nurse Shahla looked surprised. But she complied with the order and disappeared through the door into the hall.

"Mr. Mohammajon, you look well today. Certainly well enough to leave the hospital."

"That is my decision, Colonel Khan," Doctor Zafar interjected.

Khan turned toward the doctor.

"I read your notes in the patients' charts. Did you not write that Mr. Mohammajon and Mr. Mustafa were stable?"

"Yes, I wrote that. But being stable and being ready to leave the hospital are entirely different matters."

"Well you have your criteria, Doctor, and I have mine. I'll decide when the patients are ready to leave. Doctor, please excuse us for a few minutes."

Doctor Zafar strode from the room. He closed the door behind him. Colonel Khan stared down menacingly at Mohammajon.

"Mr. Mohammajon, I'm going to give you one more chance to cooperate. Why did you come to Pakistan?"

"I told you, Colonel, we came to the Khyber Pass to hunt for bin Laden." Khan turned toward Mustafa.

"Mr. Mustafa, I assure you that carrying on with this charade will have the direst consequences. If you cooperate, we may be able to help you. If not, we will confine you to the Rawalpindi military prison. So your mission is over in any case. You might as well cooperate."

"How many times must we tell you? There is no mission."

"Very well. We have methods to convince your kind to cooperate." Khan turned and strode to the far side of Aman's bed.

"Your friend here's another matter."

"Leave him alone!" Mustafa shouted, as he leapt from the bed.

One of the soldiers jumped in front of Mustafa and grabbed his arm. Another ISI officer pulled his pistol from its holster.

"Unfortunately, the prison doesn't have advanced medical facilities. We are likely to be at war with India soon. I head up the emergency triage committee in this hospital. This bed will be needed for soldiers who have a chance of recovery."

Khan pulled a pair of large shears from his pocket. He held them up for the men to see.

"What's your mission, Mr. Mustafa?"

Mustafa did not respond. Without further warning Khan opened the blades of the shears, slid them around the breathing tube in Aman's mouth, and severed the tube. A shrill alarm sounded from the respirator.

"Pig!" Mustafa shouted.

He tried to push past the soldier holding him. The other soldier seized his left arm and they held him, as the third soldier aimed his pistol at Mustafa's head.

The respirator diaphragm continued to rise and fall. Aman took a few shallow breaths. Suddenly, the heart monitor went into an erratic pattern and a ringing alarm sounded. A moment later, the monitor went into a flat-line pattern with an occasional weak spike.

"Pity," Khan muttered, as he slid the shears back into his pocket.

"You bastard!" Mustafa bellowed, as he fought against his captors. He broke loose for a moment, only to be tackled by one of the guards.

The door flew open and Dr. Zafar and Nurse Shahla raced into the room. They both ran directly to Aman's bedside.

"He's dead," Khan uttered in a matter-of-fact tone. "Do not resuscitate him."

Khan walked away from the bed. The doctor and nurse stood helplessly looking down at Aman's body. The doctor flipped a switch on the cardiac monitor and the alarm went silent. He flipped another on the respirator and the bellows stopped.

Colonel Khan stepped to the foot of Mohammajon's bed and leaned over with both of his hands on the footboard.

"You Tajiks have until tomorrow. Then you'll be transferred to Rawalpindi Prison."

He turned toward his men.

"Let him go."

The soldiers released Mustafa's arms. Their comrade kept his pistol trained on his chest.

"Doctor, you come with me," Khan ordered.

Colonel Khan smirked and stepped out of the room. The ISI soldiers retreated into the hall behind him with Dr. Zafar in tow.

Mustafa rushed around the end of the bed to Aman's side. He pulled back the blanket. His friend lay motionless with the cut end of the breathing tube protruding from his mouth.

"Pashtun pigs!" Mustafa screamed, as he grabbed a jar full of cotton balls from the counter and hurled it against the wall. It shattered into a hundred pieces.

Mohammajon tried to calm him. He placed his arm on Mustafa's shoulder.

"It is Allah's will, Mustafa."

"Allah's will!" Mustafa shouted.

Mustafa's face was red with rage. He pushed Mohammajon aside and paced across the room to the corner where the flower arrangement was hanging from the ceiling. He slammed his fist into his palm and glowered toward the hidden camera.

"Death to Pashtun! That is Allah's will!"

Fatima sat down on the edge of the bed next to her mother. She lifted a spoon from the bowl to her mother's mouth.

"Mother, eat some of this curry."

The old woman didn't respond. She opened her mouth and Fatima slipped in the spoon. She chewed, swallowed, and opened her mouth again. Fatima fed her one spoonful after another until the curry was nearly gone.

"Mother, would you like to get up and walk around the house a bit?"

She peered at Fatima with an expression of total confusion.

"I'm tired. Leave me alone."

The old woman rolled away from her daughter. Fatima wiped tears from her eyes with her sleeve. She spread the blanket across her mother.

"Okay, Mother. I'll let you rest now."

Fatima closed the door to the bedroom and went to check the crib. Nadir smiled up at her. She leaned over and kissed him on the forehead. He reached up and playfully tugged at a lock of her hair. Fatima gathered him into her arms and nuzzled him against her neck.

"My little Nadir. Your mommy loves you. I pray Allah's blessing and that your life will be filled with true love and happiness."

There was a rap on the front door. Fatima looked at her watch. It was a few minutes after four in the afternoon.

"I'll be right there," she called out, as another knock echoed through the apartment.

"Who is it?"

"Fatima, it's Janisa."

Fatima unbolted the door and opened it. Janisa smiled wearily and stepped past her into the apartment. Fatima locked the door behind her.

"You're early. I wasn't expecting you until after 5 P.M."

Janisa unwrapped her scarf and slipped it into her pocket.

"It was a slow day. I want to get home and prepare dinner. It's my husband's birthday."

"Please sit down. Would you like a cup of tea?"

"No thank you. I can only stay a minute."

Fatima couldn't suppress her curiosity any longer.

"Did you find Ahmed Jan?"

Janisa frowned. She knelt down on the blanket next to Nadir and rubbed the little boy's back.

"Fatima, the Tajik Ahmed Jan is in the hospital. The Minister of Agriculture is arriving for surgery tonight. They needed the space in the satellite. They moved Mr. Jan out of the satellite to the regular 3-E ward this afternoon."

"Are you sure?"

"I'm positive. Three-east had four admissions today. They requested an additional nurse, so I volunteered to go myself. I saw him with my own eyes. They say the Taliban tortured him. They placed him in the satellite so they would have access to the special equipment they needed for his surgery. He's in room 312, Fatima, but there's an armed guard."

Fatima smiled down at her friend.

"Thank you, Janisa. You're such a wonderful friend."

Janisa bit her lower lip, as she peered up. She shook her head ruefully.

"What is it, Janisa?"

"Fatima, something terrible happened today. The Tajik man named Aman died."

Fatima grimaced, as she held Janisa's stare.

"It's terrible, but we expected it. He's been unresponsive for weeks."

"No, that's not what happened. Colonel Khan killed him. He issued orders for the other two Tajik patients to be transferred to the military prison in the morning."

Fatima stared down in wide-eyed silence.

"Fatima, there's nothing more you can do. I want you to stay away from the Tajiks."

Janisa stood up and leaned forward until she was face-to-face with Fatima. She whispered.

"Fatima, there's tension in the air. I felt it descending across the hospital like a fog. Something terrible is going to happen. I want you to stay home tonight. I arranged for one of the nurses from the pool to relieve you. I told the night supervisor you were sick."

Fatima raised her hand and brushed her hair back from her face. She nodded.

"Perhaps you're right. I can't remember when I've been this tired. May Allah bless you for all you've done."

Janisa hugged Fatima.

"I love you like a sister, Fatima."

Janisa motioned toward little Nadir on his blanket.

"Think of your son, Fatima. He'd be alone if something happens to you."

"You're right, Janisa. You're always right."

Janisa kissed Fatima on the cheek. She smiled.

"I'll see you on Wednesday. Get some rest."

Fatima led her to the door and unbolted it.

"Goodnight, Janisa. Thank you for everything."

Janisa kissed Fatima one last time on the cheek and disappeared out the door into the night. Fatima closed the door and locked it. She pressed her back against the door and stared blankly across the room.

CHAPTER TWENTY-THREE

R ahima returned to the apartment fifteen minutes before ten. Fatima was sitting cross-legged on the floor with Nadir in her arms when the key slid into the lock and the door opened.

Rahima smiled, as she removed her coat.

"Sorry I'm late, Fatima. The road was blocked off for a convoy of military vehicles."

Fatima stood up with Nadir in her arms. She kissed the little boy on the forehead and passed him to Rahima.

"I just fed him and Mother ate about a half hour ago. I'll see you in the morning. I need to hurry to make the ten o'clock bus."

Fatima fetched a bag from the floor. She opened the door and stepped outside.

"Goodnight. Kiss Nadir goodnight for me," she called back with an apprehensive smile.

Fatima closed the door and locked it behind her. She stepped off the porch and turned away from the street toward the back of the apartment complex. She took a few steps and turned onto a path leading to a closed door illuminated by a naked bulb. She opened the door, stepped inside the musty laundry room, and flipped on the light switch. She closed the door behind her.

Fatima fished the burqa out of her bag. She ducked her head inside and adjusted the headpiece so she could see through the silk mesh. She discarded the bag in a trash can, switched off the light, and shut the door behind her.

Fatima took a few steps toward the main path. The patter of footsteps echoed from the distance and the hair on the back of her neck stood on end. She turned to retreat to the laundry room, but it was too late. The woman who lived next door stepped around the side of the building carrying a laundry basket.

"Oh, hello," the woman called out cheerfully with a curious expression on her face.

Fatima did not reply. She slid past the woman and headed up the main path toward the front of the building. She glanced down the street in one direction and then the other. The restricted view from inside the burqa made it difficult to see in the daytime. It was nearly impossible to get about in the darkness.

Fatima crossed to the opposite corner, carefully avoiding rocks and potholes, as she meandered along the path toward the bus stop. There was a man standing in the darkness smoking a cigarette outside the covered hut at the stop. The block was otherwise deserted. The man glanced toward her. He flicked the ash from his cigarette and looked up the road the other direction. Fatima sat on a bench and waited in silence.

Fatima hadn't worn a burqa in years. Like many other Pakistani women, she detested the stuffy and cumbersome traditional garment. A scarf was acceptable head cover in the area where she lived and worked. There were, however, large areas of Pakistan where any woman who eschewed the traditional Islamic dress ran the risk of public humiliation, or worse.

In short order the bus appeared over a rise in the distance. It squealed to a stop and the door opened with a loud hiss. Fatima stepped up the stairs and glanced toward the front of the bus. A dozen people were scattered in the seats behind the driver. She peered through the mesh toward the rear. Mr. Advani was sitting near the back of the bus on the right side. He was reading a newspaper. He glanced toward Fatima over the top of the paper, but resumed his reading without acknowledging her.

Fatima scooted toward the back using the seatbacks for support. She caught a glimpse of the end of a blue canvas bag on the floor, as she slipped into the seat in front of Advani.

The bus pulled away from the stop and bumped along the road through the city for several kilometers. All of the markets and bazaars were deserted. Only an occasional restaurant was still open. The bus stopped a few times along the route. Finally, it turned onto the access road that led to the main hospital entrance and pulled into the circle outside the front door.

Two guards were stationed on either side of the front door. Unexpectedly, however, an ISI soldier was stationed at a table at the entrance. A woman in a nurse's uniform was standing nearby watching the guard sort through her belongings.

"Allah help me," Fatima muttered to herself.

Fatima's thoughts raced, as she glanced over her shoulder at Mr. Advani. He stared back with his jaw clenched without speaking. She bent over, pulled the bag from the floor, and wedged it into the space beside her. She unzipped the bag, slid her hand inside, and groped around the bottom. The bag was nearly empty, but she clutched two plastic tubes in the bottom. Fatima glanced around to make sure no one was watching. She retrieved the tubes from the bag, pulled her right arm inside the burqa, and stuffed them into the pocket of her nurse's uniform. She pushed the bag onto the floor, kicked it beneath the seat in front of her, and stood up to exit the bus.

Fatima was the last one off the bus at the hospital. She stepped down and shuffled to the end of the line. One-by-one, the guard questioned those ahead of her. He carefully searched through every bag and purse. Fatima stepped up to the table when her turn finally came.

"What is your purpose here at the hospital?" the guard demanded gruffly.

"I'm a nurse on ward 2-E."

"Let me see your identification."

Fatima reached into her purse and pulled out her ID. Her hand trembled, as she handed the ID to the soldier. He looked at it for a moment, before handing it back.

"Let me see your purse."

Fatima handed him the purse. The guard rifled through the bottom and searched the side pocket. He handed it back.

"You may go."

Fatima walked past the two guards posted at the front door. She walked down a long hall toward the back of the hospital and ducked into an empty bathroom at the rear of the building.

She yanked the burqa over her head, stuffed it into the bottom of the garbage can, and covered it with a wad of paper towels.

Two technicians were walking past the bathroom, as she stepped back into the hall. One of the women recognized Fatima. She smiled and waved, before continuing her conversation.

Fatima hustled to a nearby bank of elevators and pushed the call button. The door opened and she stepped into the empty car. She pushed the button for the basement. The door rolled closed and the elevator lurched downward. It jerked to a stop and the door rattled open.

There was a dimly lit hallway extending in both directions outside the elevator doors. Strings of bare light bulbs hung down from the water-stained ceiling to the right and left. Fatima headed to the right. A large bucket was positioned beneath a leak in the ceiling half way down the corridor. The kerplunk of drops hitting the water echoed through the hall.

The corridor served as a storage area for discarded and rarely used hospital equipment. Dozens of spare beds and old medical instruments lined both sides of the hall. Most of it was antiquated junk.

Fatima hurried to the end of the hall where several mattresses were stacked against the wall. She scooted the outermost mattress away from the stack and ducked into the space behind it.

The floor was cold and damp. Fatima lifted her arm. The luminescent dial on her watch read ten minutes after eleven. She leaned her head against the mattress behind her and sighed.

Time passed very slowly. As Fatima sat listening to her own breathing, she became aware of recurring scratching and tapping noises. At first she couldn't identify the sounds. Suddenly, a series of squeaks came from her right. Fatima jerked toward the sound. A cat-sized rat peered at her out of the shadows.

Fatima suppressed the urge to scream. She yanked at the mattress in front of her and the rat scampered away.

Fatima drew her legs beneath her and stood up between the two mattresses. She fumbled in her pocket, withdrew one of the plastic tubes, and broke off the sheath that protected the tip. She crouched back down on the floor.

"Allah, give me strength," she muttered in the near darkness.

She heard another scratching noise and jerked her head to the right. Another enormous rat was staring at her with black, beady eyes. A chill ran up her spine.

The rat inched toward her along the edge of the mattress. Fatima sat absolutely rigid. The pounding of her heart seemed deafening, as the bold creature crept within arms length. Fatima shrieked and lunged at the rodent. She jabbed the tip into the rat's backside. The syringe hissed. The rat took a few uncoordinated steps and collapsed. Fatima recapped the needle and leaned her head against the mattress. She took a deep breath.

Fatima nodded toward sleep several times during the next hour, only to be jolted awake by the screech of nearby rodents. She held a syringe at the ready each time the noise grew louder, relaxing her guard once the ruckus subsided.

Fatima peered at her watch in the darkness. Nearly two hours had passed since her vigil began. She jerked to attention, as the elevator door rumbled open down the hall. The sound of footsteps, distant at first and then steadily nearer, echoed toward her. In an instant, the mattress in front of her slid away and she was exposed.

The Chinese orderly grasped the mattress with both hands and heaved it up off the floor. He glanced back over his shoulder, as he turned toward the elevators.

"What in the...?" he blurted. "What are you doing back there?"

"Sorry, my dear fellow."

Fatima lunged forward with the syringe. The needle hissed against his arm. The orderly's expression melted to shocked disbelief. He crumpled across the mattress before he could utter another word.

Fatima re-capped the syringe and slid it into her dress pocket. She grabbed the orderly by the ankles and pulled him off the mattress. She set the mattress back on edge, slid it forward toward the door, and leaned it against a broken table. She grabbed the second mattress, pulled it away from the stack, and leaned it against an old cart on the opposite side of the hall. She winced at the sight of rodent droppings scattered on the newly exposed cement floor. She brushed the refuse away with her shoe.

Fatima pushed and pulled the unconscious man across the floor by the ankles until he was positioned against the third mattress in the line. She retrieved the second mattress and pulled it back against the stack to conceal them both. Out of breath, she slumped to her knees.

The elevator door rattled open a few minutes later.

"Xiadong, are you down here?" a clearly irritated woman called out.

Softer footsteps echoed down the hall toward them.

"Wait till I get my hands on that loafer."

The sound of the mattress screeching across the floor was followed by the rattle of the elevator door. The hall grew silent once again.

Fatima fought to stay awake, as she periodically checked the orderly. He remained in a deep sleep for just over an hour and then began to stir. He moaned, lifted his head off the floor, and looked confusedly around him.

Fatima checked her watch. It was 1:45 A.M. She snapped the cap off the syringe and pressed it against the man's forearm. It hissed once more and the man slumped back to the floor.

Fatima scooted around the end of the mattress. She checked to make sure the orderly was completely hidden and walked away toward the elevator.

The elevator rattled open on the third floor. Fatima walked to the main corridor and peered around the corner. The hallway was empty in both directions. She strode purposefully into the 3-E ward and commandeered a wheelchair that was parked against the wall. Room 312 was on the right. Fatima retrieved the syringe from her pocket, uncapped it, and pushed the wheelchair through the door.

An ISI guard was sitting in a chair behind the door. He bolted to his feet.

"What do you want?"

"They repaired the CT scanner," Fatima replied cheerfully. "They called Mr. Jan for his study."

The guard frowned and looked at his watch.

"I wasn't told about this."

"Well, it was ordered by the doctor this morning. He wants to make sure there's no bleeding. You can go down to radiology with us. Help me get him into the wheelchair."

"Wait right here. I'll be back in a moment."

The soldier reached for the door and Fatima thrust the syringe against his arm. The man grabbed at the syringe with a puzzled expression on his face. Suddenly, his eyes rolled back into his head and he crumbled to the ground. Fatima pulled the guard along the floor by the ankles and slid him beneath the bed.

"Mr. Jan, Mr. Jan," Fatima whispered, as she shook the Tajik's arm.

Ahmed opened his eyes. Blurry-eyed, he stared up at Fatima.

"What is it?"

"Mr. Jan, I'm here to take you to Mustafa."

Ahmed bolted upright in the bed. He grimaced with pain.

"Mustafa?"

"Yes. He's here in the hospital. We must hurry. Let me help you into the chair."

Ahmed swung his legs over the side of the bed. Fatima helped him to his feet and he hobbled to the wheelchair.

"Where are your clothes?" she asked.

"This is all I have except for my parka. It's in the closet."

Fatima fetched the parka and set it in his lap.

He peered up with a puzzled expression, as if it were all a dream.

"Are we leaving the hospital?"

"Yes. Your friends are waiting for you outside the hospital entrance."

Ahmed pointed to the counter.

"I need that box. The key is on the counter."

Fatima handed Ahmed the small metal box and Ahmed tucked the key in his pocket. He placed the box in his lap and covered it with the parka.

"Okay, I'm ready."

Fatima shoved the wheelchair through the door. The hall was still empty. She pushed the wheelchair back to the elevator. She hit the call button and the elevator door rolled open. Fatima wheeled Ahmed's chair inside and selected the second floor.

The elevator door lurched open on the second floor. Fatima pushed the wheelchair across the corridor and through the door into the storeroom.

"Stay right here, Mr. Jan. I'll be back in a few minutes. Be very quiet and don't come out of this room for any reason until I return. Do you understand?"

Ahmed grasped her arm.

"Thank you for helping me. I'll do as you say."

Fatima ducked out of the storeroom and headed for the main corridor. She glanced at her watch. It was 2:20 A.M. She turned the corner and walked toward the 2-E station. A nurse sitting at the nurses' station looked up from a chart.

"Hi, Zora, how are you? I haven't seen you in months."

"What are you doing here, Fatima? Janisa called me in to take your shift. She told me you were sick."

"It was nothing but a bad stomachache. I feel better now. They had three admissions on 3-E. The supervisor called and asked if I could come in. Have you seen my yellow teacup anywhere?"

"I haven't seen any cups around here."

"That's funny. I could have sworn I left it here yesterday. Maybe the guard in the surveillance room has it. I'll just check."

Zora smiled amusedly.

"Oh, your teacup, huh? The guard asked about you when I first got here."

"He did?"

"Yes, he did. He was disappointed you weren't here. I'd say you're his cup of tea from the looks of it."

Fatima chuckled and shrugged. She walked back to the surveillance room and knocked on the door. There was no answer. She knocked again and looked toward the nurses' station. Zora was still sitting at the desk watching with a mischievous grin on her face.

Fatima leaned against the door, as if listening. She turned the knob and pushed the door open. The room was empty.

"Oh, hello," she called out loudly. "I was looking for you."

She darted into the room and shut the door. Her heart was pounding.

Fatima looked up at the video monitors. Mustafa and Mohammajon were asleep in their room. She ran to the tape cabinet in the back of the room. Fatima selected tapes from the night shift two days earlier and pulled the cases from the shelf. She pushed the eject button on each machine and removed the tapes. She replaced them with the older tapes and pushed the rewind buttons. Both machines hummed loudly. Fatima placed the ejected tapes in the cases and returned them to the shelf.

Each of the tape machines clicked to a stop just over a minute later. Fatima pushed the play buttons. Each screen lit up with electronic noise. The monitors flickered a couple of times before images of Mustafa and Mohammajon suddenly appeared on the video monitors. They were both sleeping.

The sound of footsteps echoed in the hall. Fatima leapt behind the door. The footsteps grew louder and stopped. The knob began to turn and the door opened. It was Lieutenant Qazi. His mouth gaped with astonishment.

"What are you doing in here?"

He glanced at the video monitors.

"I was looking for you," Fatima cooed with a shy smile.

The lieutenant continued to regard her sternly with his piercing black eyes. He glanced up at the video monitors once again.

"I thought you were sick."

"I was," she purred coyly, "but they needed me to come in to work. The ward was busy and I'm feeling better."

Fatima ran her finger over the cluster of medals across the guard's chest. She leaned her head back and smiled up at him.

"I'm off on Monday. The babysitter is taking my son to my mother's house in Islamabad. Would you like to come over to my apartment for dinner?"

The lieutenant's expression melted into one of glee. He reached out and pulled Fatima to him.

"I'll bring a bottle of wine I bought on the black market."

Fatima fished in her pocket for the syringe. She flicked the cover from the needle, pulled the syringe from her pocket, and wrapped her arms around him.

"I've never tasted wine. Is it good?"

Fatima jabbed the needle into the back of the guard's exposed neck. It hissed, as Qazi pushed her away. A look of shock gave way to stupor. She guided him into the corner, as he collapsed against the wall and crumbled to the floor.

Fatima patted the lieutenant on the head and opened the door. The nurse's desk was empty. She glanced at her watch. It was twenty minutes to three.

Fatima dashed past the Afghani's room toward the elevators. Colonel Khan staggered from the elevator alcove right in front of her. He reeked of cheap whiskey. He smiled lecherously, as he stumbled toward her.

"There you are, my little kitten."

He grabbed Fatima's arm and began to pull her down the corridor.

"Come with me," he chortled drunkenly, "there's something I want to show you."

"Stop it!" Fatima screamed.

She tried to pull away from his grasp, but fell to her knees.

"What are you doing?" a voice called out behind them.

It was a nurse from another ward. The woman took a few tentative steps toward them.

"Mind your own business!" Khan bellowed with a drunkard's slur.

His face contorted with rage.

"If you know what's good for you, you'll forget you saw us here. You hear me? Off with you now!"

The woman glanced remorsefully toward Fatima. She looked at the colonel. Finally, she turned and hurried around the corner.

"Come here, you little slut," Khan seethed.

Fatima tried to push his hand away. The colonel grabbed her wrist and dragged her along the floor. She tried to fight, but to no avail. He towed her past the elevator alcove to his office door. Holding her wrist with one hand, he fumbled to find his keys with the other. He slipped the key into the door, opened it, and pulled her into the office. He slammed the door closed.

Khan was on top of her in an instant. He writhed against her body and groped at the zipper on the back of her uniform, as he struggled to force her legs apart. She screamed and tried to roll him off. Khan lifted up and crashed his fist down on the side of Fatima's head.

"Shut up!" he shouted, as he pushed his pants down, lifted her dress, and shimmied between her knees.

Fatima reached for her pocket. She found the second syringe, knocked the cap off against the floor, and jabbed the needle into Khan's bare buttocks. A hiss echoed through the room.

Khan yelped and rolled off of her. He stared at the syringe in her hand. "You bitch!" he slurred.

Within an instant he dropped to the floor.

Fatima cried out hysterically and rolled onto her side. She lifted herself first to her knees and then to her feet. She smoothed her hair and rearranged her uniform. She put the syringe on the desk.

Fatima tried the top drawer on the desk. It was locked. She knelt beside Khan and began rummaging through his pockets until she found his key ring. Still on her knees, she inserted the small key into the lock and opened the drawer. She fetched the four green passports from beneath a pad of paper and stuffed them into her uniform pocket.

Still sniffling, Fatima pulled herself to her feet and stepped to the door. She yanked the door open and took a step into the hall, but abruptly stopped in her tracks. She turned around, stepped across Khan's body to the desk, and grabbed the syringe. Without hesitation, she jabbed the syringe into the back of Khan's arm. When the hiss subsided, she jabbed it into his arm again and again and again.

Fatima looked around on the floor for the cap and found it beneath the desk. She pushed the cap back onto the syringe, slipped the syringe into her pocket, and bounded out the door. She glanced at her watch. It was ten minutes to three.

Fatima ran headlong through the alcove and directly into the storeroom across from the elevators. Ahmed Jan was sound asleep in his wheelchair.

"Let's go, Mr. Jan," Fatima whispered, as she pushed the chair from the storeroom.

She wheeled him into the main corridor, down the hall, and into the Tajiks' room. Mohammajon was sitting on the edge of the bed reading when the wheelchair came through the door. His mouth gaped at the sight of Ahmed Jan. He jumped from the bed.

"Ahmed Jan! Praise Allah! We thought you were dead."

"We don't have time for a reunion," Fatima barked.

She shook Mustafa from his sleep. Mustafa bolted upright. He peered at Fatima and then glanced toward Ahmed. He swung his legs off the bed.

"Ahmed, my friend," he whispered, as he rushed to the wheelchair and patted his fellow Mujaheddin on the back. "I do not believe my eyes."

Fatima tossed both of the Tajiks their clothes from the closet.

"Put them on. Hurry, the truck will be here soon."

Mustafa and Mohammajon didn't move. The two men stood holding their clothes and staring back at her. Fatima crossed her arms across her chest.

"There's nothing I haven't seen before. Come now, we must hurry."

The two men did not budge. Fatima finally stamped her foot and spun around to face the opposite direction. She sighed.

"I will never understand men."

The clothing rustled behind her. Fatima turned around after a few moments. The two men were sitting on the side of the bed forcing on their shoes.

Mustafa finished first. He rushed across the room and threw his arms around Fatima. She returned his embrace and the two spun in each other's arms, oblivious to the others around them.

"I love you, Fatima, I love you!"

"Oh, I love you too," she whispered, as she kissed Mustafa fully on the lips.

Mohammajon looked toward Ahmed. He was sitting in the wheelchair with his mouth open taking in their jubilation. Ahmed turned to look at Mohammajon. Each man caught the other's bewildered stare.

"Don't look at me," Mohammajon uttered, "I told him she wasn't interested."

The two lovers finally released their embrace and Fatima scrambled behind the wheelchair.

"Here," she whispered, as she handed Mustafa one of the syringes. "It's a knockout syringe. Take the cap off and press it against the skin. It triggers unconsciousness in a matter of moments."

Fatima glanced at her watch. It was straight up 3 A.M.

"We must go. The truck is outside."

She pushed Ahmed's wheelchair into the hall. Mustafa and Mohammajon followed on foot. They ran toward the elevators.

"Fatima," a voice called out behind them, "what are you doing?"

Fatima turned. It was Zora. The nurse was running toward them from the station. She looked perplexed, almost unwilling to accept what she was seeing.

"Zora, didn't you hear the fire alarm? There's a bad fire on the 3-E. Get the other patients. We're going out the front door of the hospital. I'll be back to help."

Fatima shoved the wheelchair into the elevator alcove and pushed the button. As the elevator lurched downward, she looked up at Mustafa. He smiled and squeezed her hand.

The door rattled open on the ground floor. Fatima peered out of the car in both directions. The hall was empty. She wheeled the chair toward the east side of the hospital and down the corridor toward the side exit door. Mustafa and Mohammajon huffed and puffed behind her. They heard voices shouting and feet running in the hall above them. Fatima recognized Zora's voice.

"Fire, fire, get down to the first floor!" Zora yelled.

Fatima guided the group around a corner at the end of the corridor. They hurried up the hall to the side door. It was locked with a heavy bar.

"We must go out the front door," Fatima whispered, as she wheeled the chair around and retreated back down the hall. "It's the only way."

"We can't go that way," Mustafa whispered skeptically. "There'll be guards at the front entrance."

"Just get the syringe ready."

Suddenly, the nearby stairwell door burst open.

"Fire, fire, there's fire on the third floor!" Zora shouted, as she and a dozen patients in hospital gowns ran for the front entrance.

Fatima spotted the fire alarm on the wall next to her. She took the hammer hanging from the chain, broke the glass, and pressed the switch. Fire alarms began to ring throughout the facility. Within moments, dozens of staff and patients were running from the back of the hospital toward the entrance.

"Let's go!" Fatima shouted to Mustafa and Mohammajon above the commotion.

Fatima merged the wheelchair into a group of fleeing men. Mustafa and Mohammajon ran close behind.

The hospital entrance was in complete disarray. Nurses, doctors, and patients were shouting and pushing their way out the front door. Guards were shuffling through the throng and running in the opposite direction back into the facility. All the while, the fire alarms continued to clang.

Fatima wheeled the chair through the front door to the east side of the front portico. The inclined walkway was jammed with people trying to push down to the driveway. Little-by-little, the Tajiks made progress until finally they made it to the street.

Fatima looked to the east access road. There was a white Suburban parked along the curb.

"Okay, there they are!" she shouted above the commotion.

Fatima pushed the wheelchair around the side of the building and headed for the vehicle with Mustafa and Mohammajon right behind her.

"Hey, where are you going?" a voice bellowed behind them.

They stopped dead in their tracks and turned. It was an ISI officer with a Kalashnikov rifle.

Fatima turned the wheelchair and shouted.

"We're getting away from the building! There's a fire!"

The soldier motioned with his rifle.

"Stay up here at the front of the hospital with the others."

The four renegades took a few steps back toward the guard. Suddenly, Mustafa leaped forward. He jabbed the syringe against the soldier's arm. The syringe hissed and the man collapsed to the ground. Mustafa grabbed the rifle and sprinted to the Suburban.

The driver door opened and Advani jumped out. He opened the rear door.

"Hurry, get in!"

Fatima helped Ahmed into the back seat. Mohammajon and Mustafa jumped into the second seat. Advani slammed the door shut. He jumped into the driver's seat, put the Suburban in gear, and rammed his foot down on the gas pedal.

"Get down!" Advani yelled. "We're going to run the gate!"

A crowd of people stood in the road near the front entrance to the hospital. Advani veered the Suburban up on the grass to avoid the knot. He knocked over a direction sign and skidded back onto the main road toward the entry gate.

A soldier with a machine gun jumped in the road to block their escape. He aimed and fired as the Suburban bore down on him. A burst of bullets sprayed across the vehicle and shattered the windshield. The soldier dove out of the way at the last moment. The Suburban exploded through the gate, skidded onto the highway, and headed east.

"Everyone okay?" Advani yelled above the whistle of the wind whipping through the vehicle.

Mustafa looked over the seat behind him. Fatima nodded, as Ahmed grinned and tried to catch his breath. Mustafa glanced at Mohammajon. He was crouched on the floor behind the driver's seat with his eyes closed. He was chanting.

"Yeah, we're all okay," Mustafa shouted back.

The Suburban raced down the highway for several kilometers before Advani skidded off the highway onto a gravel road and into a clump of trees. The truck bumped and shook along the rutted path for a hundred meters. Advani steered toward a clearing and skidded the truck to a stop.

"This is it!" he shouted. "Everyone out! The helicopter will be here any moment."

Advani jumped out of the front seat and ran to the middle of the clearing. He set an electronic homing device on the ground. He scanned the dark sky, as he strode back to the group.

The three Tajiks climbed out of the vehicle. Mustafa helped Fatima get out after them. She stepped down into his arms and clung to his chest.

"I love you, Mustafa. Allah is my witness. I wish I could go with you."

Mustafa held her away by the arms.

"What do you mean, Fatima? You are going with us!"

Tears began to well in her eyes. She shook her head.

"There's no room in the helicopter."

Mustafa turned to Advani.

"There must be room. I will not leave her here."

The whirl of a helicopter, faint at first, but growing louder, approached them from the south.

Advani shrugged.

"There's room."

Mustafa turned back to Fatima. He drew her into his arms.

"Did you hear, Fatima? There's plenty of room."

Fatima pulled away. She slipped the passports into Mustafa's tunic pocket, brushed the tears away with her sleeve, and grasped both of Mustafa's arms.

"I can't come with you, Mustafa. I won't abandon my son and mother. You must go without me."

The helicopter descended out of the darkness, its engines roaring. It settled to the ground with two spotlights illuminating the clearing beneath it.

"Let's go!" Advani yelled above the din.

He patted Mohammajon on the back. Ahmed and Mohammajon trotted across the clearing and disappeared into the helicopter door.

"Are you coming, Mustafa?" Advani yelled.

"No, you go ahead!" Mustafa bellowed above the roar of the helicopter. He wrapped his arm around Fatima.

"I'm not leaving you!" he shouted.

Fatima jerked around and jabbed Mustafa in the arm with one of the knockout syringes. Mustafa gawked at her in open-mouthed horror. Fatima stared back woefully, as Mustafa slumped to the ground in front of her.

Fatima, her eyes brimming with tears, began pulling Mustafa by the legs toward the helicopter. Two soldiers in camouflage parkas leaped from the helicopter. They lifted Mustafa from the ground and rushed toward the side door. Another man inside the helicopter helped them ease Mustafa onto the floor. The soldiers leaped back inside.

Ahmed climbed down from the helicopter to the ground. He embraced Fatima.

"Allah will bless you, Fatima. I'll never forget what you've done."

One of the soldiers reached out and tugged Ahmed's sleeve. He broke away and the soldiers pulled him into the helicopter. The gunner began to slide the door closed.

"Wait!" Fatima screamed above the engines.

Fatima pulled the golden falcon and chain over her head. She leaned into the helicopter and slid the medallion around Mustafa's neck. She kissed him on the cheek.

"Tell him I love him!"

Ahmed smiled regretfully and nodded, as the helicopter door slid closed.

The engines on the helicopter began to whine anew and the wind swirled around the aircraft. Fatima ducked away, holding her scarf with one hand and her dress with the other.

The blades accelerated and the giant bird lifted from the ground. It hovered for a moment, before fading across the clearing. The helicopter reversed direction and soared back across the treetops. Fatima stood in the middle of the clearing shielding her eyes. She waved her arm.

Two military trucks sped into the clearing and stopped behind her. Half a dozen armed soldiers jumped from the bed of one of the trucks and surrounded her. The whine of the helicopter engines faded into the night.

CHAPTER TWENTY-FOUR

CIA headquarters, Langley, Virginia, January 2, 2002

Robert Richards, a bandage wrapped around his left ankle, wobbled into the CIA situation room on crutches a few minutes after 9 A.M., looking a little worse for wear. He sported a crumpled, pinstriped shirt with a prominent coffee stain across his belly and wrinkled gray slacks. His bulbous red nose and crimson cheeks set off his scruffy gray beard and mustache. The ever-present half-chewed cigar hung limply from the side of his mouth.

Stone Waverly and Marilyn Harrison were already sitting at the table with two assistants. Two of Richards' aides scurried ahead of him to the front of the table. One man placed a folder on the table before the deputy director's chair. The other aide handed folders to Waverly and Harrison. Richards slipped into his chair and leaned the wooden crutches against the table.

"Thank you for coming on such short notice. I almost didn't make it myself. I took Aldrich and Ames on a walk this morning. They took off after a stray cat and damn near tore my foot off."

Richards coughed several times in rapid succession.

"Excuse me. Stone, you remember Marilyn Harrison, Intelligence Chief for Central and Southern Asia."

"Yes I do. Good morning, Marilyn."

Harrison was wearing a conservative charcoal business suite with a yellow blouse and gray pumps. She stood up from the table and stepped to the screen on the sidewall of the conference room.

"Marilyn, before we talk about India and Pakistan, could you update us on the new information regarding the 9/11 investigation?"

"Yes sir, I'd be happy to."

Harrison pushed a couple of buttons on the controller and the screen lit up with the image of a brooding Middle-Eastern man with a heavy black beard and mustache. He had bushy black eyebrows with angry, dark eyes. The man was wearing brown tinted glasses with large oval frames.

"This is Khalid Shaikh Mohammed. He's a Kuwaiti member of al-Qaida and a chief lieutenant of bin Laden. He's in his mid to late thirties. We have recently developed several independent leads suggesting that Mohammed masterminded the 9/11 attacks."

Harrison changed slides and another bearded Arab appeared on the screen.

"Although funds for the terrorist attacks were provided by this man, Shaikh Saiid al-Sharif, bin Laden's financial chief, we now know that it was Mohammed who moved the money around and actually paid for the attacks."

Harrison punched the console once again and another slide with two Arab men filled the screen.

"Mohammed worked closely with al-Sharif and these two other close bin Laden associates named Abu Zubaydah and Tawfig Attash Khallad. We're certain these four men worked together to orchestrate the attacks. Khallad met personally with hijackers Khalid Al-Mihdhar and Nawaf Alhazmi in Kuala Lumpur in January 2000, just before they entered the United States for the last time. Our sources have provided solid information that Mohammed was the only al-Qaida leader who knew the full extent of the mission and all nineteen hijackers who carried out the attacks. Even bin Laden probably didn't know all the details. The State Department is now offering a twenty-five million dollar reward for each of these four men. That's all I have."

Richards swiveled back toward the table.

"Thank you, Marilyn. We must do everything we can to catch these bastards. We must continue to coordinate with the Pakistanis. I'm betting we'll find these men in the northern tribal provinces of Pakistan."

Richards picked up a stack of folders and passed them to both sides of the table.

"I received a directive from our all-knowing director early this morning. If you open to the first page of the folder you'll see a summary. It includes fairly detailed biosketches for General Pervez Musharraf, the president of Pakistan, and Atal Bihara Vajpayee, the prime minister of India."

Stone opened the folder. On one side of the page there was a photo of Musharraf and on the other side there was a photo of Vajpayee. There was a bulleted list beneath each photo.

Richards swiveled his chair toward Marilyn Harrison.

"Marilyn, give us a brief background summary about Musharraf and Vajpayee."

"I'd be happy to, sir."

Harrison pushed a button on the control panel and the portrait of a clean-shaven middle-aged Pakistani man with black hair and graying temples projected onto the screen.

"President Musharraf was born in Delhi, India, in 1943. His family immigrated to Pakistan during the partition of the Indian sub-continent. His wife's name is Sehba. They have two children and one granddaughter.

"Musharraf attended Forman Christian College, the Pakistan Military Academy, the Command and Staff College, the National Defense College, and the Royal College of Defense Studies in the United Kingdom."

The slides changed, showing Musharraf at various stages of his career.

"He began his military career commanding artillery and infantry brigades before going on to lead commando units. Musharraf rose through the military in spite of not being a member of the predominantly Punjabi officer class of the Pakistani Army. Instead, he comes from an Urdu-speaking family from Karachi. He was appointed director-general of military operations by the now-exiled former prime minister, Benazir Bhutto.

"General Musharraf became top dog in the military in 1998 when Pakistan's powerful army chief, General Jehangir Karamat, was forced to resign. At the time, some of our analysts felt that General Musharraf's promotion came precisely because he didn't belong to the Punjabi officer class. The theory was that Prime Minister Nawaz Sharif believed Musharraf's ethnic background would hinder him in building an effective power base.

"General Musharraf made regular appearances on state television during the Kashmir crisis with India in 1998. That's when his star began to rise. Musharraf is thought to be one of the principal strategists behind the 1998 crisis. He claimed the Pakistan-backed militants were only blocking Indian gains. It's clear, however, that the Pakistani military was directly involved in the confrontation. Musharraf and other senior generals became increasingly angry at the prime minister's attempts to find a diplomatic way out of the crisis.

"Musharraf seized power in a coup on October 12, 1999. Although he's a dictator, the general encourages corporate style decision-making. Important decisions are made in consultation with corps commanders. Musharraf's also a good listener. He encourages subordinates to speak their mind and remains loyal to them. He's seen as brave, unyielding, and unrelenting toward adversaries. When necessary, the general can act deviously to achieve his objectives.

"Musharraf was quick to side with the U.S. after 9/11. Some thought this was out of fear that he and everyone else in Pakistan would be annihilated in the backlash. However, many analysts inside and outside the Company believe Musharraf himself felt threatened by the rising tide of Islamic fundamentalism and extremism in Central Asia. He may have felt this was a good time to crack down on it in Pakistan. Musharraf arrested several prominent religious leaders who tried to incite anti-American demonstrations in the early days of the American attack. He also said he'd crack down on any Islamic seminaries or madrassas that preached violence or advocated terrorism to advance Islam."

Harrison pushed the controller several times until an older, pleasant-looking Indian man with silver-gray hair peered out across the room.

"Prime Minister Vajpayee is a very different bird. First of all, he never served in the military. He's an intellectual who made a name for himself in politics.

"He was born in 1926, at Gwalior in Madhya Pradesh. He was educated at Victoria College in Gwalior and D.A.V. College in Kanpur. He earned a master's degree and worked as a journalist and a social worker before he became politically active.

"Vajpayee was arrested in 1942 during the freedom movement. He was a founding member of the Bharatiya Jan Sangh, the precursor to the BJP party. People often refer to him as the moderate, liberal face of the Hindu nationalist BJP. Vajpayee first entered parliament in 1957. He's a powerful orator with tremendous charisma. These qualities led Prime Minister Nehru to single him out relatively early in his career as a future leader of India. Mr. Vajpayee is the first incumbent prime minister to be re-elected since 1971. He's now seen as the undisputed leader of India.

"Mr. Vajpayee has a reputation as a moderate. However, he surprised us all by carrying out a series of nuclear tests in 1998. These were immediately followed by Pakistani nuclear tests.

"Vajpayee made a historic bus trip to the Pakistani city of Lahore in February of last year. At the time, he received accolades for reviving the difficult peace process between India and Pakistan. Mr. Vajpayee faced his most difficult trial in May of last year when Pakistani-backed forces infiltrated Indian Kashmir. He did a masterful job of handling the crisis, but since then he's had a tough time controlling Hindu radicals intent on slaughtering religious minorities in the country."

"The December thirteenth attack on the Indian Parliament has created enormous pressure on Vajpayee. Many of the leaders in his own party are pressing for revenge. India blames the attacks on Pakistan-based Kashmiri separatist groups, including Lashkar-e-Taiba and Jaesh-e-Mohammad. There's evidence that Vajpayee himself was the main target of the terrorists who hit the Parliament."

"Vajpayee never married. There are persistent rumors about his sexual orientation, but our sources say he likes the ladies. That's all I have."

Ms. Harrison walked to her seat and sat down. Richards swiveled in his chair, still chewing on the unlit cigar. A sudden violent cough drove him to yank a worn handkerchief out of his pants pocket. He blew his nose with a resounding staccato bark.

"Excuse me. Thank you, Marilyn."

He coughed once more and jammed the handkerchief back in his pocket.

"The situation between India and Pakistan has deteriorated over the past few days. Both countries have amassed troops and military hardware along their common border despite intensive diplomatic efforts led by the U.S. and Britain. We are continuing high-level discussions with the leaders of both countries. Pakistan has made significant concessions. Musharraf froze the bank accounts of both Lashkar-e-Taiba and Jaesh-e-Mohammad. He also detained leaders of both organizations. This has included Masood Azhar and more than a hundred other activists. It's still a volatile situation. Either side could get a wild hair up its ass and decide to go for a pre-emptive strike."

Richards peered through his bifocals at Stone.

"That could include a nuclear attack. I believe it's unlikely, since the president made it clear to both countries this would result in harsh sanctions. We're continuing to monitor the situation."

Marilyn Harrison motioned with her hand.

"You'd think India and Pakistan would appreciate the restraint we've shown in not dropping nuclear weapons on Tora Bora when we had so many al-Qaida cornered there."

Richards nodded.

"A lot of us think we should have done just that. I personally agree with Senator Jackson. He urged the Security Council to pull back our troops and drop the big one on Tora Bora as a demonstration of power and future deterrence. I think the president seriously considered it. He still might do it in the appropriate situation."

Richards waved and one of the aides opened the panel covering the video screen in the front of the room. A huge map of Afghanistan, Pakistan, and India appeared on the screen. Infantry divisions, aircraft, nuclear weapons, and other military units of interest were indicated in all three countries.

"At present, our biggest concern is the effect this dispute is having on our efforts to find and destroy senior leadership of the Taliban and al-Qaida. Pakistan has already recalled several divisions that were supporting our efforts to kill or capture leaders from these groups who flee into Pakistan. There is great sympathy for the Taliban and al-Qaida in the tribal territories of Pakistan abutting the Afghanistan border. The tribal leaders see us as the enemy. We want to settle the confrontation and make sure no additional Pakistani troops are redeployed."

Richards switched off the projector and turned to face the table.

"We believe bin Laden and Mullah Omar are still in Afghanistan. Our best intelligence places them either here in the Tora Bora region or in this area outside of Kandahar. We're coordinating our efforts with Special Forces activities in these two areas. We want substantial Pakistani forces in position to support us and search out these enemy leaders if they flee south into Pakistan. Stone, you spent time in both New Delhi and Islamabad."

"Yes, I lived in both capitals from 1989 to 1991."

"Did you ever meet Musharraf or Vajpayee?"

"I met Vajpayee at a party in New Delhi just before I left Asia. He was charming and knowledgeable. I never met Musharraf. Nobody did. He came out of nowhere."

Richards chewed his cigar as he spoke. He sounded like he had a mouthful of oatmeal. "It sounds like you have a good understanding of both countries."

"Yes, I think so," Stone said. "I've continued to follow events in both countries over the past ten years."

Richards nodded his head.

"Stone, Musharraf and Vajpayee are planning to attend the same conference in Nepal. It begins tomorrow. I doubt there's any way they'll meet there. But at least the two of them will be in the same room. I want you to hand deliver a message from the president to both leaders. There's a Company plane headed for Katmandu this afternoon."

Stone struggled to conceal his disappointment.

"Do you really need me to go, sir? Today's my wife's birthday and we have reservations for dinner tonight at Café Atlantico in D.C. We planned to stay at the Mayflower Hotel in the capitol this weekend."

"Stone, I need your help with this one. We must have someone there with first-hand experience in Central and South Asia. I want to be able to tell the director we sent the best."

"I appreciate your confidence in me, sir, but couldn't Paul Mitchell do it? He's headed back to Islamabad next week anyway."

Richards peered across the table at Stone.

"Stone, I want you to take this message yourself."

"Okay, sir. I'll be ready to go this afternoon."

"Stone, I'll make it up to your wife. What's her name?"

"Julie, sir."

"Well, you tell Julie you'll be home in four days. Theater tickets and dinner are on me when you get back. Make a reservation for next Friday night. *Phantom of the Opera* is at the Warner."

"That's very generous, sir."

"It would be helpful if you're prepared to discuss several points with Musharraf about the troops deployed in northern Pakistan to block escape routes out of Afghanistan. Your meeting will be informal."

He pushed a manila envelope across the table.

"These are the points we want to get across. Read the briefing on the plane. You'll notice we are also committing an additional five hundred million dollars to offset the expense to Pakistan for deployment of the troops. We are prepared to provide more funding if there's a need to continue beyond February 1."

"Yes, sir, I understand."

"Well, you need to go pack. Say, Stone, whatever happened with those Afghanis who ended up in Rawalpindi?"

"We got them out last night, sir. They should arrive in Amsterdam today."

"Excellent work, Stone. I'll get word to my friend in Kabul. He owes us one."

"He owes us a lot more than one, sir."

"How's that, Stone?"

"Our operative sent word this morning that the Afghanis killed an ISI colonel during their escape from the hospital. Pakistani forces followed them to the pickup area. An ISI officer spotted some of our troops loading the men on the helicopter just before it took off."

The cigar in Richards' mouth was really churning now.

"Damned Afghanis! They can't shit without killing somebody!"

Richards took the cigar out of his mouth, held it beneath his nose, and then shoved it back into his mouth. He coughed to clear his throat.

"Stone, send a message to the ISI. Tell them we regret the loss of life. For God's sake, don't tell the Pakistanis we took them to New Delhi. Tell them we transported the Afghanis back to Kabul. I'll brief the director. He's going to chew my ass big time over this."

Richards shook his head and peered at the ceiling.

"Shit! What do we know about these Afghanis?"

Stone pushed a small folder across the table to Richards.

"All three men are Tajiks. The oldest is a man named Mohammajon. He's about sixty. At one time he was a Northern Alliance commander. He also taught history at Kabul University. He's a religious man with diplomatic training and experience. Then there's a young man named Ahmed Jan. His father was a Northern Alliance commander. He was killed in battle at Mazar-e-Sharif a couple of years ago. The Taliban wiped out most of Jan's family over the last few years. He had medical training in Saudi Arabia. Jan speaks and reads Arabic. He's got a reputation for being a pretty fair soldier himself. The third man is named Mustafa. He's a ruthless fighter. I'm guessing he was sent along to protect the other two."

Richards finally tired of what was left of the wet, chewed-up cigar. He tossed it into a trashcan beneath the table and fetched a new one from a cigar holder in his coat pocket. He thrust it into the corner of his mouth.

"So what the hell were they up to?"

"I'm not sure, sir. My best guess is they're planning to join several other Afghanis connected with the Northern Alliance in Amsterdam. This political consortium works to represent Northern Alliance interests throughout the world. They also solicit donations from people sympathetic to the cause. We don't have anything more on them."

Richards leaned back in his chair.

"Something stinks. Why would the Northern Alliance be sending Mujaheddin fighters to Amsterdam when there's a war going on in Afghanistan? Is this some kind of hit squad?"

Richards stared across the table in silence for a few moments and then looked up with a scowl.

"Have our agents in Amsterdam put these sons-of-bitches under surveillance. See if you can find out what the hell they're up to, Stone."

"I'll do that, sir."

"Let me know when you get back from Nepal. I want to know how things go."

"I will, sir."

Richards pulled himself up using the edge of the table. He tucked the crutches beneath his arms and nodded at Marilyn. They walked out of the situation room together.

Stone jammed the manila envelope into his briefcase. One of the aides was clearing papers from the table.

"Can I get you a cab, sir?"

"No thank you."

Stone slammed the top of his briefcase down, locked its snaps, and strode out the door.

CHAPTER TWENTY-FIVE

January 15, 2002

Mustafa sat in a rocking chair staring out the picture window in a second floor flat along the Oz Achterburgwal in the Red Light District. It was a sunny, but chilly, Friday morning in Amsterdam. All the trees along the deserted narrow sidewalk were bare.

Both sides of the street were lined with four story buildings painted in light shades of gray, taupe, and pink. The top three floors of each building were apartments for the eclectic population of "Venice of the North." Small bars, restaurants, coffee shops, and antique stores lined the street level on both sides of the canal. Scattered between them were clusters of draped windows that served as efficiency rooms where professional women plied their trade until the early morning hours. The bright morning sun quenched the pink fluorescent lights above the windows.

Two boys on bicycles laughed with glee as they chased fallen leaves that were spinning in the breeze along the quaint brick side road. A young couple strolled arm-in-arm along the footpath. The man turned and lifted the surprised woman off the ground with a bear hug. She returned his embrace and kissed him on the lips before he released her. They ran off hand-in-hand across the canal bridge.

Ahmed Jan set a plate of small sandwiches and a cup of tea on the table. He patted Mustafa on the back and sat in the chair beside him.

"Mustafa, my friend, I brought you sandwiches and tea. You must eat."

Mustafa's gaze fixed on the scene outside.

"It's so peaceful."

He knocked the ash off the end of his cigarette.

"No guns, no fighting, and no death. Just a leisurely walk along the boulevard."

Ahmed picked up one of the sandwiches and held it out. Mustafa rocked back and forth in the chair.

"Mustafa, eat one of these sandwiches."

Mustafa continued to stare straight ahead. He took a puff of his cigarette and snuffed out the butt in an ashtray.

"I'm not hungry."

"My friend, you need to eat something whether you're hungry or not."

Ahmed jerked on his shirtsleeve.

"Your shirts don't fit anymore. You sit around here all day drinking whiskey."

Mustafa turned to gaze at Ahmed. He shoved his hand into his pocket and held out a syringe with a capped needle.

"The donkey calls the mule an ass?"

Ahmed snatched the syringe out of Mustafa's hand.

"Where did you find this?"

"On the floor in the bathroom right after you walked out with your little black box."

"It's for the pain."

"What did they do to you, Ahmed?"

Ahmed didn't answer. He turned to look out the window. His breathing accelerated and grew shallow. He turned his gaze toward Mustafa.

"What happened in the Khyber Pass, Ahmed?"

Ahmed sighed and pushed his head into the chair cushion.

"Don't ask, Mustafa. Please don't ask."

Ahmed glanced out the window once again. Mustafa held the flame of his lighter against a fresh cigarette, took a few puffs, and rested his hand on the arm of the chair.

"I wonder what she's doing?"

Ahmed glanced at Mustafa and then toward the street below.

"Mustafa, you must accept the inevitable. Fatima is dead."

"Allah toys with me, Ahmed. What twisted pleasure does he embrace?"

"The ways of Allah cannot be comprehended by men. One day we may understand his purpose. It's Allah's will."

Mustafa turned his head and glared at Ahmed. He shook his head in disgust.

"How can your heart be so cold? Fatima saved your life. All you say is it's Allah's will. This is not Allah's will."

"Mustafa, I think about Fatima every day and every night. I beg for Allah's mercy. As the helicopter lifted off the ground, I pleaded with the American commander to rescue her. What else could I do?"

The vein bulged at Mustafa's temple and his face grew red with rage. He pounded the arms of the chair with his fists.

"The Americans, they do nothing. Nothing!"

"You don't know whether they have or not."

"I feel it in my heart. They haven't done anything. She's just another woman to them."

Mustafa stood up from his chair and leaned against the window frame. A boat taxi cruised by on the canal below and steered against the bank along a nearby bridge. A man jumped from the stern and held the boat against the dock while a young woman disembarked. She ran into a nearby pizzeria. The man pushed off from the dock and the boat glided away down the canal.

"My father was a hard man, Ahmed. When I was a boy he sent my brother and me out to beg for money every day. We'd stand outside the tourist hotel in our tattered clothes begging for money. It didn't matter if there was scorching heat or numbing cold. Our only purpose was to beg. My father beat us with his fists if we came home empty handed. One time he beat me so hard I couldn't think straight for three days. My mother tried to protect us. She'd wait at the end of the street for us to come home. If we didn't have money, she'd give us whatever she'd stolen from my father's pockets. I remember her holding me late in the night. She'd say, 'Little Mustafa, your mother loves you.' "

He sighed. Ahmed sat quietly listening.

"I see Fatima in my dreams, Ahmed. I see her in a cold dark place. She weeps and calls out in the night. 'I love you Mustafa. Please help me.' "

Ahmed stood up from his chair. He patted Mustafa on the back.

"I'm going to join Mohammajon at the Masjid-E-Al Karam Mosque. They have Dutch classes. You want to go?"

Mustafa didn't respond. He just sat staring at the street outside. Ahmed waited for a response. Finally, he grabbed his coat from the chair.

"See you tonight, Mustafa."

Ahmed opened the door and stepped into a narrow hall. The door at the end of the hall opened onto a small outdoor porch. He took the cement steps in two strides and headed off on the sidewalk.

Mustafa watched, as Ahmed ambled down the street and glanced in the windows of the shops along the way. He turned toward the stone bridge at the end of the street. The joy of freedom was evident in the spring of his step. He half skipped and half trotted across the bridge, before disappearing around the side of a building.

Mustafa reached inside the collar of his sweater and pulled out the golden falcon medallion. His index finger traced down the bird's back and along its wing. He gazed at it for a few moments before tucking it back beneath his collar.

He walked to the kitchen, opened a cabinet, and fetched a bottle of Johnny Walker Black from the shelf. He poured the last few drops of whiskey into his glass, drank it in one gulp, and slammed the glass down on the counter.

"It is Allah's will."

CHAPTER TWENTY-SIX

January 26, 2002

Mustafa and Ahmed sat on opposite sides of the living room of the apartment. Ahmed was scanning a Dari newspaper at the dinner table, as Mustafa rocked in a chair in front of the window.

It was nearly midnight. The fluorescent lights over windows on the street emitted an eerie glow that bathed the darkened street in pink. Women in lingerie lounged on stools in the four windows directly across from the apartment. From time to time, a man would wander past on the walk in front of the windows and scrutinize each woman before wandering away. Three of the women sat expressionless, while the fourth beckoned to each prospective client. One young man passed slowly by all four women and then retreated to the first window. He motioned and the woman hopped down from her stool. She cracked open the door at the bottom of a short stairwell next to the window. A few seconds of bargaining ensued before the woman opened the door and the man disappeared inside. The window shade drew closed a moment later.

A key slid into the front-door lock. Mohammajon held the door open for a middle-aged man wearing jeans and a tan parka. The guest was rather plump, with a balding head and prominent aquiline nose. Mohammajon shut the door behind them. Both of the men slipped off their coats, as Ahmed got up from the table to greet them.

"Ahmed, this is Awar Mohammed. He's from a village north of Taloqan. Awar is director of the Tajik International Aid Foundation based here in Amsterdam."

Ahmed reached out to shake his hand.

"I'm honored to meet you, Awar. Thank you for your help."

Awar held Amed's hand in both of his own.

"It is I who am honored. Our Tajik community welcomes the son of the great Tajik commander Jan. I once played a game of chess with him at a club in Kabul. I'm afraid I wasn't much competition. He was a master."

Awar glanced around the room.

"I hope your apartment is comfortable. I wish we could do more."

"It's fine, Awar. It's a luxurious palace compared to the compound in Afghanistan. Awar, this is Mustafa. He's from Badakhshan."

Mustafa stood up from the chair and stepped across the room. For once he was sober.

"Mohammajon told me you have lived here since the Russian invasion. Amsterdam must feel like home to you now."

"Not quite, Mustafa."

He motioned toward the window.

"As you can see, this city is unlike any other. Women sell themselves like cattle on one street and work as bankers on the next. I plan to return to Kabul this spring. Come, let's get started. I depart for London early in the morning."

Awar, Mustafa, and Ahmed sat around the table. Mohammajon poured each of them a glass of water and sat at the end.

"Can I see the papers you found?"

"They're in Arabic."

"I lived in Yemen for ten years. Let me see them."

Ahmed fetched the manila papers from the inside pocket of his jacket. He handed them to Awar. Awar unfolded the papers and held them up to the light above the table. He read for several minutes, as the others sat in silence. Finally, he folded the papers and handed them back to Ahmed.

"I understand the mullah's concern. This pestilence would destroy the new government in Afghanistan. I favor contacting the Americans."

Ahmed frowned and shook his head.

"No! We are not going to the Americans! If there's a leak, this shipment could be diverted and thousands of our people would die. At one time, I myself favored involving the Americans. I've changed my mind and the mullah agrees. We can trust only ourselves."

Ahmed stared at Awar. Awar nodded.

"Carnevale begins in only five days," Ahmed continued. "All we know is that agents of al-Qaida will go to the Danielli Hotel to pick up the shipment.

Mustafa and I will leave for Venice in two days. Awar, I want you to purchase the airline tickets. Here's my credit card."

"I will take good care of it, sir."

"Please return the card tomorrow. We also need a place to stay in Venice. Put us in a hotel near the Danielli beginning on January thirtieth."

"No problem, sir."

"Awar, are there any Tajiks living in Venice who can help us?"

"There's a small Tajik community outside of Padova. It is only a few kilometers from Venice. There's a former Tajik Mujaheddin who runs an Islamic religious school there. You can count on him to help you."

Ahmed nodded.

"See if one of the Tajik's can get a position at the Danielli Hotel. They must use extra workers for Carnevale."

"I'll see what I can do, sir."

"Are there any Tajik fighters living here in Amsterdam?"

"Yes, I would guess there are at least twenty who came here during the days of the Taliban."

"Give Mohammajon a list of names and phone numbers before you leave tomorrow. Mohammajon, you remain here in Amsterdam. I'll call you on the cell phone if we need help. Find three former Tajik fighters among the community here in Amsterdam. They should be ready to leave with you on a moment's notice."

Mohammajon nodded his understanding. Ahmed turned toward Awar.

"We'll unearth these Arab worms who dare to harm our people and crush them beneath our heels. There's a place reserved for them in hell."

Ahmed glanced at Mohammajon. He was listening in stunned silence.

"What is it, Mohammajon?"

Mohammajon shook his head and looked away.

"Nothing."

"Mohammajon, what's the matter? Do you disagree with the plan? I want your opinion."

Mohammajon shrugged.

"It's not the plan, Ahmed. I'm wondering what happened to the idealistic dreamer who thought our countrymen could live together in peace and build a new nation."

Ahmed glanced across the table at the old Mujaheddin fighter. His dark, baggy eyes were sad. His leathery face was creased with deep frown lines extending down from the corners of his eyes and his mouth. He seemed much older now than he did just a few months earlier.

Ahmed peered down at the tabletop. After a moment, he lifted his head and stared into Mohammajon's eyes.

"He's dead, Mohammajon. The dreamer died in Khyber Pass."

Awar's gaze drifted to Ahmed's scarred and twisted left hand and then back to the commander's eyes. He pushed his chair back and stood up from the table.

"Let me know if there is anything else our countrymen can do to help you, Commander Jan. We're grateful for your sacrifice. May you walk with Allah."

"Thank you, Awar. I hope you and I will someday play chess in that street café in Kabul. May Allah bless you."

CHAPTER TWENTY-SEVEN

Fatima could barely make out the dark and cloudy skies of Rawalpindi through the small mud-strewn windows that lined the rear compartment of the truck as it bumped along the winding gravel road. It was the first time she'd seen a hint of sky in the four weeks since her capture and trial. Drizzle accumulated on the window and formed drops that streaked down between the mud splatters.

Fatima was dressed in drab cotton prison garb that covered her from head to toe. Her hair was tied in a tight bun on the back of her head. A brown scarf covered her head and draped across her face so only her eyes were visible. Her hands were cuffed behind her back and her legs were bound with ankle irons. She struggled to maintain her balance on the hard metal bench, as the truck squealed to a stop.

The guard fumbled with the lock on the back door. The door screeched open on rusted hinges and the dark-skinned prison guard motioned toward her.

"Out with you now!"

Fatima struggled to her feet and shuffled toward the door, her chains rattling beneath her. The guard grabbed her arm and pulled her down the steps to the muddy rock-strewn ground.

Fatima peered out from beneath her scarf. A drab, windowless, flat-roofed cinderblock building lay before her. The sign over the door read "Rawalpindi Central Prison." The squat building was flanked on both sides by a double line of twelve-foot high chainlink fence. Each fence was topped with glistening razor wire. There were menacing guard towers in the no-man's-land at each end of the fence. Fatima spotted a machine gun muzzle protruding from the covered platforms at the top of one of the towers. Off to the right behind the fence, she could make out several lines of one-story cinderblock barracks with barred windows. Two uniformed guards were standing near a door at the end of one of the barracks. Each man was holding a Kalashnikov rifle.

The guard pulled Fatima up the single step to the porch of the entry building past an armed guard and through the open door. There was an older guard sitting at a wooden desk behind a counter inside the door. He stood up, put his clipboard down, and walked to the counter.

"Papers," he grunted.

The truck guard handed him a stack of papers fastened together with a paper clip. The desk guard looked through the first few sheets. He shook his head and looked up over his reading glasses.

"Life with hard labor for the murder of an ISI officer and aiding and abetting prisoners in an escape. We've got just the place for her."

He turned and looked at a diagram on the wall peppered with different colored pushpins. Two younger guards stepped through a side door into the office, as he studied the board. The desk sergeant selected a red pushpin from the tray below the bulletin board and jammed it in.

"High security building 5, cell 13."

The two younger guards stepped through a swinging door next to the counter. One of them grabbed her by the arm.

"Sir, can I have a different cell?"

The sergeant looked up from the stack of papers with surprise. His expression melted into annoyance.

"All of the cells are the same. This ain't no hotel."

"Thirteen is unlucky, sir. I don't want to spend my life there."

"There's no luck here in Rawalpindi Central Prison."

He turned toward the younger guard.

"Get her out of here before I send her to solitary."

"Come on," one of the younger guards growled, as he jerked her by the arm.

The two guards led her to a locked door at the end of a short passageway. One of the guards selected a key from the chain on his belt and unlocked the door. He directed Fatima through the door to the prison yard and slammed it closed behind them.

They directed her along a cement walk between two of the cinderblock barrack buildings. There was a gate in the middle of a chainlink fence at the end of the path. One of the guards opened the lock on the gate. The other man led Fatima through and locked the gate behind them.

They approached a metal door in a windowless, single-story cinderblock building just to the right of the gate. A sign above the door printed in black block letters read "High Security Processing." One of the guards pushed a button to the side of the door and a loud buzzer sounded inside the building. A small trap covered with a grate opened in the door a few moments later. A pair of black eyes peered out through the trap. The lock clanked and the door creaked open.

A squat man in a wrinkled uniform stood in the doorway. He took a yellow paper from one of the guards and glanced at it. He nodded and stepped aside, as one guard guided Fatima into the office by the arm.

The short man stepped up in front of Fatima. He was dark-skinned with a pocked complexion. Prominent bushy eyebrows framed his dark eyes. A thin mustache with a gap in the middle curved down toward the corners of his mouth. There was an angry, red pustule on the bridge of his nose. He grinned at Fatima with yellowed teeth and a prominent gold crown.

"I'm Abdulla Mufti, the assistant superintendent in charge of the high security lock-up. We expect you to immediately follow all orders here. Do you understand?"

Fatima nodded.

"All questions from prison staff will be answered 'Yes, sir.' We expect an immediate verbal response. Is that clear?"

She nodded again. Mufti slammed his fist on the counter. Fatima's eyes widened with fear.

"I didn't hear you!"

"Yes, sir," she shuddered.

"That's better. We'll issue you a prison uniform and a blanket. Take care of them. They'll be the last ones you get for the next five years. You'll get three meals a day. Eat the food or not, we do not care. But if you throw the food, you'll get three months of solitary confinement. Do you understand?"

"Yes, sir."

"Good. Once a week you'll have a chance to shower. You should report lice to the medical officer at that time so you can be treated. You'll have access to the exercise yard thirty minutes each day. The prisoners who thrive here at Rawalpindi Prison make good use of this time. There is no exercise period in solitary confinement."

"You'll be issued one copy of the Quran. Take care of it. It's the only one you'll receive. You can have two visitors per month. Each visit lasts thirty minutes. You can write two letters per month. The letters can be no longer than two pages each. Any mail that arrives here will be given to you on Monday of each week. Both the letters you write and the letters you receive will be censored. Do not write anything about the conditions here in the prison. Do not mention any punishment you receive or anything about the design of the prison. Do you understand?"

"Yes, sir."

"If at any time you raise your voice to prison staff, you will receive ten lashes and solitary confinement. You will get thirty lashes and six months solitary confinement if you throw anything or assault a staff member in any way. Solitary cells are six-foot square pits. The solitary food is restricted to soup three times a day. Some prisoners do not survive solitary. You don't want to do anything to earn yourself a stint in solitary. Do you understand me?"

"Yes, sir."

"Good."

The guard stepped to the desk and pressed a button on a console. He spoke into a monitor.

"Greta, we have a new prisoner."

A heavy, white woman dressed in a prison uniform entered the room through a doorway in the back a moment later. Her short hair was pulled back in a bun secured with a rubber band. She wore heavy black boots and a ring of keys hung from her belt. She walked over and took Fatima's arm from one of the guards.

"This way," the woman barked, as she took the yellow paper from the assistant superintendent. She glanced at the paper and guided Fatima out of the processing office and down a long hall.

"Right here," the female guard ordered, as she stopped at a metal door. She unlocked the door, opened it, and pushed Fatima inside. The door slammed shut behind them.

The windowless room was lined with open cabinets. There were prison uniforms arranged in a series of cubbyholes on one wall. Shelves along another wall were filled with stacks of tan-colored woolen blankets. There was a table in the middle of the small room.

"My name is Miss Buchler. I'm the day warder here in the high-security block. You do what I say and we'll get along just fine. Have a seat there."

Fatima sat down in a wooden chair near an internal door. A sign over the door read "showers."

"I'm guessing you'd wear a small."

The guard stepped across the room and pulled a top, pants, socks, and a scarf from the top of the stacks. She handed them to Fatima.

"Let me see your shoes."

Fatima kicked off each of her shoes. The woman leaned over and picked them up. She examined the soles on each of the shoes and tossed them down at Fatima's feet.

"You can wear those a while longer. Here's your blanket."

She stepped over to a cabinet and opened it. She took a copy of the Quran off the top shelf and handed it to Fatima.

"I'm going to take off your handcuffs and ankle chains so you can take a shower. There's a shelf with plastic green bottles next to the shower. Use the soap to bathe and wash your hair. It kills lice. Lice are a big problem in this prison, so I recommend you use it every week."

Buchler bent down and unlocked Fatima's ankle chains. She stood up and unlocked her handcuffs.

"Leave your clothes on the table in the shower room. I'll take care of them."

Fatima stood up from her chair. Warder Buchler unlocked the heavy metal door to the showers and pulled it open. She paused to peer at Fatima staring out from behind her scarf with expressionless eyes.

"Why'd you kill the colonel?"

"He raped me."

Buchler snickered and shook her head.

"What about the escape?"

"They were patients from Afghanistan. I was their nurse. The colonel killed one of them and nearly beat another one to death. I helped them escape from the hospital."

"What happened to them?"

"They were rescued by a helicopter. I don't know what happened to them after that."

Buchler shook her head.

"Dummkopf. Go ahead and take your shower and change into the prison uniform. I'll be back in a few minutes to take you to your cell."

Fatima staggered into the shower room carrying her prison uniform and blanket. Warder Buchler slammed the door shut behind her and locked it.

There was a short hall bounded by a three-meter-high wall lined with drab gray tile. The end of the hall opened into a large, gray-tiled room lined with showerheads.

Fatima set her things down on the table at one end of the room. She stripped off her clothes, folded them onto the table, and stepped across the room. She turned on the shower. The stream was little more than a trickle. The water was cool, but pleasant, as it ran down her body. It'd been weeks since her last bath.

Fatima took a plain green bottle from the shelf and set it on the floor beneath her. She ducked her head beneath the showerhead and let the water run through her hair. She bent down, picked up the green bottle, twisted off the top, and poured some of the soap into her hand. Smearing the soap on her arms, she wiped it across her chest. The soap smelled of solvent and stung her skin. Fatima poured more soap into her hand and worked it into her hair. She heard the door to the shower room clang open, as she ran her fingers through her hair.

"Hello?" she called out.

No one answered.

Fatima stepped beneath the showerhead to wash the soap from her hair. She turned her back to the water stream and bent her head back so the water ran through her bangs and down her face. She relished the purity of the water, as it cascaded over her body.

Fatima heard a rustle in front of her. She opened her eyes. Abdulla Mufti, the assistant superintendent, was standing across the room ogling her with a toothy grin. His pants were down around his ankles. He was masturbating.

Fatima screamed and turned her back to him beneath the shower.

"What do you want? Please leave."

"You, my dear, are a goddess. I have the power to make your stay here at Rawalpindi Prison more pleasant. In return, I only ask only for an occasional favor."

Fatima scurried to the end of the room. She took a towel from the open cabinet, wrapped it around her, and stepped behind the table.

"Please leave!"

"*Sir.* You will end your sentences with 'sir' when you address me, woman."

"Please leave, sir."

"Think it over. If you cooperate with me, I'll see you get a job in the office, plenty of food, frequent showers, and books from your country to read. I'll see you have everything you want. You'll learn to enjoy me. I've had many lovers."

Mufti grinned and the gold tooth glistened in his mouth.

"I appreciate your offer, sir. But I am a religious woman. I cannot engage in sex outside of marriage. Please leave, sir."

The sound of the lock clanking open resounded through the shower room. Mufti bent over, pulled up his pants, and zipped his fly. He grinned.

"We'll discuss it later. Think it over."

Mufti turned back into the hall.

"There you are, Greta," Mufti's voice boomed through the shower room. "Take the prisoner to her cell. I want to discuss the maintenance schedule for next week. Come to my office when you get a minute."

"Yes, sir. I'll be there shortly."

Fatima finished wrapping her hair. She tied it back and covered it with the cotton scarf. Warder Buchler rounded the corner from the hall into the shower room. She caught sight of the tears running down Fatima's face.

"You best save your tears, dearey. Only the strong survive Rawalpindi. Get your shoes on and I'll take you to your cell."

Fatima wiped the tears from her face with the towel.

"I'm sorry, I miss my son."

Fatima slipped on her shoes. She picked up her blanket and walked past the Warder. Buchler picked up her Quran and tailed her back into the hall. She led Fatima down the corridor and unlocked the door that led outside the building to the prison yard. They followed a cement sidewalk past a cluster of single-story cinder block buildings. The last building had a large 5 painted on the side. Buchler guided Fatima up the walk to the door.

She pushed a buzzer on the wall next to the door. A security panel opened and the door clanged open. An old guard with a book in his hand stood in the entryway. Warder Buchler guided Fatima into the building by the arm.

"Mrs. Asefi, this is Block Warder Sarfraz. She's assigned to cell 13."

The guard nodded without speaking. He used a key chained to a board to unlock an inside metal door. The door led to a long dimly lit hall that ran fifty meters to the other end of the building. Buchler guided Fatima into the hallway. Sarfraz locked the main door behind them and strode ahead down the hall.

The dingy, yellowed hall was lined with doors. Block numbers were printed on the wall above each one. Each of the doors was equipped with a small porthole. A shrill laugh echoed through the block.

"Shut up, Sundi!" Sarfraz shouted.

Sarfraz stopped at cell 13. He inserted the key into the lock and opened the door. He stepped inside, turned on a light, and glanced around the room. He stepped from the cell.

"Okay," Sarfraz muttered. "This is your cell."

Fatima stepped inside and Sarfraz slammed the door behind her. He locked it. The echo of the guard's footsteps faded back down the hall. The door at the far end of the hall slammed shut a moment later. Distant chanting echoed through the cellblock.

Fatima stood just inside the door and scanned the windowless, cement-walled cell. It was about three meters wide and four meters long. A naked lightbulb was hanging from the middle of the ceiling. A raised platform to one side of the cell served as a bed. There was no mattress or bedding, just cold, bare cement. The cement floor had a metal, grate-covered drain to the rear. A squat toilet was set in a back corner of the cell. The old porcelain bowl was yellowed with dark stains.

Fatima took a deep breath and sighed. She spread the blanket across the raised platform and lay down on her side with her head resting on her arms. A tear tracked across the bridge of her nose and down her cheek.

CHAPTER TWENTY-EIGHT

February 12, 2002

The setting sun's last rays scattered purple beneath a cloudy sky and danced across the waterway reflection of the majestic domes of the Chelsa di San Giorgio Maggiore and the Santa Maria della Salute.

The canal at the Venice waterfront was teaming with taxis and vaporetti. Every other imaginable vessel, some barely seaworthy, weaved past each other on their way to and from the Grand Canal. Masses of people wandered among the street vendors displaying all manner of cheap hats, statuettes, and glass artifacts beneath the balcony of the Hotel Danielli.

Al-Zadir peered down from his balcony at a young couple stepping into a gondola at the water's edge. They were both festooned in colorful seventeenth century period costumes. The garments were adorned with intricately beaded masks, feathered fans, and flowing white wigs.

The young man lifted the bustle of his lover's dress, as the woman tiptoed to the safety of a middle seat in the gondola. The sleek gondolier, dressed fully in black, offered his arm to the young man. The beau dismissed him with a wave of his hand and stepped into the gondola beside his sweetheart. He wrapped his coat around her against the chilly breeze.

The gondolier glided to the stern and used his oar to ease the craft away from the shore. He guided the craft between a pair of taxis and turned toward the Grand Canal.

Al-Zadir watched until the gondola disappeared into the canal. His gaze wandered to the Basilica of the Santa Maria della Salute and its majestic domes that dominate the Dorsodoro skyline. He lifted a teacup to his lips and sipped the green tea without diverting his gaze.

"Infidels," he muttered beneath his breath. "Allah willing, we will one day rid the world of this blasphemy."

A cell phone rang. Al-Zadir opened the cover and lifted it to his ear. He listened without speaking for a moment.

"Carnevale," he finally offered.

He listened in silence, as the caller identified himself with a predetermined code and relayed a brief series of directions. Al-Zadir pressed a button on the phone to disconnect the call. The entire discourse lasted only twenty seconds.

Al-Zadir lifted the cup again and sipped the remaining tea. He sat the cup on its saucer, grasped the table's edge, and pulled himself to his feet. Leaning over the balcony railing, he scanned the busy crowd below. Then he peered across the darkening horizon and turned to step back across the threshold into his room.

He paused at the nightstand to pocket a key attached to a red tassel and silently cracked the door open. Al-Zadir stepped into the empty hall and replaced the privacy sign on the knob, as he stooped to the floor and leaned a matchstick against the bottom of the door.

The lift directly across from the room was open. Al-Zadir stepped in and pushed the first-floor button. The doors rumbled closed and the elevator lurched downward. The doors opened a few seconds later and al-Zadir scooted out between two young men engrossed in an animated conversation in Italian. The men stepped into the elevator and the doors closed. Al-Zadir watched the floor indicator until the car reached the top floor. Finally, he turned and strode toward the lobby.

An exquisite red carpet marked the meandering path to the lobby of the Hotel Danielli. Al-Zadir paused on the balcony and scanned the tables in the bar beneath delicate Murano glass chandeliers. The tables were filled with men and women wearing every sort of colorful costume. One cackling, obese women caught his eye. Dressed in a low-cut, purple velvet gown, her jowls and bosom rippled as she laughed.

Al-Zadir strode down the stairs toward the reception desk and into an adjacent room. The suite was filled with racks of clothing. Several women at sewing machines glanced up at him before going back to their work.

A small dark-skinned young woman appeared from behind one of the racks. She was beautiful with large, almond-shaped brown eyes and long curly hair. Her high cheekbones accentuated a dazzling smile.

"May I help you, sir?"

Al-Zadir scanned across the racks of clothing. He smiled and replied with a heavy Arab accent, "I was told this was the place to rent a ball costume for this evening."

The woman motioned toward a rack in the back of the room without the slightest hint of surprise.

"We have several excellent costumes still available. There's not much time for alteration, but we should be able to find something suitable. Did you have a period in mind?"

Al-Zadir followed her toward the last rack, as he admired the woman's slender waist and perfect proportions.

"It's for the ball at the Palazzo Pisani Moretta. I understand it's a rather formal affair."

"Yes, of course," she smiled, "you'll require eighteenth-century attire."

She sorted through several garments before selecting a green knee-length coat trimmed in gold braid. The costume was adorned with large brass buttons and knee-length pants to match. The woman selected a long-sleeved, white silk shirt with a grand ruffled collar and full cuffs from a box on the table.

"This costume is very handsome. Let's try the shirt."

Al-Zadir slipped off his black shirt to reveal a muscular hairy chest. The young woman smiled and held the shirt out. Al-Zadir threw the shirt across his shoulders and buttoned it. It fit perfectly. He slipped on the coat.

"We'll need to shorten the coat three centimeters," she said, as she tugged at the sleeves.

The woman used a tape to measure his waste and inseam. She measured his foot and pulled a pair of shoes from a rack.

"Try on these shoes. Then choose a hat from the shelf against the wall. I suggest a simple black mask, but there are a number to choose from on the counter."

Al-Zadir tried on the shoes. They fit perfectly. He settled on a large, black, triangular hat and took her advice on the mask.

"Please send these to room 201 when the alterations are done. I need them by nine tonight at the latest. Can you bill my room?"

"Yes, sir, of course. They'll be done within the hour. Let me know if there is anything more we can do to make this an experience you'll always remember."

* * *

Al-Zadir laughed, as he admired himself in the full-length mirror. He had to admit the young woman had made a perfect choice. He looked like a proper eighteenth century Venetian nobleman. Al-Zadir took one more look in the mirror and opened the door to his room.

Al-Zadir checked the hall. It was empty. He crouched and replaced the matchstick against the door, before taking the stairs to the lobby and exiting through the revolving main door.

The cobblestone street outside the hotel was already buzzing with revelers in costume. Al-Zadir wove through the throng to the canal and hailed a waiting gondola.

"Palazzo Pisani Moretta," he called out, as he stepped into the boat.

The canal was crowded with dozens of gondolas waiting to dock. A slight breeze drifted across the water. It was a cool, but comfortable, evening.

The oarsman guided the gondola through the choppy waters of the bay and into the Grand Canal. Al-Zadir sat in silence, as the gondola glided past grand marble palazzos with varying architecture from Venetian Byzantine to Gothic Romanesque. Many of the palazzos were hosting festive parties with hundreds of costume-adorned guests. Al-Zadir sneered at the ostentatious display of wealth.

"The infidels celebrate while my countrymen die," he muttered out loud.

"Sir?" the oarsman queried.

Al-Zadir turned toward the oarsman.

"The palaces ... they are beautiful at night."

The gondola glided up to a majestic palazzo with an imposing pink marble facade and leaded-glass windows. The archway leading to the front door was particularly grandiose. A small orchestra on a stand regaled the arriving revelers with a waltz.

"Palazzo Pisani Moretta, sir," the gondolier called out.

The doormen lowered the gangplank onto the gondola and helped al-Zadir step on shore. He paid the oarsman and strutted toward the archway. Dozens of men and women dressed in period costume were gathered at the entryway. The women were adorned in colorful, full-length dresses sporting beads, bows, and lace. Many wore shoulder-length gloves, with beautiful jewels and elegant hair-dos. Everyone wore masks in the grand tradition of the Carnevale.

Al-Zadir waited in line patiently until he reached the receptionist.

"Your name, sir?"

"Mohat Shah."

The woman shuffled though several pages. She checked off his name on the list.

"Welcome to the Pisani Moretta, Mr. Shah. You're seated at table seven for dinner. Appetizers are being served in the foyer."

Al-Zadir meandered through the entrance and waded into the crowded foyer. A group of entertainers were dancing a minuet to the music of an accompanying quartet. He filled a small plate with hors d'oeuvres and stood to one side, taking in the splendid spectacle of dancers, poets, and magicians.

Al-Zadir set his plate down and wandered into the ballroom. One of the entertainers approached and asked him to dance. He took the woman into his arms and glided across the dance floor to a spirited waltz. Al-Zadir enjoyed demonstrating his considerable dancing skills. He thanked her when the music ended and made his way back to the foyer.

Al-Zadir took a soda and watched the entertainers dance a quadrille. A man standing behind him snorted with laughter. When al-Zadir turned his head to look, he spied a young woman dressed in a beautiful red velvet gown with a beaded mask that matched her feathered hat. She was standing alone, her eyes sparkling with excitement. She glanced toward al-Zadir and smiled. He stared for a moment and then nodded. The woman sauntered toward him and curtsied.

"Kind sir, could I be so bold to ask for a waltz before your card is filled? I'm afraid there are few men at the ball who dance with your skill."

"I'd be delighted. My name is Shah. And your name is…?"

She offered her hand.

"Miss Estalanza."

Al-Zadir took her hand and kissed it with a slight bow.

"I'm afraid you overestimate my dancing ability," al-Zadir teased with a smile.

"Perhaps you're right, but you'll just have to do. I'll have you up-to-speed in no time."

Al-Zadir smiled.

Miss Estalanza's skin was smooth and dark. The low cut of her gown revealed an ample bosom that drew his gaze.

As if on cue, the orchestra began to play the *Blue Danube Waltz*. The young woman curtsied again and al-Zadir took her hand and led her to the ballroom. They glided across the floor in perfect harmony to a medley of waltzes. The two of them danced and made small talk about nothing in particular. The orchestra played several waltzes before a hostess stepped to the microphone.

"Dinner will presently be served on the second floor. *Buon apetito!*"

"Thank you, Shah. It's been delightful."

"It has been my pleasure, Miss Estalanza. Perhaps we should dance again later."

"Please, call me Cassandra. I'll hold you to that, Shah. I'll meet you in the ballroom after dinner."

She turned and disappeared into the crowd. Al-Zadir chuckled and shook his head. He made his way up the stairs to his table along with the rest of the guests.

The table was decorated with a grand centerpiece, dozens of sparkling crystal glasses, and the finest silver. Nine other revelers were already seated at the table in classic high-back chairs. There were three couples and a trio of two women with an older man. Al-Zadir was assigned a seat facing the stage. He insisted one of the couples exchange places with him so they'd have a better view of the entertainment. The seat that was left lent al-Zadir an unobstructed view of the door into the room.

An efficient team of waiters served the five-course gourmet dinner. They served fine wine, Beluga caviar, spinach salad, bow-tie pasta, and tender pheasant. While they ate, a dance troop in period costumes strutted, bobbed, and curtsied in a grand exhibition of period entertainment.

Al-Zadir kept mostly to himself. He had a brief conversation with one of the couples about the wines of Italy. The woman said he looked a lot like Omar Sharif. Al-Zadir also spoke with one of the women in the trio. It turned out the two women were a couple and the man was their neighbor. They'd all decided to come to Carnevale to celebrate the gentleman's sixtieth birthday.

The dessert and coffee table was in the adjoining room. It was adorned with an enormous crystal fountain rising nearly to the ceiling. Al-Zadir approached the table filled with silver platters of pastries, cakes, cookies, and candies. He placed a few truffles and a slice of cake on his plate.

A dark-complexioned man in a burgundy suit and mask approached the table. He selected a few small pastries.

"They say it will rain tomorrow in the desert," the man whispered, as he set one of the pastries on his plate.

"The desert is most beautiful in the rain," al-Zadir uttered.

The man leaned across a corner of the table to take a pastry. As he did so, he slipped a small envelope into al-Zadir's pocket. The man selected one more pastry and then strode away with his plate. He vanished into the adjoining room.

Al-Zadir wandered back to his table with the plate of pastries. He took his time with desert until two of the couples at the table finished dinner and moved to the ballroom. Finally, he bid the trio a good evening and walked toward the stairs and down to the main entrance of the palazzo. Cassandra caught sight of him at the bottom of the staircase. She excused herself from a conversation with another gentleman and wove toward him through the throng of people in the main foyer.

"There you are, Shah. You aren't leaving this early are you?"

"I wanted to say goodbye, Cassandra. I have an early departure in the morning."

She frowned and feigned shock.

"Shah, you can't leave before the Carnevale Waltz."

Al-Zadir extended his arms in mock consternation.

"Of course not. How boorish of me."

Cassandra took al-Zadir's arm and tugged him gently toward the ballroom. She smiled and squeezed his hand.

"You're fortunate I'm looking out for your reputation. It would be most unfortunate if word got out you had a problem with prematurity."

The orchestra was concluding a beautiful medley of waltzes by Strauss. Al-Zadir and Cassandra stood arm in arm until the music ended. The master of the ball, resplendent in a grand green and gold coat, approached the microphone.

"And now ladies and gentlemen, the Carnevale Waltz."

The orchestra began to play the *Emperor's Waltz*. Al-Zadir guided Cassandra to the middle of the ballroom. The couple bowed slightly and began to glide around the dance floor. They flowed, as if they'd danced together for years. The other dancers opened up the dance floor to give them room.

"You're a wonderful dancer, Shah," Cassandra whispered into al-Zadir's ear. "I believe we're being watched."

"No, my lady, it is you who's wonderful. It's a simple matter for a man to look good with a woman of such beauty in his arms."

"I love your accent, Shah. Where did you receive your training?"

"I attended both high school and college in Boston. At one time I wanted to be a surgeon, but my hands are too big. I took my degree in political science."

She smiled up at him, as he twirled her in his arms. When the dance ended, they applauded and left the dance floor.

"Thank you for a wonderful waltz, Shah."

"Thank you, Cassandra. Now I must go. I'm departing early tomorrow for London."

Cassandra pouted.

"If only my charms were sufficient to convince you to stay. I'm staying at the Danielli. Where do you stay?"

"I'm also staying at the Danielli."

"What a happy coincidence! I guess I've had enough decadence for one evening. Perhaps we could share a gondola?"

"I'd be happy to accompany you. Are you alone?"

"No, I'm here with several friends, but I'm quite sure they're not ready to end the evening. I already told them I might leave early. I'm ready to go."

"Let's go then."

Al-Zadir took her arm and they strolled toward the entrance to the ballroom. A woman in a colorful silk costume was standing behind a small table near the door with cards spread out before her.

"A Tarot card reader!" Cassandra squealed. "It'll only take a minute. Please wait for me, Shah."

She grasped al-Zadir's hand and pulled him to the table. Cassandra smiled at the old woman.

"Please, can you tell me what the cards say?"

"As you wish," the old woman replied with a deeply accented voice.

The woman picked up the cards and reshuffled several times. Then she turned over several cards sporting different figures and symbols and set them on the table.

"I see that you're a kind and gentle woman who's well-educated. You are financially independent and you have many wonderful friends and a loving family. I see you are a romantic woman who loves dance, theater, and art."

Cassandra moved closer to al-Zadir and smiled broadly. The woman turned a few more cards.

"I see a new relationship in your life — a romantic relationship. Beyond that, the cards do not say."

Cassandra laughed with delight.

"Shah, let her read the cards for you."

"No, Cassandra, I don't want to know my future. The future will take care of itself."

He tugged on her arm to pull her toward the door.

"Oh please, Shah. Just a few cards."

She pouted and pulled him back toward the table. He reluctantly acquiesced.

"Okay, just a few cards. Then I must go."

The old woman shuffled the cards again. She laid a few cards face-up on the table.

"You are a man of strong conviction. You are a loner with just a few good friends. You don't allow just anyone close to you."

She turned over three more cards.

"You work very hard and sacrifice your personal life for your work because you believe strongly in your principles."

She turned over several more of the cards.

"I see a new relationship."

Cassandra smiled up at al-Zadir.

"Okay, that's enough," al-Zadir demanded, as he pulled Cassandra away from the table.

Cassandra resisted his pull.

"Please, not yet Shah. Just a few more cards."

"Okay, just a few more. Then I must go."

The woman turned more cards.

"It's a business relationship involving many men."

"That's enough!" he blurted.

Al-Zadir pulled Cassandra away from the table into the foyer.

"Shah, don't you want to know?"

"No, I don't want to know. The future will care for itself. I don't believe the cards."

The old woman at the Tarot card table turned over one more card. It was a human skeleton holding a sickle. She stared down at the card for a few moments and then looked after the couple, as they disappeared into the foyer.

"Doorman, a gondola to the Danielli Hotel please."

"Right away, sir!"

A gondola was waiting at the ramp. Al-Zadir guided Cassandra toward the oarsman, helped her into a seat, then stepped into the gondola and sat beside her. The gondolier used his oar to push the boat away from the landing.

Waves lapped gently at the sides of the Gondola as they passed another spectacular eighteenth century palazzo on the Grand Canal. The two of them took in the beauty in silence. Cassandra leaned against Shah's chest. She looked up at him and smiled.

"I'm glad you came to the ball tonight, Shah. It was a wonderful evening."

"It's been a long time since I enjoyed such pleasure. My mother used to say one must dance from time to time to feel alive. Thank you, Cassandra."

The gondola slid along the Grand Canal past brightly lit palazzos teeming with partygoers celebrating Carnevale. Festive music echoed across the water. Cassandra gazed up at the moonless sky. The stars sparkled in brilliant accompaniment. Cassandra snuggled against the cold and pointed across the waterway.

"Look, there's my favorite, the Basilica of the Santa Maria della Salute. This basilica was built in the seventeenth century in honor of the Virgin Mary's delivery of the citizens of Venice from the plague. More than one third of the people in Venice died before the Blessed Virgin's miracle. Isn't it spectacular?"

Al-Zadir glanced at the Basilica, but did not speak.

The oarsman soon docked at the Danielli. He stepped from the gondola and helped Cassandra onto the shore. She took al-Zadir's arm and they wove through hundreds of costumed revelers who were still celebrating loudly on the walk outside the hotel. The couple ducked through the revolving door into the deserted lobby. Al-Zadir glanced at his watch. It was nearly two in the morning.

"What's your room number Cassandra?"

"Two-twenty-five, what about you?"

"Two-oh-one, I'll walk you to your room."

They walked arm-in-arm up the red-carpeted stairs to the elevator. They stepped in and al-Zadir pushed the button for the second floor. The doors closed and the car jerked upward.

It was only a few steps to al-Zadir's room. Al-Zadir took both of Cassandra's hands in his and smiled.

"It was a wonderful evening."

She clung to him and he returned her warm embrace.

"Let me walk you to your room Cassandra."

"Are you trying to make a liar out of the Tarot cards?" she whispered.

"I'm flattered such a beautiful woman finds me attractive. But—"

Al-Zadir stopped short, as Cassandra took a step back and removed her mask.

"You!" he laughed, with a shake of his head.

She was the young beauty who'd helped him select his costume in the lobby shop of the hotel.

"I told you it would be a wonderful ball."

Cassandra threw her arms around his neck and kissed him passionately on the lips. Al-Zadir kissed her ear and she moaned softly. Cassandra traced small kisses down his neck, as she ruffled the hair on the back of his head with her fingertips.

Al-Zadir slid the key into the lock and pushed the door open. Without breaking their embrace, he guided Cassandra into the room and kicked the door closed behind them.

He kissed her on the lips and caressed her breasts with his fingertips. She guided his hands to the hooks on her gown. The dress fell to the floor.

Cassandra turned in his arms and lifted his hands to her chest. He fondled her with a feathery light touch, as she ran her hands down his sides. Turning in his arms once more, she slipped his coat off and let it fall to the floor. She unbuttoned his shirt.

"I want you," she whispered.

Cassandra squatted to the floor in front of him. She unhooked his pants, as he arched backward and stared at the ceiling. She pulled his briefs to his ankles and lightly kissed his stomach. She traced her fingernails up the inside of his thighs.

Cassandra stood up and kissed al-Zadir on the lips. She took him by the hand, led him to the bed, and pushed him onto his back. She straddled his chest with her knees and whispered in his ear.

"Casanova once said, 'Until you have made love in Venice, you have not made love.'"

Al-Zadir smiled. He closed his eyes and relished Cassandra's feathery kisses. She drifted down his neck and across his chest. Suddenly, she leapt from the bed.

Al-Zadir opened his eyes. The barrel of a pistol was pointing at the middle of his forehead.

"Move and I'll blow your head off!" Mustafa hissed.

The young woman darted to the corner of the room. Al-Zadir squeezed his fists and grimaced.

"Bitch!"

Mustafa's fist pounded down on al-Zadir's nose before the word fully passed his lips.

"Shut up!" Mustafa ordered. "Where is it?"

Al-Zadir did not respond. He continued to stare at the gun barrel.

Mustafa pressed the gun against al-Zadir's forehead and retrieved a knife from a sheath on his belt. He jabbed the razor-sharp point against al-Zadir's eyelid.

"Where's the pestilence?"

"There is no Allah but Allah, and Mohammad is his prophet," al-Zadir mumbled barely above a whisper.

Mustafa thrust the knife through the Arab's eyelid. The contents of al-Zadir's eyeball squirted onto his cheek. He cried out and thrust his hands to his face.

"In the coat. It's in the pocket," he cried.

"Check it!" Mustafa ordered.

Cassandra searched through each of al-Zadir's pockets. She fished a small metal cylinder that looked like a cigar container from his breast pocket. She held it up.

"This is all there is."

"Don't open it. Who gave you this?"

Al-Zadir continued to writhe in pain.

"I don't know. I'm only the courier."

"Where were you to take it?"

"London. I was ordered to deliver it to the main mosque in London."

Mustafa pressed the gun barrel against the Arab's forehead.

"Give my regards to Allah."

CHAPTER TWENTY-NINE

Two months later, April 3, 2002

Shane cringed involuntarily as he recognized the man striding diagonally across the street toward the door to the coffee shop. Mustafa was an imposing figure dressed head-to-toe in black, with neatly tailored slacks and a long-sleeve silk shirt. Thin black sunglasses curved around his temples, hiding the piercing jet-black eyes and bushy eyebrows that imprinted on Shane's memory at their first encounter. Shane had yet to see the faintest smile to betray a trace of humor in the Tajik's disposition. Mustafa's close-cropped beard only partially masked the jagged keloid scar that ran down across his chin.

The throng on the street appeared to sense danger. A path opened ahead of Mustafa among the motley mix of vagrants, students, tourists, and vendors perusing the never-ending variety of cafes, sex shops, and shows in the Red Light District of Amsterdam. A beggar stepped toward Mustafa, but dropped his cup to his side, as the menacing figure brushed by. Mustafa glanced toward both ends of the street and darted through the door.

Shane was sitting at a window table in the Bombay Coffee Shop. Mustafa ignored him and made his way through the hazy room to a stool at the bar. The pungent odor of cannabis emanated from the smoke that drifted cloud-like from several of the tables and along the carved wooden ceiling. Mustafa sat with his back to the bar and ordered an espresso from a bartender in a tee shirt and faded jeans.

Mustafa's gaze drifted from one table to the next through the dimly lit room. He analyzed each face in the half dozen groups scattered throughout the shop. Almost all of the patrons appeared to be young students. One young man bellowed to be heard above the din, as his mates swayed in unison to the deafening techno music that pulsated to the core of Shane's internal organs.

Three men were standing in a darkened cove in the rear of the room scanning a menu. A man sporting dreadlocks nodded and pulled a Tupperware box from a cabinet behind the glass display case. The man balanced several dried buds on a creased square of wax paper resting on a scale. He carefully transferred the contraband to a Zip-lock bag and handed it to the tallest of the men. The youth handed him several euro bills.

The group wove its way through the room to an empty table. Another youth with a shock of blue hair took the bag and carefully sorted, spread, and rolled the hemp. He finished the joint and stuck it in his mouth. One of his mates lit the end with a lighter. The man took a long drag and passed it to his friend.

Mustafa nodded almost imperceptibly toward Shane. The Tajik stood and wove through the tables to the alcove in the back of the room. Shane followed from his own table. He stood a pace behind Mustafa, as the Tajik perused the cannabis menu. Mustafa spoke at a level that was just audible above the din in the room.

"Are you at the Amstel Hotel?"

"Yes, the Amstel Intercontinental."

"What's your room number?"

"Two-oh-eight."

"Meet me in the Ruby's Palace bar at 11:15 tonight. Place an extra key beneath the door when you leave the room. Put the 'Do Not Disturb' sign on the doorknob. Do you understand?"

"Yes."

"See you tonight."

Mustafa put the menu back on the counter, brushed past the bartender, and darted out the front door.

The bartender beamed an ivory-toothed smile at Shane. He brushed an errant dreadlock from his eyes and spoke with a thick Jamaican accent.

"What's your pleasure, man?"

"Do you have pre-rolled pot?"

"Plenty, man. I recommend Northern Lights — it's mellow with an edge."

The last few words flowed from the man's mouth like honey.

"Is it legal to take this back to my hotel?" Shane stammered, with a hint of embarrassment.

The Jamaican smiled and nodded with rhythm

"Legal? You are in Amsterdam, man. Everything is legal, man."

The bartender pointed toward an emerald-green glass sphere sitting prominently on the bar.

"I've looked into my crystal ball, man. I seen a hot little Thai babe meeting you in your room. You look like you need to loosen up a little bit, man. Expand your horizons... you know what I mean? What hotel you live at man? Sweet Jasmine, she love the Northern Lights."

He laughed again and brushed dreadlocks out of his eyes.

"No thank you," Shane mumbled uncomfortably. "Just a couple of joints."

The bartender grinned.

"Suit yourself, man. Let me know if you change your mind. Northern Lights be the most excellent aphrodisiac. Stay away from the girls in the windows, man. They are not clean."

He darted behind the counter, opened a cupboard door, and pulled out two of the largest joints Shane had ever seen. Conical in shape, each was at least six inches long and a half-inch in diameter at the thick end.

"Northern Lights. That be eighteen, man."

Shane handed him twenty euros and stuffed the joints in his coat pocket. "Can you call me a taxi?"

"No taxi in the Red Light District, man. There's a stand across from the Grasshopper."

He smiled, baring a gold incisor among a sea of ivory.

"You need some ecstasy or a lude? How about Viagra?"

"No thank you," Shane stammered, as he turned without further reply and wove his way between the tables toward the door.

A bear of a man with an English accent yelled drunkenly at a tablemate sporting a green mohawk streak across his shaved head.

"They should level fucking Baghdad! They should nuke the fucking bastards."

The man slammed down a half-pint glass, launching beer across the table and onto the floor.

Shane slipped gingerly past the last table and out the door. He stopped and looked in both directions down the crowded street. Mustafa was nowhere in sight.

Shane ignored a pair of beggars with outstretched hands and retraced his steps back toward the edge of the Red Light District. When he reached the main boulevard, he stepped off the curb and waved at an approaching taxi. The taxi slowed to a stop and Shane opened the rear passenger door. He climbed into the back seat, slammed the door, and leaned his head back against the cushion. The driver sped away into the traffic.

"Where to?" the driver asked.

"Amstel Hotel."

Without another word, the driver made a sharp U-turn and crisscrossed at high speed through a series of narrow streets. He honked at any car that appeared to have the slightest intention of pulling in front of him. After crossing a narrow bridge over the canal, the car turned onto a dead-end street and pulled to a stop in front of the Amstel Intercontinental Hotel.

Shane fished in his pants pocket and handed the driver ten euros. The doorman opened the door and Shane stepped out onto the curb.

"Welcome back, sir. Will you be needing a cab later this evening, sir?"

"Yes. Thank you. Around eleven tonight."

"I shall hail the cab at half past ten, sir. It could take half an hour. There's a big convention in town. What's your destination, sir?"

"I'm meeting a colleague at a bar called Ruby's Palace."

The doorman's expression betrayed a hint of surprise, but he quickly regained his proper demeanor.

"Top-notch establishment from reports I've heard, sir. But do be careful, sir. Several hotel guests have complained about unauthorized charges to credit cards. Hardly the type of thing one can make much fuss about, if you know what I mean, sir?"

"Thank you. I'll be sure to carry cash," Shane called out, as he took the stairs in two giant steps and pushed through the revolving door.

"Have a good afternoon, sir."

Shane exited the revolving door into the lobby and headed directly for the lift. The door opened a moment later and an immaculately dressed older couple stepped from the elevator. Shane waited while the old woman used her walker to wobble past him. He stepped into the car and selected the second floor.

The doors opened to a grand hall with textured, hunter green wallpaper and antique, marble-topped tables. Shane strode to his room and put the key in the door. He stepped inside and closed the door behind him.

The bed had been turned down and his garment bag was hanging in the closet. His suitcase was resting on a stand. Classical piano music was playing on the stereo.

Shane kicked off his loafers and tossed his jacket on the chair. He reached into his pocket, pulled out one of the joints, and put it in an ashtray on the nightstand. He stacked three of the pillows against the headboard. Settled at last, he leaned across to the opposite nightstand for the TV remote and began searching through the channels. He scanned past two sex channels and finally settled for an old re-run of *Cheers* with Dutch subtitles.

Shane reached for the joint, lit the end with a match, and took a heavy drag. It burned his throat and triggered an involuntary coughing fit that made his eyes water until tears cascaded down his cheeks.

It took a minute to recover. He took another hit. A heightened awareness began to slowly envelop his body. He took puff after puff until the giant joint was half gone.

Shane's gaze drifted around the suite from one exquisite furnishing to another. French vitrenes were sitting on either side of an early nineteenth century roll-top desk. The walls were graced with reproductions of Flemish masterpieces. Shane recognized one as a self-portrait by Rubens. He studied the lines on the old master's face.

Shane set the joint down in the ashtray and pressed his head into the pillows. He stared up at the intricately painted ceiling. The detailed concentric circles seemed to be revolving.

He switched off the TV. Only then did he notice the rhythmic tapping on the wall behind him and the soft moaning of a woman in the room next door.

"What in the hell am I doing here?" he muttered to himself, as he stretched out across the bed and closed his eyes.

CHAPTER THIRTY

S hane startled awake at the ring of the phone. He squinted at the alarm
clock. It was 11:00 o'clock.

"Shit!" he barked, as he rolled across the bed and lifted the receiver.

"Hello."

"Sir, your cab is ready."

Shane recognized the doorman's distinctive dialect. He cleared his throat
with a cough.

"I'll be down in a moment! Hold it there!"

"Yes, sir, I'll do that, sir."

Shane lunged from the bed and into the bathroom. Turning on the light,
he leaned toward the mirror. Two blood-shot eyes stared back at him.

"Damn it!"

Shane splashed water onto his stubbled face and smoothed his hair back
with his fingertips. He wiped his face with a hand towel and tossed the towel
on the counter. He put a drop of Visine in each eye and ran to the closet.

Fumbling with the buttons, Shane removed his wrinkled polo shirt to
expose a dark, muscular torso. He unzipped his garment bag, selected a white
cotton shirt, and pulled it over his head. He stared in the mirror and shook
his head.

"You look like crap," he muttered.

Shane tried to smooth the wrinkles out of his pants. It was no use. He
slipped his feet into his loafers. Feeling for the wallet in his back pocket, he
opened the front door and sprinted toward the elevator. The elevator door
opened before he had a chance to push the button. An attendant carrying a silver
tray stepped out.

"Hello, sir."

Shane brushed by the man and got into the elevator.

He pushed the button for the lobby. As the doors began to close, he suddenly remembered Mustafa's instructions.

"Shit!"

Shane got off of the elevator. The attendant stopped and craned his neck to peek around his tray.

"Anything wrong, sir?"

"No," Shane blurted, as he hurried past the attendant. "I forgot my coat."

"Sorry, sir," the attendant called after him.

Shane rushed around the corner to his room and opened the door with his key card. He rummaged beneath some brochures on the desktop and found the small folder they'd given him at check-in. He pulled out the second room key.

Retracing his steps, Shane placed the 'Do Not Disturb' sign on the doorknob and eased the door shut. He knelt in front of the door, but then bolted upright, as the door across from his opened and the room service attendant stepped out of the room. The attendant stared at him quizzically.

"Is there a problem, sir?"

"No. Everything's fine," Shane stammered, as he sped around the corner toward the elevator.

"Sir, you forgot your coat!" the attendant called after him.

Shane slapped his palm against his forehead and reversed course back toward the room.

"Thank you. Premature Alzheimer's."

Shane smiled and rolled his eyes, as the attendant walked on toward the elevator. Once again, Shane slid the key into the lock, opened the door, and stepped back into his room. He pressed his ear to the door and waited for the elevator doors to rumble closed.

Shane grabbed his leather bomber jacket off the bed. He waited a few more seconds before opening the front door once again. Stepping back into the hall, he silently eased the door closed and stooped to slide the second key beneath the door. Finally, he hastened once again toward the elevator.

The doorman had changed into evening dress. He looked much more formal in his black tails and top hat. He opened the door for Shane.

"Sir," he offered with his proper accent, "I believe a sports coat is appropriate for Ruby's Palace."

Shane stopped in his tracks.

"A sports coat?"

"Yes, sir. No tie, I should think, but I believe a coat is in order."

Shane glanced at his watch. It was 11:15. He took a deep breath and puffed his cheeks. He retreated back through the entrance and across the lobby to the elevator. The door opened and out stepped the same room service attendant. This time, a female colleague carrying a champagne bucket filled with ice accompanied the man.

"Sir?" the attendant queried, as Shane stepped past them into the elevator. The doors began to close.

"I forgot my coat," Shane stammered.

The attendant glanced down at the leather jacket in Shane's hand, as the doors rattled closed. He turned to the other attendant and whispered.

"That lad is a strange one."

"What makes you think so?" the young woman whispered back, as she adjusted the position of the bucket in her arms.

"He's American, isn't he? That's more than sufficient."

The attendant shrugged and pushed the service cart down the hall.

Shane ducked into the back seat of the cab and the doorman closed the door. The doorman stuck his head in the passenger window and whispered to the driver. The cab sped away from the hotel. The young punk cab driver glanced up at Shane in the rearview mirror, as he negotiated around a moving van parked in the right lane.

"*Guten abend. Sprechen sie Deutsch?*"

"English," Shane muttered.

The driver shook his head.

"No English."

He reached back across the seat to hand Shane a sheet of paper. Shane took it and turned it over. It was an advertisement adorned with scantily clad women. Across the top was printed "Dutch Treat — Your Wildest Fantasy." The same phrase was repeated in several languages, including Chinese characters. There was a map at the bottom.

Shane handed it back to him.

"No, Ruby's Palace."

The driver pushed the paper back toward Shane.

"Is better."

He smiled and nodded in the rear view mirror.

"Ruby's Palace," Shane repeated gruffly.

The driver shrugged his shoulders and replaced the advertisement in a folder on the passenger seat next to him. Shane turned his head and peered out at the bustling crowd on the sidewalk along van Baerlestraat.

Shane picked a few specks of lint from his sports coat and brushed his hair back with his fingertips. He leaned back into the seat cushion and closed his eyes. His thoughts drifted back to the first time he met Mustafa.

It had been at an Anthropology Society meeting in New Orleans the month before. Shane had been standing in front of his poster on race lineage and DNA sequence organization. A deep, accented voice startled him as he was pulling down the poster at the end of the session.

"Dr. Kalakan?"

Shane turned his head to rely. The stranger's piercing eyes took him aback.

"Yes?" Shane had finally responded.

"My name is Mustafa. May I speak with you privately?"

Shane's initial inclination was to decline the invitation. But his curiosity got the best of him. He agreed to meet the dark stranger for a few minutes. The two of them walked a short block to Emeril's restaurant and they sat at the bar in the trendy Warehouse District establishment.

Mustafa was direct. He worked for wealthy clients who wanted to remain anonymous. They had a son who was a graduate student in molecular anthropology at an unnamed European university. Shane listened with increasing skepticism, as Mustafa explained that the son had taken ill with hepatitis. The family was concerned that their son wouldn't complete his work and earn his degree. They wanted Shane to finish the research project.

Shane rejected the overture outright, but Mustafa persisted. Shane's resolve weakened as Mustafa outlined the handsome offer. Shane would receive a half million dollars in cash, all expenses to conduct the research, and one-half million dollars a year for five years to support his research program upon completion of the project. Half the cash would be provided up front, with the rest paid upon completion.

Even a month later, Shane's hair stood up on the back of his neck when he thought about the proposal. It was essentially ten years of tax-free salary, along with the equivalent of two grants from the National Institutes of Health for five years.

Despite the handsome offer, Shane took the moral high ground. The proposal cut against the grain of years of training regarding academic integrity. Then there was the keen uneasiness he felt with the bearer of the proposal. It was a visceral response, like one might feel upon hearing the telltale rattle of a snake. The stranger seemed the embodiment of danger.

Shane told Mustafa he'd consider the offer and the Tajik agreed to call him at the hotel the following evening. Shane intentionally missed the appointed time. He'd been relieved to find no messages when he returned to his room. Then the phone rang later that night. Shane answered the phone in a sleepy daze and bolted upright in his bed when he recognized Mustafa's voice.

"Dr. Kalakan, don't play games with me. We expect your assistance with this matter."

Shane sat in churning silence for nearly a minute.

"You'll be a rich man, Dr. Kalakan."

Shane finally uttered the word he still regretted a month later.

"Okay."

Shane had become an accomplice. A package with details about the project would arrive at his home within a week. Two days passed before Shane realized Mustafa hadn't asked for his home address.

Shane returned home a few days later to find a manila envelope wedged through the mail slot in the front door at his houseboat. There was no postage on the envelope and there were no detailed instructions. Instead, there was a business class ticket to Amsterdam for the following week. The note indicated that the client had been unable to obtain approval to enter the United States. There was also a confirmation for three days at the Amstel Intercontinental Hotel, instructions for meeting Mustafa at the Bombay Coffee Shop, and a quarter million dollars in used one hundred dollar bills. The letter ended with an admonition about maintaining absolute confidentiality.

So here Shane was in Amsterdam a week later. He took a deep breath and shook his head. He felt more like the nutty professor than James Bond.

The car turned onto a darkened street that ran along a canal and lurched to a stop beneath a porch. A single overhead beacon lit up the steps. Shane handed the driver twenty euros and the attendant opened his door.

"Welcome to Ruby's Palace, sir. Have you visited Ruby's before?"

"No, this is my first visit to Amsterdam."

"Well, you've found the best Amsterdam has to offer, sir. Mr. Alan will assist you at the top of the stairs."

Shane glanced at his watch. It was 11:40. He stumbled near the top of the stairs, but regained his balance as he stepped into the foyer. Ostentatious was the first word that came to mind. The establishment had high ceilings with antique furnishings and marble floors. There was detailed ironwork on the stairs. It was unlike any bar Shane had seen before.

A distinguished man dressed in long tails approached Shane as he stepped into the foyer.

"Welcome to Ruby's Palace, sir. May I show you to a table?"

"I'm meeting a colleague, a Mr. Mustafa."

"Oh, yes sir. Mr. Mustafa is at the bar. Right this way."

The man motioned to an arched doorway. Shane followed him into a huge room with a long, mirrored, mahogany bar and several dozen tables and couches. A massive stone fountain extending at least twenty feet toward the ceiling adorned the center of the room. The song *Painted Black* by the Rolling Stones reverberated from enormous speakers in the back corners of the room. At least thirty young women wearing evening gowns were scattered around the room. There were blondes, brunettes, and redheads; caucasians, asians, and blacks. They all had one thing in common. Every single one was a striking beauty, elegantly bejeweled. Some of the women were sitting with men. Most were lounging alone or with other women.

Shane spotted Mustafa sitting alone on the far side of the bar. He made a beeline for the seat next to him.

"You're late," Mustafa scowled.

"I'm sorry, I overslept."

His icy stare made the hair stand up on the back of Shane's neck. Then a hint of a smile replaced the look of scorn.

"The night is still young. Tomorrow we work, but tonight we'll partake of the finer things life has to offer."

Shane scanned the decadent scene around him. Nearly every one of the women in the room was staring at him. Each one smiled invitingly when he glanced her way.

The bartender approached them.

"What would you like to drink, sir?"

"What do you recommend?"

"How about a vodka martini, straight up, dirty, with olives. It's the house specialty."

Shane nodded and the bartender set out preparing the drink. The man filled a martini shaker with crushed ice and poured a dash of vermouth. Then he inverted the closed shaker and poured out the excess vermouth. He added two jiggers of vodka and shook the concoction with vigor until there was a layer of frost on the outside of the metal shaker. Finally, he poured the drink into a pre-chilled martini glass and added two plump olives and a splash of olive juice. He set the glass on the bar and slid it in front of Shane.

"Dirty martini, sir! Let me know if you would like a particular lady to join you."

Shane lifted the glass and took a drink. It was delicious. He stared at the drink in silence for a few moments. Mustafa took a drink of his whiskey and set his glass on the bar.

"You are not comfortable, Dr. Kalakan?"

Shane continued to stare at his glass. He took another sip.

"I haven't felt comfortable since I landed in Amsterdam. Hell, I haven't felt comfortable since New Orleans."

"That will change with time, Dr. Kalakan. Amsterdam is a city unlike any other. You must relax and allow its many pleasures to sweep you away."

With that, Mustafa emptied his glass. The bartender filled it again with whiskey.

"Dr. Kalakan, are you gay?"

Shane smiled at his glass and shook his head.

"No," he chuckled uncomfortably, "I'm not gay."

He glanced at Mustafa. His expression hadn't changed. Mustafa bore the stare of an experienced poker player.

"You're not married?"

"No, I'm not married."

"Well, Dr. Kalakan, this will be a fantasy evening neither you nor I will soon forget. My client wants you to enjoy yourself here in Amsterdam."

Mustafa waved at the bartender. The man strode from the opposite end of the bar.

"Yes, Mr. Mustafa, how can I serve you?"

"We'd prefer the company of the blonde in the red dress and the brunette in the blue dress."

"Certainly, Mr. Mustafa."

The bartender walked across the room and whispered to each of the women. Both beauties stood up and walked across the room. The statuesque blonde smiled sweetly and offered her hand to Shane.

"My name is Melinda. And you are?"

"Shane, Shane Kalakan."

Shane shook her hand awkwardly and then released it.

"Shane, that's a very strong name," she purred.

The brunette was an exotic-looking Indian woman. She offered her hand to Mustafa and spoke with a British accent.

"Hello, my name is Lana."

Mustafa took her hand and kissed it. He stood up from the barstool and pointed toward an empty couch on the opposite side of the room.

"I think we'll be more comfortable on the couch."

The two women followed, as Mustafa swaggered across the room to a couch behind the fountain. Mustafa reclined at the end of a plush leather couch with a woman on either side.

Shane sat near the other end of the couch. The bartender set fresh drinks on the table in front of them, including two fluted champagne glasses for the ladies.

"My handsome friend is shy," Mustafa said, as he motioned toward Shane.

Lana slid across the couch against Shane and rested her hand on his leg. She smiled.

"I love shy men," she whispered. "The shyness often hides an inner fire."

Shane laughed uncomfortably. She cuddled against him and kissed his ear lobe. He shook his head and smiled.

Lana had almond-shaped, green eyes with stunning olive skin and full lips. Her ample cleavage was adorned with a ruby pendant necklace. Her alluring smile was perhaps her finest feature, but she had many charms.

She kissed Shane on the lips. Her hand drifted slowly with feathery pressure down his chest, and came to rest once again on his thigh. Her gaze remained fixed on his eyes all the while. She smiled bashfully.

Shane felt a hint of warmth in his groin. He smiled and looked toward the waiter. The man was carefully pouring champagne into the two fluted glasses. Shane looked to his right. The blonde was kissing Mustafa's chest beneath an unbuttoned shirt. Mustafa glanced over the young woman's shoulder and grinned.

"This is a night you'll never forget," the brunette whispered into Shane's ear. "I'm an expert in the lover's art of Kama Sutra. Your wish is my command."

Lana sighed and kissed Shane on the earlobe. She nuzzled his ear and rested her hand on his chest. Shane glanced across at Mustafa. He and the blonde were smiling with amusement.

The champagne flowed and the music reverberated, as the two beauties gradually ensnared the men with laughter, caresses, and suggestive whispers. Shane began to loosen up, as the bubbling golden nectar blunted his anxiety. He found himself succumbing to the captivatingly sensual beauty clinging to his side.

Two hours passed, before the blonde finally took Mustafa's hands and pulled him up from the couch.

"Let's go, big boy. The penthouse beckons."

Lana tugged Shane to his feet and guided him through the doorway behind the other couple. Mustafa, arm-in-arm with Melinda, stumbled up the first few steps of the circular staircase. Shane walked with Lana to the bottom of the stairs.

Suddenly, Shane stopped and dropped his arm from Lana's waist. He stood for a moment regarding Melinda and Mustafa. Lana tried to coax him with a gentle tug on the arm, but Shane held his ground. He smiled apologetically.

"I'm very drunk and very tired. I need to get some sleep."

The brunette wrapped her arms around him.

"Come with me, Shane. I'll give you a massage in the Jacuzzi. Don't be bashful, it'll be just you and me."

Lana tried to kiss him, but Shane pulled away.

"No. I'm sorry, it's been a long day."

Mustafa stopped. He peered down from the landing half way up the stairs.

"Dr. Kalakan, you just need a warm bath and another bottle of champagne. Let yourself go."

"No, I'm very tired. Thank you for an enjoyable evening. What time tomorrow?"

Mustafa shrugged his shoulders and held out his arm. Lana scurried up the stairs to his side. Mustafa wrapped his arm around her waist and stood for a moment gazing down at Shane with an arm around each beauty. He smirked drunkenly.

"Suit yourself, Dr. Kalakan. I'll meet you at your hotel room at three tomorrow afternoon."

Mustafa turned and guided the women toward the upper flight of stairs. Suddenly, he lost his balance and stumbled backward. The two women pulled him down onto his backside to keep him from tumbling down the stairs. Lana and Melinda giggled uncontrollably, as they rolled over on their hands and knees and became entangled in their gowns. Mustafa cackled on his back for a few moments, before turning over. He pulled himself to his feet and helped the cackling women get up from the floor. Mustafa wrapped an arm around each beauty and the giggling trio disappeared up the stairs.

Shane smirked and shook his head. He turned to find the doorman standing behind him.

"Perhaps another time, sir. Ruby's car is waiting for you."

Shane nodded and the attendant opened the door. A black Mercedes limousine was waiting on the street with the rear door open. Shane walked down the stairs and climbed into the back seat. The doorman shut the door.

"Where to, sir?" the driver queried.

"The Amstel Intercontinental."

The car whisked away from the curb and into the night.

Shane found a manila envelope sitting on the desk inside his hotel room. It contained a report that was about a dozen pages long. He scanned through the first few pages. Too tired to continue, he tossed the report back on the desk.

It only took a short time for him to undress and hang his clothes in the closet. He took a hot shower and slipped on a pair of pajamas. Finally, he slid into bed between the crisp, cool sheets.

Shane lay in the darkness staring at the blinking red light on the smoke detector in the ceiling. His mind wandered back to Ruby's Palace. For an instant, he felt the alluring brunette blowing into his ear. He smelled her intoxicating perfume and stroked her silky smooth skin. He felt a twinge of remorse and then sleep overcame him.

CHAPTER THIRTY-ONE

There was a knock on the hotel room door at 3 P.M. on the button. Shane got up from the desk and slipped the bundle of papers into the manila envelope. He walked to the door, peered out through the peephole, and opened the door.

Mustafa had another man with him. The two men stepped into the room and Shane closed the door behind them.

"Dr. Kalakan, this is my client, Ahmed Jan."

Shane took Ahmed Jan's outstretched hand and shook it.

"Good to meet you, Mr. Jan. I was beginning to wonder if you really exist."

Ahmed returned his handshake with a reserved smile.

"I'm sure you understand our need for discretion, Dr. Kalakan. My family is from Afghanistan. It has been difficult to travel to the United States since the attack on your country last September."

Ahmed turned to look for a place to sit down. It was then Shane noticed Ahmed's scarred and contracted left hand. The fingers were contracted into a permanent semi-fist. Three of the fingers had been cut off at the tips.

Shane motioned toward the sitting room. The two men sat on the couch and Shane sat in the high-back chair across from them.

"Would you like something to drink, Mr. Jan?"

"I'll take a glass of water, thank you."

Shane opened the mini-bar and fetched a bottle of water. He poured three glasses and set them on the coffee table. Ahmed took a sip and placed the glass back on the table.

"Dr. Kalakan, I appreciate your agreeing to help with my studies. I've been ill for almost a year now. I'm afraid it'll be a long time before I can return to the university to complete my research. I conceived and designed the project, but considering the events of the past seven months, I may never be able to complete the work. My father is most anxious for me to complete my degree, but he also wants me to return to Afghanistan. I need your help to complete the research and obtain my degree."

Shane nodded his head. He took a sip of his water and set the glass back down on the table.

"I found the project to be very interesting."

"So you've read my summary?"

"Yes, I reviewed it this morning. The approach is novel, but it should be straightforward."

"It's a relatively simple project, but one of practical interest to my family and me. It will have useful applications in Afghanistan."

"In what way?"

"My country is composed of many tribes. I am a Tajik. There are several Tajik tribes that make up the Northern Alliance. Even though the Pashtun Karzai is the new interim leader of Afghanistan, the Tajiks continue to dominate the north. My native village is in the Panjshe Valley in the northeast of Afghanistan. We dream of one day establishing an independent state ruled by Tajiks where our people can live in peace, raise their families, and die with dignity. Identification of this unique sequence will allow us to rapidly screen the local population for those who are of certain Tajik ancestry."

"I see. If there's a unique Tajik sequence, it certainly could be used in that way."

"Is the design clear?"

"Yes, it is very straightforward. There should be little difficulty identifying unique sequences if they exist."

"That's encouraging. I'd like to briefly review the details with you to make sure there are no misunderstandings."

"Sure. Let me get the protocol."

Shane retrieved the folder from the desk. He sat down and resorted the pages. Ahmed reached into his coat pocket and retrieved a square plastic container about the size of a man's wallet. He handed the box to Shane.

"You'll find twenty samples of DNA in this container, Dr. Kalakan. I removed all of the DNA sequences that were present in two or more copies before I got sick. Thus, only single copy sequences are represented in the DNA from each donor."

"That certainly makes my job a lot easier."

"Six of the tubes are marked A1 to A6. These contain DNA isolated from Tajiks from my homeland. The fourteen remaining tubes are labeled B1 to B14. These DNA samples were obtained from members of other tribes in my country. You are to isolate a unique sequence that is present in all of the A1 to A6 Tajik samples, but which is not present in any of the B1 to B14 samples from other Afghani tribes. The unique sequence should be at least one hundred DNA bases in length. Is that clear?"

"Yes, it's very clear."

"How long will it take you to finish?"

Shane pressed his lips together, as he mulled over the question.

"It should only take a couple of months to determine whether such a unique sequence exists in the DNA of the Tajiks. I must warn you though, it may not be possible to identify a unique sequence if there's been intermarriage among the tribes."

"There has been no intermarriage in the individuals who provided the Tajik samples. All of these people can trace their Tajik ancestry for at least five hundred years."

"Can I get more of each of these samples if I need them?"

Ahmed shook his head.

"No, these samples are irreplaceable. Please protect and conserve them. How soon will you start the work?"

"I'll have one of my post-docs get started next week."

Ahmed shook his head again.

"Dr. Kalakan, no one other than you is to be aware of this project. You must do every bit of this work yourself."

Shane's eyes widened with surprise.

"But I don't do bench work anymore. I haven't worked in the lab in nearly ten years. I design the experiments and write papers and grants, but my post-docs do all the bench work."

"You must work on this project by yourself, Dr. Kalakan."

Shane ran his fingertips through his hair and sighed.

"I don't understand why I can't have just one post-doc work on the project."

"My family is paying you well to maintain secrecy. A post-doctoral student would expect to publish the results. A technician would ask too many questions. The only way to maintain high secrecy is for you to do the work yourself."

Ahmed stared into Shane's eyes.

"Have we not paid you well enough?"

Shane took a deep breath and nodded.

"Yes, your offer is very generous. I can do it, but it'll take longer."

"We need you to complete the work as soon as possible, Dr. Kalakan. The remaining two hundred fifty thousand dollars will be paid when we get the sequence and confirm it. The funding for your lab will be provided as a sponsored research agreement from a company here in Amsterdam. Are we in agreement?"

"I'll do the best I can."

"I must catch a plane. Mustafa will provide you with further details. Thank you, Dr. Kalakan."

Ahmed nodded once more at Shane. He stood up and opened the door. He disappeared into the hall and closed the door behind him.

Mustafa waited a few moments before speaking. He took a cigarette pack from his coat pocket and took out a cigarette.

"May I smoke?"

Shane, still flustered, waved his hand in approval.

"Sure, whatever."

"You broke the heart of the beautiful brunette last night, Dr. Kalakan."

Shane shook his head.

"I doubt she shed a tear. I trust you had a good time after I left."

Mustafa smirked.

"It was truly an evening to remember. I admire your morality, Dr. Kalakan. Beautiful women are my weakness."

"It had nothing to do with morality. I was exhausted."

"Perhaps I should have gone with you. Now I'm the one who's exhausted."

Mustafa took a drag off the cigarette and set it in the ashtray.

"Dr. Kalakan, I want to review a few more details with you. You'll receive a check for fifty thousand dollars at your office next week. It will be from a company called Genetracker here in Amsterdam. These funds are for the project itself. The paperwork with the check will indicate that the funds are an award for your research."

He handed Shane a card.

"This is an international calling card. There's a phone number written on the back in invisible ink. The number will only appear if you place the card over a steaming teapot for a few moments. It'll disappear a few minutes later. You can steam the card over and over again."

Shane turned the card over. The back surface of the card was embossed with a trademark, but was otherwise blank.

"Call the number when you're done with the project. You'll get the rest of the cash and the funding contract for your laboratory once the work is verified. You can also call this number if you have any problems with the project. I want to make sure there's no misunderstanding. No one else is to have knowledge of this project. Is that understood?"

"Yes, I understand."

Mustafa stood up and pulled a small digital camera from his coat pocket.

"Dr. Kalakan, to keep this project secret, it may be necessary for you to order some items without revealing your true identity. I'll leave that for you to decide. I'd like to take a photo of your face. We'll use it to generate new identity documents, including a new passport. For, example, this could be used to rent a mailbox under a different name. Is there another name you'd like to use?"

"Do you really think it's necessary?"

"You never know. But if I don't take the photo, you won't have the documents if you should need them. Stand against this wall."

Shane backed up to the wall and Mustafa took a series of photographs with the digital camera. He looked at the monitor after each shot. Some he saved, but most he discarded.

"What about the name, Dr. Kalakan?"

"I've always wanted a name that was easy to spell. How about Steven Nelson?"

"Okay, Steven Nelson it'll be."

Mustafa stood up from the couch and extended his hand.

"It was a pleasure to meet you, Dr. Kalakan."

"Please, call me Shane."

"Okay. Thank you, Shane."

Mustafa walked to the door and opened it. He nodded and stepped out into the hall.

Shane listened at the door as Mustafa's footsteps faded down the hall. He picked up the cigarette and ground it out in the ashtray. He felt for the plastic box in his coat pocket and pulled it out. The plain black container looked like a cigarette box. He put the box back in his coat pocket and began to pack his bags.

CHAPTER THIRTY-TWO

April 10, 2002, CIA headquarters in Langley, Virginia

R ichards scanned through the pages of a briefing report he'd received just before the meeting. With one hand he flipped through the pages, while he spun his cigar around in the corner of his mouth with the other.

"Okay, Marilyn, what do you have for us?"

Marilyn punched a button on the controller and the image of an old Afghani man with a beard appeared on the screen.

"This is ex-King Zahir Shah of Afghanistan. We're preparing for his return to Kabul sometime next week. He's been in exile in Rome for thirty years. You may recall his reign was the last period of peace in Afghanistan. We uncovered a plot to assassinate him just as he arrived in Afghanistan. Dozens of Pashtun with links to the Taliban were arrested the past two days. Zahir Shah will preside over the opening session of a Loya Jirga, or grand council of elders. It's scheduled for June. The Loya Jirga will decide whether Karzai and the interim administration stay or a new government is put in place. The plan is for the interim government to run the country until elections are held in two years. We've trained fifty bodyguards to protect Zahir Shah. He's the only man with sufficient support among the elders of the Pashtun clans to provide some stability in the country. Many of the warlords have pledged their allegiance to him. Our preference is for the king to support Karzai staying in power.

"See he stays put in Kabul when he gets there. The more he moves around, the more likely his enemies will take him out. Marilyn, summarize what we know about the whereabouts of high-level al-Qaida leadership."

"Sure, Mr. Richards. There have still been no confirmed sightings of Osama bin Laden. A new tape of bin Laden was released last week. We've examined it in detail and it appears to be old footage shot shortly after 9/11. There are persistent rumors bin Laden died during the bombing of Tora Bora, either from injuries sustained during the bombing itself or as a result of interruption of his treatment for severe kidney disease. One report indicated he was undergoing kidney dialysis and the equipment was destroyed in the bombing. If he were on dialysis, he'd only last a short time without treatment. Our agents are looking for confirmation. The longer we go without a new video or other evidence he's alive, the more likely it is that he's dead. It's important for al-Qaida operatives around the world to hear from him to keep the organization alive."

Richards pulled the cigar out of his mouth and chuckled.

"What's so funny, sir?"

"I was just thinking how appropriate it would be if the son-of-a-bitch drowned in his own piss. I'm betting he's somewhere in the Pakistani tribal territories."

"We have no credible information indicating he's escaped into Pakistan, but we have CIA paramilitary units working with American, British, and Australian commandos scouring the tribal provinces along the Pakistani border. Some Qaida leadership is being sheltered there and we now have Pakistani permission to pursue these elements. We may find bin Laden hiding there. *Al-Quds al-Arabi* newspaper in London claimed it received an e-mail message from bin Laden. The style and content are suggestive, but we have no confirmation. There's also been a report he's being sheltered by the religious leaders in an Iranian village near the Afghani border."

"What about his immediate family members?"

"We don't know what happened to the other bin Laden family members. Some of them may have been killed in Tora Bora. It's possible some escaped into Pakistan. They'd find strong support among the Pathan tribes in northwestern Pakistan. These tribes are basically the same heritage as the Pashtun. Male Pathan live by the same ancient tribal code as the Pashtun. It's called Pashtunwali. Pashtunwali values courage, personal honor, resolution, self-reliance, and hospitality. They're no more likely to give up bin Laden than the Taliban is. We're continuing to search for bin Laden and his family members with the assistance of the Pakistani military. Some Qaida members being held in Cuba were captured in Tora Bora. We're interrogating them, but thus far there's little useful intelligence."

Richards yanked the cigar out of the corner of his mouth.

"Shit. There haven't been this many phony sightings since Elvis died."

Stone Waverly chuckled. He closed his report and tossed it on the table.

"Go on, Marilyn," Richards ordered.

"Ayman Al-Aman was the number two man in al-Qaida. Strong intelligence from several sources indicates he was killed in the bombing of the caves in Tarin Kowt Valley near Kandahar in March."

Marilyn pushed a button on the monitor. A young Arabic man with a close-cropped beard and mustache appeared on the screen. He was wearing glasses.

"This is Abu Zubaydah. He's believed to be the number three man in al-Qaida. There's evidence he's been controlling the organization since we overran Afghanistan. He is under a death sentence in Jordan and he participated in many al-Qaida operations against U.S. interests. He also has close ties to the Palestinians. He may have had a role in some of the recent suicide bombings in Israel. We helped the Pakistanis track him to Faisalabad two weeks ago. He got shot trying to escape, but he's recovering. He's been transferred to Islamabad and we're participating in his interrogation. He's been talking about dirty nuclear bombs and attacks on American banks and shopping centers. We're not sure how much is real and how much is idle boasting. He's an arrogant son-of -a-bitch."

"Get the Pakistanis to extradite the bastard to Jordan. We'll see how arrogant he is with a noose around his neck. We did that with a terrorist from Hamas a few years back. He's been singing a different tune ever since."

Harrison punched the advance and three Arab men peered down from the screen.

"These are the other three chief architects of the 9/11 attacks. Shaikh Saiid al-Sharif, bin Laden's financial chief, Tawfig Attash Khallad, a bin Laden confidant who met with several of the hijackers, and Khalid Shaikh Mohammed, the man who actually masterminded the attacks. Special forces and CIA operatives in northern Pakistan are closing in on them. Mohammed is definitely under surveillance. He's living in a small town up in the mountains in the tribal area north of Peshawar. The other two have also been seen in the area. They appear to be making an effort to stay apart most of the time. It's only a matter of time before we track them down. That's all I have. Stone, do you want to do the update on Venice?"

"Sure. Do you have the photo of Abdullah al-Zadir?"

Marilyn pushed the advance on the monitor. A clean-shaven Arab with a sinister-looking scowl came up on the screen. Stone cleared his throat.

"This is Abdullah al-Zadir. He's an Egyptian who's been accused of having a direct role in plotting the U.S. embassy bombings in Kenya and Tanzania. He's a known senior al-Qaida operative."

Richards nodded.

"Stone, didn't this guy disappear right after we started bombing Afghanistan? As I recall, our intelligence placed him in a city near the Iranian border."

"Yes, that's right. He was hiding out in Zaranj in western Afghanistan. There's even some evidence the Iranians let al-Zadir into their country for several weeks after 9/11. We finally caught up with him. Someone executed him in the Hotel Danielli in Venice during Carnevale. He was traveling with a fake passport as 'Mohat Shah.' Our operatives in Italy confirmed it was indeed al-Zadir. He was seen the night before dancing with an unidentified woman at a Carnevale ball. A Tarot card reader saw him leave with her. The maid found him in his bed the next morning with a bullet hole between the eyes. Whoever killed him beat him up pretty bad first."

"What the hell was he doing there?"

Stone punched another button on the monitor. A photo of three men appeared on the screen.

"This is where it gets interesting. These are the three Afghanis we brought out of the military hospital in Pakistan. Remember, you asked me to keep an eye on them? I put a team of agents on them in Amsterdam. They're living in a flat in the Red Light District. They've been seen visiting the Masjid-E-Al Karam Mosque and an office called the Tajik International Aid Foundation."

Stone advanced the slide. It was a photo of an older man with a gray beard and balding head.

"This is Awar Mohammed. Mohammed is the director of the Aid Foundation. At one time he was a Tajik fighter. He visited them at their apartment right after they arrived."

Richards picked up his cigar and put it back in his mouth.

"So what are these jackasses up to, Stone?"

Stone pointed at the photo on the screen.

"This is Ahmed Jan and this is Mustafa. They flew to Venice on January thirtieth and returned to Amsterdam on February third. They stayed at a hotel near the Danielli. Their reservation was for November thirtieth to February eleventh, but they left early.

"So that means they left right after al-Zadir was killed. Did they do him?"

"We don't know, sir. No one remembers seeing them at the Danielli. But it would be an amazing coincidence if they weren't the ones who killed him."

Richards rubbed his temples. He smacked on the cigar, as he rolled it with his tongue in the corner of his mouth.

"They killed him all right. The only question is why?"

"We don't know, sir. Maybe they had a grudge against al-Zadir. We just don't know."

"Hell, maybe we should feed these Tajiks some names and locations of other al-Qaida members. Keep an eye on them. These bastards are up to something. Find out where al-Zadir was between the last sighting in Zaranj and the time he arrived in Venice."

"I'm looking into it, sir."

"Okay, that's it. We need to cancel next Wednesday's meeting. I'll be in Pakistan. Oh, by the way, Stone, good work in Nepal. I understand your efforts had a lot to do with India and Pakistan beginning a new dialogue. For what it's worth, the director sent his personal thanks."

"Thank you, sir. But I really didn't accomplish anything. War could still break out any minute."

"Did you take your wife out to dinner?"

"I did, sir. Julie told me to thank you for the theater tickets. It was a great show."

"My pleasure. Let's meet again two weeks from today. Let me know if you find out anything about those Tajiks."

CHAPTER THIRTY-THREE

April 15, 2002

B uster burrowed beneath the covers and crawled behind his master's legs. The Dalmatian stood up beneath the covers, spun around, and finally plopped his head down on the back of Shane's knees.

Shane lifted his head off the pillow and squinted at the alarm clock. It was a little past eight. Shane rolled out of bed and parted the drapes to find a cloudy spring day in Seattle.

He took a long hot shower and pulled on jeans and a polo shirt. He glanced at a photo jammed into the frame of the mirror, as he reached for his watch on the dresser. He pulled the photo out and held it up. Shane and Buster were sitting on a park bench next to a pretty woman with long brown hair. She was smiling and rubbing noses with Buster. Shane jammed the photo back into the frame and shut the dresser drawer. He strode into the kitchen.

He poured two cups of dry chow into Buster's dish and filled the water bowl. The automatic coffee pot was just finishing its cycle. The aroma of fresh-brewed Starbuck's filled the kitchen. Shane poured a cup and added a dash of milk. He took a big gulp and carried the cup to the bedroom.

Shane fetched the box of DNA samples from its hiding place in the closet. He slipped it into the side pocket of his backpack and headed for the kitchen. Buster was still crunching down his food. Shane patted him on the head and stepped out the door onto the porch. The screen door slammed behind him.

Shane's houseboat was one of five that shared a common walk down from the street. His was the last in the row and the only one with an unobstructed view of Portage Bay. It was light blue with white shutters.

Shane maneuvered his kayak off the dock and into the water. He tucked the backpack into the stern.

"Hey, Shane. How was Amsterdam?" his neighbor called out from the adjoining houseboat.

"Hi, Dan. I'll come by and fill you in this afternoon. I have a little work to do at the lab. You still having that party tonight?"

"Yeah, it's going to be a good one. You going to come by?"

"If I can get my work done. I'm on a tight schedule with a new project."

Shane slipped into the kayak and used his oar to push away from the dock. Dan strolled over to the edge of the dock.

"Terry Cummings is coming with her roommate."

"So what? You're the one who's hot for her."

"Damn right, but rumor has it she's got her eye on you. You'll show up if you have any sense in that head of yours."

"We'll see. What should I bring?"

"I've got the food covered. Just bring a six-pack."

"I'll try to stop by."

Shane drew the oar through the water and turned toward the opposite bank. He wove his kayak between a pair of boats headed toward the cut to Lake Union. It only took a few strokes to reach the opposite bank. He hauled the kayak up on shore next to a line of canoes. It was a five-minute walk to his lab in the K-wing at UW.

The elevator door opened on the third floor and Shane stepped into the empty hallway. There wasn't a soul around.

Shane's windowless office was relatively large for a space assigned to an assistant professor. Still, it was meager by most academic standards. He sat down and pulled open the desk drawer. There were several phone books and a manuscript scribbled with edits in the bottom. Shane pushed the phonebooks to one side, retrieved the small black box from his backpack, and placed it beneath the manuscript. He locked the drawer.

It took several minutes for his computer to boot up. He opened a new word processing file and began to develop a strategy for isolating the unique Tajik sequence based on similar techniques he'd used for several projects in the past.

DNA is composed of four building blocks called nucleotides. Amazingly, this four-letter alphabet, containing the letters A, T, G, and C, codes for all of the information needed to develop and maintain a rose, a dog, or a human.

The structure of DNA is like a twisted ladder, with the rungs of the ladder being formed by the pairing of A on one side of the ladder with T on the other side or G on one side with C on the other side. The DNA of a human contains tens of millions of these nucleotide pairs. Each gene of the tens of thousands in a human or dog is specified by a unique sequence of these four letters stretching from hundreds to thousands of letters long.

Shane's job wasn't to find a needle in a haystack, his charge was to find a needle in the Pacific Ocean. He was being paid handsomely to identify a stretch of letters shared by the Tajik DNA samples that was not present in any of the others. It didn't matter what gene the unique letters came from, as long as they were found only in Tajik DNA.

The technique of choice was called genomic subtraction. The first step would be to break down the DNA in each sample to a size that was easier to handle than the long and sticky DNA strands in normal human cells. This was easily accomplished by dissolving the DNA in solution and breaking it apart with high frequency sound waves produced by an instrument called a sonicator. The longer the exposure to the sound waves, the smaller the average size of the resulting DNA fragments. Shane decided to use a sonication time that would give DNA fragments about three hundred bases long. Sonication isn't strong enough to tear the two halves of the ladder apart; it merely produces a lot of short ladders from the very long ladder that makes up each human chromosome.

The next step was to melt the small ladders apart by boiling them. The high temperature of boiling would break apart all the AT, TA, GC, or CG pairs that form the rungs of the ladders. When the solution was subsequently cooled, the pairing sequences that were originally bound together would eventually find each other in the solution and reform the small ladders.

In subtraction hybridization, the small melted DNA ladders of one person, called the driver, are mixed with the small melted DNA ladders from another person, called the tester. But the driver DNA and tester DNA are not mixed in equal amounts. The driver ladders are at twenty times higher concentration in the mixture than the tester ladders. Because the driver sequences are much more common in the solution than the tester, the melted driver ladder halves find each other much more quickly to reform complete ladders. The same is true of any ladder sequences in the tester that happens to be the same as ladder sequences in the driver. The bulk of the DNA in the tester would fall into this category, since all humans, regardless of race, have most of their DNA sequences in common. Thus, all of these identical sequences in the driver and tester would find each other quickly. However, any unique sequences in the lower concentration tester would have a difficult time finding their mates among all the millions of other sequences in the solution, since they would be present at less than one-twentieth the concentration.

If the solution of melted ladders from the driver and tester were kept at the cooler temperature for just the right amount of time, all of the identical ladders would have mated back together and many of the unique sequences would still be searching for mates. At that point, the solution is passed through a special material that separates the reformed double-stranded ladders of DNA from the still separated single-stranded half ladders. In this way, the unique sequences in the tester DNA could be isolated. The unique ladders of the tester are then read by sequencing so that their specific sequences of A, T, G, and C are known.

Shane would use the B-labeled DNA samples as the high concentration driver and one of the A-labeled Tajik DNA samples as tester. He actually planned to mix several of the B DNA samples together to form a universal driver to eliminate isolation of sequences that were not present in one B sample, but which might be present in another. In the end, Shane would go back and use the polymerase chain reaction, a powerful amplification method abbreviated PCR, to make sure each isolated A sequence was present in all six A-labeled Tajik DNA samples, but not in any of the B-labeled DNA samples. He anticipated that many of the sequences he identified in the initial experiments wouldn't turn out to be unique to the Tajiks, but according to the deal he only needed to find one unique sequence. If he did that, his job would be finished.

The scheme sounded simple and it would definitely work. The problem was Shane had committed to work alone and, therefore, it could take months.

He finished putting the details of his plan together and copied the file to a CD. He locked the CD in the drawer with the DNA samples and deleted the plan from his computer.

Shane was startled by the cackle of two of his students in the adjoining lab. He glanced at his watch. It was nearly 3 P.M. He turned off the lights in his office and slipped out the side door next to the elevator.

Shane rapped on the screen door and shuffled into Dan's houseboat. His neighbor was sitting at the kitchen table scanning the entertainment section of the *Seattle Times*.

"Hey dude, what's up?"

"I got done a little early. Thought I'd come by."

"Grab a beer. The cooler's over there next to the refrigerator."

Shane opened the cooler and pulled out a Rolling Rock. He scooted into the bench behind the table and popped the cap.

"So, tell me about your trip."

"Well, let's just say Amsterdam's one hell of a city. You ever see the Red Light District?"

Dan tossed the paper on the table.

"Hell no. I've never been anywhere in Europe. Tim Nelson went to a convention there last year. He told me it was one wild-ass place."

"That's an understatement. It's sort of Sodom and Gomorrah of the twenty-first century."

"What was going on there?"

"I went to meet a client. He hired me to do some work for him."

"Why Amsterdam?"

"That's where his company is based. The head guy has a thing about traveling to the U.S. since the World Trade Center. So they paid my way."

"Good riddance. I hope they all stay out. Too damn many people here already."

Dan got up from the chair and tossed his beer bottle in the trash. He opened the cooler and grabbed another one. He twisted the top off and sat back in his chair.

Shane recounted the events of the evening at Ruby's Palace. Dan listened attentively.

"And you just walked away? Just like that?"

"Just like that."

Dan shook his head incredulously and took another swig. He set the beer down and stared across the table at his friend.

"So, Shane, you seeing anyone?"

Shane took a swig of his beer. He leaned back in the chair and sighed.

"No, Dan, I'm not seeing anyone."

"Why the hell not? You're a good-looking guy with a great job and a nice house. Hell, there are women all over Seattle who'd jump at the chance."

"I guess I just haven't met the right one."

Dan tossed his bottle in the trash.

"That's horseshit. Listen buddy, I know you've been through hell. But you've got to get back on that horse and ride again."

"I'm just not ready yet, Dan."

Dan stared at Shane in silence for a few moments.

"It's been two years now, Shane. You've gotta get on with your life, buddy."

"How many times do I have to say it, Dan? I'm not ready."

Shane stood up and walked across the kitchen to the window. He looked out across the water on the bay.

"Dan, when Annie died, my heart died too. I don't think I'll ever get over her. It's as simple as that."

Shane turned around. The two men stared at each other without speaking. Dan downed the rest of his beer.

"I can't comprehend it, man. How could I know what it would be like to watch your fiancée get cut to pieces by the prop on a damned boat? I just wish I could help. I lost my two best friends that day."

Dan stood up from the chair and strode across the room to the open door. The channel was full of boats of every type and size. He rested his hand on the doorjam and stared out at the water.

"I just wish there was something I could do for you, Shane."

Shane downed the last of his beer and tossed the bottle in the trash.

"I gotta get going, Dan. Thanks for the beer."

"See you tonight?"

"We'll see. I'm thinking about heading up to Anacortes to get some work done on my boat."

"Okay, see you later."

Shane stepped out onto the deck and the screen door slammed behind him.

Dan shook his head and tossed his empty bottle in the trash.

CHAPTER THIRTY-FOUR

Mohammajon rose to his feet and rolled his prayer rug. He tailed along with a group of the other men toward the back of the mosque. He put the rug back in the cabinet where dozens of other rugs were lying in neat stacks. He followed the group through the main door leading to the garden and then turned away along the pathway toward the mosque offices.

It had become Mohammajon's custom the past two months to attend prayers five times a day. He'd become quite active in the Islamic community of the Masjid-E-Al Karam Mosque during that time. He dutifully accepted tasks assigned to him by the mullahs and carried them out with enthusiasm. Among these was his role in directing the writing and printing of the weekly newsletter. He'd become quite close to the mullahs as a result of his dependability and dedication.

Mohammajon shuffled through the door to the basement office and sat down at a desk. He booted up the early model IBM computer and opened a newsletter file. He began updating information about the events scheduled for the coming week.

The door opened with a creak. Mohammajon looked up from his work, as Mullah Baloch stepped in from an adjoining office carrying a donation basket.

The mullah was a middle-aged Egyptian with just a hint of a potbelly and a dusting of gray in his temples. His full beard was black. His baggy eyes belied a dynamic temperament.

"Good evening, Mohammajon. I hope you're feeling better today."

"Allah has blessed me, Mullah. I've been sick the past few days, but I feel much better today."

The mullah sat at an adjacent desk and began sorting through donations. He placed the checks in one pile and the cash in another. He tossed the coins into a sorting machine.

"Mullah, I'm almost finished with the newsletter. Is there anything special you'd like to add about the food drive for the poor?"

The cleric looked up from the desk and smiled.

"Why don't you include a notice about our need for volunteers to seek donations at the entrance to the Shippol Airport on Sunday at noon?"

The mullah leaned back in his chair.

"I don't know what we ever did without you here at the Mosque, Mohammajon. How are you getting along in Amsterdam?"

Mohammajon smiled ruefully.

"I guess I'm adjusting. Amsterdam is a city filled with sights I never imagined before I left Afghanistan. It's been quite a shock."

The mullah laughed.

"It was for me too, when I came here from Egypt seven years ago. You'll get used to it. There's a lot of Allah's work to be done."

"I miss my country. I find myself longing to return to Afghanistan now that the war is over."

"To see your family?"

"I have no family, Mullah. They all died in the war. But there are stories in the newspaper every day about sweeping change in Afghanistan. I fear I'll return some day as a stranger in my own land."

"As I would feel if I returned to Egypt. Many changes have occurred in Cairo since I left seven years ago. What brought you to Amsterdam?"

"I came to assist my young countrymen. I follow Mullah Habid's instruction."

"I see."

The mullah stood up from the desk. He wrapped rubber bands around several stacks of cash and slipped them into a zippered bank bag.

"Mohammajon, there is talk among the men at the Mosque."

"What talk, Mullah?"

"Just the kinds of rumors idle men embrace. Some suspect you are on a mission related to the war in Afghanistan."

"These are the words of an old fool with only air between his ears! Zulfiqar stirs this talk. He weaves gossip like an old woman."

"I must admit you're an odd threesome. The man named Ahmed Jan comes to the mosque only occasionally and the other young man not at all. Mohammad Qazi pointed out the Tajik named Mustafa to me last week. He was leaving a bar near the main square. He was too drunk to stand."

"The young Tajik has a heavy heart. He yearns for his lost love."

"None of you has a job, yet you live in an expensive apartment and do not want for money. Even a blind man would be suspicious."

Mohammajon stared at the mullah for a moment and then nodded his head. He looked down at the computer screen and went on with his work on the newsletter.

The mullah sat back down and watched him for a time before speaking again.

"It's a shame about the Taliban."

Mohammajon looked up from the computer.

"I bear no regret for the Taliban. They reaped what they sowed."

"The Taliban had virtuous intentions at the start. They were only students who sought to follow the teachings of the Quran and to establish a pure Islamic state in Afghanistan."

"The Taliban are blood-thirsty lackeys of the Pakistan ISI and al-Qaida. They murdered thousands of my people. They even butchered their own women and children on the basis of mere allegation. The Taliban destroyed Afghanistan, Mullah."

"Come now, Mohammajon, Afghanistan was destroyed long before the Taliban. The Taliban only destroyed a couple of Buddhist statues and killed a few people in the soccer stadium to set an example. Most of the changes they made were in accordance with the words of the Prophet."

"The Taliban are Pashtun. The Pashtun slaughtered my wife and sons before they called themselves Taliban. My oldest son was only nine. The murdering dogs slit his belly open and left him to die. Was this in accordance with the words of the Prophet?"

"I understand your hatred, Mohammajon. No man should bear such heartbreak. These are the evil deeds of a few cowardly criminals, but that doesn't mean the entire movement is rotten."

The mullah sat silently for a few moments before speaking again.

"Allah's will be done. If there is some mission, I only ask you to re-evaluate its relevance in the light of the changes occurring in your country. The war is over. The new government represents all people. Tajiks, Pashtun, and Uzbeks are represented among the highest officials. Friends and former enemies alike are striving to set aside differences for the good of the whole. I pray your charge is not to destroy the delicate peace that is even now in its infancy. Would you strip the bark from the tender shoot?"

Mohammajon looked up from the computer. His heavy eyes locked with the mullah's in a muted stare. Mullah Baloch waited for a few moments for Mohammajon to respond. Mohammajon only sat and stared.

Finally, the mullah stood and picked up the cash bag.

"I'll see you tomorrow, Mohammajon."

Ahmed unlocked the apartment door. He pushed the door open with his leg and carried a box of groceries to the kitchen table. He set the box down and walked back across the room to shut the door.

"Mohammajon, I found fresh lamb and vegetables. How about if we have stew tonight for supper?"

Mohammajon was sitting on the couch reading from the Quran. He looked up and waved his hand without speaking. Ahmed began putting the food away in the cabinet and refrigerator. He was nearly finished before Mohammajon spoke.

"Ahmed, it is written, if your enemy puts down his weapons you should not kill him."

Ahmed closed the cabinet door and slid the box on top of the refrigerator before stepping into the living room. He sat down in the armchair across from Mohammajon.

"What's your point, Mohammajon?"

"I'm wondering if we should reevaluate our mission?"

Ahmed's eyes bulged with bewilderment. He reached into his coat pocket and pulled out a plastic bag.

"Mohammajon, do you remember this?"

He pulled the two papers from the bag and held them out.

"Perhaps I should read them to you once again? The Pashtun did not lay down their weapons. The guns were torn from their bloody hands."

Ahmed shook the papers for emphasis.

"They planned to massacre the Tajiks by the hundreds of thousands. Men, women, and children, they made no distinction. The bloodthirsty murderers sought nothing less than to wipe the Tajik people from the face of the earth."

"Al-Qaida was planning to kill our people. That's all that can be concluded from these papers."

Ahmed shook his head with dismay.

"Al-Qaida and the Pashtun, they are the same, Mohammajon. Did it not suit primarily the Pashtun intentions to experiment with the vector on our people? If it was just a demonstration they sought, why not choose an infidel population?"

"It was not all the Pashtun. Hamid Karzai is searching for Mullah Omar and other Taliban leaders to punish them. I read it just yesterday."

Ahmed shook his head in disbelief.

"Wake up, Mohammajon. Moderates like Karzai will not prevail. The Taliban are only biding their time. They will seek their revenge as soon as the Americans leave Afghanistan. Even now they regroup around Kandahar. The Taliban convinced the Arabs to unleash this horror on our people. They are responsible and have brought this pestilence upon their own heads."

Ahmed held up his scarred left hand.

"I myself have felt the wickedness of their ways."

The sound of footsteps echoing on the wooden floor in the hall hushed their conversation. The doorknob jiggled for a few seconds and then stopped. It jiggled again and stopped.

Ahmed pulled a pistol from his waist and walked to the door. He yanked the door open.

Mustafa was standing in the hall bent over at the waist with his legs wide apart. He had a key in his hand. His breath reeked of whiskey.

Mustafa looked up at Ahmed with narrow, bloodshot eyes and grunted before stumbling past him through the door to the rear of the apartment. A crash echoed from the bedroom a few moments later. Ahmed rushed to the bedroom with Mohammajon close behind.

Mustafa was lying face down on the hardwood floor. Pieces of ceramic lamp were scattered around him.

Ahmed stooped to pick up the shards from the floor.

"Help me get him into bed."

Ahmed tossed the broken lamp into the trashcan and helped Mohammajon lift Mustafa onto the bed. Mohammajon pulled off Mustafa's shoes and took off his jacket. Mohammajon shook his head.

"He's killing himself."

Ahmed looked up at Mohammajon.

"The Pashtun did this too. They ripped his heart from his chest."

CHAPTER THIRTY-FIVE

May 1, 2002

Fatima was sitting on the raised platform in her cell reading the Quran. The naked bulb in the ceiling provided just enough light to make out the words on the page.

She was exhausted from a long day of hard labor in the kitchen where thousands of meals were prepared for the prisoners every day. It was her job to stock the supply room and clean the pots and pans the cooks used to prepare the food. There were perks. Now and then she managed to supplement her own meager diet with a morsel of food that stuck to one of the pots.

Fatima's life had sank into a numbing routine during the three months she'd been in Rawalpindi Prison. A bottle of water and a portion of naan were dropped into the box in the bottom of her cell door shortly before dawn. She was taken to the food preparation center twenty minutes later. There she'd work under guard until after dinner when the last pot was clean and all the shelves were restocked for the following day. Sometime between 8:30 and 9:00 at night she'd be led back to her cell. This grueling cycle continued seven days a week and was only interrupted by thirty minutes of daily exercise and a weekly shower.

Fatima hadn't received a single letter or visitor during the entire time. She'd heard nothing of Nadir or her mother. It was as if they'd vanished from the face of the earth. She felt a constant ache in her heart for them, and the man for whom she'd sacrificed everything.

The weather had begun to change. Already the May temperatures were approaching the mid-90s. The torrential rains of winter transformed the Rawalpindi Prison into little more than a mud pit. Fatima could only imagine the stifling heat of the approaching summer.

The clank of a closing door echoed in the distance. The sound of footsteps grew steadily closer and then stopped outside the door. Fatima looked up with surprise, as a key slid into the lock on her cell door. The heavy metal door creaked open and Warder Malik stepped inside.

"Come with me, Fatima."

Fatima stood up and turned around with her back to Malik. The warder shackled her arms behind her and led her into the hall. An unsettling cry echoed through the cellblock.

Warder Malik unlocked the door at the end of the hall. He led her through the office and out the front door into the prison yard. Spotlights bore down from the tops of the buildings and fence posts on the perimeter of the yard. Malik locked the door behind them.

"Where are we going, sir?"

"The assistant superintendent's office. He wants to see you."

A chill ran up Fatima's spine. She hadn't seen or heard from Abdulla Mufti since her first day at the prison. Malik pushed her along the path toward the windowless cinder-block building where the superintendent's office was located. He grabbed her by the arm and turned her toward him.

"Fatima, you must do whatever Superintendent Mufti wants you to do. Do you hear me? One word from him can change your life. He even has the power to set you free someday."

They arrived at the side door and the Warder pushed the buzzer. The door opened a moment later. It was Mufti.

"Thank you, Warder. I want to talk with the prisoner alone. Stay here in the yard. I'll call for you when we're finish with our chat."

"Yes, sir."

Malik guided Fatima up the stairs into Mufti's office. Mufti locked the door behind her.

The room was hot. The dark skin on Mufti's forehead glistened with beads of sweat. He smiled. The gold crown adorning his worn and yellowed teeth sparkled.

"Have a seat on the couch, my dear. I'll be off the phone in a minute."

Fatima sat down. She stared straight ahead, as Mufti resumed an animated conversation at his desk. The desktop was cluttered with papers. Large stacks of files were strewn across a countertop in back of the room.

Fatima listened to Mufti argue against the transfer of a group of prisoners from Islamabad. His bushy eyebrows shot up and down, as he squabbled with the unseen party at the other end of the line. He intermittently rolled his beady black eyes at points he found particularly outrageous. Finally, he agreed to a lesser number and hung up the phone.

"Damned ISI."

Mufti stood up from behind his desk. He smiled, walked over to the couch, and sat down beside Fatima.

"Hello, my dear. I bet you thought I forgot about you. I had to go to the North for a while to train a new superintendent. I just got back yesterday. I've been thinking about you. How do you find life in the prison?"

"Very hard, sir. I miss my son."

Mufti's eyebrows shot up.

"Your son? I thought you weren't married."

"Oh yes, sir. I have a two-year-old boy. I don't know what happened to him. I haven't seen him since the day I was arrested."

"And your husband? What has become of him?"

"I don't know, sir. I'm not sure if he knows where I am."

Mufti's eyes narrowed with anger.

"Don't lie to me woman! I read your file. Your husband was killed years ago in Iran. You lied to me about sex outside of marriage. Your son is a bastard!"

Tears welled in Fatima's eyes. She looked down at the couch without speaking. Mufti lifted her chin with his fingertips.

"Stop your crying! I forgive you."

He ran his fingers through her hair.

"You really are a beautiful woman, Fatima."

Fatima turned her head away defiantly. He gripped her jaw with his hand and forced her to look at him.

"I could force you to submit to my will. But that wouldn't be nearly as satisfying. I want you to enjoy me willingly."

Mufti let go of her chin and Fatima looked back down at the couch.

"My dear, this is what's expected of you. Each week we'll spend a delightful evening together here in my office. We'll share French champagne, the best food, wonderful music, and passionate romance. This will become your oasis from the harsh monotony of this prison. I'll see you get plenty of good food and a job as a nurse in the infirmary. I'll also see to it your son is cared for in a madrassa in Islamabad. Look at me."

Fatima looked up. Her beautiful almond-shaped eyes overflowed with tears. She wiped her cheek on her arm.

"And if I do not comply with your wishes, sir?"

"Then Rawalpindi Prison will become your own private hell."

Fatima clinched her fists in rage.

"I will not do this, sir!" she yelled, her voice quivering with fury. "I will not sacrifice my soul, even for my son whom I love so dearly. I will not be your whore, sir!"

Mufti placed his hand on Fatima's knee. She stiffened to his touch and gruffly pushed his hand away.

"You are so wrong, my dear."

He grabbed her chin with his hand and forced her to look at him. Mufti gave her a knowing smile and nodded his head.

"You'll change your mind with time. You'll beg for my attention. I'll see to it you have all the time you need to reconsider."

Mufti stood up from the couch and strode across the room. He unbolted the lock and opened the door.

"Warder Malik."

"Yes, sir."

"The prisoner swore at me. Sixty days in solitary. Bread and water."

"Yes, sir."

Malik marched into the office and jerked Fatima up from the couch. He pushed her out the door and led her along the path past her cellblock. They proceeded through the yard to a rear gate. Malik unlocked the gate and pushed Fatima into a fenced enclosure. There in the shadows, Fatima could make out the forms of four cement-block huts. Each hut was set several meters from the nearest neighbor. He shoved her along a narrow cement path to the first hut.

"Damn it, woman. I told you to do what he wanted."

Malk opened the heavy door to the cement block hut. The foul stench of human feces surged from the two-by-three meter cell. The warder shined a flashlight inside. Cockroaches scattered across the damp, brick floor. He scanned toward the back of the cell. There was an open hole in the floor in the back corner.

Malik pushed Fatima to the floor inside the cell. The door slammed with a resounding clang and the bolt clattered shut. Malik's footsteps faded into the night.

Fatima leaned her back against the wall and pulled her feet beneath her. She struggled to suppress the urge to vomit, but she began to retch uncontrollably. She'd descended to the very depths of hell.

CHAPTER THIRTY-SIX

June 11, 2002

S hane picked up each plastic tube in succession and zapped it with a vor-
tex mixer before returning it to the ice bucket. He looked up at the clock
on the wall. It was a few minutes before four in the morning. Shane
decided to store the samples in the freezer as soon as the centrifugation was finished. He needed to get a few hours sleep before the department meeting scheduled for 11 A.M.

Shane had worked non-stop on the project for nearly two months. He
arrived at the lab a little after midnight almost every night and toiled until close
to 5 A.M. He often wanted to work later, but one of the postdoctoral students
in an adjoining lab had the irritating habit of showing up at the crack of dawn
almost every day. The ambitious lab rat even worked on Saturdays and Sundays.
Shane didn't want to run the risk of arousing suspicion, so he planned his
schedule accordingly.

Shane made remarkable progress on the project. He completed separate
subtraction hybridizations on three of the A-labeled samples. He isolated more
than a dozen candidate sequences for each of the A-labeled samples. He
sequenced each of these and found three unique sequences that were present in
all three A-labeled tester samples. Then he designed PCR primers to detect each
of the candidate sequences. He was preparing to retest all of the A-labeled and
B-labeled DNA samples to confirm his findings.

Shane picked up an ice bucket from the benchtop and carried it to the
other side of the lab. He set it next to a refrigerated microcentrifuge, lifted the
top, and began inserting the tubes. He was about half done when a young
woman's voice startled him from behind.

"Working late again, Dr. Kalakan?"

Shane spun around. It was a graduate student from Josh Peterson's lab named Teresa Daniels. She'd taken two of Shane's lecture courses during her first year of training. Teresa was a shapely blonde with a mischievous personality and big blue eyes. She had a reputation for being a hard-working student with unlimited potential. She was also a heart breaker in tight-fitting blue jeans and a tank top.

"Hi, Teresa," Shane stammered. "What are you doing here so early?"

Teresa walked across the room. She glanced at the ice bucket and then at Shane.

"Dr. Peters got an industry contract for some circadian studies. He assigned one of the experiments to me. The samples need to be collected at all sorts of inconvenient time points. I had to come in several times in the middle of the night the past two weeks. You were here working every time. What are you up to?"

Shane felt his face flush red.

"Oh, nothing," he stammered. "It's just a little pilot study on the use of genetic differences to distinguish Eskimo populations."

She smiled sweetly and peered around him at the samples in the centrifuge. Then she glanced at her watch.

"So let me see if I have this right. You're working here at almost four in the morning on a little linkage study in Eskimos when you have four postdoctoral students, two graduate students, and two technicians working in your lab? You know, Dr. Kalakan, I probably would have fallen for that nonsense a year ago, but the reason I didn't choose your lab for my thesis work was because you have a reputation for never working at the bench. So you're going to have to do better than that."

She smiled again and brushed her long hair away from her face. Shane felt his face flush again.

"We ... well, that's the truth," he stammered. "I need to get the project done quickly and there's no room in the lab during the day."

"Uh huh, right. So why didn't you ask Ben Caruthers to do it? He told me he's been begging for a new project. You know why I think you're here in the middle of the night Dr. Kalikan? I think you're either A, making illicit drugs or B, working on something really hot and you don't want to share the glory. Since I don't smell any solvents, I think it's the latter."

Shane had recovered his composure. He was getting a little irritated at the young woman's insolence.

"Look, Teresa, this is my lab. I'm a faculty member and you're a graduate student. I don't have to tell you anything about my work."

"That's true, Dr Kalakan, you don't have to tell me anything."

She began backing away toward the door. Suddenly, she turned and scurried toward the bench on the other side of the lab.

"But let's see what your notebook says!"

Shane sprinted after her.

"Don't touch my notebook!"

Teresa screamed like a schoolgirl playing a prank. She got to the notebook first and thrust it behind her back to keep him from wresting it away from her. She broke free and scooted around the bench to the desk. She skimmed through the first page of the notebook before Shane reached the desk.

"Give me my notebook, Teresa!"

She turned her back to the desk with the notebook behind her and smiled.

"Make me."

Shane tried to reach around both sides to snatch the notebook. He pressed her back against the desk to keep her from bolting once again.

"Sexual harassment! Sexual harassment!" she screamed out with a giggle. "Dr. Kalakan is sexually harassing me!"

Shane backed away.

"Shh!! Okay, what do you want?"

Teresa smiled broadly with triumph and tossed her hair back behind her. She batted her eyes.

"I want you to cut the bull, Dr. Kalakan, and tell me what you're working on."

Shane held his hand out.

"Okay. Give me the notebook and I'll tell you."

"That's so sweet of you. I'll tell you what. I'll give you the notebook if you cook dinner for me this Friday night. I'll bring the wine and you can tell me what you're really working on. Deal?"

Shane smiled. He continued to hold out his hand.

"You know where I live?"

"Sure, you live next door to Dan Murphy. Right? I went to a party at his place a few weeks ago."

"Okay, you've got a deal."

Teresa smiled coyly and handed Shane the notebook. She sauntered toward the door and opened it.

"I'll see you at seven this Friday, Dr. Kalakan."

"Do you want fish or beef?"

She smiled.

"I'll leave that up to you. Just don't work too late Thursday night. I don't want you falling asleep on me."

Teresa smiled one last time and shut the door behind her. Shane shook his head, as he loaded the last of the tubes into the centrifuge.

* * *

Stone Waverly reached across his desk and picked up a file. He opened it and began reading through a summary of recent intelligence on al-Qaida. One paragraph in particular caught his eye. There were reports from several independent sources that bin Laden died of kidney failure during the bombing in Tora Bora. One CIA analyst was suggesting that Abu Qatada, a London-based Muslim cleric wanted in Jordan for terrorist offenses, was likely to assume command of the organization. Djamel Beghal, a jihadist associated with al-Qaida confessed to learning about Jihad or holy war from Qatada at the Baker Street mosque in London. Qatada's teachings were also found in the Hamburg apartment of Mohammad Atta, the presumed leader of the 9/11 attacks, right after the attacks on the World Trade Center and Pentagon.

The photo of Qatada drew Stone's gaze. He was a menacing man of Middle-Eastern descent with a large head framed by a long dark beard and mustache. Bushy brows emphasized his ominous black eyes.

The phone rang on Waverly's desk. Stone picked up the receiver and cradled it against his shoulder.

"Waverly."

"Hello, Stone, Richards here. How's the family?"

"Great Mr. Richards. We just found out Julie's pregnant again."

"That's wonderful news, Stone. Give her my regards. Stone, I'm calling you on a secure line. Did you get that recent summary on the Iraqi defector?"

"I just got it. I'm reading the Qaida synopsis right now. I'm going to read that one next."

"Well, this guy Huwaidi had a senior position on the staff of Nassir al-Hindawi. Al-Hindawi was a key player in the development of the Iraqi biological weapons program. Al-Hindawi was arrested in January of this year trying to get out of Baghdad using a forged passport. It appears he was executed. Huwaidi managed to escape from Iraq by driving to a Kurd-controlled area in the North."

"Sounds like he should have details about the biological weapons program."
"He's a gold mine. We got specific information about the location of a major anthrax lab and storage facility. Iraq also has stores of smallpox and Ebola in another lab and they've been stockpiling weapons grade material. But what really caught my attention was the information Huwaidi provided about a biological vector development laboratory just outside of As Salman in southern Iraq. That's why I'm calling you. Apparently, the lab was set up by a young Saudi Arabian scientist who got his training at the Pasteur Institute in Paris."

"Another case of the Western world providing the tools for our own destruction."

"Exactly. Huwaidi told us that this scientist was engineering custom vectors to use for biological warfare. There's one particular vector they made a lot of progress on. We've code named it the Armageddon vector. This vector was engineered as a hybrid between the influenza and Ebola viruses. It's transmitted by inhalation and apparently the active virus is infectious as hell."

Stone sat dumbfounded. He couldn't believe what he was hearing.

"Here's the kicker. The Armageddon vector was engineered so it can only integrate into victims who have a particular sequence of DNA in their chromosomes. The integration sequence is engineered into the virus and can be selected to function in particular populations by picking out unique DNA sequences. So, for example, it could be engineered to work only on Kurds and have no effect on other Iraqi populations. Once infected, the victim is symptom-free for a period of three to four weeks while he's unknowingly spewing infectious virus into the air wherever he goes. Then the virus goes lytic about a month after the infection and the victim has a classic Ebola total-body meltdown. Blood oozes from every orifice."

"God help us," Stone muttered. "A virus like that could send the world back to the Dark Ages."

"Are you sitting down? This is where it really gets ugly. Huwaidi told us the Iraqi secret police tried to deliver a stock of the Armageddon vector to al-Qaida in February. It was supposed to be delivered in Venice, but the Qaida agent was killed and the vector disappeared."

Stone gasped.

"I'll be damned. Now we know what the Tajik sons-of-bitches were doing in Venice. I wonder how they found out about it?"

"Who knows? Maybe they found something in an al-Qaida compound we bombed in Afghanistan. I already ordered in several operatives to shadow the three of them in Amsterdam. I hate to do this to you, Stone, but you're the best man for the job. I want you to go to Amsterdam and find out what the hell they did with the vector."

"I understand, sir. I can leave immediately. What about the source in Iraq?"

"That's up to the president. For now he doesn't want information about the vector released to the public. He's concerned there could be panic if the word gets out. He'll be raising world awareness of the danger of the Iraqi weapons of mass destruction over the next few months without mentioning this specific weapon. He'll be trying to rally world support for a military attack on Iraq. I'm betting he'll order a military strike on the facility where the Armageddon vector is produced, irrespective of the support of our allies."

"How do you want me to travel to Amsterdam?"

"I'm putting one of our jets at your disposal. The pilot has filed a flight plan to leave in three hours. Let me know as soon as you find anything. Don't hesitate to call me personally for backup. Stone, this is top secret. Don't put anything on paper about the Tajiks that could end up on the director's desk. He'll chew my ass out good if he finds out we sprung the Tajiks from Pakistan."

"I'll keep that in mind, sir."

"Stone?"

"Yes, sir?"

"Watch your ass. I'm not sure if the Iraqis know about the Tajiks yet. If they do, you can bet they'll be gunning for them. I don't want you getting caught in the crossfire."

"I'll be careful, sir."

Stone hung up the phone. He sat for a minute digesting his conversation with Richards, before gathering up several of the files from his desk and locking them in his briefcase. He strode from his office toward the parking lot. He had three hours to pack his bags, kiss his wife goodbye, and return to CIA headquarters in time to make the flight for Amsterdam.

CHAPTER THIRTY-SEVEN

S hane lifted the top on the potbelly barbeque grill, but the coals weren't ready yet. He plopped the top down and scooted the plate of shrimp and filet onto the picnic table. He sat down and took a deep breath.

The dancing reflections of the afternoon sun shimmered across the gentle wake of a sailboat that was inching forward in anticipation of the drawbridge opening. The captain turned the wheel to make yet another broad turn. Shane waved as the boat skirted by the front of his deck.

Suddenly, a floral fragrance enveloped him and a pair of soft hands covered his eyes.

"Guess who?"

"Don't tell me. Carmen Elektra?"

Shane slid his hands into Teresa's and pulled them away from his face. He stood up from the bench. Teresa was wearing a purple halter-top and white shorts. Her long blond hair was pulled back with a barrette.

"Wow!" Shane blurted out, before he could catch himself.

He bowed and swept his hand in mock homage.

"The stars blush at your splendor."

Teresa's smile was radiant. She leaned forward and kissed him lightly on the cheek.

"So does that mean you approve, Dr. Kalakan?"

"You're just full of surprises, Teresa Daniels."

Teresa batted her eyes with false modesty. She unwound a net bag hanging from her shoulder and pulled out two bottles of wine.

"I brought a chardonnay to start and a merlot for the main course."

Shane smiled and took the bottles.

"Have a seat. I'll get some glasses and a bottle opener."

Shane opened the side door into the kitchen and Buster bounded onto the patio. The Dalmatian ran directly to Teresa. He sniffed her hand and began to spin around and around, all the while wagging his tail with jubilation. Shane walked out onto the deck a few seconds later.

"He's beautiful. What's his name?"

"Buster. Don't pet him unless you really want to. He won't leave you alone once you start."

"I love dogs. My parents raised border collies. I'd have one now, but my landlord doesn't allow pets."

"Where do your parents live?"

"I grew up in Southern California. My father owns a bioengineering start-up in Laguna Beach. He got his degree here at UW in the seventies. He's the one who decided I needed to go to UW."

"You could've gone anywhere you wanted."

"Not if I wanted any support from him. My dad's a control freak."

"Yeah, well you shouldn't look a gift horse in the mouth. I'm still paying off my school loans."

"Your family didn't help you through school?"

"My parents were killed in a car accident when I was twelve."

"I'm sorry."

"That's okay. They were on their way to pick me up from a little league game. A drunk driving a pickup truck ran a red light at an intersection. I lived in a string of foster homes until I was eighteen."

"God, how horrible. Do you have any brothers and sisters?"

"I had a younger sister. Her name was Ali. She got adopted by one of our foster families. They took us both at first. We lived with them for three years. My foster dad lost his job just when things were getting back to normal. They had three kids of their own and they couldn't keep us both. I'm not sure what happened to them."

Teresa didn't know what to say. She turned and gazed out across the water. Shane set the glasses on the table and picked up the chardonnay.

"Do you have any brothers or sisters?"

"I'm the youngest of five. They all live in California."

"I always envied people with big families. I want half a dozen kids someday."

Shane turned the corkscrew into the wine bottle and yanked out the cork. He poured two glasses and handed one to Teresa.

"What should we drink to?" Shane asked, as he held his glass up.

"How about happier times?"

"Okay, to happier times."

Teresa smiled and clicked his glass. They both took a sip of the wine. Shane set his glass on the table, took the top off the grill, and hooked it on the rim. The filets and shrimp sizzled as he pushed them off the plate and onto the grill. He replaced the cover and smoke billowed from the vents.

Teresa wandered to the edge of the dock. She closed her eyes and turned her face to the wind, as the gentle breeze gusted through her hair. She opened her eyes and gazed out toward the bridge. Shane walked up beside her and took a sip from his glass.

"It must be wonderful living here," she half-whispered, without diverting her gaze from the water. "There's something about the smell of the water and the squawk of the seagulls."

"I've dreamed of living on the water for as long as I can remember. I always imagined myself living in some grand villa. This little place is all an assistant professor can afford in Seattle."

Teresa turned and pouted.

"Oh, you're so mistreated. My apartment looks out over a McDonald's parking lot."

"Yeah, I guess I was lucky to find it."

"What's for dinner? I'm starving."

Shane turned and walked toward the table.

"The chef has prepared fresh oysters, followed by a fresh spinach and bacon salad, and topped off with a beef filet and shrimp garnished with asparagus and teriyaki mushrooms."

"Yum, it sounds wonderful!"

"You sit here facing the water. I'll get the oysters."

Shane fetched the oysters from the refrigerator. He served them on a bed of greens garnished with a horseradish sauce.

The dinner conversation was lively and sprinkled with laughter. They finished the white wine with the salad and the red with the main course.

"You're incredible, Shane. I was expecting cheese sandwiches or burgers."

"Cooking's a hobby of mine. I took some classes at a chef school here in Seattle. It's relaxing."

Teresa smiled.

"We'll, you can cook for me anytime you want."

"Dessert?"

"Please, don't tempt me."

"How about chocolate cheesecake with strawberries? It's such a beautiful evening on the water. Why don't we take the boat out on the lake and sip a glass of port beneath the lights of downtown Seattle."

"That sounds wonderful!"

"Okay, let's go."

Shane fetched a cooler from the deck. He pulled off the cockpit cover, set the cooler on the seat, and started the engine. He flipped on the running lights.

"All aboard!"

Teresa took Shane's hand and stepped into the sailboat.

"Sit back here in the cockpit. I'll let you take over when we get her out on the open water."

Teresa ran her hand along the beautiful teak wood detailing and tossed her hair back with a shake of her head.

"This is such a beautiful boat. The detailing is so fine. Who built it?"

"It's a Swan 40 from Finland. I worked at a yacht club when I was going to college. I fantasized about owning a Swan someday. I bought it for my twenty-seventh birthday, right after I got my job at UW."

"What's it called?"

"*View Corridor.*"

"*View Corridor,*" she laughed. "Why would you call it that?"

He chuckled.

"When I first moved to Seattle I was living over on Juanita Bay sharing a house with one of the other faculty members. I had a J22 sailboat and some of the neighbors tried to keep me out of the slips at the community dock because they claimed the mast obstructed their view corridor to the water. I got into a nasty rhubarb with this old woman who kept bringing me up before the architectural control committee."

"What a nightmare."

"The funny thing was, this lady didn't even live on the water. She got the board to take away my dock lease. I had to take it to court to force the community to let me moor the boat there. The judge ruled in my favor. He said I could keep any boat I wanted there as long as it didn't exceed the length specified in the community covenants. I bought my Swan at the boat show the next weekend and named it the *View Corridor.*"

He grinned.

"It really pissed them off. I can't change the name now. It'd be bad luck."

Teresa laughed and shook her head.

"Remind me not to piss you off."

"I'm a teddy bear most of the time. But you don't want to make me mad."

Shane pulled the throttle back and the boat glided from the dock between a pair of pylons. He eased the throttle off and signaled twice with the horn.

"What's that for?"

"It's to let the man on the bridge know we want him to open it."

Ten minutes passed before a horn sounded and the bridge began to open. Shane steered the boat between the soaring steel arms into Lake Union.

It took nearly twenty minutes to reach the center of the lake. Shane turned off the engine and set the boat adrift beneath the skyscrapers of downtown Seattle. He cued the CD player. The soaring vocals of Sarah Brightman and Andrea Bocelli singing *Time to Say Goodbye* seemed to float on the breeze.

Teresa looked up at Shane and smiled.

"Sarah Brightman. I love it. I once dreamed of becoming a star on Broadway. Unfortunately, I got my dad's voice."

Shane chuckled as he swung the wheel around. The nearly-full moon was rising above the rooftops of the buildings along the east side of the lake. He ducked into the cabin.

"Look at the moon," he called out, as he disappeared down the stairs. "I'm getting the port. The cheesecake is in the Tupperware pan."

Teresa gazed up at the moon, as she pulled the top off the Tupperware. She scooped up a piece of cake and set it on a plate. Shane re-emerged from below deck with two glasses and a bottle. He pulled the cork and poured smoky-colored port into each glass. He handed one to Teresa and raised his glass.

"To sparkling summer nights in Seattle. Thank you for an incredible evening."

Teresa stood up behind the wheel next to Shane. She smiled, clicked his glass, and took a sip of the port. Shane savored his sip while gazing at the glimmering skyline. Teresa set her glass down next to the plates. She wrapped her arms around his chest and snuggled against his back. She stood on her toes, kissed him on the back of the neck, and ducked beneath his arm.

"Dr. Kalakan, you take my breath away."

She gave him a lingering kiss on the lips. Shane wrapped his arms around her. He sat back on the seat without breaking the kiss. Teresa sank to the deck between his knees. She ended the kiss with a tender embrace. She sighed.

"God, I've wanted to do that for so long!"

Shane lifted her chin and kissed her once more on the lips. Teresa took the glass from his hand and set it on the deck. She entwined her hands behind his neck.

Shane pulled her close and pressed his mouth against her soft red lips. Her tongue danced with his in an eager duel of ardor. She kissed him lightly on the forehead and the chin, before once again pressing her mouth to his.

Shane ran his hands beneath her blouse and caressed her silky skin. His fingertips traced feathery circles around both of her breasts. Teresa bit her lip and moaned. Then she clutched his wrists and pulled his hands down around her back. She peered into his eyes and smoothed his hair back with her fingers.

"Please, Shane," she whispered, "stop."

Shane laughed uncomfortably.

"Are you serious?"

Teresa nodded her head.

"I'm saving myself for marriage or until I turn twenty-five. It's a promise I made to my grandmother before she died."

Shane dropped his hands down to his side. He took a deep breath and sighed.

"Okay, I can handle it. I saw a bumper sticker last week ... 'Celibacy cultivates creativity.' "

Teresa smiled apologetically. She cuddled against his chest and reached up and kissed him on the cheek. She glanced at her watch.

"It's almost two. I've got another one of those time points at 6:30 tomorrow morning. I've got to get some sleep."

Shane stood up and started the engine. He turned the boat and headed back toward the Aurora Bridge. Teresa laid her head on his shoulder, as he guided the boat through the winding channel to Portage Bay. Neither one spoke as the boat glided along the glassy water.

The bridge was just opening for a sailing yacht as they motored past Ivor's Salmon House. The Swan slipped through the gap and into the mouth of Portage Bay.

Shane edged the sailboat into the slip and jumped off to secure the lines. He leaped back in and shut the engine off before helping Teresa step off the boat. She turned and embraced him.

"Thank you for dinner, Shane. It was wonderful."

Shane leaned over and kissed Teresa on the lips. He put his arm around her back and led her around the side of the house past Dan's front door. All of the boathouses along the walk to the street were dark, except for a string of lights draped along the path.

"Where did you park?"

"Just across the street. That's my Audi."

Shane walked her to the car. Teresa unlocked the door with the controller on her key chain and opened the door. She turned and kissed him.

"Thank you again for a great time."

"Have a nice weekend."

She crouched into the driver's seat, closed the door, and started the engine. Shane knocked on the window. She smiled and opened it.

"Can I see you again, Teresa?"

"Of course. How about Sunday?"

"This Sunday?"

"Why not? It's my birthday. I'll make you a deal. If you'll take me sailing, I'll make you dinner. Do you like sushi?"

"I love it. What time?"

"How about two?"

"I'll see you then. How many candles should I get for the cake?"

She smiled sweetly.

"Twenty-five."

She giggled and drove away from the curb before Shane had a chance to reply.

CHAPTER THIRTY-EIGHT

June 15, 2002

Stone Waverly set his coffee cup down and turned to the next page in the newspaper. He was on his third latte. It was a pristine summer day in Amsterdam. A warm breeze gusted through his hair. Stone looked up at the cloudless sky and then glanced at his watch. It was a few minutes shy of noon.

He watched a young couple saunter past along the brick path that ran along the canal. The young woman whispered into her boyfriend's ear. He laughed and swatted her behind.

Stone glanced back across the canal just in time to see Mustafa emerge from the Tajik flat and scamper down the steps to the street below. He was wearing jeans and a polo shirt. Stone peered over the top of his newspaper, as Mustafa peered down the street behind him.

Mustafa wandered slowly along the canal toward the bridge, glancing in each window as he passed. He ambled to the middle of the bridge and lingered overlooking the canal as a passenger boat cruised beneath the span. He turned and waited for a man on a bicycle to pass, before heading off along the walkway.

Stone pulled a couple of bills from his shirt pocket and slid them beneath a saucer on the table. He stood up, tucked the newspaper beneath his arm, and strode toward the bridge. He hurried to the end of the block, as Mustafa disappeared around the corner.

Stone darted through the main entrance of the corner shop and headed toward the side door. He emerged from the shop just in time to catch a glimpse of Mustafa, as he disappeared into a bar on the opposite side of the street. Stone waited for a taxi to pass, before he ambled across the street. He looked up at the sign. It was The Gatsby Pub. Stone glanced down the street, before darting through the door into the bar.

Mustafa was sitting alone at a table by the window. He was the only customer in the bar. Stone lingered near the door until the waiter set a bottle of Johnny Walker Black in front of the Afghani and strode away.

Stone made a beeline toward the Tajik's table. Mustafa gawked with surprise, as the American pulled out a chair and plopped down across from him.

"Mr. Mustafa?"

"Yes."

"I have some news for you about Fatima Asefi."

Mustafa's eyes widened for a moment and then narrowed with skepticism.

"Who are you?"

"My name is John Rush. I work for the U.S. government."

Mustafa stared at Stone in silence. He took a sip of whiskey. Although he appeared outwardly calm, beads of sweat began to accumulate on his forehead.

"Where is she?"

"She was convicted of murdering an ISI officer and abetting prisoners in an escape. She's been sentenced to life in prison. They've got her locked up in Rawalpindi Prison."

Mustafa downed his whiskey and poured another shot from the bottle. His hand quivered, as he clutched the gold falcon medallion hanging outside his shirt.

Stone motioned for the waiter.

"What can I get you, sir?"

"Bring me a beer. Do you have Beck's?"

"Yes, sir."

"I'll take a Beck's."

The waiter ambled away. Mustafa downed another shot and waited until the waiter was out of earshot.

"What about Fatima's son?"

"Her son's fine. A family in Rawalpindi took him in. Ms. Asefi's mother died of a stroke shortly after her arrest."

The waiter strode back to the table and set the beer down in front of Stone. He poured another drink for Mustafa and set the bottle of Johnny Walker Black in the center of the table before strolling off toward the bar. Mustafa gulped down the shot and poured another. He glared across the table at the American.

"What do you want?"

"I was hoping we could work out a deal."

Mustafa regarded the American for a moment. He glanced over his shoulder.

"What kind of deal?"

"Mr. Mustafa. I work for the CIA. Have you heard of the CIA?"

Mustafa nodded. He took another sip.

"I'm listening."

"Mr. Mustafa, we know about the vector. We know you killed the Arab in Venice."

Mustafa's expression didn't change. He wiped a sleeve across his forehead.

"I'm still listening."

"Your mission's over, Mr. Mustafa. Mr. Ahmed and Mr. Mohammajon are also under surveillance. We just want the vector. If you tell me where to find it, we'll use our influence to get Fatima Asefi's prison sentence shortened."

Mustafa stared into Stone's piercing blue eyes, taking the measure of the man. He lifted the bottle and refilled his glass. He took another sip.

"No deal. I'm familiar with CIA tricks. What did you say your name was?"

"John Rush."

Mustafa struggled to control the rage within.

"Well, Mr. Rush, your word means nothing to me. Do you think we've forgotten how you Americans abandoned us after the Russians left our country? You stood by and did nothing while the ISI and their Taliban puppets raped and slaughtered our women and children. You did nothing while they killed our leaders and stole our land. You did nothing! New York was a party compared to what the Taliban did to my people the past five years. You'll abandon us again just as soon as it suits your purpose."

Mustafa's speech was becoming slurred. He threw back another shot of whiskey without diverting his red-eyed stare from Waverly.

"Here's my offer. Take it or leave it. Get Fatima out of prison. Once she's out, I want you to take her and her son to Santa Fe, New Mexico, and set them up with a place to stay and enough money to live comfortably. I'll give you what you want as soon as my conditions are met. Do you understand?"

"Mr. Mustafa, Fatima Asefi murdered a Pakistani colonel. We can petition the Pakistanis for leniency, but we can't just get her released."

"He was a dog! If Fatima killed him, he deserved what he got! This is my offer. Take it or leave it. The vector is in a safe place. Set up Fatima in Santa Fe and I, Mustafa, will tell you where to find it."

Waverly sat for a moment pondering the Tajik's offer. Finally, he nodded with trepidation.

"We can't do this overnight, Mr. Mustafa. It'll take some time."

"I've got all the time in the world."

"You must not tell anyone about our deal. Do you or your colleagues have plans to leave Amsterdam?"

"There are no plans to leave Amsterdam for the next month."

"Is the vector here in Amsterdam?"

Mustafa shook his head.

"I have nothing else to say. I'll tell you what you want to know when Fatima is in Santa Fe."

"Okay, I'll meet you here a week from today. Two o'clock. Don't expect too much. I'll update you on whatever progress we've made."

"Mr. Rush, the vector is already activated. It'll be released if you expose me. Don't mess with me."

"Mr. Mustafa, we won't mess with you, as long as you don't mess with us. I'll see you here next Saturday."

Stone stood up and put a bill on the table. He nodded at Mustafa and strode from the bar.

Shane carefully transferred three rectangular agarose gels to the ultraviolet viewing box. Each gel had PCR amplifications from all six A samples and all fourteen B samples generated with primers designed from the sequences isolated by subtraction hybridization. Each gel also had a sizing sample containing multiple standardized bands that ranged in length from one hundred to one thousand base pairs.

Shane pulled his goggles down and flipped the light switch on the viewing box. He peered down at the first gel. All six A samples had a clear, fluorescent pink band of the appropriate size. Ten of the B samples didn't have the band, but four did.

He moved the second gel over the UV light source. Four of the A samples and eight of the B samples had the appropriate band. Shane looked up toward the ceiling and took a deep breath. He sighed and smacked his hand down on the bench top.

"Shit!"

He moved the first two gels off the box and slid the third agarose gel over the light source. All six A samples had bright bands two hundred base pairs in length. The band was missing from all fourteen B samples.

Shane clutched his fist and pumped his arm in the air.

"Yes!"

He leapt and skipped across the room in a dance of joy.

"It worked! I did it!"

It took a few minutes for Shane to regain his composure. He rotated a digital camera with a UV filter over the light box and recorded several images of the gel. He labeled the print.

Shane unwrapped a disposable scalpel and carefully cut out one of the A bands from the third gel. He transferred the sliver of agarose to a plastic tube and snapped the top closed.

He glanced up at the clock on the wall. It was a little after two in the morning.

Shane retrieved a pair of boxes from the refrigerator and sorted several reagents out on the bench top. He isolated the amplified DNA from the sliver of gel and inserted it into a special bacterial DNA tool called a plasmid. The plasmid was designed to link with DNA fragments amplified by PCR. He purified the bacterial plasmid containing the A DNA with reagents from the second kit. He inserted the plasmid-A DNA hybrid into a bacterial host and plated it on several agar plates to allow it to replicate.

He was done! He'd isolated a DNA sequence unique to all of the A DNA samples and absent in all of the B DNA samples. He'd cloned the sequence and inserted it into host bacteria. All he had to do was provide Ahmed Jan with the sequence of the unique fragment, the PCR primers, and a sample of the bacteria containing the clone.

Shane carried the plates into the side room in his lab. He opened the door to an incubator, placed the plates on the bottom shelf, and shut the door. He ambled back to the main lab and began to open the door, but suddenly froze in his tracks. He pondered for a moment, before returning to the incubator. He opened the door, took the top plate from the stack, and shut the door.

Shane walked to his office and unlocked his desk drawer. He retrieved the bound notebook labeled "Amsterdam" and slipped out of the office. He jogged to the elevator. The door rumbled open as soon as he punched the call button. He stepped in and selected the third floor. He glanced at his watch. It was just short of five in the morning.

Shane stepped out onto a corridor extending nearly a third of a mile from the K research wing to the hospital. He walked along the deserted hallway into the nearby H-wing. The first door on the right was the Microbiology Core. He fetched a magnetic card from his wallet and slid it over an entry panel to the right. The lock clanked open and he pushed through the door.

He flipped on the lights. The room was filled with dozens of incubator cabinets, flask shakers, and refrigerators. Shane picked up a marker pen from the desk. He wrote "Dr. Kalakan lab" on the plate and set in on the bottom shelf in the first 37-degree incubator.

Shane opened the door to the hall. An elderly policeman was standing outside the door writing on a clipboard. The cop looked up with surprise as Shane turned off the lights and shut the door. Shane walked down the hall toward the exit.

"Excuse me sonny!" the policeman called after him. "I need to see your I.D."

Shane turned and pulled his wallet from his back pocket. He fumbled through the credit card holder until he found his university I.D. card. He handed it to the policeman. The old man glanced at it, recorded the employee number on his clipboard, and handed the card back.

"Working a little late for a Saturday night, aren't you, Doc?"

"My grant renewal's due in two weeks. I'm trying to get a few last-minute experiments done."

"I admire your determination, laddie. What specialty are you?"

"I'm a molecular anthropologist."

"Whew, that's a mouthful. Which end do you work on?"

"Which end?"

"Does an antapoligist work on the upper or the lower?"

Shane cocked his head with a quizzical expression.

"I still don't understand what you're asking."

"Do you work near the mouth or the near the bum?"

Shane mused for a moment. Suddenly, he tilted his head back and laughed.

"I'm not a medical doctor, I'm a researcher. I study gene pools in North America."

The old man scratched his head.

"Well, I'll be damned. But I guess somebody needs to study those pools. Why ain't you working in the oceanography building?"

"I work where my chairman tells me to work. They ran out of space over in oceanography."

"Well, keep your nose to the grindstone, sonny, and someday you'll get into medical school. It took my next-door neighbor's grandson three tries to get in. You work hard enough and you will too. Well, I gotta skedaddle. My shift is over soon. I hope you get that grant, sonny."

Shane shrugged his shoulders and smiled. He watched the old man limp away toward the K-wing, before turning to head for the parking lot.

It took Shane ten minutes to drive from the medical school to his boat-house. He crawled into bed a little before six in the morning. Exhausted from a long night of work, he was asleep before the grandfather clock in the living room began to chime.

CHAPTER THIRTY-NINE

I t was a crystal clear day with temperatures in the low eighties and the lake outside was teeming with sailboats, powerboats, and kayaks. Shane felt exhilarated. This would be the first day in nearly two months he didn't awake with the unfinished project weighing on his subconscious. It was also Sunday … Teresa's birthday. He felt a sudden twinge of doubt.

"Watch, she probably won't come," he mumbled to himself.

It was damn near impossible to sleep with Buster romping and barking in the living room. He was ready to get out on the sailboat where he could get a better view of the other hounds scampering and barking along the boat decks. Shane threw his covers off and jumped into the shower. It was just before noon.

Shane decided to wait until Monday before calling Ahmed Jan in Amsterdam. He wasn't sure what the response would be when he relayed the good news about the project. The Afghanis might decide to jump on a plane immediately. He knew they had a contact in the area. No sense risking the arrival of unwanted guests. Especially today.

He slipped on a pair of jeans and a sailing shirt. He pulled on leather boat shoes and donned a sailor's hat with the bill cocked slightly to one side. Finally satisfied with his image in the mirror, he stepped into the kitchen.

Buster was barking at the picture window, as he jumped back and forth across the couch. Two kayakers were paddling just beyond the end of the dock. A snow-white poodle adorned with a blue bow was spinning and yapping on the bow of the lead kayak.

"Buster, get down off the couch!"

Buster howled one final time and jumped down with his tail wagging. He ran to the kitchen and sniffed his empty bowl.

"Are you hungry, boy?"

Buster cocked his head to one side and howled even louder.

"You want a cookie?"

The Dalmatian spun around with mounting excitement. He threw his head back and howled once again. Shane opened the pantry and pulled a couple of large dog biscuits from a box on the top shelf.

"Sit."

Buster sat and Shane balanced one of the biscuits on the end of his nose. The Dalmatian sat perfectly still with the biscuit resting in front of his eyes.

"Okay."

Buster flipped the biscuit skyward and grabbed it out of the air. He wagged his tail, as he chomped the treat down.

"Good boy!"

Shane tossed the second biscuit on the floor and scooped food into Buster's bowl. Buster finished off the second biscuit and began crunching down his breakfast.

Shane opened the freezer and fetched a container of coffee. He filled the automatic coffeemaker with water, measured eight scoops of French roast, and pushed the switch to start the cycle. The coffee-maker began to sputter.

He dragged a cooler out of the pantry and poured two bags of crushed ice into the bottom. He fetched two bottles of Veuve Clicquot Yellow Label from the refrigerator and plunged them into the ice. He gathered up three blocks of cheese, an assortment of fruit, and three submarine sandwiches. He stacked the food in the cooler with plastic plates, a knife, and a couple of champagne glasses. Finally, he took a Tupperware cake box out of the refrigerator and set it on top.

Shane closed the top on the cooler and secured the latch. He grasped the handles and hauled the cooler out the front door.

"What a day!" he whispered, as he scurried across the dock.

He put the cooler down on the edge of the dock next to the sailboat and raised a hand to shelter his eyes. The Windex on the top of the mast was pointing due south. He gauged the breeze at just over twelve knots.

"Perfect!"

It took him just a minute to pull off the cockpit cover. He lugged the cooler down into the cabin and stowed it beneath the table.

Shane opened several windows on the starboard side of the boat. He checked to make sure the electrical cord was plugged in, before turning on the air conditioner and bounding up the stairs to the deck.

He scurried back to the kitchen and poured himself a cup of coffee. He added a dash of condensed milk from the refrigerator and took a bite out of an old-fashioned glazed donut.

"Buster! Where are you?"

Buster barked from behind the closed bedroom door.

"How'd you get in there?"

Shane walked toward the bedroom.

"Looking for something?" a female voice purred.

He whirled around toward the unexpected voice. Teresa was standing in the middle of the living room in a short, baby-blue terry robe with her hair tied up in a French twist. There was a huge white bow tied around her waist. She was grinning from ear to ear.

"Wow, you look great!"

Teresa pouted her cherry red lips.

"You didn't call me."

"I tried to call several times yesterday. I kept getting a busy signal."

"Really? My roommate must have been on the phone. Okay, then, I forgive you."

"You're early."

"I know, I'm sorry. I just couldn't wait to see you."

Shane smiled.

"I've been watching the clock for two days myself. What's with the bow?"

"I brought you a present."

"Oh yeah, what is it?"

"You've gotta unwrap it."

Shane grinned and stepped across the room. He pulled the bow. The robe fell open and Teresa let it slide off her shoulders to the floor. She was wearing a metallic blue micro bikini with a thong bottom that highlighted her perfect hourglass figure. The top barely covered her ample breasts. She was stunning.

Shane's mouth dropped open. Teresa wrapped her arms around his waist and kissed him on the lips. She cuddled against his chest. Shane wrapped his arms around her and kissed her again. He ran his hands down her back and kissed her on the neck and shoulders. Suddenly, he dropped his hands to his side and stepped back.

"We've gotta stop. I can't take this anymore."

Teresa smiled and took his hand.

"What time is it?"

Shane glanced at his watch.

"Twelve forty-five."

"Well, grandma, I just turned twenty-five."

Shane shook his head and grinned. He picked Teresa up in his arms and carried her to the window. He drew the curtain, kicked the front door closed, and shuffled to the couch. He sat down in the middle of the couch and turned Teresa around to face him. He kissed her again, as he pulled the tie loose on her bikini top. It dropped across his thighs.

"God, you're beautiful!"

Teresa stepped from the bathroom wearing a black Speedo one-piece. Her hair was pulled back in a ponytail. She smiled, gave Shane a hug, and kissed him on the cheek. Buster whimpered and nuzzled her leg. He ran off toward the front door and scampered back into the bedroom a moment later. Teresa chuckled.

"I think Buster's ready to rumble."

"He's been ready since the sun came up this morning. Right, Buster? You want to go sailing?"

Buster threw his head back and howled. He barked and scurried away toward the front door.

"What happened to the blue bikini?"

Teresa held up her sports bag.

"It's in here with the sushi. I don't want you to run your precious boat aground."

"More likely we'd never get away from the dock."

She smiled.

"I'll bring it along just in case."

"In case what?"

Teresa fluttered her eyes and grinned.

"In case you get bored with the conversation."

She wrapped her arm around Shane's waist and kissed him again.

They headed out the front door and Shane locked the deadbolt behind them. Buster ran ahead and jumped into the boat. He edged along the starboard side onto the bow. He barked twice and spun around to make sure they were following.

"He's ready to go," Teresa chuckled.

"He's been this way ever since he was a pup. I lived on a sailboat in San Diego when I was a post-doc. He grew up on the water."

Teresa crawled over the side of the boat into the cockpit. She fished through her bag, found a pair of sunglasses, and slipped them on.

Shane untied the lines from the cleats and jumped on the stern. He turned the key and the engine sputtered to life. He revved the engine, pulled the throttle back, and edged away from the dock. The boat cleared the pylons and he turned to starboard and motored toward the cut.

The sunlight sparkled on the water, as the boat skirted over the wake of a yacht headed in from Lake Washington. Buster ran from one end of the bow to the other, barking and frolicking in the breeze. Teresa smiled and leaned her head against Shane's shoulder.

"What a great birthday gift. Thank you, Shane."

Shane leaned over and kissed her on the forehead.

"Me too. It's rare to have an ideal wind day in the summer. You must be a lucky charm. I couldn't imagine a better way to spend my birthday."

Teresa shielded her eyes from the sun and looked up at Shane.

"It's your birthday too?"

Shane grinned.

"Tomorrow is my thirtieth."

Teresa frowned.

"Why didn't you tell me?"

"You didn't give me a chance. You drove off before I could say a word."

Shane kissed her and brushed her hair back across her ear with his palm.

"Besides, this is all I really wanted."

Shane turned the wheel and fell in line behind a yacht. There were dozens of kayaks and canoes darting across the channel at the end of the cut. Shane slowed to let them pass, before motoring on toward Lake Washington.

"Look!" Shane yelled, as he pointed toward the south.

Mount Ranier, capped with snow, jutted majestically above the Evergreen Bridge.

"It's so beautiful," Teresa said. "I've never seen it from the water."

Shane turned the sailboat directly into the wind once they made the last channel marker.

"Teresa, keep the boat headed for the mountain. I'll raise the sails. Buster, come!"

Buster scampered along the port side of the boat and jumped into the cockpit. The sail luffed in the stiff breeze, as Shane hauled it up the mast and secured the line. He released the line on the jib sail, unrolled it, and wound the line around the winch on the port side. He leaped back into the cockpit.

"Okay. Get ready to duck!"

Shane turned toward the east. The wind caught the sails and the hull sliced through the water like a knife. The balmy breeze gusted through Teresa's hair. She turned her head and relished its warmth against her skin.

Shane and Teresa spent the day sipping champagne, sampling cheese and sushi, and sailing back-and-forth from one end of Lake Washington to the other. Shane pulled in the sails for a couple of hours in the late afternoon and dropped the anchor. They sunbathed on the bow and whiled away the afternoon to a medley of ballads by Jimmy Buffet, Don Henley, and Jackson Browne.

"This music reminds me of my dad," Teresa mused. "During the summer we'd drive along the beach in his convertible blasting the stereo. He loved Don Henley. I was trying to think of the song that always reminds me of the beach."

"*The Boys of Summer?*"

"That's it! I love that song."

"My foster dad taught me to love this music. He owned a sailing school. I worked on the boats and listened to these songs for weeks on end."

The sun plunged beneath a line of fluffy clouds and set behind the hills that line the west shore of Lake Washington. It was a spectacular sunset with crests of orange, blue, and crimson. The *View Corridor* drifted toward the north end of the lake and the clouds changed to shades of violet that reflected across the water. Teresa snuggled up to Shane and took his hand. The sun slipped away on one side of the boat and the full moon rose on the other. She took a deep breath and sighed.

Shane started the engine, motored into Juanita Bay, and maneuvered between a pair of yachts that were anchored just beyond the boardwalk. Their gentle wake was the only ripple in the bay. He dropped the anchor and flipped on the anchor lights.

"Ready for some cake?"

"You got a cake?"

"Sure, I baked it myself. It's my specialty."

"You're just full of surprises, Shane Kalakan."

He bowed, swept his hand in a wide arc, and pointed to the cabin.

"Lady Teresa, the chef requests the pleasure of your company in the galley."

Teresa stepped gingerly down the stairs into the cabin. It was furbished in teak wood and leather with an oval table and couch to one side. Buster whimpered until Shane lifted him down from the deck. He jumped up onto the bed in the bow and curled up to take a nap.

Teresa sat on the couch, while Shane opened one of the cupboards over the stove and pulled down a Tupperware cake container. He placed the container on the table and pulled off the top to reveal a two-layered cake covered with candles.

"German chocolate! That's my favorite."

"It's mine too," Shane laughed.

He struck a match and lit each of the candles.

"Okay, make a wish and blow them out."

Shane looked down at Teresa. Tears were streaming from her eyes. He sat down and wrapped his arm around her.

"Teresa, what's the matter?"

She picked up one of the napkins and blotted her cheeks. She smiled.

"I'm sorry. Nothing's wrong. I'm just so happy."

"Well, it won't do for you to cry on your birthday. Make a wish and blow them out."

She smiled, blew out all the candles with one breath, and kissed him on the cheek.

"Do you want to know my wish?"

"Don't tell me. If you tell, it won't come true."

Shane cut two pieces and transferred them to the plates. Teresa took a bite.

"It's so good!" she mumbled with wide eyes and a full mouth.

They each ate a piece and shared another. Shane opened the second bottle of champagne and poured two glasses.

"So, Shane, are you going to tell me what you're working on in the lab?"

Shane folded his arms across his chest and leaned back into the seat.

"I told you the truth. I'm trying to find a way to distinguish subgroups in a heterogeneous population by using genetic polymorphisms."

"Why all the secrecy?"

Shane sat up and turned toward Teresa. He took a deep breath.

"Can you keep a secret?"

She nodded.

"Of course."

"Promise me."

"I promise. I won't tell a soul."

"Okay. A company in Amsterdam hired me. They came to me with an idea for identifying specific genetic variations that can be used to distinguish the ancestry of a subgroup of a heterogeneous population. They hired me with the stipulation that I would do all the work myself. They forbade me from even using people in my own lab to help."

"Why'd you agree to do that?"

"It's interesting work and the pay is great. I finished the project yesterday. The pilot worked just the way I designed it."

"That's great, Shane. So you've already finished the project?"

"All I need to do is send them the data and the clone. They paid me an advance. I get the rest of the money once they verify the sequence. Please, don't tell a soul."

"My lips are sealed."

"How about spending two weeks with me in the San Juan Islands to celebrate?"

"I'd love to! When?"

"As soon as I get paid. How about August? We'll take the boat and spend a couple of weeks island-hopping from Victoria to Orcus Island. We can spend a few days each in Friday Harbor, Roche Harbor, and Rosario. Have you ever hiked up to the observation tower on the top of Mount Constitution?"

"No, I've never even been to the San Juans."

"We've gotta fix that. From the observation tower you can see Vancouver, Mount Baker, and most of the islands."

"It sounds wonderful."

Shane kissed her on the cheek.

"Now let me ask you something."

"Sure, anything you want."

"Why me?"

"What do you mean?"

"I mean, you must have men ask you out all the time."

She gave him an impish smile.

"I don't know. You seemed so sweet when I was in your class."

"Really! So when did you decide you wanted to get to know me?"

"Over a year ago. I had an awful crush when I took your class."

"Come on! I thought you showed up at my office to ask questions out of a burning interest in science."

"Yeah right, Dr. Kalakan. You're the only person who didn't know. Someone slipped an anonymous note into my textbook suggesting I might be more successful getting you into bed if I sat in the front row with a short skirt and no underwear."

"I'm sure that would've piqued my interest."

"No, I tried. It didn't work."

Shane looked at Teresa with a wide-eyed expression of shock.

"I'm kidding. Actually, the note was much more blunt. I think the exact words were something like, 'You might have more success getting Kalakan if you sit up front and wear that short Levi skirt without the thong. Bitch!' "

"Really?"

"Yeah, I still have the note somewhere. I suspect it was Natalie Frontiare. She had a crush on you too."

"Where was I when this was going on?"

"I thought you were just a typical brilliant scientist living in your own private Idaho. Then I heard about your fiancée."

Shane stood up and began to clear the plates from the table in silence. He filled the sink with soapy water, washed the plates and utensils, and put them back in the cabinets. Teresa waited patiently.

"You heard about Abby?"

"I heard some people talking about her at work last summer. I'm sorry if I touched a nerve."

Teresa stood up from the table and gave him a tender embrace.

"Are you okay?"

Shane smiled glumly and nodded his head. He took both of her hands in his.

"I'm better now than I've been for a long, long time. I feel alive again, thanks to you Teresa."

Teresa smiled and traced the back of her hand across his chest.

"How about a little more therapy?"

Shane turned his head and looked over his shoulder. Buster was rolled up among the pillows on the bed. He was sound asleep.

"I've got an idea. How about if we motor back to my house? I'll let Buster sleep in the boat."

Teresa mocked shock with a wide-eyed look. She put her hand to her mouth and smiled.

"Are you trying to get me into bed, Dr. Kalakan?"

"Absolutely. I'll make you a deal. I'll take you out to breakfast in the morning."

"Sounds great! How about the Boat Street Café? I heard they have a fantastic brunch."

"Should I pick you up in the morning or just roll over and give you a nudge?"

Teresa grinned and playfully tickled his side.

"I'll spend the night at your place under two conditions, Dr. Kalakan. First, you take the day off tomorrow. Second, you let me take you out to dinner for your birthday tomorrow night."

"That's a deal. Come on, help me pull up the anchor."

Shane eased the boat into the slip and threw the engine in reverse to bring it to a stop. He leaped out to the deck and tied the bow and stern lines. He climbed back down the stairs into the galley and filled one of Buster's bowls with chow and another with water. Buster stared up, as Shane hoisted the cooler to the top of the ladder.

"You're sleeping in here, Buster. See you in the morning."

Shane closed the door and stepped onto the dock next to Teresa.

"I feel bad, Shane. Don't leave Buster out here. He can sleep in the house with us."

"He's fine. He loves the boat. He'll whine all night long if we don't let him sleep in the bedroom."

Teresa wrapped her arm around Shane's waist.

"See you in the morning, Buster," she called out.

"What's up, Shane?"

Shane and Teresa jumped at the sound of the male voice behind them. It was Dan. He was standing in his swim trunks with his arms folded across his chest, smiling like a Cheshire cat. He motioned toward them with a bottle of beer.

"What the hell's going on here?"

"Hey, buddy. We've been out on the lake. When did you get home?"

"Just a couple of hours ago. I was just washing my boat down when I saw your running lights."

"How was Lopez?"

"It was phenomenal. There wasn't a cloud in the sky for the past seven days. The sailing out on the sound was great."

Dan smiled at Teresa.

"Hi, Teresa."

"Hey, Dan."

"I didn't know you two knew each other."

Teresa smiled coyly, as she clung to Shane's side and brushed her hair back from her face.

"So I leave town for a week and I come home to find my erstwhile buddy shacking up with the woman of my dreams. Teresa, let me know if he doesn't treat you right. Mine's bigger than his."

Shane rolled his eyes.

"Goodnight, Dan."

"I meant my boat! Listen, I got a bottle of Southern Comfort on the boat. You two want to party?"

Teresa grabbed the belt loop on Shane's shorts and pulled him toward the front door of the boathouse.

"Come on, stud."

Shane shrugged his shoulders. He smiled and followed obediently, as Teresa dragged him past Dan to the door. She fished the keys out of Shane's pocket, unlocked the door, and yanked him into the living room.

Dan hadn't moved. He stood dumbfounded with astonishment.

"Goodnight, Dan," Teresa called out, as she waved and closed the door.

CHAPTER FORTY

June 18, 2002

A hmed set his bags down on the hardwood floor and unlocked the apartment door. He pushed the door open with a shoulder and slid the bags through the doorway into the foyer.

Mustafa was slouched over in one of the high-back chairs in the living room. A half-empty bottle of Johnny Walker Black sat on the table next to him. He was holding a shot glass in his hand. Ahmed tried to ease the door closed with his suitcase, but the catch wedged against the door jam. He kicked the door closed with his heel. The bang startled Mustafa awake.

Mustafa peered bleary-eyed through the darkness, before leaning his head back against the chair. He closed his eyes without speaking.

Ahmed carried his bags into the bedroom. The bed was dishoveled and smelled of vomit. Blankets, sheets, and pillowcases were piled on the floor in one corner of the room. A soiled terry towel was lying near the head of the mattress. It was weighed down with a phone book and several magazines.

Ahmed set his bags down near the closet and headed back to the kitchen. He opened a cabinet door, but the shelves were empty. He fetched a dirty glass from the sink, rinsed it with tap water, and took a drink.

"Where've you been?" Mustafa called out from the darkness.

Ahmed walked into the living room and flipped on a lamp. Mustafa was slouched in the same chair with his eyes closed. His hair was a matted mess.

"I left for a few days to take care of some business."

"Mullah Habid called last night from Kabul. There's a message on the answering machine. He said he'd call back around ten tonight."

"You sick again?"

"Yeah, I've been sick for the past few days."

"You'd feel better if you'd stop drinking. You're poisoning yourself, Mustafa."

"I'd feel a lot better if you and Mohammajon would just mind your own damned business. It's none of your concern, just like it's none of my concern if you want to keep shooting up with whatever you keep hidden in that little black box."

Ahmed clinched his teeth in anger and grabbed Mustafa by the collar. He jerked Mustafa's head around.

"Listen to me, you drunken fool! You *are* my business! You're jeopardizing the mission. Half the time you're passed out and the other half you're stumbling around in a drunken stupor shooting your mouth off to whores all over the Red Light District. Fatima should have left you to the ISI. She gave her life. For what?"

Mustafa cocked his head to one side and leered up at Ahmed. His puffy red eyes were like road maps. He gripped Ahmed's hand and strained to pry his fingers open, but he didn't have the strength. He clutched the golden falcon around his neck.

"You're right, Commander Jan. You're always right. Only the whiskey drowns the guilt and pain I feel within my heart."

Mustafa put his arms on the chair and tried to rise to his feet. Ahmed pushed him back down into the seat and held him there with his arm.

"Let me up, damn it!"

"Go back to sleep."

After a few moments of futile struggle, Mustafa stopped fighting and eased back into the chair. He picked up the whiskey bottle in his trembling right hand. The bottle clattered against the lip, as he slowly refilled the glass.

Ahmed swung his free hand and swiped the bottle into the air against the wall. It shattered into pieces across the living room floor.

"Bastard!" Mustafa bristled. "You're just like your father!"

Ahmed shook him by the collar.

"Look at you! You're a disgrace to our people! I'm cutting off your support. You can scrounge around in the gutters with the other worthless drunks."

The door flew open behind them. It was Mohammajon.

"Shut up! Both of you! I could hear you shouting from across the street. Ahmed, let go of him!"

Ahmed dropped his arm.

"I'm sick of him sitting around here stinking drunk. We can't rely on him anymore. Have you been in the bedroom? He puked his guts out all over the mattress."

"Awar Mohammed did that. He spent the night here last night. He's been sick as a dog. I had to take him to the emergency room early this morning. The doctor thinks he has liver cancer."

Ahmed took a deep breath and shook his head before walking into the kitchen and opening the refrigerator. There was a bag of bagels on the top shelf. He grabbed a plain bagel and took a bite. He mumbled with a full mouth.

"Mustafa's got a week to shape up or get out. I'm not putting up with anymore of his drinking and whoremongering."

Mohammajon stooped to the living room floor and picked up the glass. He placed the pieces onto an unfolded newspaper. He carefully rolled the newspaper into a ball and carried it to the kitchen. He opened the broom closet and tossed the newspaper into the trashcan.

"Ahmed, where've you been the past three days?"

"I had to take care of some business."

"Where's the vector? The vial isn't in the dresser."

"Don't worry. It's in a safe place."

"Have you taken it upon yourself to make all the decisions about this mission?"

"Mullah Habid ordered me to secure the vector. Taliban forces are regrouping in the South around Khost. Several interim government leaders disappeared from the area around Kabul the past few weeks. Some were Pashtun tribal elders loyal to Karzai, but two were Northern Alliance generals. Mullah Habid believes it's only a matter of time before the country erupts into renewed fighting."

Mohammajon leaned against the kitchen counter with his arms extended, facing away from Ahmed.

"So that's it? After all we've been through, you don't need us anymore."

"Mohammajon, this mission is for you and all the Tajik people. If, as you believe, the Pashtun moderates maintain peace with the Tajiks, then this mission can be aborted at any time. If not, then we will use this weapon to defend our people."

"This plan is against the teachings of the prophet."

"Mohammajon, in the name of Allah, the Taliban and al-Qaida planned to use the vector on the Tajiks. For all we know, they already have a new supply. We can't afford to sit back and wait to see what happens. The evidence is clear. The Taliban and al-Qaida are still operating in Afghanistan, and they're bent on nothing less than the total annihilation of our people. They'll take revenge in any way they can. It is their way of life."

"What about the thousands of innocent women and children who will die? Have you no pity left in your heart, Ahmed Jan?"

"I regret the killing of the innocent. I pray Allah will prevent it."

Mohammajon turned to face Ahmed. The two men stared into each other's eyes.

"Ahmed, you have the power to protect the innocent."

"You've changed Mohammajon. Where do your loyalties lie? No man can serve two masters."

Ahmed pulled a telegram out of his pocket and handed it to Mohammajon.

"This is a message from Mullah Habid. He orders you and Mustafa to return to Afghanistan immediately."

Mohammajon shook his head. To Ahmed's eye, his Tajik comrade appeared at least a decade older than he had on the wintry day they first met in Kabul. His eyes were heavy and his face drawn. Mohammajon glanced at the message and turned away.

"I need two weeks to get my affairs in order here in Amsterdam. I'll return to Afghanistan the first of July."

"Will you take Mustafa?"

"That'll be up to him."

"I'll continue his subsidy for two weeks. He'd be better off in Kabul, far from the temptations that have been his undoing. He'll be dead in less than six months if he stays here."

"I'll talk with him."

Ahmed strode across to Mohammajon and grasped his arm.

"Mohammajon, I'm sorry it had to go this way."

Mohammajon nodded without speaking.

"I'm leaving again for a few days, Mohammajon. I'll be back in time to purchase your airline tickets. Here are two hundred euros."

Mohammajon did not reply. Ahmed put the bills down on the countertop and walked out the front door.

CHAPTER FORTY-ONE

I t was surprisingly cool for an early summer afternoon in Amsterdam. The heavy rain of the early morning hours had dissipated into a nearly perfect day. A light breeze fluttered through colorful flowers in hanging baskets lining the narrow, brick street.

The sidewalk was teeming with tourists and shoppers. Mustafa glanced over his shoulder toward the bridge, as he crossed the street. A gang of rambunctious boys was enjoying the first day of summer break by peddling through the Red Light District on bicycles fitted with playing cards clamped across the spokes of their wheels. The chatter of the cards and the cheery shouts of the boys rose to a crescendo, before fading away into the distance. An old couple pushed a grocery cart filled with flowers along the sidewalk on the opposite side of the street.

Mustafa ducked through the doorway into the Gatsby Bar. Half the tables were occupied by an assortment of tourists and regular customers. Stone Waverly was sitting at a table near the back of the restaurant. He looked up from his newspaper.

Mustafa made a beeline across the bar and sat down at the table facing the door. His breathing was labored and there was perspiration beading on his forehead.

"Sorry I'm late. I had to wait for my countryman to leave the apartment."

"No problem. You don't look well. Can I buy you a drink?"

"Thank you. I'll have a glass of orange juice."

Stone called the waiter over and ordered the juice and another Heineken for himself. They made small talk about the festival in the center of the city until the waiter brought the drinks with a tray of nuts.

Mustafa took a drink of his orange juice and set the glass down on the table. He wiped his mouth with a napkin and blotted his forehead.

"Do you have news?"

"Yes, I have very good news for you, Mustafa. We made a deal with the Pakistani government. Fatima was released from Rawalpindi Prison three days ago."

"How is she?"

"As well as could be expected. She's got dysentery and she's lost a lot of weight. We have doctors taking care of her. They expect her to fully recover. She refuses to talk about her experience in the prison. I can't imagine what it must have been like."

"Where is she now?"

"She arrived with her son yesterday in Santa Fe. The agency put them up in an apartment with enough money to buy clothing, food, and other necessities. She'll continue to receive support until she gets her nursing license and a job. Of course, that also depends on you living up to your side of the deal."

Mustafa smirked and shook his head incredulously.

"What are you shaking your head about?"

"You sons-of-bitches would do anything to get what you want. You don't give a damn how much you have to lie and cheat."

"Mr. Mustafa, I'm telling you the truth."

'I don't believe you. Those ISI bastards would never let her out of prison this quickly. You're trying to take me for a fool."

Stone lifted his briefcase off the floor and placed it on the table. He unlocked it and pulled out a small electronic device. He positioned it on the table in front of Mustafa and released a catch on the top. A screen popped out. He pushed a button on the top and the screen began to flicker. Fatima appeared on the screen a moment later. She looked frail and her hair was cut short. She was wearing a tee shirt and jeans.

Fatima held up a newspaper. The camera zoomed in and scanned the page. It was the *Santa Fe New Mexican* dated June 21, 2002. The camera zoomed out. Nadir was clinging to her side. Fatima looked up at the cameraman. Tears ran down her face, as she began to speak.

"Mustafa, my darling, I can never repay you for what you've done. I still can't believe Nadir and I are here in Santa Fe together. I don't know where you are or what you are doing, but I pray you will come to Santa Fe soon. I know I'm not much to look at, but my heart belongs to you."

With that the screen went blank. Waverly pushed the top down on the video player and stashed it back in his briefcase. He sat back in his chair and took a swig of beer.

"That doesn't prove anything. You can manipulate a video any way you want."

"You saw the newspaper."

"Yeah, but so what. It still doesn't prove she's in Santa Fe."

Stone reached into his breast pocket and pulled out a piece of paper and an international calling card. He handed them to Mustafa.

"She's waiting by the phone in her apartment. Here's her phone number."

He pointed toward a hallway on the other side of the restaurant.

"There's a pay phone back there. I'll wait here while you give her a call."

Mustafa opened up the piece of paper. He looked at Waverly, pushed his chair back from the table, and strode toward the hallway. The telephone was in an enclosed booth. He inserted the card into the phone, held the receiver to his ear, and pushed 00. The operator answered a moment later.

"International operator, may I help you?"

"Yes, can you tell me the area code for Santa Fe, New Mexico, in America?"

"Just a moment please. That area code is five-zero-five, sir."

"Okay, can you connect me?"

"What number are you trying to reach, sir?"

Mustafa called out the number. After a short pause, the phone began to ring. Someone answered the phone before the first ring ended.

"Mustafa?" she asked hopefully.

"Is it really you, Fatima?"

"Oh Mustafa, I can't believe it. I haven't been able to do a thing since Mr. Peters told me you'd call. I love you, darling."

She began sobbing uncontrollably.

"Who's Mr. Peters?"

"He's the American who's taking care of us. Where are you?"

"Fatima, I need to ask you a question."

"Of course, my love, anything. What is it?"

"Where are you?"

"We're in Santa Fe, New Mexico," she blurted, with a bewildered tone. "I thought you knew."

"Do you remember when you first told me about Santa Fe?"

"Yes, it was in the hospital in Rawalpindi."

"Why did you want to live in Santa Fe?"

There was a prolonged silence on the other end of the line. Mustafa waited for her reply.

"Because I saw a TV program about all the artists who live in Santa Fe."

Mustafa closed his eyes and took a deep breath. He smiled gratefully and clutched the phone against the side of his head.

"Fatima, forgive me for doubting you. It's just too good to be true. I'm in Amsterdam."

"Mustafa, I love you. I don't know how you got me released from prison or how you arranged for Nadir and me to get out of Pakistan. I only know you saved my life."

"Fatima, my darling, I can only repay the smallest measure of what you've done for me."

"Mustafa, come to Santa Fe. Come live with us here."

"I will come soon. I have a few things to finish up here in Amsterdam. I will be there in your arms soon. My love, there is one more thing I've ached to ask since the last time I saw you."

"Yes, Mustafa."

"Will you be my wife?"

The phone went silent and then Fatima began to sob on the other end of the line. She sniffled for a few moments, as she struggled to compose herself. Finally, she managed to murmur through the tears.

"Yes, my love. I'll willingly be your wife."

"Then Allah truly blesses me."

"Do you still have the falcon I gave you, Mustafa?"

"Of course, it never left my neck. It has been my strength all these months."

"It is the eternal symbol of my love and devotion to you, Mustafa. Nadir and I will wait for you here in Santa Fe with open arms."

The line beeped twice to indicate the time was about to expire on the calling card.

"I love you, my darling. I must go now. I'll call you again soon. Goodbye."

"Goodbye, Mustafa. I will pray Allah protects you."

Mustafa hung up the phone. He strode back into the dining room and across to the table. Waverly was sitting impatiently staring at his watch. He looked up, as Mustafa sat down.

"Are you convinced?"

"I still can't believe it."

"Mustafa, I'm losing my patience. Tell me where to find the vector."

Mustafa glanced around the room at the groups of diners. He leaned forward and spoke with a hushed voice.

"First, you must promise to let me stay in Santa Fe with Fatima. I'll work to support us. But I can't return to Afghanistan as a traitor against my people. I just want you to promise I can stay. Then I'll tell you all I know."

"I've arranged refugee status for you. You can stay in the United States as long as you obey our laws."

"Okay. I'm not certain where the vector is right now."

Waverly sighed loudly. He threw his head back and stared at the ceiling.

"Mustafa, I'm not putting up with any more of your crap. I've delivered my side of the bargain. Now, either you tell me where the vector is or I'll see that Fatima's on the next plane back to Rawalpindi."

Mustafa grabbed Stone's arm.

"I'm telling you the truth. Ahmed Jan, my countryman, removed it from its hiding place in our apartment earlier this week. He was gone for three days. But I think I know where he took it."

"Where?"

"I think he took it to Seattle."

Stone's eyes widened with disbelief.

"Shit! The vector's in the United States?"

"I can't be certain, but we've been working with an American scientist living in Seattle. He's working on a Pashtun code for the vector."

"What's the American's name?"

"Shane Kalakan."

"What else do you know about him? Do you know where he lives or where he works?"

"I just know he lives in Seattle and he works at a university. That's all I know.'

Waverly fetched a pen and small notebook from his coat pocket.

"How do you spell his last name?"

"K-A-L-A-K-A-N."

Waverly scribbled in the notebook and put it back in his pocket. He took a card out of his shirt pocket.

"Okay. I'm going to check this out. Put this card away. I want you to call this number in two days. If we find the vector, I'll make sure you get your refugee status and a visa to get into the United States. For Mrs. Asefi's sake, I hope you're not bullshitting me."

"Bullshiting you? What does it mean, 'bullshitting you'?"

"You better not be lying."

Waverly reached in his pocket and pulled out a twenty euro bill. He placed it on the table.

"There's one more thing I want to tell you, Mr. Rush."

"Yes? What is it?"

"Ahmed Jan discovered plans of the Taliban and al-Qaida to use this vector on the Tajik people in Afghanistan. Al-Qaida plans to test the vector there and then use it on Americans. This vector is still available to our enemies. We never discovered the identity of the men who brought the vector to Venice. The Arab told us he was to deliver it to a mosque in London. You must find the men who created this virus and destroy them before they kill my people."

"Mr. Mustafa, the United States will use every weapon at its disposal to eliminate this vector and all of those who are responsible."

Stone pushed his chair back and stood up.

"Call the number in two days."

Stone picked up his briefcase and strode from the restaurant. Mustafa watched the American disappear out the door. Only then did he notice a man with a long beard sitting at a table near the door. Their eyes met for just a moment. The man stood up and picked up his bag. He pushed the door open and disappeared into the crowd outside.

CHAPTER FORTY-TWO

June 22, 2002

T eresa," Shane bellowed from beneath the mast, "haul in the jib!"
Teresa released the jib sheet and pushed a button on the console. The jib sail gathered around the automated jib stay. Shane dropped the mainsail and flaked it on top of the beam. He tied three lines around the sail and secured the cover, before jumping into the cockpit next to Teresa. He took the wheel and eased in behind two other sailboats waiting for the Montlake Bridge to open.

Shane glanced at his watch. It was straight up 2 P.M. The bell sounded and the traffic gates closed atop the bridge. The last few cars cleared the metal grating and the arms of the drawbridge began to rise.

The two boats ahead of the *View Corridor* eased through the expanding gap in the center of the bridge. Shane glanced to the stern and eased the throttle forward. The graceful sailboat glided toward the opening. Teresa waved as they passed a group of children sitting on the wall lining the cut.

The mast was less than twenty meters from the gap when the red warning lights on the bridge started flashing and the siren began to wail. The arms of the bridge stopped and then began to close.

"Son-of-a-bitch!" Shane shouted. "Teresa, get below! Run!"

Teresa scurried down the ladder. Buster, sensing alarm in his master's tone, twirled and barked in the cockpit.

It was too late to turn. Shane jammed the throttle all the way forward and steered between the falling arms of the bridge. He peered upwards as the gap grew ever more narrow. The mast slipped through a moment before the bridge slammed shut.

Shane turned and gawked out over the stern in horror. The catamaran in the line behind him was attempting to turn in a sweeping arc. It didn't make it. Its mast collided with the center of the bridge and snapped off at the deck like a child's toy. The wood exploded like a cannon shot.

Shane threw the throttle in reverse and maneuvered his boat back toward the bridge to render assistance. Teresa hurriedly climbed up the stairs from below. She caught sight of the mast and sail floating in the water beneath the bridge.

"Oh my God! What happened?"

"The watchman closed the damned bridge! There'll be hell to pay for this."

Within seconds, two powerboats pulled along side of the stricken sailboat. Shane watched until he was certain the crew was safe, before easing his throttle forward.

Three fire trucks raced across the bridge with sirens blaring a moment later. A pair of rescue trucks tailed close behind.

"I wonder what's going on?" Teresa shouted.

"Something's going on at the medical school. Look, there's smoke!"

The *View Corridor* glided into the westward end of Portage Bay. It cleared the trees that lined the cut and the medical school came into view.

"Son-of-a-bitch, the K-wing is on fire!"

Teresa turned from the beehive of activity surrounding the ill-fated catamaran to behold an even greater horror. Flames were leaping from the windows of the upper floors of the K-wing of the medical school and ominous black smoke was billowing into the air above the campus.

The *View Corridor* passed beyond Jensen's boathouse and the full extent of the disaster became apparent. More than a dozen fire and rescue trucks with lights flashing were parked along the access road. Two more fire trucks rounded the corner from Pacific Avenue with sirens wailing. Two firemen were already directing streams of water into the windows from hoses along the access road. Two hook-and-ladder trucks had taken up positions along the curb. Both trucks were extending ladders toward more than a dozen screaming people leaning out of the windows on the top floors.

Shane turned the sailboat into the university marina directly opposite the burning building and steered the boat toward an empty slip against the shore.

"Where are you going, Shane?"

"I've got to get the clone."

"Shane, you can't go in there!"

Shane jumped from the boat, tied the port lines to cleats on the dock, and sprinted up the main dock to the shore. He ran along the sidewalk past the bow of the boat, shouting to Teresa as he went.

"There's a backup culture in the microbiology core in the H-wing. I'll be right back. Stay here with the boat."

Teresa watched as Shane sprinted across the parking lot and up the driveway. He disappeared around the corner next to Jensen's Boathouse.

Several more police cars and fire trucks arrived at the entry gate. The access road was choked with a solid mass of emergency vehicles. The fully extended ladders from the two trucks plucked a group of people from the upper bank of windows of the K-wing.

Shane was gone for nearly fifteen minutes before Teresa spotted him jogging down the sidewalk from Pacific Street. He ran down the driveway and leaped onto the bow of the boat.

"The whole damned K-wing is on fire," he puffed excitedly.

Shane released the lines and jumped back into the cockpit. He eased the throttle back and steered the *View Corridor* past a line of boats and into the bay.

"Is everyone okay?"

"I think so. Johnny Kline and Roger Clark were outside on the sidewalk. They were the only ones in the lab. Roger was working in the confocal facility when he heard an explosion. The flames had already spread into the hall by the time he opened the door. They think the fire started in my lab."

Teresa shook her head. She took his hand.

"Shane, did you get the clone?"

Shane reached into his pocket and pulled out a glass tube with a black cap. He held it up and then tucked it back into his pocket.

"They tried to keep me out of the H-building, but I took the stairs down to the basement and snuck in through the mechanical room. The electronic lock was disabled on the entry door to the microbiology core. I had to break the window on the door to get in."

Shane eased the boat into the slip next to his boathouse and threw the throttle in reverse. The boat slowed to a stop. He turned off the engine and secured the lines.

He helped Teresa onto the dock. The two of them stood on the end of the dock watching as firefighters poured water through the windows and onto the roof of the K-wing. A loud explosion echoed across the water. Smoke began to billow from the windows on the first floor a moment later.

"I wonder how it started, Shane?

"Some piece of equipment must have shorted out. I just hope no one was hurt."

"God, Shane, I'm so sorry."

Shane shook his head and turned away.

"I can't watch it anymore. Let's go inside. Buster!"

Buster was standing on the bow of the boat trying to maneuver close to a family of ducks in the water below. He showed no signs of obeying Shane's command.

"He's fine. He'll come in when he gets bored."

Sirens continued to blare across the bay. Shane put his arm around Teresa. She leaned her head against his shoulder, as they walked across the dock to the sidewalk and headed for the front door. Shane reached into his pocket for his keys.

The door burst open, just as Shane reached for the doorknob. A dark-skinned Arabic man holding a machine gun leaped onto the porch and motioned them inside.

"Get in the house!"

The Arab shoved Teresa through the door with the barrel of his gun. He turned and pointed the machine gun at Shane. Shane put his hands up and stepped into the living room behind Teresa.

"Don't shoot. We'll do whatever you ask."

Another Arab with a gun was crouched behind the door. Both men were dressed in long-sleeved white shirts, blue jeans, and tennis shoes. Their faces were clean-shaven.

Shane glanced around. Every cabinet and drawer in the kitchen was open. China, food, and household supplies were strewn across the floor into the living room. All the cushions from the chairs and couch in the living room were ripped open. There was foam scattered everywhere.

The bedroom door was open. The mattress had been pulled off its frame and was leaning against the headboard. Bedding and clothing were piled on the floor just inside the doorway.

The second man stood up and trained his machine gun on Shane. He spoke in perfect English.

"Give me the vector, Dr. Kalakan."

"What vector?" Shane stammered, as he scanned the jumbled room.

Without warning, the man turned his gun toward the kitchen and pulled the trigger. A burst of automatic fire sounded from the machine gun. Bullets pierced the refrigerator and blew the door completely off its hinges.

The man coolly turned back toward Shane. He made a menacing motion toward Teresa.

"I'm going to give you one more chance before I blow your pretty girl-friend's head off, Dr. Kalakan. Where's the vector?"

"Please, don't shoot. Just let me slip my hand in my pocket."

The leader motioned with his gun. Shane stared straight into the Arab's harsh and ruthless eyes. He slid his hand into his pocket, pulled out the vial, and held it out.

"I think you may be looking for this."

The Arab reached out and grabbed the vial. He raised the tube up to the light.

Suddenly, the front door crashed open. Two booming shotgun blasts blew the intruder off his feet. Shane and Teresa dove for cover behind the furniture. Buster bounded through the door. He growled viciously and leaped at the Arab leader. The man sidestepped his charge and butted Buster in the head with his gun. Buster collapsed to the floor.

Dan dove through the door and rolled across the floor. He fired another shotgun blast, just as the Arab pulled the trigger on his machine gun. The shotgun blast caught the intruder full in the face. The burst from the Arab's machine gun tore through Dan's abdomen. There was silence for a few seconds before Shane struggled to his feet.

"Oh my God, Dan!" Shane cried.

He knelt at his friend's side and pressed a dishtowel against his stomach. Blood poured from a gaping wound. It was futile.

"Teresa, call the paramedics!"

Dan tugged at Shane's arm. He peered up with glassy eyes.

"You owe me one, buddy."

Dan took a halting breath, grimaced, and closed his eyes. His body went limp.

"They killed him!" Shane screamed in anguish. "The bastards killed him!"

Shane grabbed the shotgun off the floor and pumped it. He aimed it at the leader's chest and fired off a blast. He pumped the gun again, turned, and fired another blast into the second man's lifeless body. He tossed the gun down.

Shane looked around and spotted the vial on the floor next to the Arab leader's body. He picked it up and stuck it in his pocket.

"Teresa, get on the boat!"

"Shane, call the police," Teresa pleaded.

"No, Teresa, they'll find the money."

Teresa took his head in her hands. She stared into his eyes.

"Shane, what is this? What are you involved in?"

"I don't know, Teresa. They paid me cash for the clone. I'll go to prison if they find the money here. I need time to think."

Shane sprinted to the bedroom. He slid the bed frame against the closet doors. He bent down, lifted a trap door in the floor, and fetched a briefcase from a hidden compartment. Shane slammed the door shut and pulled the frame back to the center of the room.

Buster was beginning to rouse on the living room floor. The disoriented canine tried to pull himself to his feet, but wobbled and fell back to the floor.

"Teresa, carry this briefcase to the boat. I'll get Buster."

Shane scooped up Buster and ran out the front door toward the dock. Teresa followed with the briefcase.

Across Portage Bay the fire trucks were still clustered around the K-wing of the medical school. Firemen were pouring water through the windows and onto the roof. A wisp of white smoke rose skyward from the top of the building. Sirens wailed, as a hodge podge of police and emergency vehicles rushed to and from the disaster.

Shane jumped on the sailboat and laid Buster down on the deck in the cockpit. He turned and helped Teresa into the boat before starting the engine. He leaped onto the dock, untied the lines, and jumped behind the wheel. The boat glided past the last pylon toward the middle of Portage Bay.

Shane guided the sailboat between an assemblage of boats of every size and shape adrift in the bay. Dozens of spectators crowded the decks and watched the inferno at the medical school in stunned silence. None of them gave the *View Corridor* more than a passing glance. Shane put the engine in neutral and sounded the horn.

Two police cars with flashing lights skidded to a stop on the street in front of Shane's row of boathouses. A uniformed officer leapt from each car. One of the cops brandished a pistol and the other carried a shotgun. The two men crept along the walkway toward the water. They knocked on the door of the house closest to the street. A man stepped out on the walkway and pointed down the line of boathouses. The two cops, guns at the ready, pushed the man back into his house and crept down the walkway toward the water.

The traffic alarm sounded and the guardrails lowered on the bridge. Shane glanced toward the shore one last time, as the bridge began to open. The cops reached his houseboat. One peered through the front windows, as the other crouched just outside the door. Shane pressed the throttle forward. The *View Corridor* accelerated through the gap in the bridge and skirted past Chihuli's boathouse into Union Bay.

Shane restarted the engine, as the Ballard lock gate began to open. One of the lock workers along the wall untied the lines and threw them onto the deck of the sailboat. The yacht in front of the *View Corridor* started its engine and cruised out of the gate. Shane pushed the throttle forward and fell in line behind it.

Teresa hadn't uttered a word since the sailboat left the dock at Portage Bay. Shivering uncontrollably, she huddled against Shane's side. Buster was curled up beneath Shane's feet. Teresa reached down and patted him on the head.

"Shane, what was that all about?"

Shane shook his head.

"I have no clue, Teresa. All I know is some Arab bastard just killed Dan. They were after some vector. It must have something to do with the clone."

"What's in the briefcase?"

"It's half-payment for the cloning work. I'll call the man who hired me when we clear the last channel marker."

It was a pleasant, sunny day on the Strait of Juan de Fuca. The winds were blowing out of the east at ten to fifteen knots and the swells were at two to three feet. Shane took the direct route up the strait. He programmed the autonavigation system for Friday Harbor and set the radar to warn of anything that approached within five hundred meters.

Shane fetched his wallet out of his back pocket. He slid a card out from between two photos and pointed across Teresa's lap.

"Hand me the cell phone."

Teresa grabbed the cell phone out of the cup holder and handed it to him. Shane got up and stepped down the ladder to the galley.

"Where are you going, Shane?"

"I've gotta steam this card to read the phone number. Keep an eye out for any boats in front of us."

Shane climbed out of the galley a few minutes later. He pressed the send key on the phone and held it to his ear. It took close to a minute for the call to go through.

"Mr. Jan, this is Shane Kalakan."

Shane listened for a moment before clinching his fist and pounding it on the seat.

"This *is* an emergency, damn it. Some bastard just killed my best friend with a machine gun."

Shane held the phone between his neck and shoulder. He stood up behind the wheel and looked up the strait.

"I have no idea who they were. They looked like Arabs."

He punched a button on the GPS and peered at the screen.

"No, I never saw them before. Two of them broke into my house. They were waiting for us when we got home. They were looking for something they called a vector."

Shane reached across and took Teresa's hand. He shook his head in dismay.

"They're dead. My friend shot both of them. The building that housed my lab at the university also burned down today. They probably did that too."

Shane paused again to listen.

"No, we left before the police arrived. I've got the clone with me."

Shane listened silently for several minutes. He became more agitated the longer he listened.

"Yeah, I guess we are in danger. Thanks for the timely warning," he retorted sarcastically. "Listen, pal, this wasn't part of the deal. You never said anything about somebody trying to kill me."

Shane turned the wheel slightly to the starboard to steer the boat along the shore of Lopez Island and reset the autonavigation system.

"I'm not telling you where I am! Mr. Jan, you haven't been straight with me and it almost got us killed. I'm calling the shots from now on. I'll call you at this number in two days to let you know where to meet me. You bring the rest of the money and I'll tell you where to find the clone and the sequence information. After that, I never want to see or hear from you again."

Shane listened for a few more moments.

"Just a second."

He motioned to Teresa.

"Teresa, hand me something to write on from the drawer beneath the TV in the cabin."

Teresa hustled down the stairs and returned with a pen and notepad. She handed them to Shane.

"Okay. What's the number?"

Shane wrote a number on the paper.

"Okay, I got it. I'll call you."

He hung up the phone.

"Damn it."

"What happened, Shane?"

"That was the guy who hired me to isolate the sequence. Guess what? He says we're in danger. Like yeah, I guess so."

"Did he know who those men were?"

"He thinks they might have been al-Qaida operatives."

"Al-Qaida? Why would they want the clone?"

"He wouldn't tell me over the phone. He wants me to meet him on Monday in Vancouver and give him the clone. He thinks al-Qaida will be searching for me. He told me to get a new cell phone. I'm not supposed to use this one anymore."

Shane tossed the cell phone over the side of the boat into the water.

"Shane, this doesn't make any sense."

Shane bit his lower lip and gazed out over the bow. Finally, he shook his head and pressed his face into his hands.

"I don't know what the hell's going on anymore, Teresa. I'm so sorry I got you into this mess. Kenmore Air flies out of Friday Harbor. I'll drop you off there so you can catch a seaplane to Seattle. I want you to stay with your parents in California until this is over."

"No, Shane, I'm staying with you."

"Listen to me, Teresa. Dan's dead. Do you hear me? He's dead. This isn't some game. I got myself into this and I need to get myself out."

"Shane, you need to call the police."

He shook his head.

"No. Not until I get the money and find a place to stash it. I'm going to lose my job over this. There's no doubt about it."

Teresa slipped her hand into his. She leaned her head against his shoulder.

"Shane, I love you. Wherever you go, I'm going too."

"Teresa!"

"Shhh," Teresa insisted, as she pressed her finger against his lips. "There's no way you're getting me off this boat, Shane Kalakan."

"Damn, you're a stubborn woman, Teresa Daniels."

He shook his head and hugged her against him. She held her hand out in front of Shane's face. She was still shaking.

"I think I need a drink."

Shane checked the autonavigation before scurrying down the stairs into the cabin. He reemerged with two frosty martini glasses filled with pink liquid. He handed one of them to Teresa and sat down beside her.

"It's a Cosmopolitan martini. I thought we could use a good stiff drink."

Teresa held out her glass.

"To Dan, our true friend and hero. As a wise woman once said, 'Tis better to die young in pursuit of fleeting adventure, than to live a lifetime of tranquil monotony.' "

Shane leaned back into the seat, sipped his martini, and peered out across the sparkling water. He took a deep breath and downed the last of the elixir.

"I'd settle for some monotony right now. Who said that?"

Teresa leaned over and kissed him on the cheek.

"I did."

CHAPTER FORTY-THREE

June 23, 2002

A hmed bounded up the stairs to the apartment two steps at a time. He paused outside the front door and pulled a pistol from the waistband beneath his coat. He switched off the safety and slid the gun beneath his belt. He fished a key from his pocket, unlocked the door, and stepped inside. Mohammajon was sitting in the living room reading a newspaper. He looked up.

"Good morning, Ahmed."

Ahmed looked back over his shoulder toward the bedroom.

"Where's Mustafa?"

"He left the apartment yesterday morning. He said he'd call you. He needs the money to leave Amsterdam."

Mohammajon could sense the urgency in Ahmed's tone.

"What's wrong, Ahmed?"

"The American Shane Kalakan was attacked this morning in Seattle. It sounds like the Arabs found him."

"How do you know this?"

"Haven't you heard? It's all over the news. They're saying it was a terrorist attack. The Arabs killed the American and burned down the lab at the medical school in Seattle."

"What about the vector?"

"That's a good question, Mohammajon. What about the vector? Do you have any idea how the Arabs found the American?"

"No, Ahmed, I don't know, but there's something I must show you."

Mohammajon reached into his shirt pocket and fetched an envelope. He handed it to Ahmed.

Ahmed opened the envelope and pulled out several photos. The first photo showed Mustafa sitting at a table with a Caucasian man. There were drinks on the table. In the second photo Mustafa was peering at an electronic device. The next photo showed a man handing Mustafa a piece of paper. Ahmed scowled, as he shuffled to the last photo. Mustafa was standing at a pay phone making a call.

"Where did you get these?"

"From my colleague at the Mosque. He saw Mustafa with this man at a bar. He happened to have a new camera with him."

"When were they taken?"

"Yesterday."

Ahmed sighed and shook his head. He reached into his pants pocket, retrieved a manila envelope, and handed it to Mohammajon.

"Here are three thousand euros. It'll cover your expenses for the flight home. Mullah Habid expects you next week. I paid the rent for one more week. Have you shown these photographs to Mustafa?"

"No, he hasn't been here since yesterday morning."

"Tell him to call me on my cell phone if you see him. Don't mention the photos or anything about the American."

"You will kill him?"

"Yes, if I find him, I must kill him. He betrayed our people."

Mohammajon nodded, as he regarded Ahmed's face.

"This is a decision you must weigh carefully, my son. Be wary. Mustafa is a cunning and ruthless fighter. Weak men did not survive on the front in Mazar-e-Sharif. He can do no further harm and whiskey will kill him soon enough. Where will you go?"

Ahmed shook his head.

"I don't know. I'll wait for Mullah Habid's orders."

"All that happens is Allah's will. You must remember this, Ahmed."

"Is it Allah's will for the Arabs to have the vector and use it to kill our people? No, Mohammajon, I will never accept this. Never!"

Ahmed offered his hand.

"Allah be with you, Mohammajon. You and I, we are both Tajik. But we view the world through very different eyes. Perhaps I will see you one day at a café in Kabul and we will share a loaf of naan and drink a toast to the adventure we shared."

Mohammajon stood up from his chair. He took both of Ahmed's hands in his own.

"I will not forget you, Ahmed Jan. I pray Allah will give you strength tempered by wisdom. Our people need such leaders."

"Pray for all of our people, Mohammajon."

Ahmed glanced at his watch.

"I must go."

Ahmed turned and walked to the foyer. He looked back at Mohammajon one last time. He nodded and walked out the door.

Stone Waverly scooted his chair up to the desk. The teleconferencing monitor was blank. The screen began to flicker. Deputy Chief Richards suddenly appeared on the screen. He looked even more disheveled than usual. The ever-present cigar was dangling from the corner of his mouth.

"*Guten tag,* Stone. When did you arrive in Seattle?"

Stone glanced at his watch.

"A little over six hours ago, sir. I've been out to University of Washington and Dr. Kalakan's houseboat. I just left a meeting with Brad Johnson, the FBI chief here in the Seattle office."

"Stone, this is a secure line. Marilyn Harrison and I are here in the situation room. You can speak freely. What the hell's going on there?"

"It's a fucking nightmare, sir. Two Arabs were killed in a houseboat owned by the American scientist. A dead American was found in the same house. The place was ransacked and all the furniture was torn apart. The Arabs were probably searching for the vector. The dead American was initially thought to be Shane Kalakan. But the FBI just I.D.'d him as a man named Daniel Murphy. He was the next-door neighbor. The FBI is searching for Kalakan."

Richards tossed his cigar butt into an ashtray.

"Damn it, Stone. We sent the FBI a copy of Kalakan's driver's license photo yesterday. Bunch of damned provincials. You tell Johnson I'm going to talk with his boss. The whole lot of them are bumbling idiots."

"Don't be too hard on them, sir. The first agents on the scene didn't have the photo. They weren't on the Kalakan case. The police called them as soon as they found the dead Arabs. The agents on the Kalakan case were at the medical school talking with Kalakan's boss when the fire started. It took them a while to put it all together."

"Stone, what about the fire?"

"A research building in the University of Washington School of Medicine was destroyed by an inferno at just about the same time. Someone set off an incendiary device in Dr. Kalakan's laboratory."

"Hell of a deal. Stone, what about the Armageddon vector?"

"No sign of it sir. It could have been destroyed in the fire. There was no sign of it in the house. The dead Arabs were probably not the only al-Qaida involved in this operation. They came from a cell we uncovered after 9/11. Seven of the known cell members have been under arrest since late September. There were at least five other al-Qaida operatives in the cell. The FBI has been searching for them the past nine months. Two of the five were killed in Kalakan's houseboat. We don't know whether Shane Kalakan escaped with the vector or the other members of the Qaida cell got him. No car was found in the neighborhood. Another neighbor reported seeing two Arabs in a van after the gunfire erupted. We think they were al-Qaida members driving a getaway vehicle. State records indicate Kalakan had a sailboat called the *View Corridor*. It's also missing. So they may have the vector, but we're not sure."

"How did the Arabs find him, Stone?"

Stone hesitated. He stared into the teleconferencing monitor.

"Stone?"

"Sir, I think we might want to discuss this later."

"Go ahead, Stone. I want your opinion. No use dicking around now."

"Well, sir, the killings in the boathouse occurred less than five hours after I called you about Dr. Kalakan. The timing suggests a CIA leak. I guess it's possible the leak occurred in the FBI."

Richards leaned back in his chair and pulled the cigar out of his mouth. He glanced at Marilyn Harrison.

"I already did some checking, Stone. The Arabs were killed less than half an hour after I called the FBI. There wasn't enough time for anyone from the FBI to alert al-Qaida in time for them to carry out this operation. I'll tell you what I think, Stone. We've got another damned mole here in the CIA. Only a handful of our people had access to the information. I've launched an internal investigation and I've asked the FBI to do the same. I'm going to have the bastard's balls."

Richards pulled a new cigar out of his shirt pocket and stuck it in his mouth.

"What's your next step, Stone?"

"I'm working with the FBI field office here in Seattle. We have agents looking through the rubble in Kalakan's lab and we're searching for Dr. Kalakan. There was a call from his cell phone to a cell phone in Amsterdam a few hours ago. The FBI should know by now where the call originated from and who was being called. So Kalakan may be alive or someone else may be using his phone. We're also looking for his boat."

"Stone, what about the Arabs?"

"We found a laundry slip on one of the dead Arabs. It led us to a house in a suburb of Seattle called Kirkland. The Arabs were living on Lake Washington. The FBI is going over the house with a fine-tooth comb."

"All right Stone, keep me posted. I'm meeting with the director and his staff in an hour to go over plans we're preparing with the chiefs of staff for the president's decision on an attack on the Iraqi installation at As Salman in southern Iraq. We've developed information from several sources confirming the information we got from the Iraqi defector. We're certain the vector was produced and stored in that facility. We're also going after Saddam Hussein. Ultimately, that's the only way to put an end to this crap. I expect the operation to be carried out within days."

"Hopefully they haven't distributed the vector around the country."

"They may well have. But the operation has also been planned to simultaneously neutralize the scientists working on the project. We aim to cut the head off the beast by eliminating the responsible Baath Party leadership and the scientists who created the vector."

"What support can I expect here in Seattle, sir?"

"I'm sending twenty-five field agents to Seattle, Stone. They'll all work under your supervision. The FBI director told me he was putting more than one hundred agents on this case. So you should have all the manpower you need. Let me know if you need anything else. You've got a blank check on this one."

"What happened at the Loya Jirga in Afghanistan, sir? I didn't see anything in the paper."

"Karzai was re-elected for another eighteen months. That certainly simplifies things for us. How's the family, Stone?"

"They're fine, sir. I haven't seen them for a while, but I keep in touch by phone."

"You better take that pretty wife of yours on a long vacation to Tahiti when this is over. You know, sort of a second honeymoon. Damned good woman you have there Stone. You better hang on to her."

"I'm trying to, sir."

* * *

Ahmed's cell phone rang. He set his newspaper down on the desk and flipped opened the phone.

"Ahmed."

He bolted upright in his chair.

"Where are you, Mustafa?"

Ahmed listened for a few moments. Then he leaned over and pulled a note pad and pen from the top of the desk.

"Yes, Mustafa, I've got money for you. I'm at the Rembrandt Residence Hotel at Herengracht 255. Call my room from the house phone when you get here. Don't call me on this phone again. I'm getting rid of it right after we hang up. The hotel phone number is 20-6221727."

Ahmed listened for a few more moments. He doodled on the notepad with a pen until Mustafa finished speaking.

"I understand. You need to be here within an hour. I'm leaving Amsterdam this evening."

Ahmed hung up the phone. He knelt next to the bed and slid the cell phone between the mattress and the box springs. He yanked his 9-mm semi-automatic Glock from his belt. He released the clip, ejected the bullet from the firing chamber, and reloaded it back into the clip. He reinserted the clip in the pistol and pulled back the action to transfer the first bullet into the firing chamber. He slipped the gun back beneath his belt.

Ahmed went through a mental checklist. His bag was packed and lying on the bed. He unzipped it and checked through his clothes. He re-zipped the bag. The photos of Mustafa were in an envelope in his coat pocket. His airline tickets were in his pants pocket.

He walked across the room to a recliner. He sat down, leaned back in the chair, and waited for Mustafa to arrive.

The phone rang a little over thirty minutes later.

"Hello. Yes, I'll be right down."

Mustafa was sitting on a couch in the lobby when Ahmed stepped from the elevator. He rose to his feet and strode toward Ahmed with enthusiasm. His face was clean-shaven and his hair was neatly trimmed. He gripped Ahmed's arm.

"My friend, it's good to see you once again."

"You look well, Mustafa. It's good to see you taking care of yourself."

"Allah is great, my friend. He cast out the devil and his whiskey. I've taken work at a restaurant in the west of Amsterdam. You are in a hurry. I will not delay you."

Ahmed reached into his pocket. He frowned.

"I'm sorry, I left the money in the room. Come upstairs and I'll get it for you."

The two men stepped into the elevator. The elevator churned upward and stopped on the seventh floor. Ahmed's room was a few short steps down the hall. He unlocked the door and held it open.

"Please, Mustafa, have a seat there at the table. Would you like orange juice or a Coke?"

"No, thank you. I ate lunch at the restaurant. They're expecting me back soon for the dinner shift."

Ahmed sat on the opposite side of the table from Mustafa. He slipped the gun from his belt and rested it in the chair beside him. Mustafa sensed Ahmed's unease.

"What is it, Ahmed?"

"Tell me how the Arabs found Dr. Kalakan in Seattle."

Mustafa blinked with surprise. He stared into Ahmed's eyes. His mouth went dry.

"What would I know of this?"

Ahmed reached into the breast pocket of his jacket and pulled out the envelope. He pushed the envelope across the table toward Mustafa and rested his hand on the gun.

Mustafa picked up the envelope and pulled out the photographs. His expression froze with shock, as he spied the first print. He shuffled through the four photos.

Beads of sweat began to accumulate on Mustafa's brow. He set the prints down and stared across the table. Ahmed returned his stare. The tension rose as the seconds passed. Ahmed slipped his finger onto the trigger.

"Mustafa, how could you betray your people to the enemy? You might as well slit the throats of every Tajik man, woman, and child in Afghanistan."

Mustafa's right eyelid began to twitch uncontrollably. He rubbed his brow with his hand.

"I told only the Americans, Ahmed. I did not tell the Arabs."

"Who is this man in these photos?"

"He told me he was CIA."

"Why do you come to me for money? Why didn't you get it from your

CIA friend? If he is CIA."

"I didn't ask him for money, Ahmed."

Ahmed pounded his fist on the table. His face contorted with rage.

"Then why, Mustafa? Why did you betray our people? Why did you betray me?"

Mustafa lowered his head with shame and looked toward the photos on the tabletop. He swallowed hard and coughed into his hand.

"It was the only way to save Fatima. I was desperate, Ahmed."

Mustafa wiped the sweat from his brow with his sleeve.

"Ahmed, have you ever really loved a woman? Because if you haven't, then there is no way you could understand the heartache I felt. Everything else faded to insignificance. I never knew I could ever love anyone this way."

Mustafa waited for Ahmed's response. There was none, so he continued.

"I remember when our forces ran out of water during the Taliban siege on the hills surrounding Mazar-e-Sharif. We got just a small ration each day. It was barely enough to wet a man's mouth. The waterfalls near my home in the Hindu Kush were constantly in my thoughts those two weeks. I felt the mist on my skin and the splash of the water cascading into the pool below. I even dreamed of water when I slept. Losing Fatima was far worse. I love Fatima with all my heart, Ahmed. I would have done anything to free her."

"So for this one woman you sacrificed the lives of millions of your own people?"

Mustafa gripped the side of the table. Ahmed raised the gun off the chair and pointed it at Mustafa. Mustafa peered down the barrel.

"I did not sacrifice our people, Ahmed. Only the Americans can reach the evil men who created this vector. Only the Americans can permanently end this threat to our people. You lash out, blinded by your thirst for vengeance against the Pashtun. This mission will not end the threat to our people."

Ahmed shook his head.

"Mustafa, you're a fool. This man was not CIA. He was a stoolie of al-Qaida. Fatima will not be released from Pakistan. She will remain in prison and our people will still die."

"You're wrong Ahmed. Fatima has been released. I've seen her and I've spoken with her. She's no longer in Pakistan. The American kept his promise."

"Then the Americans have traitors of their own!" he shouted. "After all we've been through together! You should have come to me, Mustafa! We could have found a way together!"

Ahmed pulled the hammer back on the pistol.

"I can't believe you did this, Mustafa."

Mustafa lowered his head. He sat silently. A tear ran down from the corner of the eye of the hardened Mujaheddin warrior. He brushed it away with his sleeve.

Mustafa took a deep breath and sighed. He looked up at Ahmed and nodded his head.

"You are right, my friend. I should have come to you. My judgment was clouded by whiskey and heartbreak. I'm a traitor and I accept my fate."

Ahmed held the gun on Mustafa for several moments. Then he dropped the barrel and slipped the gun beneath his belt. He reached into the breast pocket of his jacket and fished out his wallet. He opened it, pulled out a wade of one hundred euro bills, and pushed them across the table.

Mustafa looked down at the stack of bills. He looked up at Ahmed.

"Go on, Mustafa. Take the money. Get out of here before I change my mind."

Mustafa stood up from the table and scooped up the bills. He walked to the door.

"Mustafa!" Ahmed called after him.

Mustafa turned. Ahmed was still sitting at the table with his back to the door.

"Yes, Ahmed."

"Give Fatima my regards. Tell her I'll always be grateful. I'll always honor her name."

Mustafa stood for a moment with his hand on the doorknob.

"I will, Ahmed. I will."

Ahmed nodded. Mustafa opened the door and stepped into the hall. He eased the door closed behind him.

CHAPTER FORTY-FOUR

Teresa opened her eyes and stared up through the vented window above the bed. The darkness was yielding to a crystal clear morning. She glanced at the clock on the nightstand. It was a little after six.

She fetched her robe from the hook beside the bed and gathered it around her. Then she slipped on her boat shoes and wandered bleary-eyed into the galley.

The automatic coffeemaker was just finishing the last sputter of its cycle. Teresa fetched two mugs from the dish drainer. She filled the cups with coffee and topped them off with a splash of canned milk.

Teresa started up the ladder and set the mugs on the deck, before hurrying up the remaining stairs. Shane was sitting at the bow with his knees pressed to his chest, gazing toward the end of the bay. Buster was curled up beside him.

Teresa squatted to pick up the mugs. She tiptoed along the port side of the boat. Shane heard her footsteps. He turned and gave her a weary smile. Teresa handed off one of the mugs and knelt down beside him.

"Good morning, my sweet," Shane yawned, as he leaned over and kissed her on the cheek. "Fresh brewed coffee always smells better on a boat."

Teresa set her coffee down and massaged Shane's neck and shoulders with both hands. He flexed his neck backward to ease the tightness.

"Morning coffee's better, period. You must be exhausted. Why'd you get up so early?"

"I wanted to check out the other boats anchored in the bay."

The mirror-like water in the bay yielded to a sandy tree-lined shore on the opposite bank. Two Bayliner cruisers were anchored along the west shore. There was no sign of activity. The sun's first rays were just beginning to peek above the heavily forested hilltop to the west.

"It's beautiful here. Where are we, Shane?"

"We're in the Canadian Gulf Islands just north of the San Juans. This bay divides North Pender Island from South Pender Island. We're close to Port Browning. I'd guess we're about fifteen miles from Vancouver."

"Sorry I fell asleep on you last night. How did you find this place in the dark?"

"It was easy with the GPS. Dan and I used to come up here all the time. North Pender Island was his favorite vacation spot. We'd spend the weekend drinking beer, eating fresh boiled crab, and telling tall tales about the ones that got away."

"Do you mean fish or women?"

Shane snickered and wrapped his arm around Teresa's shoulders. He picked up the mug and used it to warm his hands. Then he took a drink of coffee and set the mug down on the deck.

"I can't believe Dan's really gone. It all seems like a bad dream."

Teresa leaned her head against him and watched a formation of geese fly across the bay heading south. The honking faded into the distance.

"He saved our lives, Teresa."

"It took great courage to do what Dan did, but he should have called the police."

"There wasn't time. He heard the machine gun and knew we were in trouble. That's the way Dan was about everything. If you needed help with something, he was always the first one there. I, on the other hand, just stood there and watched."

He pounded a fist into the palm of his hand.

"I should've jumped that Arab son-of-a-bitch as soon as Dan blew the other one away. It happened so quickly."

"Shane, there wasn't a thing you could have done. He would have shot you both."

They sat in silence for several minutes sipping their coffee and watching the sun clear the treetops. Its warm rays took the edge off the morning chill.

"Maybe you're right. Come on, let's go get something to eat. The people on those Bayliners will be stirring soon. They probably just anchored here for the night. We'll take the skiff over to Port Browning once they head out. There's a small grocery store next to the marina. I need to pick up some supplies and fill those five-gallon fuel tanks."

Shane flipped on the TV. He surfed through the channels until he found a morning exercise program. He glanced at his watch. It was nearly 6:30. "The news comes on in five minutes. Let's see if they say anything." The exercise program was followed by a series of commercials. There was a lead-in for the morning news between two of the commercials. "*Stay tuned for special coverage of the terrorist strike at the University of Washington.*"

Shane sat at the table and Teresa scooted in beside him. The commercial ended and the introduction began for the newscast. A blonde newscaster picked up the story.

"*We want to begin our coverage with the developing story from Seattle. There's been a terrorist attack at the University of Washington. The FBI has confirmed the fire in the K-wing of the medical school started in the laboratory of Dr. Shane Kalakan, a member of the faculty.*"

A video of the burned out K-wing appeared on the screen.

"*Two people died in the fire. Dr. Freeman Goode had been on the faculty at the medical school for twelve years and Felicity Rodriguez was a fourth-year medical student who worked in Dr. Goode's lab. A graduate student named Teresa Daniels is still missing. Rescue workers continue to search through the rubble.*"

A photo of Shane's boathouse appeared on the screen. It was surrounded by yellow police investigation tape.

"*In what is now believed to be a related incident, two Arab men with ties to al-Qaida were shot to death in the houseboat of Dr. Shane Kalakan, the same researcher whose lab was firebombed at the University of Washington. Another man was also found shot to death in the home. The third body was initially thought to be that of Dr. Kalakan. Investigators are now reporting the third man was Daniel Murphy. Mr. Murphy lived in the boathouse next door. Police believe Mr. Murphy was involved in a shootout with the Arab men.*"

Shane's image peered back at them from the television set.

"*Investigators still haven't located Dr. Kalakan. FBI spokesperson Brad Johnson had this to say about the situation.*"

Agent Johnson appeared on the screen.

"*At the present time the FBI has no information regarding the whereabouts of Dr. Shane Kalakan. We're concerned about Dr. Kalakan's safety. The FBI is also looking for three other al-Qaida members who belonged to the same terrorist cell as the dead Arabs.*"

Photos of the Arabs peered out from the TV.

"*They are Muhummud al-Sadir, Mohammed al-Qaetra, and Saeed al-Bal.*

We believe Dr. Kalakan may have been abducted by one or more of these al-Qaida operatives."

The blonde newscaster returned to the screen.

"The FBI remains uncertain why the terrorists targeted the University of Washington or Dr. Kalakan. The FBI admitted they've been searching for the two dead Arab men, as well as the three Arabs who are still at large, since shortly after the attack on the World Trade Center. All five are thought to be members of an al-Qaida sleeper cell based in the Seattle area. The FBI is also searching for Dr. Kalakan's forty-foot sailboat named the View *Corridor. If you have any information related to this case, you are asked to call the FBI.*

"Early this morning two men held up a bank in Bellevue..."

Shane switched off the TV.

"Jeez Louise. It sounds like they've got the entire FBI looking for me."

"Shane, I think you should call them."

"Not until I get the rest of the money from Ahmed Jan. I worked my butt off on this project and I'll be out of work once the facts come out. I'll have to fess up when this is over."

"Shane, I need to call my parents. They must be frantic."

Shane thought for a minute. He took a deep breath.

"You're right," he sighed, "you need to get word to them. Do you have any close friends who live near your parents?"

"Let's see, Nancy Hastings was my best friend in high school. She lives just around the corner from my parents."

"Can you trust her?"

"Sure, I can trust Nancy."

"We can't call your parents' house. The FBI would trace the phone call in a matter of minutes. There's a pay phone over in the harbor. I'll buy a couple of calling cards. Call Nancy and tell her you're safe. Ask her to tell your parents you're camping with friends in Mt. Ranier National Park and you saw the story about the fire at UW on the news. That way they'll stop worrying about you without alerting the FBI."

"That's not going to work, Shane. My parents will wonder why I didn't call them directly. They'll still be suspicious."

"Tell Nancy you tried to call your parents, but the line was busy. It probably is anyway."

Teresa shook her head and rolled her eyes.

"What a schemer you are, Shane Kalakan."

Shane wrapped his arms around Teresa and kissed her on the lips.

"I'll call Ahmed Jan at the same time. I promise, I'll contact the FBI as soon as I find a way to hide the money."

"That's not going to be easy Shane. The FBI will want to know why the Arabs came after you and where you've been since the K-wing burned down."

"I'll tell them the truth. I freaked out when I saw my friend murdered by the Arabs. I came to the Gulf Islands to hide until I knew it was safe to come in."

"But why are the Arabs trying to kill you?"

"I'll tell them the truth about that too. I'll tell them about everything but the money. Come on, let's go."

Shane lifted the seat cover and pulled out a bundle of beach towels. He fetched a Mariner's baseball cap from the same hold and pulled it down over his head. He handed an LA Dodger hat to Teresa.

"What's with the beach towels?"

"Let's drape them over the stern to cover the name of the boat. No sense taking a chance some boater recognizes the name and calls the FBI. Buster, stay!"

Shane climbed up to the deck and glanced out across the inlet. Both of the motor yachts were gone. He closed the hatch behind Teresa and locked it. They draped the towels over the stern. Shane untied the skiff, activated the winch, and lowered it into the water.

"Get in, Teresa, and I'll hand you the fuel tanks."

Teresa crawled down the ladder into the skiff. Shane passed down the tanks and she stacked them in the bow. Shane climbed into the stern. The engine started on the second pull. He put the engine in gear.

It was a bright sunny day without a cloud in the sky. They rounded a point and headed toward Port Browning. The masts of the sailboats moored in the marina came into view a few minutes later.

Shane steered the skiff along the dock to the temporary moorage area behind the grocery store. He squeezed the skiff in between two others and turned off the engine. It took a couple of minutes to tie the line to a cleat, pull the fuel tanks up to the dock, and head for the shore.

Shane and Teresa rounded the corner toward the front door of the store. Shane stopped in his tracks. He turned without speaking and walked back around the corner of the building. Teresa followed in hot pursuit.

"Where are you going, Shane?"

"Shhh! Did you see the newspaper rack? My smiley little face is on the front page."

"Oh God, what are we going to do now?"

Shane pulled two hundred-dollar bills from his pocket. He handed them to Teresa and yanked her hat down over her forehead.

"You can do it. Buy some meat and vegetables, a half-gallon of milk, and whatever else you want to eat. We need enough to last a few days. Get two twenty-dollar calling cards and the newspaper. Pre-pay for ten gallons of diesel fuel. I'll wait for you over by that bench. We can get the fuel and make the phone calls once we load the groceries into the skiff. Oh, get a ferry schedule too."

Teresa ambled toward the front door of the market. She rounded the corner carrying a large box twenty minutes later.

"Let me carry that. How'd it go?"

"Fine, as far as I could tell."

"Did you remember the ferry schedule?"

"Yeah. It's in my pocket with the calling cards."

Teresa scooted into the skiff and Shane passed down the box. He filled the tanks with diesel fuel while Teresa went to make her phone call. He had the tanks stowed in the skiff by the time she returned ten minutes later. Teresa had tears streaking down her face. Shane leapt out of the skiff and wrapped her in his arms.

"What's wrong?"

"I'm a terrible liar, Shane."

"How'd it go?"

"Nancy had just left my parents' house. My entire family and most of our friends have been at my parents' house since early this morning. My dad and brother flew to Seattle last night."

Shane turned and looked skyward.

"God help us!"

"What's the matter, Shane? I did what you asked me to do."

"Teresa, you have to go home. Give me that ferry schedule. The ferry to Vancouver leaves just after noon. You can catch an early afternoon flight to California and get to your parent's house early this evening."

Teresa grabbed Shane's hand and spun him around.

"Shane, I'm not leaving until you do. I told Nancy I was having an affair. I told her we'd be camping until next Sunday and that I'd borrowed another camper's cell phone to make the call. That should be plenty of time. Nancy's going back to my house to let everyone know I'm safe. Then she's going to call the police in Seattle and tell them I'm okay. Everything's going to be fine. I want to stay with you."

Shane shook his head.

"What a mess. When first you practice to deceive. I need to make my phone call. You stay here with the skiff. I'll be back in a few minutes."

Shane jogged away down the dock. Ten minutes later he returned, stepped down into the skiff, and started the engine.

"Did you reach him, Shane?"

"Yeah, I reached him."

He backed the skiff away from the dock and headed toward the inlet.

"What happened?"

"I'm meeting Ahmed Jan at a restaurant in Vancouver tomorrow afternoon. He's going to give me the money. I'll give him the clone and that'll be the end of it."

"What if he steals the clone and doesn't pay you?"

"I'm not stupid enough to take it to the meeting. I'll get a motel room and leave the clone there. I'll call him after he pays me and tell him where to find it. We'll hide the money and then go to the police."

CHAPTER FORTY-FIVE

June 25, 2002

Shane locked Buster in the cabin of the *View Corridor* early the next morning and took Teresa with him on the skiff to Otter Bay on North Pender. They planned to board the ferry to Tsawwassen near Vancouver. The morning air was crisp. The slightest breeze wafted through the trees along the shore and the water on the bay was glassy calm. The two of them waited at the terminal for more than an hour before the ferry finally appeared in the distance. Ten minutes later the ferry inched toward the dock.

The captain reversed the engines as the big boat edged through a line of pylons and slowed to a stop. Teresa and Shane sat on a stone wall next to the gangplank while the crew tied the lines to mammoth cleats along the dock.

More than a dozen people were waiting to board. The foot passengers disembarked first and headed for town. A line of cars and trucks began to file out of the vehicle deck shortly thereafter. An attendant opened the boarding gate and Teresa and Shane made their way across the gangplank and onto the upper decks with the other passengers.

A group of seagulls drifted above the ferry. An old woman tossed a few crusts of bread off the upper deck and into the water below. Dozens of the squawking gulls plunged toward the surf in a frenzied struggle.

Teresa huddled against Shane and kissed him on the cheek. He put an arm around her shoulders and combed his fingers through her hair.

"Are you afraid?" she whispered.

"A little, but everything will be over soon."

"Be careful, Shane. Remember, I love you just the way you are. My father always told me money only clouds the good things in life."

The ferry rounded northern tip of the Penders and made its way into the channel between Galiano and Mayne Islands. Once it cleared the tips of the islands, it headed due east toward Vancouver.

The ferry docked at the terminal in Tsawwassen two hours later. Teresa and Shane disembarked and boarded a bus for the depot in Vancouver. From there they took a taxi to a Holiday Inn Express in North Vancouver.

Shane used the counterfeit U.S. passport in the name of Steven Nelson to rent a room in the rear of the hotel. It took a few minutes to find the room and make themselves comfortable. Shane drew the curtains and checked the dead-bolt on the door.

"Are you hungry, Teresa?"

"Not really, honey. Are you? I packed two turkey sandwiches in your bag."

"No thanks. I'll get something at the restaurant. You eat those if you get hungry."

Shane glanced at his watch.

"Well, I better get going. I'm meeting him at a café across the street from the Centennial Pier. It's called the Maritime Diner. I should be back in an hour or so."

Shane reached into his pocket and pulled out the vial. He handed it to Teresa.

"This is the bacteria expressing the DNA clone. I'm leaving it with you. Stay here in the room until I get back. I'll call you here if I need any help."

Teresa locked her hands around his waist and cuddled against his chest.

"Please be careful, Shane."

He lifted her chin. Tears were welling up in her eyes. He kissed her tenderly.

"Don't worry, my sweet. Everything's going to work out."

The taxi dropped Shane off directly in front of the Maritime Diner. He glanced across the street toward the Centennial Pier. There were several old windowless warehouses lining the waterfront. A freighter named the *Lady North* was docked directly across from the largest building. Shane watched the enormous crane lift a bundle of lumber off a railcar and transfer it into the hold of the giant ship.

Shane opened the front door of the diner and stepped inside. The restaurant was buzzing with a lunchtime crowd of seamen and laborers from the docks. The small café held fewer than ten tables. The place was alive with laughter and conversation. Shane approached a young woman standing behind the counter.

"May I help you, sir?"

Shane peered toward the rear of the restaurant. He spotted Ahmed sitting at a booth in the back. Ahmed was talking on a cell phone.

"I'm meeting a friend here for lunch. I see him there in the back."

Shane waited for a group of men to pass and then made his way through the crowd. Ahmed Jan hung up the phone as Shane neared the table. He smiled and thrust out his hand.

"Dr. Kalakan. Thank you for coming. I hope you didn't have a hard time finding this place."

"Not at all. The taxi brought me."

Shane scooted into the booth and Ahmed sat across from him. A waitress dressed in a worn blue uniform slid two glasses of ice water onto the table.

"Are you ready to order?"

Shane glanced at the menu on a board above the counter.

"I'll have a bowl of the clam chowder with iced tea."

"And you, sir?"

"I'll have the same."

The waitress stepped away and clipped the order to the end of a line hanging outside the kitchen window. A long-haired cook in a tee shirt reached out through the window and grabbed the first ticket.

The two men stared at each other for a moment. Ahmed took a sip of water and set his glass back down on the table.

"Well Dr. Kalakan, I guess you're a little confused right now."

Shane leaned across the table.

"I don't think confusion quite covers it. I'm pissed as hell! My best friend got killed and my career is ruined."

Ahmed leaned back in the booth and nodded sympathetically.

"Would you allow me to fill in the details?"

"I'm listening."

"Dr. Kalakan, I'm not a student."

Shane rolled his eyes.

"Mr. Jan, tell me something I don't know."

"I am a Tajik of the Northern Alliance."

Ahmed paused to wait for Shane's response. There wasn't one, so he continued.

"Dr. Kalakan, you must have some feeling about why we contacted you? Yes?"

"I thought you hired me because I did research using methods similar to those needed to isolate the DNA sequence."

"That was part of it. But there are many scientists with these skills. There were special reasons we picked you."

Ahmed reached into his bag and pulled out a plastic sleeve. He slid it across the table. It contained a yellowed photograph of a man with a full beard wearing a military uniform. He was sitting on a horse holding a sword. There were dozens of men crowding around. They were all reaching up to touch the man's hand.

"Do you recognize this man, Dr. Kalakan?"

Shane studied the photograph. He shook his head.

"No, I never saw him before."

"His name is Habibullah Kalakani. He was a great Tajik king of Afghanistan. Habibullah led our people to victory against the Pashtun in 1929. Nadir Khan killed him, along with many of your family members, less than a year later. He was a fierce warrior. Our people cherish his memory to this day. He was your great uncle, Dr. Kalakan."

Shane peered down at the photo. As he did, the waitress rushed to the table and put down her tray.

"Two bowls of clam chowder and two ice teas," she said, out of breath. "Will there be anything else?"

"No, thank you," Ahmed replied.

The woman finished the check and tore it out of her book. She placed it on the table.

"Thank you. Have a nice day."

She hurried off to another table. Ahmed's phone began to ring. He lifted it to his ear.

"Ahmed Jan."

He listened to the caller for a few moments.

"Good. I'll speak with you later."

Ahmed hung up the phone. Shane was studying the photograph. He set it on the table.

"How do you know this man is my great uncle?"

"Dr. Kalakan, the Kalakanis were among the most influential Tajiks in Afghanistan. Your grandfather was Mohammad Kalakani, the youngest brother of Habibullah Kalakani. Mohammad left Tajikistan in 1945 to escape the Russian oppression. The Russians slaughtered our people by the thousands. Several members of your family disappeared during the Great War. Most of them were never seen again. Mohammad took your father Awar Kalakani to New York to start a new life."

Shane picked up the photograph again and stared at the man's face. The resemblance to his father was uncanny.

"Mohammmad died just a year later. Your father Awar moved to Chicago in 1965 and changed his name to Adam Kalakan. He worked for many years as a clerk at Rush Memorial Hospital in Chicago. He married a young Tajik woman in 1970 and you were born in Chicago in 1972. Your sister Ali was born in 1977. Your parents were killed in a car accident in Chicago in 1984. You and your sister lived together in foster homes until one of the families adopted her in 1986. You moved from one foster home to another until you were eighteen. You studied at the University of Chicago and took your job at the University of Washington in 1998."

"I took my job in 1999. How do you know all of this?"

Ahmed reached into his bag and pulled out a hardback book. He slid it across the table.

"This book was written by Khalilullah Khalili. He was an Afghani poet who worked with your great uncle Habibullah Kalakani. It's a historical biography about your great uncle. It was written in 1978. It details everything up to the time your father was living in Chicago. It even has a paragraph about you and your sister Ali. You can keep that copy."

Shane picked up the book and thumbed through it. It was written in a language he didn't recognize.

"Are you sure? Father never mentioned a brother."

"I'm certain, Dr. Kalakan. Our leaders in Afghanistan maintain lists of leading Tajik families throughout the world. A Tajik mullah in Kabul gave me your name when we needed someone to help with this project."

Shane shook his head.

"So what's the real reason for isolating the Tajik DNA sequence?"

Ahmed scanned the restaurant and leaned across the table.

"Dr. Kalakan, I'm afraid we misled you. The A samples were not Tajik. They were Pashtun. The B samples were Tajik."

Shane peered at Ahmed with a bemused frown and shook his head again. "I don't understand."

Ahmed slid two crumpled papers across the table.

"Dr. Kalakan, I found these papers hidden in the jacket of an Arab of the Qaida just after the fall of Kabul last November."

Shane picked up the papers. He glanced at them and set them back on the table.

"They are written in Arabic, Dr. Kalakan. These papers describe a new vector that was to be delivered to al-Qaida. They planned to use it on the Tajik people and other enemies of al-Qaida, including the Americans."

Ahmed pulled a notebook binder from his pack and pushed it across to Shane.

"We intercepted the vector along with the translated information in this notebook. It was on a microfilm hidden within the cap of the vial. Dr. Kalakan, your father must have told you about the Tajiks and the long struggle with the Pashtun?"

"My father never spoke about the past. He forbade my mother to even mention Afghanistan. I remember him saying no good could come from the past. He always told me to keep my eyes on the future. I knew my grandfather was Tajik and that he died in New York City. That's all I knew about him until today."

Ahmed took a deep breath and exhaled.

"That's a pity. How can I expect you to understand where we are today?"

"Why don't you just start at the beginning? I've got some time."

"Dr. Kalakan, the Tajiks and the Pashtun have fought for more than a thousand years. The Taliban are Pashtun. We Tajiks are part of the Northern Alliance."

"I've read a lot about the Tajiks in the newspapers since 9/11."

"Dr. Kalakan, this new vector was to be delivered to the Taliban. They planned to use it to wipe out the Tajiks throughout Afghanistan and the surrounding countries. It was designed to spread only to people who share a unique DNA sequence inserted into the vector."

Shane's face transformed to stunned realization.

"You plan to use my sequence to direct this vector against the Pashtun."

Ahmed didn't answer. He stared at Shane with steely resolve.

"You're crazy. I want no part of this genocidal madness."

"Dr. Kalakan, as the Americans like to say, you are already up shit creek without a paddle."

"I'm through with you and all of this nonsense," Shane bellowed. "Forget about the rest of the money. You can keep it."

Several men at an adjacent table stopped talking. They all turned and stared at the two men. Shane stood up from the booth and fished through his pockets. Ahmed grasped him by the arm.

"Sit down, Dr. Kalakan," he said just above a whisper. "I'm afraid it's not going to be that easy. You'll have a hard time convincing the FBI you didn't know about the vector."

"Bullshit! Let go of my arm."

"Did you report the money we paid you? What's your revenue department called? The IRS? Then there's al-Qaida. You can bet they'll be searching for you, Dr. Kalakan."

Shane stared at Ahmed for a moment. He slid back into the booth.

"Do whatever you want, Mr. Jan, I'm not giving you the sequence."

Ahmed leaned across the table and spoke in a muffled voice.

"Dr. Kalakan, I'm disappointed you don't feel some empathy for your people. The Taliban and al-Qaida are regrouping in Afghanistan. It's only a matter of time before they use this vector against the Tajik people. We need your assistance. Please help us."

"I'm an American, Mr. Jan. Your petty tribal fighting is no longer my concern. I will not be a party to genocide."

"Dr. Kalakan, young Americans are still dying in Afghanistan. Your president would never admit it publicly, but he is a reasonable man. He'd applaud our efforts."

"The president of the United States would never condone the killing of innocent women and children. I'm leaving. I want no part in this."

Shane stood up once again and took a step to leave. Ahmed grabbed his arm and pulled him back to the table.

"I'm afraid you must be part of this, Dr. Kalakan. You will cooperate, if you ever want to see your woman again."

"Don't threaten me."

"It is no threat. Dr Kalakan, did you notice the man who got into the cab when you got out? He called a minute ago. Your woman is safe and will be treated well. We'll return her when you finish your work. Would you like to speak with her?"

"You bastard! If you harm her, I'll kill you!"

"Dr. Kalakan, we have no intention of harming her. But it's your own fault she's in this situation. You promised me in Amsterdam you wouldn't involve any other person in this project. Remember?"

"What do you want?"

"Dr. Kalakan, this gives me no pleasure. I only want your help for our people. You have nothing to fear, as long as you agree to help us."

"What do you want?"

"I want you to insert your DNA sequence into the vector and prepare the active virus. The details you need are in this manual. It shouldn't take you long. In return, I'll pay you the remaining quarter million dollars, plus an additional hundred thousand dollars for the additional work."

Shane stared at the table for nearly a minute. Finally, he nodded his head in capitulation.

"I need to hide my boat somewhere."

"Dr. Kalakan, you don't appear to fully grasp your situation. You can never return to your former life. It's only a matter of time before the police locate your boat. What do you call it, the *View Corridor*? It's been on the news for three days. Did you get rid of the cell phone?"

"I threw the phone in the water. My dog is on the boat. I won't leave him."

"Where's the boat now?"

"It's anchored in an isolated bay in the Canadian Gulf Islands."

"Go get the dog. Do not delay. This will be the last time you can ever go near your boat. You must sink it."

"I'm not sinking my boat. Are you crazy?"

"The authorities will find the boat. It'll put them on your trail. You must assume your new identity from this moment on. You are Steven Nelson and I am Saaed. I'll also provide a new identity for your woman."

"And just where am I going to do this work?"

"We control a lab here in Vancouver. We have full access to the facility. It's stocked with all the equipment and supplies you could possibly need. I'll take this manual with me and give it to you later at the lab."

Shane ran his hands across the three-day growth of stubble on his face. He took a deep breath and sighed loudly.

"I apparently have no choice. When do we start?"

"Pick up your dog and we'll start tomorrow. Do you still have the passport I sent you?

"It's in my pocket."

Ahmed reached into his bag and pulled out several items bound together with a rubber band.

"These papers document your Swiss bank account and the $350,000 deposit. My authorization is required to access the account. You'll be able to access it without my signature as soon as you finish the project. There's also a Washington driver's license and a Social Security card in the name Steven Nelson. Give me anything you have that identifies you as Shane Kalakan."

Shane took his wallet out of his pocket. He removed the money and a few photos before handing it to Ahmed. Ahmed stuffed the wallet into his bag.

"Mr. Nelson, you have a room at the Touch of English Bed and Breakfast. The address and phone number are on this key. You're in room five. Call me on my cell phone when you're ready to start."

Shane took a drink of ice tea. He stared into Ahmed's eyes.

"How do I know I can trust you?"

"You don't, Mr. Nelson."

Ahmed stood up from the table and walked away.

It took just over seven hours for Shane to return to the Gulf Islands by ferry, take the skiff to the boat to retrieve Buster, and return to Vancouver. He managed to put together a suitcase full of clothing and other personal effects, in addition to the briefcase full of cash. He considered sinking the sailboat, but just couldn't bring himself to do it.

It was nearly 9 P.M. before he sat down on the edge of the bed and called Ahmed Jan's cell phone. Ahmed answered on the second ring.

"Yes?"

"This is Shane Kalakan."

"I'm sorry. You must have the wrong number. I don't know anyone by the name of Kalakan."

Shane began to protest, but then recovered.

"This is Steven Nelson. May I speak with Saaed?"

"This is Saaed."

"I want to start work now."

"Now, Mr. Nelson? Perhaps the morning would be better."

"I want to start now!" Shane bellowed.

Ahmed went silent for a few moments. When he finally spoke, it was with a calm voice.

"Okay, Mr. Nelson. The driver will pick you up in front of Touch of English in twenty minutes."

"One other thing."

"Yes."

"I will not do this work unless you bring Teresa to the lab to work with me."

"That's not possible, Mr. Nelson."

"Then there's no deal."

"Mr. Nelson, you are in no position…"

Shane cut him off.

"If I'm going to trust you, Saaed, or whatever your name is, then you must trust me. Bring her to the lab. She can help with the work. I'll cooperate fully, as long as you treat her well."

Ahmed did not respond, so Shane continued.

"The work will go faster. We'll work around the clock until the project is finished."

There was another long silence. Finally, Ahmed responded in an unruffled tone.

"Okay Mr. Nelson. The driver will pick you up in twenty minutes. Bring your dog and all your other belongings with you. Ustad will search you before taking you to the lab. I'll bring your woman to the lab later tonight."

"Then I will cooperate."

"I hope so for your sake, Mr. Nelson. I hope so."

Shane was standing in front of the hotel exactly twenty minutes later. An early-model Chevrolet Impala bumped into the driveway and screeched to a stop in front of him. The driver leaned across the front seat and rolled down the passenger window.

"My name is Ustad. Get in."

Shane opened the back door and tossed his luggage into the seat. He snapped his fingers and Buster jumped inside. Shane ducked into the seat and slammed the door.

Ustad sped out of the driveway and made a right turn. He wound through a series of streets that ran along the bay until he reached an industrial park in North Vancouver. He pulled the car to the curb on a darkened street.

"Get out, Mr. Nelson. I need to search you."

Shane got out of the car. Ustad turned him around and patted down his shirt and pants. He opened the back door and unzipped the suitcase. Ustad went through the clothing and toiletries, before rezipping the suitcase. The briefcase was locked.

"What's in here?"

"The money Saaed gave me."

"Open it."

Shane unlocked the briefcase with a key on his keychain and flipped open the top. The inside smelled of newly printed money. Packets of one hundred dollar bills were neatly stacked inside. Ustad closed the briefcase and locked it. He tossed it into the back seat.

"Okay. Get back in the car."

Not another word was spoken. Ustad drove along a major thoroughfare that cut through the middle of the industrial park. It appeared to be a new development. The farther they drove, the more scattered the buildings became. Ustad drove to another section where there were just a few structures. Most were just steel frames.

The Chevrolet finally turned into a long cul-de-sac. The first few lots on either side were vacant. They slowed in front of a building at the end of the cul-de-sac that was under construction. Just the steel frame had been completed.

Ustad pulled the car into the driveway and drove along the side of a ten-foot wall to the back of the lot. A two-story, mirrored-glass building was hidden in the back behind a fence that demarcated the construction zone. "Bioeng Corporation" was spelled out in block letters above the front door. The building was only about one quarter the size of the unfinished structure at the front of the lot. The windows were dark and there were no cars or other signs of activity outside. Ustad pulled to a stop next to the front door.

"This is it. Knock on the door."

Shane stepped out of the car. He called Buster out of the back and grabbed his things. He slammed the door shut and the car bounced out of the driveway and sped away.

Shane stepped up the darkened walkway to the glass door. He rapped on the glass. A beam of light appeared down the hallway a moment later. A man with dark features walked to the door and unlocked a dead bolt.

"My name is Mohammad. Come with me, Mr. Nelson."

Shane stepped in and followed him down the hall. Buster scampered behind with his tail wagging. Mohammad held a card against a security panel on the wall next to the door and the lock clicked open. He opened the door.

Shane stepped into an enormous, brightly lit room. Ten parallel lab benches extended from the front to the rear. Dozens of instruments were arranged on the benches and along the walls on all four sides of the room. The cabinets over the benches were filled with supplies of every sort. It was the most impressive molecular biology lab Shane had ever seen.

Mohammad led him between two of the lab benches toward the back of the room. The manual Ahmed Jan had shown him earlier was sitting at a workstation about half way down the bench. Mohammad pulled out a stool. He wandered off to the back of the room and sat at a desk along the wall.

"Buster, lie down," Shane ordered.

The Dalmatian curled up beneath the bench. Shane scooted the stool up and began skimming through the manual. Once he'd surveyed the organization of the manual, Shane returned to the first page and began to read for detail. The first section discussed the molecular structure of the vector and its construction. The following section detailed the use of subtraction hybridization to isolate and insert a population-specific homing sequence. A third section provided instructions for packaging and testing the infectious virus. The final section was brief. Just two pages were devoted to the release of the active virus.

Shane had nearly made it through the binder when the door at the front of the room opened. He stood up and looked over the top of the cabinets that ran down the middle of the bench. Teresa stepped through the door with Ahmed Jan behind her. She was holding a large department store bag in each hand.

"Teresa!" Shane called, as he rushed across the room and picked her up in his arms. He gave her a long hug and then set her down.

"I'm so sorry, Teresa."

Teresa was clearly puzzled. She looked at Shane and then at Ahmed. Shane took her hand.

"Teresa, I've been crazy since this morning. I couldn't bear the thought of not seeing you again."

"Not seeing me again?"

Teresa glanced at Ahmed again. She looked back toward Shane and shook her head with exasperation.

"What are you talking about, Shane? Ustad picked me up at the hotel. He told me you were tied up with Ahmed. He took me shopping at Pacific Centre Mall. He said you wanted me to buy a new wardrobe."

She handed Shane one of the bags.

"I felt guilty spending so much on myself. I got you three pair of jeans and a couple of polo shirts. I hope they fit. I didn't know what sizes you wear. The other bags are in the car."

"Mohammad," Ahmed ordered, "get the bags for the lady."

Shane glanced at Ahmed Jan. Ahmed had a sheepish grin on his face. "Saaed, what's going on here?"

"Mr. Nelson, I told you our intentions were good. You will be treated well as long as you help us assemble the vector."

"Shane, what vector are you talking about? Everyone keeps talking about a vector."

"It's a long story, Teresa. These men want us to clone my sequence into a viral vector and package it for them. They want us to stay here until we're done."

"Why's he calling you Mr. Nelson?"

"It's my new name. Mr. Steven Nelson. It sounds English. You'll get a new identity too. I think Molly Nelson sounds appropriate. I'll tell you all about it while we work. The sooner we start, the sooner we finish."

Teresa set her bag down on the floor. She wrapped her arms around Shane's neck and kissed him on the lips. Shane took her hand and led her back to the bench. He pulled another stool over to the workstation.

"Do you have the clone, sweet?"

Teresa slipped her hand into her front pocket and pulled out the vial. She handed it to Shane.

"The vector has a multi-cloning site. There are two unique cloning sites that match up with splice sites in the plasmid vector I used to clone the DNA sequence. We can use them to insert this sequence into the vector. Then we'll use an engineered human cell line to produce infectious virus. The manual recommends immortalized B lymphocytes in culture."

"Shane, what are they planning to do with this vector?"

"The vector's a killer, Teresa. It's designed to spread through any population that shares the DNA sequence I isolated. The sequence acts as a homing device to allow viral insertion into the cellular DNA."

"Who do they plan to kill?" she asked skeptically.

"They duped me, Teresa. The sequence I isolated is specific for people of Pashtun ancestry. That includes the Taliban in Afghanistan and one of the largest groups in Pakistan. They plan to use it as a deterrent. If the Pashtun use the vector on the Tajiks, the Tajiks will use it on them."

"That's just great," Teresa muttered disapprovingly. "Now we're card-carrying bioterrorists."

CHAPTER FORTY-SIX

June 26, 2002, Langley, Virginia

Stone was reading through a report on the current situation in Afghanistan. He'd been waiting for nearly thirty minutes in a secure conference room near Richards' office. The deputy director was late.

Richards had ordered Stone to return to Langley for a face–to-face meeting. Stone caught a red-eye flight back to Virginia. His plane arrived early in the morning. There'd been barely enough time to drive home, take a shower, and change out the clothing in his suitcase. He managed to have a quick breakfast with his family before heading off to CIA headquarters. It was the first time in three months he'd seen his three-year-old son and pregnant wife.

The door opened with a hiss. Richards strode into the room with Marilyn Harrison behind him. Harrison pushed a button on a console next to the door and the door slammed shut with a metallic echo. Richardson sat down across from Stone at the table. Harrison took a seat next to Richards.

Richards' cigar butt was dangling from the corner of his mouth. His cheeks and nose were bright red. He didn't look well.

"Good morning, Stone. Good to see you. How's the family?"

"Fine, sir. I got a chance to see them this morning."

"Glad to hear that. Stone, I know the last few months have been tough on your family. Hell, it's been tough on all of our families. I asked you to come to Langley to discuss the situation in the Northwest. I wanted to meet in a secure environment."

Richards coughed to clear his throat.

"We initiated an internal investigation after al-Qaida hit Shane Kalakan and the University of Washington, but we still have no clue how the damned

Arabs beat us to Seattle. I'm damned sure not taking any more chances. Where do we stand?"

"Sir, I wish I had better news. We haven't been able to locate Shane Kalakan. We don't know if he's alive or dead. The Mounties found his sailboat in the Gulf Islands near Victoria yesterday. There was no sign of him. We found four different sets of fingerprints on the boat. One set belonged to Shane Kalakan. We're trying to run down the others. Someone made a couple of calls from Kalakan's cell phone on the twenty-fourth. The phone was in the San Juan Islands just north of Seattle when the calls were made. The receiving phone was in Amsterdam. The call was made to a satellite phone number that belongs to a Tajik expatriate living in Amsterdam. Neither phone has been used since the last call. I checked all the harbors close to where the boat was found. I showed at least two hundred people the photos of Kalakan. Nobody recognized him. My gut tells me he's dead."

"What makes you think so?"

"Well, his lab was burned down with an incendiary device. We're certain the Arabs did it. Several different people saw suspicious looking Middle-Eastern types lurking around that wing of the medical school just before it burned down. A road crew working at the school saw at least two men who fit the same description. They were driving out of the parking lot in a van around the same time. They nearly ran over a flagman trying to hold them up for cross traffic. These same workers heard the explosion in Shane Kalakan's lab less than five minutes later."

"But that doesn't mean Kalakan is dead, Stone."

"We're not sure whether the Arabs found the vector or not. I'm guessing they didn't. The shootings at Shane Kalakan's houseboat occurred about fifteen minutes later. We're certain of the timing because a neighbor called 9/11 when he heard machine gun fire. I figure the Arabs wouldn't have bothered going after Shane Kalakan if they'd found what they were looking for in the lab."

"Maybe they found the vector and tried to kill Shane Kalakan to eliminate anyone with knowledge about the plan."

"I guess that's possible. We just don't know at this point."

Richards leaned back in his chair, tilted his head up, and stared at the ceiling. He worked the cigar butt around and around in the corner of his mouth. He removed the butt from his mouth and tapped it on the table. Finally, he sighed loudly, sat up in the chair, and leaned his elbows on the table with his chin in his hands.

"Was it an expensive sailboat?"

"Yeah, one of the best. It's a custom-made Swan from Finland."

"What do we know about these Arabs?"

"They originally came from Saudi Arabia. They've been living in a two-bedroom house in Kirkland for at least the past three years. That's about fifteen miles from the university. The two dead ones worked at a money transfer service in a city called Bothell up until 9/11. That's just north of Seattle. The service was suspected of funneling funds to al-Qaida and the FBI closed it down. They disappeared with three other men linked to al-Qaida. That's about it."

Richards sat for a moment looking at Stone and turning the cigar butt in the corner of his mouth. He pulled it out and held it in his hand.

"I'll tell you what I think, Stone. Shane Kalakan is still alive. He's somewhere in Canada. The Arabs would've sunk the boat as soon as they got to Canada. Why would they take a chance of someone finding the boat and using it to narrow the search? A true sailor like Kalakan wouldn't have the heart to sink it. It'd be like killing your firstborn child. Focus your search on Vancouver. Kalakan himself was using that cell phone. I'll bet you dinner at Clancy's. Have the Mounties put a blanket over Vancouver. Make sure they have photos up at the airports, train stations, and cruise ship terminals. You find Shane Kalakan and you'll find the vector."

"I'll do everything I can, sir. "

"What about the Tajiks in Amsterdam? What happened to them?"

"Our informer Mustafa is now in Santa Fe. We enrolled him and his new wife in the FBI witness protection program. We know the Tajik named Mohammajon returned to Kabul. We lost track of the man named Ahmed Jan. We had two men on him in Amsterdam. He was in a hotel in the center of the city five days ago. He met with Mustafa just before we flew him to the U.S. Jan left the hotel that evening and managed to shake the tail. They haven't seen him since. There's no way Jan left using his real name. It's possible he got away with a new identity. Mustafa thinks Ahmed Jan was called back to Afghanistan."

"Shane Kalakan was likely calling him in Amsterdam."

"That's my guess, sir."

"Stone, you've got to find this vector before someone gets the chance to activate it."

"We're doing everything we can, sir."

"Stone, I have some other news for you. The military pulverized the laboratory at As Salman in southern Iraq last night. They hit it with smart bombs and then decimated the surrounding area with daisy cutters. Our sources tell us the Saudi scientist who designed and constructed the Armageddon vector was killed. His name was Omar al-Bakr. Hopefully, we got all the aliquots of vector. They could have stored some of it in other labs in Iraq, but killing the main scientist should hinder further development."

"I didn't hear anything about an attack on Iraq."

"They aren't talking and neither are we. The president sent Saddam a message after the attack. He let him know we're aware of the vector and that we'll go nuclear if anyone ever uses the vector on the U.S. or our allies. Marilyn, what's the latest from Afghanistan?"

"There's still a lot of activity around Gardez. U.S. forces bombed the daylights out of a group of caves up in the mountains. Most of the fighting is centered on complexes that are only ten kilometers from the village of Shah-i-Kot. The altitude is twelve thousand feet and there's been a bitter storm there the past four days. Several British soldiers were killed yesterday. We're making some progress, but it's going to be slow going until the weather clears."

"Any sign of the big fish there?"

"Senior leaders of al-Qaida and the Taliban are believed to be directing the fighting. There's a rumor bin Laden and his deputy Ayman al-Zawahiri are holed up with them. The U.S. command blocked all routes to and from the area. They're determined not to repeat the fiasco at Tora Bora."

"Okay, keep me posted. I've got a twenty-year-old cigar I'm saving for the day we kill that bastard. A staffer at the Department of Defense gave it to me."

Richardson looked at his watch. It was nearly ten o'clock.

"Stone, why don't you stay home until tomorrow morning? You've earned a little R-and-R. I want you to head back to Seattle tomorrow. Call Kitch Morgan in the FBI office right away. Tell him to meet with the Mounties about the investigation in Vancouver. I want them to search all the labs in both the universities and private sector where someone could work on the Armageddon vector."

"Thank you, sir, I'll give Kitch a call. There's a flight to Seattle tomorrow morning. I'll be on it."

"You're a good man, Stone. Remember, find Kalakan and you'll find the vector."

"Sir, if he's alive, we'll find him."

CHAPTER FORTY-SEVEN

August 18, 2002

Shane and Teresa worked on the vector night and day for seven weeks. Ahmed made sure they had everything they needed. He brought supplies, food, fine wine, and even movies.

Ahmed converted the lab director's office into a bedroom, complete with a queen-sized bed, oversized pillows, and cable TV. There was an attached bathroom with a shower. It made a surprisingly cozy bungalow for the young lovers. He even bought a cushioned dog bed for Buster.

Ahmed brought them coffee and rolls with orange juice every morning. One of the three Afghanis who watched over them brought restaurant fare for lunch and dinner. Ahmed also brought them magazines and newspapers to ease the tedium. They followed the investigation of the fire at the University of Washington and the search for Dr. Shane Kalakan. Coverage had slowed to a trickle. There had been no new developments in the case since the first few days following the attack.

Teresa called her parents two days after their arrival in Vancouver. Ahmed gave her a new cell phone to use for the call. It was gut wrenching. She told her parents she'd fallen in love with a rock star and had left with him on a tour of Europe. The tour was due to last through the Christmas holidays and then she expected to return to the United States. Her father ranted and raved about irresponsible behavior. Her mother just cried. She told them she loved them and hung up the phone. It was the only time she felt more than a twinge of regret.

Ahmed shared nearly every meal with Shane and Teresa. Almost invariably, the conversation turned to Afghanistan and the long and arduous struggle of the Tajik people. Ahmed regaled Shane with the exploits of his great uncle

Habibullah Kalakani, the Tajik king of Afghanistan. Over time, a palpable bond developed between the two men. They both came to relish the hours they spent together. Shane came to accept, if not embrace, the need for the vector. Ahmed convinced him it was the only way to provide some measure of assurance the weapon wouldn't be set loose on the Tajik people.

The typical workday lasted fourteen to sixteen hours, but Shane and Teresa sometimes labored for stretches of twenty-four to thirty-six hours, depending on the task at hand. They made steady progress constructing the vector and verifying its sequence. That turned out to be the easy part.

The final phase required them to set up a cultured cell packaging system. This step and all subsequent handling of the virus required the use of a high-level containment facility situated on the second floor of the building. Theoretically, the completed vector would infect only the cells of those whose DNA bore the unique Pashtun sequence isolated from the blood samples, but Shane and Teresa weren't taking any chances.

The final phase began with a time-consuming series of botched experiments. Neither Shane nor Teresa had previous experience with the crucial cell culture system. One problem after another was solved through painstaking attention to detail and hard work. It took nearly two weeks to sort out this final glitch. A stroke of luck allowed them to sidestep the final hurdle, just as tempers had reached the boiling point. They prepared three independent batches of high titer virus once the protocol was worked out.

The last task was to test the virulence of the virus on transformed white blood cells isolated from individuals of differing racial backgrounds. Ahmed brought in blood samples from many different donors. Shane isolated lymphocytes from each sample and infected them with Epstein-Barr virus, a virus that transforms a subgroup of the white blood cells and makes them grow rapidly in culture. Clones of transformed cells were selected from each of the cultures and frozen for final testing of the virus.

Ahmed let himself in through the front door of the facility. He was carrying two garment bags with hangers. He made sure the door closed behind him and strode to the elevator. The elevator door opened on the second floor and he walked down a long hall to the furthest corner of the building. He approached a wall at the end of the hall with a porthole window. Through the window, he could make out two figures wearing garments that looked like space suits. The two people were sitting at a tissue culture hood. One of the scientists was using an automated dispenser to transfer a clear liquid into a series of culture plates that were lined up on the bench inside the hood. Each plate contained a layer of red fluid.

Ahmed pushed an alert button on the wall. Both of the scientists turned to look toward the window. The one holding the dispenser stood up, walked to an intercom box next to the window, and pushed a switch. It was Shane.

"Hi, Ahmed, what's up?"

"Are you almost done? I have a special surprise planned for you and Teresa."

"We'll be done in ten minutes. We're just infecting the last batch of cells with the third aliquot of vector. We need to clean up the lab and shower. It'll take forty-eight hours for the cytopathic changes to develop. Then we'll know."

"No problem. I'll wait for you in the lab."

Teresa and Shane strolled hand-in-hand into the lab a few minutes later. They were wearing jeans and tee shirts. Shane walked up and placed his hand on Ahmed's shoulder.

"Hey, dude, nice tuxedo. You look like Mr. GQ. What's up?"

Ahmed shut down the computer and stood up from his chair. He smiled.

"I think you two might enjoy a night on the town."

Ahmed handed each of them a garment bag. He glanced at his watch.

"Go freshen up and put these on. The car will be here in forty-five minutes."

Teresa glanced at Shane and smiled. He took her hand and gave it a squeeze.

"We'll be ready! What's the occasion?"

Ahmed grinned and shrugged his shoulders.

"It's a surprise, my friend. Let's just say it's your reward for a job well done. I'll wait for you here."

Shane and Teresa hustled off to their living quarters to dress. Buster pranced around their feet the entire time. He could sense the excitement in the air.

It took them just over half an hour to get ready. Teresa was holding Shane's arm and laughing hysterically, as they sauntered back into the lab. Shane was wearing a black tux with a blue cummerbund. Teresa wore a blue sequined evening gown with a plunging neckline. She was absolutely ravishing. Teresa curtsied and Ahmed kissed her on the cheek.

"You look so beautiful, Teresa. Are you ready?"

Shane patted Ahmed on the back.

"We're ready! I was just telling Teresa about the last time I wore a tux. It was at my high school homecoming. I got a little carried away on the dance floor and ripped the seat out of my pants."

"This I would have paid money to see," Ahmed chuckled.

They strolled to the foyer and stepped through the same door they'd entered seven weeks earlier. It was a warm and beautiful Vancouver evening. A black stretch limousine was idling at the curb. The driver opened the door and the three of them crawled into the back.

The limousine accelerated away from the facility and meandered through the industrial park. Less than fifteen minutes later, they were cruising along the Vancouver waterfront, as the bright orange sun set behind a regatta of sailboats dueling on the bay. The car made a left turn into the parking lot of a marina and glided to a stop in front of a waterfront restaurant. A doorman helped the three of them out.

A red carpet led from the driveway and up a flight of stairs to the front door of the restaurant. A brass plaque next to the entry read "The Admiral's Perch." The doorman opened the door and the three of them stepped into the foyer.

The restaurant was decked out with crystal chandeliers and fine linen. It had ceiling to floor windows overlooking the marina. The maître d' led them to a table next to the window and seated Teresa in a high-back chair looking out over a line of grand yachts of every size and shape. The last remnant of the sun set behind a row of masts.

"Saaed, it's beautiful!" Teresa exclaimed with a smile. "I've missed the water so much. Thank you."

The waiter was a tall, distinguished-looking man wearing long tails. He smiled, as he handed each of them a menu.

"Welcome to The Perch. Can I offer you a cocktail?"

Ahmed Jan smiled at Shane and Teresa. He reached across the table and took Teresa's hand with his left and Shane's hand with his right."

"This is a special night for my friends. I'd like to start with a bottle of your finest champagne."

"We have a rare bottle of Krug rosé at twenty-two hundred dollars. I'd be happy to bring that for you, sir. What is the occasion, if you don't mind my asking?"

"It's a celebration of friendship."

"That is indeed a special occasion. The Krug is a perfect choice, sir."

"That will be fine."

The waiter strode away. They looked out over the marina without speaking for a few moments. An Azimut 68 Plus motor yacht was tied up in the temporary moorage for diners directly below them. Its sleek profile and beauty gave Shane chills. She was named the *Pacific Princess*.

"Saaed, this is very special. Thank you. We'll feel like idiots if the project doesn't work out."

"It wouldn't be because you haven't put your heart and soul into the work. I can't begin to tell you how much I appreciate what both of you have done. I wanted to do something special for you. These past two months I have come to love you like a brother and sister."

Shane reached across the table and rested his hand on Ahmed's arm.

"You're a good man, Saeed. Teresa and I hope you find happiness and fulfillment. We will always be grateful for the way you've treated us. I've had a lot of time to think things over the past few weeks. I know you saved our lives. God knows what would've happened if the Arabs found us. You reintroduced me to my heritage and gave us the time we needed to think about our future. We want you to be the first to know. Teresa and I are going to marry."

Ahmed beamed and took Teresa's hand in his.

"Ahh. This is great news. A perfect occasion for champagne."

The waiter set a silver ice bucket on the table and displayed the label on the champagne. Ahmed nodded and the waiter opened the bottle. He poured a taste for Ahmed. Ahmed took a sip and smiled.

"It's very fine."

The waiter poured the golden bubbly nectar and scurried away. Shane lifted his glass.

"I want to propose a toast. To Tajiks everywhere. May our people find peace and happiness."

"And I would like to toast to the marriage of my friends and to the *Pacific Princess*. May she bring you a lifetime of pleasure."

Shane stared at Ahmed with a perplexed expression.

"The *Pacific Princess?*"

"I feel deep regret over the loss of your friend, your boat, and life as you knew it. I wanted to do what little I could to make it up to you in the name of the Tajik people."

"Saeed, I still don't understand."

Ahmed held out his hand toward the yacht below.

"The *Pacific Princess*. This is your new home."

Both Teresa and Shane suddenly dropped Ahmed's code name.

"Oh my God, Ahmed!" Teresa squealed. "It's beautiful."

"Ahmed, I can't accept this. It's too much."

"I only wish I could do more. You've been uprooted from your life, your friend was killed, and you lost your sailboat. It's the safest place for you to live for the next few years. Besides, the American government paid for it."

"The American government?"

"Your government provided the Northern Alliance with hundreds of millions of dollars for reconstruction since the war started in Afghanistan. I would say this is reconstruction of the highest quality."

Shane lifted his glass and shook his head in disbelief.

"To the *Pacific Princess* and the American government."

They clicked their glasses and sipped the fine champagne. Shane took a deep breath and gazed with awe at the dazzling yacht below.

"Thank you, Ah..." Shane caught himself. "Thank you Saaed. I'm speechless."

"That alone is worth the price of the yacht."

The waiter returned and took their orders. They talked and laughed like the oldest of friends, as they finished the bottle of champagne and went on to a meritage.

"Can I ask you something, Saaed?"

"Sure, my friend, ask me anything you want."

"I'd like to know the whole story of the vector. I feel like we're part of this now."

"You are a big part. I will tell you what I can. My father was a commander of the Northern Alliance under our great leader Commander Massoud. Our people were under blistering attack. Our forces were under siege by the Taliban and al-Qaida in the northeast corner of Afghanistan and many of our leaders were killed. My father died in battle near Taloqan. It was only a matter of time before we would have been overrun. An al-Qaida death squad posing as journalists assassinated Commander Massoud. He died on September ninth of last year. It was our bleakest hour. Two days later, al-Qaida destroyed the World Trade Center and damaged the Pentagon. That turned out to be the beginning of our rebirth."

Ahmed proceeded to give a detailed account of the prior nine months.

They dined on crab cakes, endive salad, and lobster tails, as he told them of the events in Kabul with Mullah Habid, Mustafa and Mohammajon, the journey through the Khyber Pass, their incarceration in the Military Hospital in Rawalpindi, Fatima, and the apartment in Amsterdam. Teresa and Shane sat in silence listening to the implausible tale of sacrifice, courage, and betrayal. Ahmed finally sat back and folded his hands.

"All of this occurred in just over twelve months. I was transformed from a boy to a man in this one year."

"It's an incredible story, Saaed. Can I ask what happened to your hand?"

Ahmed held up his twisted and scarred hand.

"The Taliban and al-Qaida did this when they captured me at the battle for Taloqan, but it was nothing compared to the torture they inflicted in the Khyber Pass."

"I can't imagine. What happened to Mustafa?"

"I cannot tell you where he is, but I think he and Fatima have found happiness."

"And Mohammajon?"

"He returned to Afghanistan. Allah willing, he too will find peace."

"So where do you go from here, Saaed?"

"I can't tell you this, my friend. Not because I don't want to tell you, but because I really don't know. I must return to Afghanistan with the vector. I will leave as soon as you finish."

"It is my hope there will be no need to release the vector," Shane said. "But if it became necessary, wouldn't it be safer to release it in Pakistan?"

"I've considered that. But, that would drive more Pashtun refugees into Afghanistan. Then an antidote might be found before the virus spread to Afghanistan. It would also result in the killing of many innocents. I must take it to Afghanistan and release it among our enemy."

"Saaed, what can we do to help you?"

"I'll be satisfied only if my good friends live a full and happy life. I'll contact you with my address when this is finished. I'll yearn for the day the pictures of your children arrive in my mail."

Ahmed took one last sip of champagne.

"No more business tonight. Look there, dessert is waiting on the sun deck of the *Pacific Princess*. Come, let's see what you think of her."

CHAPTER FORTY-EIGHT

Shane peered into the microscope. He pushed the culture plate back and forth on the stage and then sat back. Teresa sat at a computer entering data in a spreadsheet. They were both wearing protective suits.

"This is culture 10 of viral vector batch 3. The cells are 4 plus infected. Most of them are already dead."

"Okay. That's it. Cultures 2, 6, and 10 were infected with all three batches of the virus. None of the other cultures show any evidence of infection. Batch 3 appears to have the highest potency."

"Ahmed should be here by now. It's time to break the code. I'll put one ampule from each batch in the exit port. Let's get out of here."

Teresa and Shane exited the level 4 biosafety facility fifteen minutes later and made their way down to the lab on the first floor. Ahmed was sitting at one of the desks scanning through a Dari newspaper. He looked up.

"Well, how did they look?"

"Cultures 2, 6, and 10 were infected."

Ahmed unfolded a paper from his shirt pocket. He scanned down the page, nodded solemnly, and stood up from the chair.

"Cultures 2, 6, and 10 were Pashtun samples. The others in the first ten were taken from Tajiks, Uzbeks, and a Hazara. Samples 11 through 18 were taken from three white Americans, two black Americans, two Russians, and an Arab. Was one of the vector batches more potent than the others?"

Shane nodded.

"Batch 3 appeared to be the most potent. We left a concentrated ampule of each batch in the exit port of the biosafety facility. All you need to do is break the top off the ampule and disperse the powder in an area where Pashtun are congregated. It must be a dry environment so the powder scatters. Don't use it in the rain. That's very important. I hope it never becomes necessary."

"As do I. The situation has developed rapidly over the past two days. I must leave here within an hour. Pack the things you want to take with you. I'll drop you off at the *Pacific Princess* before I go."

Shane nodded.

"We'll hurry. We can be ready in half an hour."

Shane took Teresa's hand and the two walked away toward their compound. Buster jumped off the bed to greet them when they opened the door. They pulled their luggage out of the closet and began to pack.

Ahmed waited for the inner door to close before he hastened from the lab and bounded up the stairs. There was a yellow laboratory explosive cabinet at the top of the stairs. He unlocked the cabinet door and fetched a large box from the top shelf. It was labeled "REI Outdoor Clothing Store."

Ahmed closed the cabinet door and carried the box to the end of the hall. He stopped in front of a metal door. There were large block letters on the door that read "LEVEL 4 BIOSAFETY FACILITY, DANGEROUS PATHOGENS, NO ADMITTANCE WITHOUT AUTHORIZATION."

He unlocked the door, stepped into the vestibule, and shut the door behind him. Ahmed set the box on a bench and turned the handle on a Plexiglas door in the middle of the back wall. He opened the door to reveal a small chamber about a foot long. The chamber had a door on the opposite side that opened from inside the biosafety laboratory. The chamber was empty except for three small glass ampules resting on a cloth.

Ahmed tore the top off the REI box. He pulled out a small black plastic cylinder that was a little larger in length and diameter than a cigarette. He held the cylinder against his chest with his left hand and unscrewed the tube with his right. The cylinder separated into two equal halves. The inside of each half was filled with small bits of white foam.

Ahmed set the top half of the cylinder down on the bench. He pressed the bottom against his chest and carefully lifted ampule number three out of the chamber. He held the two-inch long ampule up to the light. It was filled with a fine, yellowish-white powder. He slid the ampule into the middle of the plastic cylinder until it was buried beneath the bits of foam. He screwed the top of the cylinder back on and set it down on the bench.

Ahmed pulled a parka from the REI box and sat down on the bench. The coat was made of dark brown nylon. Ahmed tore the new garment tags off the coat and used an Exacto knife to cut a small slit along the bottom seam of one of the front panels. He slid the cylinder through the slit and manipulated it deep into the down insulation.

He sorted through the tissue paper in the bottom of the box until he found a tube of Superglue. Ahmed flicked off the tip with the Exacto knife, applied a dollop of the glue just inside the cut in the fabric, and pressed the edges together. He held the jacket up to the light. The defect in the seam was nearly imperceptible. He pressed the jacket between his two hands. The cylinder was well concealed.

Ahmed slipped on the coat, opened the door to the hall, and turned out the lights. He shut the door to the biosafety facility behind him and headed for the stairs.

Ustad loaded the last bag in the trunk and slammed it shut. He jumped into the front seat and closed the door.

"Let's go!" Ahmed ordered. "We're running out of time."

Ustad pulled the car onto the access road. Shane and Teresa turned in their seats and looked out the back window, as the building housing the laboratory disappeared behind the construction wall. Teresa sighed and slid her hand into Shane's.

"I never thought I'd miss this place," Teresa whispered. "I feel like we're leaving our first home. How about you, Buster?"

She patted the dog on the head. Buster wagged his tail and stuck his head out through the open rear window. Ahmed looked back from the front seat and smiled.

"I will never forget the time we spent together in this place."

It was a beautiful, cloudless day with a prevailing easterly wind. Ustad headed toward Vancouver Harbor. He drove through the heart of downtown and turned onto the avenue that ran along the water. They pulled into the marina less than a mile later.

The car squealed to a stop and four of them stepped out. Buster jumped down to the sidewalk and wandered over to the grass. Ustad fetched Shane and Teresa's luggage from the trunk. He ducked back into the car, leaving Ahmed, Shane, and Teresa standing on the sidewalk. Ahmed gave each of them a bear hug.

"May Allah be with you. Trust only yourselves."

"Ahmed, we left the lab notebook on my desk. Should we go back and get it?"

"There's no time. I don't need it anyway. Perhaps it will help the Americans decipher the virus and neutralize the vector."

"Is there anything more we can do to help, Ahmed?"

"No, my friend. You have done more than enough. You are a great Tajik patriot, Shane. Just like your great uncle Habibullah Kalakani."

Ahmed gripped Shane's hand.

"It's time for you to get on with your lives together. The Swiss bank account is in order. You can now access all the funds. These are the keys to the *Pacific Princess*. I hired a man to captain your boat for the next twelve months. He should be waiting for you down at the *Princess*. You must continue to use your new identities. Steven and Molly Nelson. What could be more American?"

Shane took the keyring and stuck it in his pocket.

"We'll keep the satellite phone on until we hear from you. We will hear from you, won't we, Ahmed?"

Ahmed nodded ruefully. There was a hint of sadness in his eyes. Shane waited for him to speak. Ahmed finally thumped him on the shoulder and smiled.

"Goodbye, my friends. I will contact you when I can."

Ahmed strode to the passenger side of the car and got in. Shane and Teresa watched in silence, as the car rambled away from the curb and turned out of the parking lot.

Ustad eased the car to a stop about a quarter of a mile beyond Centenniel Pier. He turned into a parking lot in front of a cluster of warehouses that lined the water and parked near an open gate. Ahmed jumped out of the car with his backpack and parka. He slammed the door shut, jogged through the gate, and headed down the walkway toward the water.

There was a freighter named the *Ocean Trader* tied up along the dock next to one of the warehouses. Two men on the dock were just pulling away the gangplank, as two sailors on the ship watched from the deck. Ahmed sprinted toward the gangplank and shouted with both hands cupped to his mouth.

"Hold it! I'm Saaed Mohammed. First Mate Timo Henderson told me to come by and speak with the captain about a cabin that might be available for the voyage to Karachi. Is that still open?"

One of the sailors lifted a megaphone and called down from the deck.

"Wait here just a moment. I'll ask the captain."

The man hustled up two sets of stairs along the starboard side of the ship and disappeared through a door leading to the bridge. He reappeared a few moments later and waved Ahmed aboard. Ahmed scurried across the gangplank and bolted up the stairs to the bridge.

There were three men on the bridge, including an old salt wearing faded blue overalls. He had leathery skin with a red nose and pitted cheeks above his snow-white beard. He was wearing a maritime officer's hat.

The man motioned Ahmed to a small windowless room containing a lone desk. He closed the door behind them and peered at Ahmed over his half-eye readers.

"Me name be Captain Torkel," he said with a thick accent. "How can I help yee?"

Ahmed reached out and shook his hand.

"My name is Saaed Mohammed. I'm looking for passage to Karachi. I met your first mate at the Mariner's Grill last night. He told me you had a cabin available."

Captain Torkel rubbed his white beard and stared at the stranger for a few moments.

"Yee ain't one of them terrorists, are yee?"

Ahmed chuckled, smiled, and shook his head.

"No, sir. I'm just trying to get home. My family lives in northern Afghanistan. I haven't seen my mother in eight years. I just got word she's very ill."

"Why don't yee take an airplane? It be's a lot faster."

"I had some trouble with the Pakistani government a few years back. They don't like my people there. I doubt they'd let me through customs."

"I see. Are yee carrying any weapons in that backpack?"

"No, sir, just clothing, a cell phone, and some kitchen utensils I bought here in Vancouver for friends and family back in Afghanistan."

"Do you mind if'n I takes me a look?"

"No, go right ahead."

Ahmed set the backpack on the desk and opened the straps. The captain looked down into the main compartment and pulled out a stack of clothing. He looked up at Ahmed and then turned the pack upside down. Dozens of can openers, bottle openers, cheese cutters, and other inexpensive kitchen utensils spilled out across the desk, along with a book of poetry.

"Glory be son. How many kin yee got?"

"I have many friends and family members in the North. I want to take a little something to each of them."

The captain thumbed through the book and then loaded the utensils back into the backpack and covered them with the clothing. He shut the flap on the pack.

"What freighter experience has yee had?"

"I haven't had any experience, sir. But I'm willing to learn."

Captain Torkel grinned and shook his head.

"Son, we be's at sea for thirty days before we be's maken Bombay. You be's cost'n me more food and supplies than I be's gettin out of yee. This ain't no maritime school."

"I'm willing to pay."

Captain Torkel's expression brightened straight away.

"Well then, why didn't yee be's sayin' so in the first place? Cash?"

"Yes, I'll pay in American dollars."

"How much this be worth to yee?"

"Mr. Henderson mentioned ten thousand dollars as the going rate."

"Yee got that kind of cash?"

"Yes."

"Well then, there be's a cabin for yee. We be's headin' for Bombay, but we's goin' on to Karachi to drop off a hundred tons of lumber. It be's best yee pay me now."

"How about if I pay you half now and the other half just before we hit port in Karachi?"

"I guess that'll be's working. I'll be askin' yee to stay aboard ship in Bombay."

"That's fine. There's one more thing, Captain."

"Yes?

"I'll need help getting on a bus in the Saddar district once we arrive in Karachi. I need to slip in without the authorities knowing. Can you arrange that?"

The old captain stroked his beard.

"That'll be's takin' some doin', son. I could get meself arrested. Don't fancy spendin' time in some filthy Pakistani jail."

The captain turned and looked out the window toward the dock. He sighed.

"I makes yee a deal, son. Any the crew ask yee, yee tell 'em yee paid me two thousand dollars for passage. That gets yee a private cabin and three meals a day. Once we gets to Karachi, we gets yee to Saddar. How's that be soundin' to yee?"

"You've got a deal."

Ahmed unzipped one of the pockets on his parka and pulled out a wad of one hundred dollar bills. He counted out fifty one hundred dollar bills and handed them to Captain Torkel. The captain stuffed the bills into his overalls and opened the door. He gestured at one of the sailors.

"Mr. Peters. Be showin' Mr. Mohammed to Donner's old cabin. Mr. Moeller, yee can shove off."

"Aye, aye, Captain."

Peters led Ahmed down the stairs to the main deck and then down another set of stairs. They headed toward the stern.

"Here's your cabin, sir."

Peters opened the door and turned on the light. The room was little more than a closet with a narrow bunk, metal table, and reading lamp. It had a single porthole window.

"This is your key. I need to get back up to the deck."

Peters jogged off down the hall. Ahmed hung his parka on a hanger in the closet and slid his backpack beneath the bed. He locked the door and headed for the stairs.

The ship had already put the dock a quarter mile behind by the time Ahmed reached the deck. The afternoon sun felt warm against his face. He shaded his eyes with his hand and scanned along the waterfront in the same way a tourist might relish his last glimpse of an exotic port.

It took just over half an hour for the freighter to ease out of False Creek and make its way into English Bay. Dozens of boats were scattered across the choppy bay enjoying the beauty of the Vancouver waterfront. One of the vessels caught Ahmed's eye. He looked up the deck and noticed one of the sailors was standing near the bow of the ship scanning the horizon with binoculars. Ahmed strode up behind him.

"Sir, can I borrow your binoculars for a moment?"

The sailor turned and smiled. He handed Ahmed the glasses.

"Sure. Take your time."

Ahmed rested his elbows on the rail. He panned across the bay and focused in on the distant boat. He scanned across to the stern and zoomed in on the name. It was the *Pacific Princess*. He scanned upward to the sun deck where Shane and Teresa were standing against the rail sipping champagne. The breeze was gusting through their hair. Teresa was wearing a dazzling, metallic-blue bikini. Shane was bare-chested above a pair of shorts. Buster ran back and forth across the deck, howling in the air. Teresa laughed, leaned against Shane, and kissed his cheek. Shane combed her hair away from her face with his fingers and kissed her on the lips.

Ahmed smiled contentedly and handed the binoculars to the sailor.

"Beautiful day on English Bay, huh sir."

"Yes, it is. It's a wonderful day on English Bay."

CHAPTER FORTY-NINE

August 22, 2002

S tone plopped down in a high-back chair in a secure room in the regional office of the FBI in Seattle. He lifted the receiver on the phone and dialed. A woman answered after a few rings.

"Central Intelligence Agency, may I help you?"

"This is Stone Waverly. I'm returning Deputy Director Richards' call."

"Just a moment, sir. I'll see if he's in."

There was a click on the line a minute later.

"You there, Stone?"

"Yes, sir. I'm calling from the FBI field office in Seattle."

"What'd you find?"

"Sir, your information was right on target. They've been working in the partially constructed research facility at the Bioeng Company in Northern Vancouver. Bioeng halted construction last November when they ran short of funding. The company headquarters is in Toronto. No one in Toronto seems to have a clue about what was going on in Vancouver. We're trying to find out how the Tajiks got access to the facility."

"How'd you miss it, Stone?"

"There was no record of the facility in the Mounties' files. The company hasn't even filed for a permit to open the lab. They were only twenty-five percent finished with the construction and the permit costs fifty thousand dollars. The facility just looked like an incomplete shell from the street. The lab where they were working was tucked in behind the construction site. We never even got close. How'd you uncover it, sir?"

"Total blind luck Stone. One of our operatives in Kabul got an anonymous tip to search the Bioeng lab in Vancouver. We passed the information on to you as soon as it came in. Did you find Kalakan?"

"No sir. The facility was completely deserted."

"Are you sure it's the right lab, Stone?"

"It's the right lab alright. We found fingerprints all over the facility. Shane Kalakan and Ahmed Jan have both been in the lab. Jan's prints matched a set we got from the ISI in Rawalpindi. I guess I owe you a dinner sir."

"Damn it, Stone, are you telling me Kalakan and Ahmed Jan got away again?"

"It looks that way, sir. There were several sets of prints we haven't been able to I.D. One set matched prints we found on Kalakan's sailboat."

"Damn it, Stone. These sons-of-bitches are making us look like the Keystone Cops. Have you got a search underway?"

"Yes sir. We have two hundred operatives working on this in Canada and the Northwest U.S. We alerted the Border Patrol. We have agents and Mounties in every airport, train station, and ferry depot in British Columbia. The Coast Guard is searching for them in the Gulf Islands and throughout the waterways in British Columbia. We've gotten photos to every bus and cab driver in the province. The Mounties are scouring all the car rental agencies. We've even set up random roadblocks on highways leading out of western British Columbia. We're doing everything we can to find them. It's a big country, sir."

"How about the lab? Anything else there?"

"We have some good news, sir. We found a lab notebook describing the construction of the Armageddon vector. Two different people made multiple entries over the past two months. One of them was Kalakan. The other writer was John Doe from the sailboat. His prints were all over the notebook. We've collected hairs and other specimens for DNA analysis. The notes indicate they finished construction of the vector using a Pashtun homing sequence and tested it on human white blood cell lines. The notes also document preparation of three batches of concentrated virus. We found several culture specimens and two ampules that contain a yellow-white powder. One was labeled "number one" and the other was labeled "number two." We sent it out for analysis at the Army infectious diseases unit at Fort Detrick. I also sent them a copy of the lab notebook."

"Tell their commanding officer we need the analysis as soon as possible. It sounds like Kalakan and Jan may have one batch of the purified viral vector with them."

"That seems like a good bet, sir."

"Good work, Stone. I'm betting Kalakan and Jan have already left British Columbia. We've got a slew of other problems that need attention. This damned investigation has diverted too many Company resources. I want you to cut back the search in British Columbia and the northwest to just enough agents to complete the investigation at the lab. The Armageddon vector can only be used in an area where there's a high density of Pashtun. I'll alert our operatives in both Pakistan and Afghanistan. Come on home and take some time off."

"Sir, are you sure you want to cut back this soon? Kalakan and Jan may still be hiding here in Vancouver."

"We got the vector, Stone. Wrap things up and come on home. The scientists at Fort Detrick can get to work on measures to counteract the vector."

"Sir, don't you think we should send out a general alert to the Pakistani and Afghani governments? This virus could kill a lot of people. It'll spread like a wildfire if they manage to release it."

"Not just yet, Stone. We don't want to create a panic. They've got plenty of problems to deal with right now. I'll talk to the director. He'll probably confer with the president."

"Sir, with all due respect, I don't think we can afford to wait. The Muslim world will blame the U.S. if the Tajiks manage to release this vector and kill thousands of Pashtun. It could conceivably kill millions. Our Muslim allies will be convinced the U.S. developed this biological weapon as a convenient way to eliminate the Taliban."

Stone waited for Richards to respond. He listened as the deputy director chewed on his cigar.

"Stone."

"Yes, sir."

"I'll handle the investigation from here. Wind things up there and come on home. That pretty wife of yours needs you here in Virginia."

"Yes, sir."

"Stone, one more thing."

"Yes, sir?"

"We never had this conversation. You understand?"

Stone sat in stunned silence.

"Do you understand, Stone?"

"Yes, sir, I understand."

"You're a good man. Take a couple of weeks off when you get back to

Virginia. Give me a call just before you come back to work. How does September twelfth sound?"

"It sounds good, sir. It's been a tough year."

"I'm sending Mickey Barber out there to take over for you. He'll be there by tomorrow night. See you in a few weeks."

Stone hung up the phone. He folded his arms across his chest, leaned back into the high-back chair, and stared at the blank white wall on the other side of the desk.

CHAPTER FIFTY

October 5, 2002

A hmed leaned against the rail on the main deck and took a long drag on his cigarette. A cool, gentle breeze wafted against his face. The *Ocean Trader* cut its engines and glided to a standstill just outside the mouth of Karachi Harbor. The clatter of heavy chains was followed by a splash as the anchor hit the water.

Ahmed flicked the butt of his cigarette overboard and gazed out across the lights of Karachi's eight million people. The flickering lights extended beyond the harbor as far as the eye could see. The eerie quiet triggered a sudden sense of foreboding.

Most of the cruise from Vancouver had been uneventful. The first month was the most peaceful period of Ahmed's young life. He had time to contemplate the future without anxiety, battle, or killing. He spent hours reading the poetry of Hafez. Ahmed came to appreciate Commander Massoud's love of the master's work. He'd reread the passage Massoud had cited from memory so many times that the page had become dog-eared.

The *Ocean Trader* had been ravaged by a squall off the coast of Indonesia thirty days into the voyage. That morning there'd been a magnificent crimson sunrise beneath a distant gathering of clouds. The first mate, Henderson, taught Ahmed the ancient maxim of the mariner: "Red sky at morning, sailor take warning."

By afternoon the freighter was forging through driving rain and raging seas. Ahmed spent those two days rocking and rolling in his cabin bunk. He retched time and again and fought uncontrollable terror as the gale built to a crescendo.

Nothing horrified the Tajik more than the thought of drowning at sea.

An alarm sounded the first night of the storm when the ship was tossing to and fro like a toy. Ahmed learned later that a wave the size of a four-story building had broken across the bow. The force of the breaker shredded the duel safety lines on a sailor struggling to secure cargo. The poor man was washed from the deck and into the furious sea before anyone knew what happened.

The storm subsided as quickly as it came, and the *Ocean Trader* made Bombay the following night. While one team of longshoremen offloaded half of her cargo of lumber, another replenished her fuel and supplies. Ahmed stayed hidden in his cabin for two days while the ship was in port. He was too close to his goal to make a stupid mistake now.

Ahmed called Mullah Habid on his satellite phone just as the ship shoved off from Bombay. It was the first time in three months he'd so much as turned the phone on. Better Bombay, India, as the ship departed, than Karachi, Pakistan, as they arrived.

The call confirmed what Ahmed had read in a Dari newspaper prior to departing Vancouver. The Taliban was regrouping throughout Afghanistan, but especially in the areas around Kandahar and Khost. They were biding their time and waiting for the Americans to become distracted in Iraq or any one of a dozen other flashpoints across the world. Karzai had been unable or unwilling to stem the buildup. The mullah ordered Ahmed to call for final orders when he arrived in Kandahar.

Ahmed struck a match and lit another cigarette between his cupped hands. He took a long drag and blew the smoke into the cool breeze. He started at the sound of the hatch opening behind him.

"Thar yee be's, Mr. Mohammed. Er yee ready to disembark?"

"Yes, Captain. Are we docking in Karachi tonight?"

"No, thar docks be's filled. We'll be's dockin' at ten hundred hours in the mornin'. A customs officer likely be's awaitin' to inspect the papers of the crew and the cargo. We going to hide yee in the cargo hold til he be's leavin'. Once he be's gone, two me men be's takin' yee to Saddar to put yee on the bus."

"That sounds like a good plan, Captain. Thank you for your help."

"Mr. Mohammed, best yee and me be's settlin' now."

Ahmed stuck his hand in the pocket of his parka and pulled out another wad of hundred dollar bills. The captain took the bills and stuffed them deep into his pants pocket.

"Yee best be's stayin' below deck when the sun come a callin'. Yee don't want no customs agent spottin' yee here on deck. Yee report to the first mate at yee cabin when yee be's hearin' the clatter'n anchor chain. Good luck to yee and yee mother."

"Thank you, Captain. Good luck to you."

Ahmed heard the clatter of the anchor chains just after nine hundred hours the following morning. First Mate Timo Henderson met him at his cabin. He helped Ahmed strip the bunk and spitclean the cabin. Once they finished, Henderson led Ahmed to the aft cargo hold with all of his belongings. The sailors had fashioned a hidden chamber against the starboard of the cargo hold using stacked bundles of lumber. The compartment was little more than a meter square.

"You stay here until I come to get you. Be quiet as a mouse if you hear the hatch open. Remember, if the inspector finds you, none of us knew anything about you. Tell 'em you stowed away in Bombay when we were offloading cargo. No sense anyone else going to prison. You pay your money and you take your chances."

Ahmed grasped Henderson's arm.

"You can count on my silence."

"God be with you, Saaed. Be careful in Karachi. There are many thieves and murderers who'd slit your throat just to steal the shoes off your feet. Convert a small amount of your money into rupees and hide the rest in your underwear."

Ahmed ducked into the hiding place. Timo used a winch to move a large bundle of lumber over the entrance to the hideaway. Ahmed hid there in the stuffy darkness for the better part of an hour before the ships engines shifted to idle.

Thirty minutes later the hatch opened and Ahmed heard voices conversing in English. He recognized Timo Henderson speaking with another man. The two men made small talk, as they shuffled down one side of the cargo hold and then the other. They walked past Ahmed's hiding place to the far end of the hold and then back again. The two were in the cargo hold for less than five minutes before their voices faded and finally disappeared. The hatch clanked shut and the hold went silent.

Ahmed heard the hatch open again a few minutes later. Henderson called out to him.

"Mr. Mohammed, stand back and I will lift the bundle of lumber away."

Henderson used the winch to shift the bundle of lumber so Ahmed could squeeze out with his things. Henderson took the backpack.

"The inspector left the ship. The longshoremen are ready to start unloading the cargo. Let's go."

Ahmed followed Henderson up three flights of stairs to his cabin. He opened the door and set the backpack on the bed.

"Wait here until I come to fetch you. I'll sneak you out on the first truck that's loaded. Here's a bit of bread. It's probably all you'll get for a while."

"Thank you, Timo. I'll be here."

Henderson shuffled away toward the main deck.

Ahmed opened his backpack and pulled out a worn shalwar kameeze. He took off his jeans and shirt and put on the traditional garment. He pulled his money out of the zippered inside pocket of his parka. He counted out fifteen hundred dollars in hundred dollar bills and stuffed the rest of the cash into his undergarment before pulling up his pants. He slid on a pair of worn shoes and wrapped his head with a white turban. Kneeling to the floor beside the bed, he stuffed his jeans and long-sleeve shirt into the corner beneath the bunk and pulled on his REI parka. He secured the straps on his backpack and sat down on the edge of the bunk to wait for Henderson's return.

Over an hour passed before Henderson knocked on the cabin door. The first mate blinked with surprise when Ahmed opened the door.

"I'll be damned. I hardly recognize you. Let's get down to the dock. The truck is loaded and waiting."

Henderson reached beneath his shirt and pulled a handgun from his belt. It was an old 22-caliber pistol.

"Here, I want you to take this. I've kept it beneath the mattress in my cabin for fifteen years and never even pulled it out once. It's loaded."

Ahmed took the pistol. He smiled and stuck it into the waistband of his shalwar kameeze.

"Thank you, my friend. I'm not deserving of your kindness."

The two men made their way down the hall and up the stairs through a hatch leading to the main deck. Ahmed shaded his eyes from the bright sunlight and peered down at the dock. It bustled with men rushing to and fro. A line of old trucks was parked along the dock. The column extended down the access road and around the corner. The truck at the front of the line was loaded with lumber. It had pulled off to one side. The driver gestured with his hand, as the two men shuffled down the gangplank to the dock. Ahmed jumped into the cabin next to the driver and Henderson leapt into the bed atop the load.

The driver jammed his foot down on the clutch and shifted the transmission into first gear. The truck lurched forward and turned onto a street that led away from the waterfront. They were ensnarled in city traffic within a block of the dock.

The truck inched ahead a few meters at a time through the narrow streets of Karachi toward the Saddar section of the city. They drove down one busy block after another. Every street was bustling with pedestrians, bicycles, cars, and trucks going every which direction. Vendors and shopkeepers were busy peddling every imaginable type of merchandise.

After nearly an hour of stop-and-go driving, the truck accelerated onto a highway on-ramp. Traffic on the thoroughfare was surprisingly light and they made good time the rest of the way to Saddar.

The truck finally turned off the highway into a more modern area of the city. Ahmed glanced at his watch. They'd driven for nearly an hour. The driver eased to a stop in the middle of a large transportation center crowded with minibuses, buses and trucks. Henderson jumped down from the bed and opened Ahmed's door.

"Saeed, first you must have rupees. Use one of those moneychangers beside the statue."

Ahmed walked across the street and approached a man behind one of the tables. He changed five hundred dollars and received just over thirty thousand rupees. He crammed the money into his pocket. Henderson was waiting behind him when he turned around.

"Okay, my friend, let's find a bus. What is your final destination?"

"I'm headed for Charman on the border with Afghanistan. Quetta would be fine. Even Sibi would get me partway there."

The two men set off together weaving through the crowd past dozens of vehicles parked along one side of the square. Drivers were standing outside calling out the names of their destinations. It only took a few minutes to find a man yelling "Sibi! Sibi! Air conditioning to Sibi!"

Ahmed approached the driver.

"How much to Sibi?"

"Five thousand rupees per person."

"Is there a bus to Charman?"

"No bus travels directly from Karachi to Charman. You must transfer in Sibi. That will cost another five to six thousand rupees."

"How long is the trip to Sibi?"

"Seven to eight hours. It's another five to seven hours from Sibi to Charman, depending on the weather."

"Okay. It's just me."

Ahmed counted out five thousand rupees and handed them to the driver. The man gave him change and helped him to stow his backpack in the baggage compartment. Henderson waited patiently for him to finish.

"All set, my friend?"

"All set, Timo."

"Okay. We'll be on our way. May God be with you."

Ahmed tried to hand him a roll of rupees, but Henderson waved him off.

"No, my friend. The captain gave me my share."

Ahmed hugged him and smiled.

"Thank you, Timo. I hope to see you again one day."

"I hope so. The *Ocean Trader* will return to Karachi in the spring. I'd enjoy hearing your stories about the Khyber Pass and the Lion of Panjshir if you need passage again. It was a pleasure to have you aboard."

He handed Ahmed a card.

"This card has the web site where our schedule is published. If Fate should return you to Karachi, I'd enjoy sharing a cup of tea and hearing about your adventure."

"Thank you, Timo. I look forward to seeing you again one day."

Ahmed turned and mounted the stairs into the bus. The cabin was stifling hot and the stench of human body odor hung in the air. Almost all the seats were occupied. Most of the passengers were men, but a few veiled women were sitting in seats next to windows with their husbands or fathers beside them. Ahmed felt the weight of dozens of eyes, as he shuffled down the aisle toward the rear of the bus. He spotted an open seat next to the window about two-thirds of the way back. The old man sitting in the isle was snoring. Ahmed stepped across him and dropped into the seat.

It became clear immediately why the seat was empty. It was directly above the wheel well. Ahmed had to assume a semi-fetal position with his legs on top of the metal protrusion. He glanced around behind him and scanned the rear of the bus. It was the only unoccupied seat.

The front door whooshed closed a short time later and the bus began to inch through the crowded square. The squat Pakistani driver honked the horn repeatedly in a futile attempt to clear the swarms of people from his path.

The bus reached the highway shortly before eleven in the morning. They headed north through dry and dusty downtown Karachi. The city was dotted with modern high-rises, antiquated apartment complexes, and decrepit structures that had been built throughout the city with no apparent attention to planning. The bus reached the outskirts of the city an hour later and merged onto a highway headed north along the Indus River.

The air-conditioning in the bus was useless. Ahmed wiped streams of sweat from his brow with his sleeves. He attempted to sleep, but the snoring of his seatmate and the cramped seat made that all but impossible.

The bus turned off the highway in Hyderabad two hours into the journey. The driver pulled to a stop at a roadside café that was nestled among a cluster of shops along the street. Most of the riders on the bus took the opportunity to stretch, use the restroom, and get a bite to eat.

Ahmed stepped down from the bus onto the dirt parking lot. He was swarmed by a group of poor Sindhi children begging for money as he headed for the café. He reached into his pocket and retrieved the coins the money-changer had given him in Karachi. An older boy tried to wrestle the coins from Ahmed's closed fist. Ahmed repelled him with his forearm and handed him a single coin.

Ahmed distributed the remaining coins to others in the mob. Another older beggar pushed a scrawny little boy away just as he reached for the last coin. The coin tumbled to the ground. The bully fetched the coin out of the dirt and jogged off laughing before Ahmed could grab him.

The young curly-headed boy began to sob, as he stared up at Ahmed with dark, pleading eyes. Ahmed pulled a one hundred-rupee note from his pocket and handed it to the boy. The dark-skinned youth wiped the tears from his eyes with a dirty sleeve. He looked down at the money and smiled up at Ahmed.

The older boy ran between them and ripped the note from the little boy's hand. He laughed, as he sprinted around the side of the café and disappeared. The smaller boy ran after him for a few steps, before falling face down on the ground. The other boys jogged by and mocked the little one, as they too disappeared around the side of the café.

Ahmed walked over to the little boy. He lifted him from the ground and brushed the dirt from his face. Tears were streaming from his eyes.

"What's your name, little mouse?"

The boy sobbed uncontrollably. He wiped away his tears with his forearm.

"Tahir."

"Why do the other boys mock you?"

"My father Christian," the boy answered in broken English. "They call me Infidel. They not play with Tahir."

Ahmed patted Tahir on top of the head.

"I'm hungry, Tahir. Are you hungry?"

The little boy nodded.

Ahmed picked him up and carried him to the café. He opened the door. Several of the passengers were crowded around a counter. Others were seated at makeshift tables in the back of the café. Ahmed carried Tahir to a line of bins filled with cookies and other pastries at the end of the counter. He set him down on his feet.

"Do you have any brothers and sisters, Tahir?"

The boy stared up with big, dark eyes.

"Two brothers and three sisters."

"Which is your favorite treat?"

The little boy wandered from one end of the bins to the other. He carefully inspected the contents of each bin, before he went on to the next. He periodically looked up at Ahmed. Each time, Ahmed smiled and motioned for him to continue.

A middle-aged man ducked out of the kitchen carrying a tray of food. He spotted the boy. He slammed the tray down on the counter and bounded across the café.

"Infidel! Get out of my café."

He reached out to grab Tahir.

Ahmed seized the man by the arm and spun him to the ground. He glared down at the man with a fierce look of admonition. Every head in the café turned.

"Leave the boy alone! He's with me. Tahir, which one do you want?"

Tahir pointed to a bin that was filled with assorted cookies.

"Fill a large bag with those cookies," Ahmed scowled at the proprietor.

The man, terror in his eyes, pushed himself off the floor. He scurried behind the counter and picked up a waxed-paper bag. He put a few cookies in the bag.

"Fill it!"

The man shook, as he filled the bag to the top with the cookies.

"Fill another bag with these," Ahmed demanded, with a point of his twisted hand.

The proprietor opened another bag and transferred pastries from the bin until the second bag was full. Ahmed pointed toward a roll of plastic bags.

"Put both bags into one of those."

The man opened a blue plastic bag and put both of the bags inside.

"Now, get me two servings of Qabeli."

The man scurried across the small café to the counter. He retrieved two cardboard containers from a shelf beneath the counter. The man glanced up at Ahmed repeatedly, as he filled each container with the dish of rice, raisins, mutton, carrots, and onions. The proprietor sealed each container and slipped them into a bag with paper towels and plastic utensils.

"How much?"

"Two hundred rupees for the pastries, sir. Ninety for the Qabeli."

Ahmed handed the man two thousand rupees and took the bags. He stepped forward and stared into the man's eyes. He whispered so only the proprietor could hear.

"You give this boy one bag of those cookies every week for the next two months. I'll return to Hyderabad in January. I'll come looking for you if you ever mistreat this boy again. Do you understand?"

The proprietor's eyes widened with fear. He nodded enthusiastically.

Ahmed walked toward the exit. The proprietor scurried ahead and held the door, as Ahmed and Tahir walked outside.

"Where do you live, Tahir?"

"Behind café," he pointed.

"Show me your home."

Ahmed followed the boy through stacks of old tires that were piled between the café and the gas station next door. The rear alley was lined with dozens of makeshift shacks fashioned from scraps of discarded metal, wood, and cardboard. Several older men were sitting on chairs outside a cluster of shacks across the alley from the café. The two older boys who'd accosted Tahir were standing nearby. They all turned to stare at Ahmed.

"Which house is yours, Tahir?"

The boy pointed across the alley toward a particularly shabby shed. Two toddlers were playing with a plastic ball on the strip of bare dirt in front of the crude structure.

Ahmed squatted beside Tahir. He playfully roughed the boy's hair and peered into his eyes.

"Tahir, always stand up for what you believe. Ignore those other boys. They are ignorant. Obey and love your mother and father, regardless of what those boys say. Do you understand?"

The boy nodded and continued to stare at Ahmed. Ahmed reached into his pocket. He pulled out a one thousand-rupee note and stuffed it into the boy's pocket. He handed Tahir the blue plastic bag filled with treats.

"Give the money to your father and take this bag to your mother. Get on home now."

Tahir smiled. He turned and ran across the alley to his home clutching the bag to his chest. Ahmed watched, as he and his brothers ducked through a blanket-covered doorway and disappeared into the shack. Ahmed glared toward the older boys, before retracing his steps to the front of the café. The bus driver waved.

"We go!" he yelled.

Ahmed walked to the bus and handed the driver the bag holding his lunch.

"Hold this. I'll be right back."

Ahmed hustled into the café and strode to a door near the back. He relieved himself in the bathroom swarming with flies. It reeked of urine.

Ahmed strode back to the bus and took the bag from the driver. He shuffled down the aisle, but his seat was occupied. There was a frail, old woman sitting next to the old man. She smiled with a toothless grin and motioned toward an empty seat a little farther back. Ahmed headed toward the back of the bus and slid into the aisle seat. He opened one of the containers and shoveled a spoonful of Qabeli into his mouth.

The bus pulled away from the café and merged back onto the highway. The route meandered north along the Indus River Valley. From time-to-time, the bus passed people traveling along the side of the road. Some groups led carts pulled by oxen or donkeys filled with belongings. Other travelers walked along the side of the road with everything they owned strapped to their backs. Many of the women wore burqas that covered their bodies from head to toe.

The bus arrived in Jacobabad five hours later. The driver announced overhead that he'd stop just long enough to refuel the bus. Most of the passengers took advantage of the opportunity to stretch and use the restroom. The bus was reloaded and careening down the highway less than twenty minutes later.

The bus finally pulled into Sibi a little after midnight. It was a typical Pakistani city, with a chaotic mixture of ancient and new. Shanty shacks were intermingled with residential buildings, with a few high-rises sprinkled here and there.

The bus wove through a series of darkened streets and finally came to a stop at the Sibi Transportation Center. It was little more than a parking lot with haphazardly scattered buses, trucks, and Suburbans. Ahmed was surprised to see drivers standing in front of vehicles calling out the destinations of cities in the middle of the night. Most of them shouted in Pashtu, the language of the Pashtun. Khost, Quetta, and Jacobabad were a few of the names he recognized.

Ahmed stepped down from the bus. He slipped on his parka and waited for the driver to pry his backpack out of the luggage compartment. Ahmed slipped the pack over his shoulders and meandered through the transportation center.

Ahmed considered finding a ride and going on to Cheman, but decided he was too worn out. He peered down one of the side roads that emptied into the transportation center. Nothing looked promising, so he walked to the next block. There was a small inn with a vacancy sign in the window a short distance up the second street. He trudged up the road and opened the door. A bell attached to the frame jingled, as he shut the door behind him.

An old Chinese man stepped through the doorway from a side room. He nodded. Ahmed spoke to him in English.

"Do you have a room for the night?"

The man nodded.

"One room. Two thousand rupees."

"I'll take it."

"Passport."

Ahmed handed him his Afghani passport and Pakistani travel papers. The man opened the forged passport. He looked at the photo and then at Ahmed, before sorting through the other papers. He wrote down some information on a pad and handed the documents back.

The man took a key from a drawer and picked up a small kerosene lamp from the counter. He led Ahmed down a short hallway past several other doors. He stopped in front of the last door, unlocked it, and pushed the door open.

The room was tiny, even by Pakistani standards. Along one side of the windowless space was a bunk with a small, frayed wicker table. The old man set the lamp down on the table. He nodded repeatedly at Ahmed, as he backed out the door and shut it behind him.

Ahmed sat on the edge of the bunk. He removed his shoes and unwound his turban. He stood up, removed the pistol from the waistband of his shalwar kameeze, and stepped toward the bed. There was a light knock on the door.

Ahmed grabbed the pillow from the bunk and used it to cover the pistol in his right hand. He stepped back across the room and opened the door.

A young Chinese man was standing in the hall. He glanced down the hall behind him, before whispering to Ahmed in fluent English.

"Mr. Mohammed, my name is Fushin. My father owns this inn. May I speak with you for a moment?"

Ahmed motioned him into the room. He slipped the pistol beneath the pillow on the bed and closed the door. The man spoke in a whisper.

"My father asked me to come speak with you."

"Yes, what is it."

"Mr. Mohammed, are you Tajik?"

Ahmed flinched with surprise, before quickly regaining his composure.

"Why do you ask?"

"At one time my father owned inns throughout the north of Afghanistan. Many of his good friends in Kabul and Taloqan were Tajik. My father fears for your safety."

Ahmed mulled over the young man's words for a moment. He decided to trust him.

"Yes, I'm Tajik."

"Mr. Mohammed, you are in grave danger here in Sibi. Many Taliban and Arab men have gathered in the hills the past few months. A few have ventured into town in recent weeks. Two Tajik families were slaughtered during the night last Saturday. One man was a good friend to my father. Even now his body is hanging in the main square. The Arabs threatened to kill anyone who touches him. There will be trouble if they find you here."

"I'll be leaving first thing in the morning for Cheman."

The Asian man's eyes widened with surprise.

"You cannot travel to Cheman, Mr. Mohammed. The roads between here and Cheman are swarming with Taliban. It is said there are thousands of Taliban hiding in the mountains south of Cheman. They search vehicles at random. They've even massacred Pashtun loyal to the new Afghan government. If they discover you…"

His voice tailed off without ending the sentence.

"Fushin, I must return to Kandahar. My mother is very sick. I must see her before she dies. Can you help me?"

"You are asking the impossible, Mr. Mohammed. I will speak to my father. You sleep now and I will wake you in the morning."

Fushin let himself out and walked back down the hall toward the entrance to the inn. Ahmed locked the door. He sat on the edge of the bunk and pulled the gun out from beneath the pillow. He checked to make sure a bullet was in the chamber and slipped it beneath his pillow. Sleep came quickly.

CHAPTER FIFTY-ONE

A hmed was awakened from a deep sleep by a knock on the door. He glanced at his watch. It was just shy of six in the morning. He sat up and tiptoed to the door with the pistol clutched in his hand. He leaned against the wall and whispered through the door.

"Who is it?"

"It's Fushin."

Ahmed slipped the pistol beneath his waistband. He unlocked the door and opened it. Fushin slipped into the room and closed the door behind him. He was carrying a bag.

"We must leave now for Cheman, Mr. Mohammed. It will take at least five to six hours. My father wants to be home before dark. Here, put this on."

Fushin handed the bag to Ahmed. Ahmed pulled a garment from the bag and unfolded it. It was a burqa.

"I will not wear this. I am a man."

"You must wear the burqa, Mr. Mohammed, if you want our help. My father and I are in grave danger. They'll kill us too if you are discovered."

Ahmed stared at Fushin and then at the burqa. He opened the garment, slipped it over his head, and rotated it so he could see out through the silk mesh.

Fushin stepped back and looked at him. The burqa was long enough to hide Ahmed's entire body down to the tops of his shoes. Fushin grabbed Ahmed's backpack and parka and opened the door.

"Let's go."

Ahmed followed him to the lobby. They slipped past two other guests and headed out through another doorway that led to the back of the inn. Fushin unbolted the door and opened it.

The alley behind the inn was littered with garbage. Old crates and boxes were stacked against the wall of the building next door. Ahmed gathered his burqa and stepped down the stairs to the mud.

An old green Suburban was idling next to the building. Fushin's father was sitting in the front passenger seat. Fushin opened the side passenger door and tossed the backpack and parka onto the floor. He guided Ahmed up into the second seat.

Fushin slammed the door and darted around the vehicle to the driver's side. He got in, put the vehicle in gear, and pulled away from the inn. Fushin's father turned in his seat. He smiled with a toothless grin and nodded at Ahmed without speaking.

Ahmed reached out and patted the old man on the arm.

"Thank you, sir," he said appreciatively.

The old man nodded again without looking back.

Ahmed peered out through the mesh in his burqa, as the Suburban wound through a series of streets lined with teahouses and shops. Even at this early hour, the street vendors were preparing their wares. They stacked clothing, blankets, and sacks of grain on tables in preparation for the crowds of people who would soon be meandering through the streets.

The Suburban reached the city limits of Sibi twenty minutes later and began to head along the highway to Quetta. The terrain was relatively flat for the first few kilometers, but then they began to wind through the foothills north of the city. The highway changed into a rutted asphalt road that coursed upward into the mountains through an endless series of steep inclines and sharp curves. The pavement was eroded away completely in some places. Long stretches of the road were strewn with rocks and boulders.

Fushin and his father remained silent for most of the trip. Now and then one of them would ask a question or comment on something they saw along the road. They seemed absorbed in their own thoughts.

From time-to-time the vehicle passed small groups of people walking or riding carts. None of the travelers paid much attention to the occupants of the Suburban. They were too preoccupied with their own challenges to care.

It took close to two hours to reach the outskirts of Quetta. The highway got better as they rumbled through a picturesque valley dotted with apple orchards and farms.

Fushin slowed at a Pakistani military checkpoint just outside the city. There were more than two dozen armed Pakistani soldiers milling around outside a mud-walled building. Ahmed guessed there were many more troops inside the garrison.

A Pakistani soldier with a Kalashnikov rifle draped across his shoulder held up his hand for them to stop. Fushin rolled down his window.

"Papers," the man demanded gruffly.

Fushin handed the soldier his father's identification and then his own. The soldier glanced at the documents and peered in the window toward the back seat where Ahmed sat in silence wearing the burqa. The soldier handed Fushin the identification and waved them through.

About a mile beyond the checkpoint the highway made a sharp curve and passed through a short tunnel that emptied out onto a plain filled with tents and shanty buildings. It was the Quetta refugee camp, home to thousands of people displaced from Afghanistan during the previous decade. Many of those dwelling in the camp had made their way into Pakistan to flee the intolerance of the Taliban. The trickle turned to a flood when the Northern Alliance and supporting Americans invaded the south. The vast majority of the people in the camp were Pashtun.

Quetta itself was delightful. The city was rebuilt in the early 1900s after a quake devastated the city. They drove into the bustling city center, past bazaars and markets full of shoppers and vendors. Tract after tract of small homes had been built to the north of the city within the past decade. They came upon a cluster of elegant estates on enormous landscaped lots dotted with prominent guard towers just outside the city limits.

The terrain flattened out for the next forty kilometers. The Suburban made good time during this stretch, as it sped along a well-maintained highway toward the Afghan border. They crossed railroad tracks sixty kilometers from Cheman. The road paralleled the tracks for several kilometers. A freight train sped past with its horn blaring just before the road turned to the south.

The Suburban began winding through a series of switchbacks just before eleven in the morning. Ahmed dozed off, as they gained altitude in the Khojak Pass to the south of the Afghani border. He was awakened by Fushin shouting in Chinese and honking at a convoy of six brightly colored trucks headed for Afghanistan. The trucks pulled to the side of the road and the Suburban sped past.

The vehicle reached the crest of the pass an hour later and headed down the other side. They emerged from a steep switchback and Cheman flooded into view below them. The city disappeared behind the canyon wall in the next turn, only to reappear around another sweeping curve.

They passed a road sign: "Cheman 5 km." Fushin, riding the brake, steered the vehicle down a steep incline and edged into a treacherous turn. The cliff to the right dropped off precipitously to the valley below and the Suburban slowed to a crawl. Fushin completed the turn into a small clearing and a group of armed men dressed in shalwar kameeze with black turbans came into view. There were at least forty fighters in the group. Most of them were carrying Kalashnikov rifles, but a few were holding rocket-propelled grenades.

"Taliban!" Fushin barked, as he slowed nearly to a stop.

Ahmed slipped the pistol from his waistband and held it at the ready beneath his burqa. A man in the road raised his hand and motioned for Fushin to stop. Fushin edged forward and rolled down the window.

"Stop!" the man yelled in English. "What is your nationality?"

"My father and I are both Chinese," Fushin answered. "We are permanent residents of Pakistan."

"Give me your identification."

Fushin handed him their papers. The fighter examined the cards for a few moments and then handed them back. The Taliban warrior stooped and peered through the window into the back seat. Beads of sweat were accumulating on Ahmed's brow beneath the burqa. He stared straight ahead through the mesh.

"Who's that back there?" the man demanded gruffly.

"My mother. We are trying to get her to the doctor in Cheman. She is very ill."

"Do you have food?"

"Just one loaf of bread."

"Okay, you may pass, but if you return this way we expect twenty loaves of bread in toll. Do you understand?"

"Yes, I understand."

The man waived them through the gauntlet of Taliban troops. Fushin rolled up his window and took a deep breath. The old man uttered something in Chinese. The younger man chuckled uncomfortably and looked back at Ahmed in the rearview mirror.

"My father says you are a lucky man."

"Why does he say that?"

"Because the Taliban steal women for wives."

Ahmed slipped his pistol back into his waistband.

"It's the Taliban bandit who's the lucky one."

The rest of the journey down the side of the mountain was uneventful. Along the way, they skirted past the Cheman refugee camp. It was little more than a decrepit tent city teeming with hungry, hopeless people. The Suburban reached the plateau less than thirty minutes later. They drove through the center of Cheman toward the border crossing into Afghanistan. Once a smuggling town, Cheman had become a busy crossing point for relief trucks bound for Afghanistan with blankets and food.

The narrow, dusty streets of the frontier city were lined with small shops and businesses swarming with humanity. Fushin pulled the Suburban to the side of the road next to a makeshift outdoor market. He leapt from the front seat and jogged to a food stand. Ahmed watched as the proprietor loaded loaves of bread into two large bags. Fushin paid the shopkeeper and carried the bags back to the truck. He opened the tailgate, tossed them into the rear, and jumped back in the driver's seat.

Fushin drove on to the edge of town. He pulled the Suburban onto the dirt and stopped when the border crossing came into view one hundred meters further down the road. He turned and smiled at Ahmed.

"Well, my friend, it looks like we made it."

"I am grateful for your kindness. Allah willing, my countrymen will welcome me and I'll gaze into my mother's eyes before the sun goes down this very day."

Ahmed held out ten thousand rupees.

"Please accept this."

Fushin's father shook his head and muttered something to his son in animated Chinese. Fushin waited until he finished, before nodding respectfully and turning back toward Ahmed.

"Mr. Mohammed, my father believes deeply in honor and tradition. Many years ago the Russians put a price on my father's head when an informant told them he was helping the Mujaheddin smuggle Stinger missiles into Panjshir Valley. The Russians threatened to kill anyone who aided him. A Tajik family living in Taloqan hid my father for two weeks until the Mujaheddin could spirit him away to the South. The Russians found out several months later. They shot the Tajik man who saved my father's life. My father does not want your money. The debt he has borne for so long is now paid."

Ahmed patted Fushin's father on the shoulder. The old man stared straight ahead, tears welling in his eyes.

"May I keep the burqa?"

"Please, it has served you well."

Ahmed slipped the burqa off over his head, folded it, and packed it into the top of his backpack. He opened the passenger door and stepped down to the ground.

The road leading up to the border crossing was almost empty. Ahmed put his arms through the straps of the backpack and pulled it up on his back.

Ahmed turned, parka in hand, and watched Fushin make a U-turn in the road. He waited until the Suburban disappeared over the rise before heading toward the border station.

Ahmed handed the guard his Afghani passport and Pakistani visa. The guard gave the documents a cursory glance and handed them back.

"The border is closed. No one can enter Afghanistan at this time."

Ahmed clasped his hands and pleaded with a look of despair.

"My mother is near death. I must reach Kandahar today."

The guard stared at Ahmed for a moment. Then he stood up and glanced to his left and right out the window.

"I may be able to help you, but it will cost five thousand rupees."

Ahmed fetched the sum from his pocket and slid it through the window. The guard retrieved the documents. He stamped them and handed them back to Ahmed.

"May Allah bless your mother."

Ahmed stepped across the border to the Afghani station less than fifty meters away. The guard was a bear of a man with a long beard wearing a white turban. He stuck out his hand and Ahmed passed him his passport and visa. The man held the passport up and read it through a pair of half-eye bifocals.

The man asked him a question in Pashtu. Ahmed shook his head.

"I don't understand. English?"

"Are you Tajik?" the man asked in Dari.

Ahmed nodded. The guard sorted through the passport until he found the Afghani exit stamps.

"What was your business in Pakistan?"

"I'm in the import-export business. I'm returning from Karachi with cooking utensils. I want to see how well they sell before making an investment in larger quantities."

The man grimaced.

"Cooking utensils? Let me see."

Ahmed lifted his backpack up on the table and opened the top. He pulled out the burqa and handed the agent his backpack. The guard glanced inside and pulled out several of the items.

"This is nothing new. It's used to open Coke bottles. This one opens food cans. What is this?"

"It's a cheese cutter."

"A cheese cutter?" he snickered.

"Yes, this metal band cuts cheese into thin slices."

The guard shook his head.

"What will they think of next?"

The man set the cutter down and picked up the burqa. He unfolded it to make sure nothing was concealed inside.

"Why do you have this?"

"It's a burqa."

"I know it's a burqa. What are you doing with it?"

"I bought it in Karachi. It's for my mother. It's made of a special fabric that will help her stay cool during the hot days of summer."

The guard stared at Ahmed. Then he began to search through each of the side pockets on the backpack. Finally satisfied, he reached for Ahmed's parka. He held it up and looked at the label.

"This coat was made in America. Where did you get it?"

"I bought it from a seaman in Karachi. I needed a new coat for the winter."

The man nodded. He checked through each of the pockets and handed it back to Ahmed. He stamped Ahmed's passport.

"You can go, Mr. Mohammed. The people of Afghanistan would be better served if you brought blankets and food. Who has use for these utensils?"

Ahmed nodded. He packed the utensils and burqa back into his backpack and strapped it shut. He slipped on the backpack, picked up the parka, and walked away from the station.

All men and women who love their native land know the special feeling of stepping onto their beloved soil after a prolonged absence. Ahmed Jan felt nothing.

The sky was overcast and there were threatening clouds on the horizon. A fall chill was in the air. Ahmed wiped a few drops from his forehead.

More than a dozen cars and trucks were parked along the side of the road within two hundred meters of the Afghanistan border station. Most were rusting heaps. Several of the drivers were congregated besides a pickup truck talking. One of them looked up and yelled at Ahmed in Pashtu.

"Kandahar? Two hundred thousand Afghanis."

Ahmed spotted a string of currency exchange businesses a few hundred meters farther up the road. He shook his head and walked on. A man in a wheelchair with a skullcap was sitting behind the counter of the first hut.

"What is the conversion rate for rupees?"

"Seventy-five Afghanis per rupee."

Ahmed fished the wad of rupees out of his pocket and placed them on the counter. The man licked his fingers and quickly sorted the bills. He counted just over eleven thousand rupees and figured the conversion on a small calculator. He lifted a metal box from beneath the counter and pulled out eight stacks of Afghani bills bound with paper. The man counted out the balance due in loose change and pushed the stack across the table. Ahmed stuffed the money into a pocket in his parka. He turned and took a few steps away from the hut. On a whim, he turned and queried the old man.

"Do you know a Tajik driver?"

The man leaned across the counter and peered up the road. He pointed.

"The blue minivan," he said in Dari. "His family is from Mazar-e-Sharif."

Ahmed strode toward the minivan. At first he didn't see anyone in the vehicle. But as he approached closer, he spotted a young man slumped across the front bench seat. Ahmed pounded on the door and called out in Dari.

"Excuse me. How much to Kandahar?"

The young man jerked up and rubbed his eyes. He stared at Ahmed from beneath heavy lids.

"How many riders?" the youth asked in Dari.

"Just me."

"Two-hundred fifty-thousand Afghanis. I have water and naan."

"Okay. Let's go."

Ahmed slid open the side door and tossed his backpack onto the seat. He climbed into the back seat and slammed the door. The young man started the engine and pulled off of the dirt shoulder onto the road headed north.

The road was peppered with potholes and craters. The driver swerved from one side of the road to the other to avoid the worst obstacles. The ride was uncomfortably bumpy, as the van rattled and creaked along the highway.

A hard rain began to fall and dusty residue on the windshield turned to mud. Driving became even more difficult, as the young Tajik strained to see the road through worn wipers that only spread the sludge from one side to the other.

They drove through the dismal town of Spin Boldak just north of the border. There were only a few people about on the nearly deserted main drag. It was a ghost town.

A kilometer north of town they came to a squalid refugee camp. Improvised tents were scattered to the horizon with thousands of despairing people wandering through the muddy squalor. The driver pointed out the window.

"That's Spin Boldak refugee camp. It's been there since the drought began five years ago. Since the bombing it has swelled to over seventy thousand people."

Ahmed stared out the window at a young mother carrying a child in her arms.

"It's horrible," he muttered. "Even Allah has forgotten them."

Less than a kilometer from the camp, they came abreast of a cluster of burned-out vehicles resting just off the pavement. Ahmed peered out the window at the twisted and blackened hulks of pickup trucks and Suburbans.

"Taliban," the driver called out.

He smiled back at Ahmed in the rearview mirror.

"American planes swat them like mosquitoes."

The farther they drove, the more ruins of war they encountered. At one point, they sped by a partially hidden compound in the middle of a stand of bare trees. All of the buildings had been pulverized beyond recognition. Wood and other debris were scattered across the surrounding terrain. The only recognizable structure was part of a dome.

The driver glanced up in the rearview mirror.

"Al-Fayat Mosque. It was an al-Qaida training facility. Many Arabs, Chechens, and Pashtun died. They say the sky rained fire."

"What's your name?" Ahmed asked.

"Awar."

"Where are you from?"

"My family lives in Mazar-e-Sharif. The Taliban killed my father two years ago. My mother lives there with my older brother, his wife, and children. What's your name?"

Ahmed glanced up at the rearview mirror.

Winter in Kandahar

"My name is Ahmed. What are you doing in the South?"

"Same as everyone else. I'm trying to make some money. You should've seen the business right after the Americans attacked Kandahar. Thousands of people traveled between Kandahar and Cheman the first few weeks. I charged seven hundred fifty Afghanis for a single trip. I couldn't keep up. Some days I drove back and forth ten or fifteen times. I made enough money to buy this new car. Business slowed to a trickle the past few months. What were you doing in Pakistan?"

"I have an import business. I was picking up a shipment in Karachi."

Awar shook his head and peered back at Ahmed in the rearview mirror.

"You are crazy to be traveling alone in Pakistan these days. Especially in the North."

"I have a partner in Quetta. His family takes care of me."

"I still would not take the chance. I've heard terrible stories from travelers about torture and killing. Even the Pashtun are not safe."

Awar drove on for nearly two hours. He maneuvered the van around pot-holes, craters, and burned-out hulks along the highway. They made small talk about the war, the weather, and the thousands killed in the earthquake in Nahrin in March.

They passed very little traffic heading away from Kandahar toward the border, just an occasional truck or car. A driving rain slowed them to a crawl. After an hour the rain slacked off and they continued on toward Kandahar at a steady clip.

Ahmed spotted a hand-painted sign next to the road during a lull in the conversation. It read "Kandahar 10 km." He glanced at his watch. It was 4:15 in the afternoon.

"Awar, I need a safe place to stay in Kandahar. Do you know of an inn where Tajiks are welcome?"

"There is a small hotel run by a family of Durranis Pashtun on the north side. It's called the Garden Hotel. I've picked up Tajiks, Uzbeks, and Hazaras there. You'll need cash, they don't accept credit cards."

"Okay, take me there."

It wasn't long before they reached the outskirts of the ancient city. Ahmed was surprised at the seeming normalcy on the streets. People were scurrying here and there among teashops, cafes, shops, and bazaars that were intermingled with bombed-out buildings. Pashtun troops loyal to the interim government were scattered along the narrow streets. They all carried Kalashnikov machine guns.

"Where are the American troops? Aren't they still in Kandahar?"

"Oh, they're still here all right. Most of them are out at the American compound near the airport. There are thousands of soldiers out there. They don't come inside the city much, but we see their helicopters and airplanes all the time."

"What of the Taliban?"

The driver stared at Ahmed in the rearview mirror.

"Many were killed or fled to Pakistan, but others are still lurking around like snakes in the grass. They mostly hide in the mountains to the north and south. Sometimes I spot groups of men traveling through the city. They do not wear the black turban, but we know who they are. It is still very dangerous. Even the Pashtun loyal to Karzai rarely travel at night. The Taliban treat them as collaborators."

He glanced at Ahmed in the mirror and drew a finger across his neck.

Awar stopped at an intersection to allow a donkey cart to pass. A young man walked alongside guiding the donkey. Ahmed glanced out over the dash at the cart piled high with furniture and clothing. There were two old bicycles tied to the back.

Ahmed glanced out the side window. A young Pashtun man about twenty-five years old was standing next to the car glaring at him through the window. Their eyes locked for a moment. The man sneered and motioned for Ahmed to roll the window down. Ahmed reached across to oblige him.

"What do you want?" Ahmed yelled.

"Tajik pig! You're not welcome in Kandahar."

"Don't concern yourself, I won't be here long. I can't stomach the smell. You stink worse when you're alive."

The man lunged toward the window. Ahmed yanked the pistol from his waistband and aimed it at the hothead. Awar hit the gas and the van sped off through the intersection. Ahmed glanced back at the Pashtun and shoved his gun back in his waistband.

"Are you trying to get us both killed?" Awar shouted angrily.

"Arrogant Pashtun — they don't know when to shut up!"

"That may well be, but this is Kandahar. The Tajiks are still few."

Ahmed's rage slowly ebbed, as Awar drove through the hustle-bustle of the city's center and into the north section.

"Awar, I've got to make a long-distance call before you drop me off at the hotel. Is there some place you know?"

"There's a new Internet café and telephone service just around the corner from the Garden Hotel. They've got phone booths where you can use long distance and international calling cards. They sell the cards there. I'll take you."

Awar turned left off the main boulevard several blocks later. He made a quick right at the next intersection and pulled to a stop in front of a small one-story building. It was the Kandahar Internet Teahouse. A sign out front, printed in several languages, read INTERNET/TELEPHONE. Ahmed slipped on his parka, pulled the hood up on his head, and stepped out of the van. The rain was falling hard once again.

"Wait for me. I'll be back in a few minutes."

Ahmed slammed the door and strode up the stairs through the front door. Several people in the small room were sitting at tables with computers. The aroma of green tea filled the air. Ahmed approached an Asian man sitting behind the counter.

"I need to make a phone call to Kabul."

"The phones are in the back. We sell calling cards for 100,000 or 500,000 Afghani. The 100,000-Afghani card gets you a five and a half-minute call to Kabul."

Ahmed counted out five hundred thousand Afghanis and the man handed him a card.

"Just dial 0-0-4-2 and the number in Kabul. Insert the card when you hear the tone. It'll ring after a few moments. Just hang up and pull the card out when you're done."

Ahmed wandered to the back of the café. There were three empty booths along the rear wall. He opened the door to the first and stepped inside. Ahmed was surprised at the modern equipment. He lifted the receiver and dialed. A tone sounded nearly a minute later. He inserted the card and the phone began to ring. It rang more than a dozen times, before an unfamiliar voice answered in Dari.

"Hello."

"I must speak to Mullah Habid. Tell him there is news from Kandahar."

There was silence for a moment and then another man picked up the phone.

"Who is this?"

"Ahmed."

"Ahmed Jan?"

"Yes."

"Ahmed, this is Osman. Mullah Habid's assistant."

"Yes, I remember you. I must speak to the mullah."

"Ahmed, Mullah Habid is dead."

Ahmed caught his breath. His throat knotted. He coughed and finally managed to speak.

"Mullah Habid is dead?"

"He was killed in an ambush yesterday morning on his way to a conference in Nahrin. It was the Taliban. They pinned a note to his chest."

Ahmed took a deep breath and sat in stunned silence.

"Ahmed, are you still there?"

"Yes, Osman, I'm here."

"Ahmed Mullah told me to order you to proceed if he did not return. The code is Kalakani."

There was again silence on the line.

"Ahmed, did you hear me?"

"Yes. Yes, I heard you, Osman. I understand. I must go now."

Ahmed hung up the phone. He sat quietly for a few moments, before pulling himself to his feet and opening the door to the booth. He staggered past the man behind the counter without saying a word and strode down the porch and across the muddy path to the van.

Ahmed opened the passenger door. He was about to climb into the seat when something across the street caught his eye. He peered through the rain for several moments. Then he ducked into the van and closed the door. Awar started the engine.

"Wait! Wait here just a second," Ahmed called out, as he rolled the rear window down.

The mud-brick building across the road appeared to be some kind of warehouse. There was a large truck parked in the driveway. Several men wearing turbans were carrying bags of rice, flour, and sugar from the warehouse to the truck. One man in particular caught Ahmed's eye. Ahmed watched as he limped away from the truck and disappeared into the warehouse. The man reappeared a few moments later carrying another bag of sugar. He hoisted the bag up to the bed and put it down, then took a deep breath and wiped his brow.

"Mohammajon!" Ahmed growled.

"What?" the driver asked.

"What do you know of that building across the street?"

"It looks like a warehouse."

"Do you know who owns it?"

"No, I've never noticed it before."

Ahmed watched the men finish loading the truck. A tall man with a long black poncho closed the warehouse door and locked it. Two of the men strode to a van parked in the driveway. The other man headed for the passenger side of the loaded truck and opened the door. There was no doubt, it was Mohammajon.

Ahmed watched as Mohammajon jumped up into the passenger seat and slammed the door. The van pulled into the street and the truck bumped out behind it.

"Follow that truck!"

"Hey, that wasn't part of the deal."

"Just do it! I'll give you another 250,000! Hurry!"

Awar gunned the engine and made a tight U-turn. He took a left turn at the corner and another left onto the main boulevard. Several vehicles crowded in between their van and the truck."

"Don't get too close," Ahmed barked, as he crouched behind the front seat.

"Who are they?"

"One of them is a man I thought I knew," Ahmed muttered. "His name is Mohammajon."

"Do you want me to pull up next to them?"

"No! I want to see where they go. Just follow them."

Awar tailed the truck, as it rumbled on through the north section of Kandahar and headed out of the city. The road wound up into the hills.

Thirty minutes into the pursuit the pavement ended and the road became rutted and narrow. The van rattled and splashed through standing water along the muddy trail. They wove from one switchback to the next. The driver of the supply truck turned on his headlights, as darkness fell.

Awar slowed the van to a crawl. He kept his distance, but followed close enough to see the glow of the taillights.

The rain began to fall harder. Awar slammed on the brakes and pulled to a stop in the middle of the road. He spun in his seat.

"I've got to turn back. We dare not go farther."

"No! Stay with them! I must see where they go."

"Look," Awar shouted, "I don't care how much you pay me! This is Taliban country!"

"Just a few kilometers more."

"No!"

Awar began to turn the wheel. Ahmed pulled the pistol from his belt and held it to the young man's head.

"If you lose them, I will kill you."

Awar punched the accelerator, nearly losing control, as the wheels spun dangerously close to the edge of the cliff.

"Whatever you say, my friend. Just put the gun down."

Awar skidded through a series of curves until he caught sight of the truck's taillights a couple of switchbacks ahead. He eased off the gas and tailed the vehicle at a safe distance.

The truck's taillights veered from the road at the bottom of a ravine and headed off across the rock-strewn, muddy terrain. Awar pulled the minivan up to the junction with a smaller trail and stopped. Ahmed, gun in hand, watched as the taillights on the trucks bumped up and down along the terrain. The brake lights went on and then the taillights disappeared altogether.

"Where are we?" Ahmed demanded.

"I'm not sure exactly. We're in the mountains north of Kandahar. That's all I know."

"Okay, I'm getting out here."

Awar jerked around in his seat.

"What? Are you crazy?"

Ahmed opened the door. He stuck the gun back in his waistband and pulled on his parka. He tied the hood around his chin and slung the backpack over his shoulders.

"I'm sorry, I couldn't take a chance on losing this man. Here's 500,000 Afghanis. Keep what you've seen to yourself."

"I will tell no one, lest they think I've lost my mind."

Ahmed slammed the door and jogged off into the pouring rain. Awar soon lost sight of him in the darkness. He flipped on his headlights, turned the van around, and headed back toward Kandahar.

CHAPTER FIFTY-TWO

October 7, 2002, Langley, Virginia

Stone opened the outer door to the deputy director's offices and stepped into the lobby. An assistant was sitting behind the counter. She finished her conversation and hung up the telephone.

"May I help you?"

"Yes, I'm Stone Waverly. Mr. Richards asked to see me."

"Go right in, Mr. Waverly. He's expecting you."

Stone stepped across the room to Richard's office door. It was partially open. He knocked.

"Come in!" Richards bellowed.

Stone pushed the door open. Richards was sitting behind his desk reading a report. An unlit cigar dangled from the corner of his mouth. He stood up and thrust out his hand.

"Stone, nice to see you. How was your vacation?"

Stone shook the big man's hand.

"It was great to spend some time with the family again, sir."

Richards closed the door and directed Stone to a seat across from the desk.

"I know exactly how you feel, Stone, I want an update on Kashmir. What's the situation there?"

"It's still very tense, sir. Indian security forces killed three more infiltrators there yesterday. The Indians think all of these extremists are sponsored by the ISI. Most of them are Pakistani, but there have been a few Chechens and Afghanis killed in Kashmir in the past few weeks. Most of them belonged to either Lashkar-e-Toiba or Al-Badr. There are daily attacks on Indian patrols, and every week or so there's an attack on Hindu or Christian civilians. It could blow at any moment."

STEVEN E. WILSON

"It's your job to see that doesn't happen. The State Department is encouraging both leaders to keep their people under control. The last thing we want is another war between Pakistan and India. The president is putting heat on Musharraf to help seek out and destroy al-Qaida hiding in the tribal areas of northern Pakistan. We don't want his attention diverted."

"I'm doing everything I can, sir."

"I know you're doing your best, Stone. Keep up the good work. There's something else I wanted to see you about. I got the final report back on the materials we confiscated in Vancouver."

"I saw the report, sir."

"That's good. I just wanted to make sure you got the follow-up you requested. Ingenious sons-of-bitches. The director and I thank you for everything you did to hunt down this vector. The Army is well on its way to developing a vaccine that'll neutralize the vector irrespective of the homing sequence. I've had nightmares about what might happen if al-Qaida manages to activate a vector with sequences that recognize segments of the American population. We've pulled out all the stops. The vaccine should be available in a few months. We'll start with the military and gradually vaccinate the entire population."

"Sir, any word on Ahmed Jan and Shane Kalakan? I understand the National Security Agency intercepted a call placed on Jan's cellphone in Bombay on October third."

"How did you hear about that?"

"Well, sir, all of the intelligence reports related to India and Pakistan come across our desk. I alerted our people in Bombay, but I have a feeling Jan already left the country."

"What makes you think so?"

"Sir, Ahmed Jan disappeared in Vancouver around August twentieth. I called Mickey Barber in the Seattle office this morning. There hasn't been even a trace of Jan or Kalakan since that time. We lost track of both of them six weeks ago."

"Yeah. So what?"

Stone pulled a paper out of his pocket and handed it to Richards.

"I looked up these shipping records for the port of Vancouver. The freighter *Ocean Trader* left Vancouver with a cargo of lumber on August twentieth. It headed for Bombay and was scheduled to dock on the first of October. It actually arrived on the second. It left Bombay on the third and docked in Karachi on the sixth. Sir, I think Ahmed Jan was on that ship. Shane Kalakan may have been with him. I've alerted the Pakistani authorities. I sent them photos of both men. I didn't mention the vector, but I think it's time to tell them."

Richards glanced at the paper. He rolled the cigar in the corner of his mouth.

"I'll look into this, Stone. Thank you for your insight."

"Sir, do you want me to prepare a secret memorandum for the Pakistanis? We should inform Musharraf immediately. Jan could release the vector at any moment."

Richards stood up and walked around the desk. He rested his hand on Stone's shoulder.

"I'll discuss it with the director this afternoon. Let me take care of it from here."

Richards peered down at Stone over his half-eye reading glasses.

"I want you to keep this to yourself, Stone. Do you understand? We can't have this leak just yet."

Stone stared up at the deputy director.

"I understand, sir."

"Good man, Stone. I can always count on you to do the right thing. We'll talk again soon."

CHAPTER FIFTY-THREE

October 7, 2002

The ominous skies opened up in an instant. Torrential rain beat against Ahmed's face as he slogged through puddles and streams swelled with runoff. He followed the truck's muddy tracks through one pass and then another. The terrain turned rocky and the trail became impossible to follow in the darkness.

Ahmed wiped the rain from his brow with his sleeve and trudged blindly around a bend in the trail. He stooped to pick mud from the treads of one boot and then the other with a tree branch. A flicker of light caught his eye as he tossed the branch away. Soaked to the skin, Ahmed headed off into the cover of the surrounding brush. He crept toward the light until he was close enough to make out a cluster of men gathered around a campfire.

Suddenly, Ahmed caught a glimpse of a silhouette leaning against a tree just off to his right. He dove to the ground and crawled forward on his belly. He watched in silence as the lone figure took a drag on a cigarette and tossed the butt to the ground. The man shouldered his rifle and headed directly for Ahmed's position. It was a lookout wearing the black turban of the Taliban.

Ahmed crawled forward a short distance and lay still behind a large rock. He drew the pistol from his waistband and released the safety. He tucked the gun in his waistband and picked up a rock from the ground.

As the fighter passed in front of him, Ahmed leaped up and bashed him in the back of his head with the rock. The man crumpled to the ground.

Ahmed yanked the Kalashnikov rifle from the fighter's hands. He raised the gun by the barrel with both hands and slammed the butt down on the soldier's forehead.

Ahmed scurried into a stand of brush near the clearing where he'd first spotted the guard. From there he could clearly see the campfire. Several men were standing around a pit beneath the protection of an overhang in the wall of the cliff. All of them were wearing the signature black turban of the Taliban.

One of the men laughed as he conversed with the others in Pashtu. He seemed to be the leader. Ahmed couldn't make out what he was saying, but the man seemed to be lecturing.

Two other men appeared in the mouth of a cave behind the fire. One was hunched over and hardly able to keep his balance. He was bare from the waist up. The other man spoke a few words to the leader in Pashtu. The leader spun around and punched the bare-chested man in the face and shoved him to the ground. Another man sitting on the ground next to the fire leapt to his feet and kicked repeatedly at the figure sprawled in the mud.

The leader shouted and motioned with his arm. Two of the Taliban grabbed the man's leg and dragged him away. They disappeared into a clump of bushes off to the right of the campfire. Two gunshots pierced the night.

The two men came back into the clearing a short time later. They were pushing a younger man in a shalwar kamese ahead of them with the barrel of a Kalashnikov rifle. The terrified man stumbled to his knees and begged for mercy in Pashtu. One of the Taliban fighters laughed and kicked him in the head, before pulling the man to his feet and shoving him toward the fire. They disappeared into the cave behind the fire pit.

Ahmed gradually worked his way around to the clearing. He slipped silently into the middle of a knot of bushes and fell to his knees. A heavy rain beat down around him.

Ahmed peered out through the bushes and caught his breath. Several bodies were scattered across a small muddy clearing. A ring of wooden posts encircled them. Ahmed counted eight men bound to posts with their arms tied over their heads and their feet dangling above the ground. One of the men whimpered in pain, as he tried in vain to ease the weight of his body by pushing his feet against the pole. A man wearing a brown turban and a plastic parka was sitting on a rocky perch holding a Kalashnikov rifle. Ahmed could clearly make out the man's face. It was Mohammajon.

Loud yelling in Pashtu resounded from the direction of the campfire. Ahmed crouched in silence, as voices drew near. He edged around to the right behind the line of poles. The same two Taliban appeared in the clearing dragging another motionless figure by the ankles.

One of the Taliban fighters shouted in Pashtu and motioned toward one of the men hanging from a pole. The man opened his eyes, scowled at the Taliban fighter, and spit on the ground. The fighter dropped the leg he was holding and fired two shots into the chest of the man on the pole.

The Taliban fighter pointed to another young man bound to a pole and shouted. Mohammajon drew a knife from his belt and cut the ropes binding the man's wrists. He dropped to his knees on the ground. The young man tried to break free, but the Taliban fighter butted him in the back of the head with the rifle. The two Taliban grabbed the man's arms and led him off toward the cave.

During the commotion, Ahmed slipped to the edge of the line of poles. The older man who'd spit on the ground screamed out in agony. Mohammajon turned and shouted in Pashtu. He bounded across the clearing and swung his rifle by the barrel. The butt cracked across the shins of the wretched man. He shrieked and fell silent.

Mohammajon sneered and turned away. He shuffled back across the clearing and turned to sit down on the rock. Ahmed leapt out of the undergrowth and rammed Mohammajon in the side of the head with the butt of his rifle. The old Tajik tumbled to the ground and Ahmed tore the rifle from his hands. Mohammajon rolled over on his backside and peered up through the darkness. His mouth dropped open with shock.

"Traitor pig!" Ahmed seethed.

"I'm no traitor, Ahmed Jan."

Ahmed kicked him in the side and pressed the gun to his head.

"You dare lie to my face, even here in this place. It's all so clear to me now. You exposed the American to the Arabs. Then you sent me to kill Mustafa for your own betrayal, didn't you?"

"Only to stop you from killing innocent people. Your mission is not according to the words of the Prophet."

Ahmed pointed to the corpses on the ground nearby.

"Is this according to the Prophet? How about the mullah? You killed Mullah Habid as surely as day follows night."

Ahmed bent down and drew a long knife from a sheath on Mohammajon's belt. Mohammajon stared up at him and then closed his eyes. He began to chant.

"There is no Allah but Allah, and Mohammad is his prophet. There is no Allah but Allah, and Mohammad is his prophet."

Ahmed thrust the knife into Mohammajon's belly. Mohammajon opened his eyes and grimaced with pain. Ahmed withdrew the knife and plunged it into Mohammajon's chest. The old Tajik gasped and toppled over face down in the mud. Ahmed withdrew the blade and stuck it in the ground.

Ahmed dropped his backpack off his shoulders and set it on the rocks. He scaled up the back of the first pole and cut the rope that bound the man's wrists. The man dropped to the ground.

"Thank you!" he whispered. "Allah bless you!"

One after the other, Ahmed cut the men down from the poles. He handed Mohammajon's Kalashnikov to one man. He passed the gun he'd taken from the guard to another.

Ahmed drew the pistol from his waistband. Several of the men ran off into the brush. As Ahmed turned to follow, the older man grabbed his arm and pleaded in broken English.

"I Mahmud Hashim."

He pointed toward the cave and spoke in broken Dari.

"Taliban. My son Zahir."

A loud shout echoed from the direction of the campfire. Ahmed took the Kalashnikov rifle from the old man. He released the safety on the handgun, handed it to Mahmud, and motioned him into a stand of bushes beside the trail. Ahmed crouched behind the rock formation near Mohammajon's body and steadied the barrel of the Kalashnikov on a boulder.

A muted moan, followed by laughter and the rustle of the bushes, signaled the approach of the Taliban fighters. The same two men in black turbans backed into the clearing dragging the young man by the ankles. Blood was running from his mouth and one eye was swollen completely shut.

Both men turned toward the ring of poles. Their smirks dissolved into horror. The leader pointed toward Mohammajon's body lying prone on the ground, as two shots rang out from Ahmed's rifle. Both men crumbled to the ground.

Mahmud rushed to the young man's side. He knelt, wiped the blood from the side of his face and comforted his son in Pashtu.

Ahmed helped Mahmud pull his battered son to his feet. Ahmed ducked beneath the dazed young man's arm. He guided him out of the clearing away from the Taliban sanctuary.

Three of the other men were waiting nearby. Two of them took Zahir between them and slogged away toward the east. Ahmed and Mahmud guarded their retreat.

The line of men hurried along a winding trail that led still higher into the mountains. Pockets of brush concealed the trail in a few areas, but the muddy ground was otherwise bare.

Ahmed trudged along near the back of the line. He looked up and caught one of the men staring. The man quickly turned his head. Twice more during the trek he noticed the man scrutinizing him. Each time the man looked away.

After two hours of slogging through the mud, the older man named Shah slumped to the ground beneath an overhang in the trail. He signaled he couldn't go on.

Mahmud directed the group to a nearby rocky enclosure nestled against the east face of the mountain. The perch was protected on three sides by steep rock walls. Ahmed climbed up into the rocks, dropped his pack, and lowered himself to the ground. He fell into a sound sleep.

Ahmed was awakened by a shake of his arm. He squinted up into the overcast sky. The old man named Shah was standing over him. He held out the gun.

"I am Shah," he said in broken English. "Mahmud say we go now. Here, you gun."

Ahmed sat up and gathered himself. He placed the pistol back in his waistband and gazed out over the rocks. The rain had stopped, but the sky was still gloomy. There was a winter chill in the air. His breath fogged as he spoke.

"I must return to Kandahar."

Shah turned to Mahmud and translated. Mahmud shook his head and spoke in Pashtu. Shah turned to Ahmed.

"Mahmud say only way back to Kandahar is way we came. Too dangerous. It is two hours to compound. Mahmud say you guest until it safe to return. He take you back to Kandahar."

"What tribe are you?"

"We Durranis Pashtun. Mahmud leader."

"Why do the Taliban kill your men?"

"Taliban Ghilzai. Tribes feud many centuries. We forbidden pass through Ghilzai land, but we must go Kandahar for food. We go over Ghilzai land. We hurt nobody. They ambush and steal supplies. They think we ally Americans. They kill six men."

Ahmed looked down at the valley below. A river meandered along the valley floor.

"Where are we?"

Shah pointed to the valley.

"That Arghandab River. This Arghan valley."

He pointed toward the peak behind them.

"Tarin Kowt Valley just over mountain."

Mahmud spoke to Shah. He turned and smiled at Ahmed.

"Mahmud ask what you name?"

"My name is Ahmed Jan."

Mahmud nodded and spoke again to Shah in Pashtu.

"Mahmud say you very brave man, Ahmed Jan. Mahmud thank you for save his son. We go now before Taliban come."

Shah lifted Ahmed's backpack and held it while the Tajik ducked his arms through the straps. A younger fighter picked up one of the Kalashnikov rifles and led the way down the steep and rocky path to the muddy trail below. Ahmed scooted down the rocks a short distance behind Mahmud.

Just as the group reached the trail, a burst of machine-gun fire rang out. The lead fighter dropped his rifle and collapsed to the ground. Machine guns clattered from beneath a nearby cluster of shrubs and bullets zipped through the air around them. Another fighter crawled out to the Kalashnikov rifle that was lying on the ground next to the dead man. He cradled the rifle in his arms and retreated toward cover. A rocket-propelled grenade exploded directly in front of him.

Ahmed retreated back toward the rocky perch. He bounded up the embankment behind two other men and knelt behind a rock. He drew his handgun. A Taliban fighter broke from behind a tree fifty meters in front of them and headed for a rock just off the trail. A Durranis fighter took aim with a Kalashnikov and squeezed off a burst. The Taliban Mujaheddin dropped to the ground.

Mahmud cupped his hands and barked in Pashtu toward the tree line. A deep voice bellowed a reply. There was a brief respite, and then a pair of loud claps echoed across the clearing.

"Mortar!" Mahmud shouted.

Ahmed ducked against the rock formation in front of him. Both projectiles exploded with thunderous blasts just short of the base of the rocky perch. Rocky debris showered down on them.

Another pair of claps resounded across the clearing. The first shell exploded harmlessly just to the right of the rocks. The second exploded into the wall of the cliff behind them. Ahmed glanced up and froze in horror, as a gigantic rock broke free and cascaded down on their position. Ahmed was buried beneath a pile of rocks and boulders.

"Shah!" one of the men called in Pashtu.

Several of the Durranis fighters set about clearing the rocky debris off the two men. One of them squatted next to Shah and pressed his fingers against his neck. He moved on to Ahmed.

"Shah's dead, Mahmud, but the Tajik still has a pulse."

A young Durranis fighter leapt to his feet and fired a series of short bursts with a Kalashnikov. Two Taliban running across the clearing tumbled to the ground. Another line of Mujaheddin sprung up in their place. The Durranis fighter fired another burst. Two more Mujaheddin fell to the ground, but two made the cover of a rock formation one hundred meters below. Suddenly, four more Taliban sprinted across the clearing with rifles in hand.

A shout echoed from their right flank, just as they reached the base of the perch. Withering machine-gun fire knocked up rocks and debris all around the Taliban positions. More than a dozen Taliban fighters were hit, as a fresh line of fighters swept across the opening below the rocky perch. One of the rescuers hurried up the rocks. He embraced Mahmud.

"Are you hurt, Mahmud?"

Mahmud looked down at his shirt. There were blood spatters across his chest. He shook his head.

"No, I'm fine. Shah's dead. Check the others."

A shot rang out from the clearing below. Mahmud turned and glanced over the rocky wall. The Durranis commander, gun in hand, stood over the body of one of the captured Taliban. He strode up to a second black-turbaned fighter and fired two shots into his head. The man crumpled to the ground. The commander waved his arm and shouted across the clearing.

"Mahmud, should we go after the others?"

Mahmud shook his head. He turned and looked down. Two of the Durranis fighters had cleared the rocks away from Ahmed's body. He was unconscious and both of his legs had grotesque bends just above the knee. One of the men pressed a rag against Ahmed's head.

"Does the Tajik live?"

"Yes, Mahmud. But he has a bad head injury and his legs are broken."

Mahmud shouted down to the commander in the clearing below.

"Mohammad, did you bring stretchers?"

The commander nodded.

"Bring one of them."

Mahmud glanced down at Ahmed.

"Khan, we will take the Tajik with us to the compound. Put him on a stretcher."

Zahir pushed through the cluster of men standing around his father.

"Father, this man will not survive. He'll slow us down. The decree from your own lips bans all men from the compound who are not of our tribe. This is your own law."

"Yes, Zahir, you are right. But the Tajik risked himself to rescue us. He saved your life, my son."

Mahmud patted his son on the shoulder.

"We value courage and personal honor above all else. We will take him to the caves. Shakiba will care for him there until he is well enough to return to Kandahar. We'll go on to the compound when the Tajik's fate is settled."

Zahir helped Hamid thread two heavy branches through loops in the wool stretcher. The two men lifted Ahmed and centered his body on the stretcher. Mahmud and Zahir took up one end of the stretcher and two other men lifted the other. The four of them carried Ahmed down from the rocky perch to the trail below.

They followed the winding trail eastward for more than three hours with a group of nearly a hundred Durranis fighters. A smaller group armed with rocket-propelled grenades and Kalashnikov rifles took up positions along a narrow pass to guard the withdrawal. The route wound upward to higher elevation along a trail that had a sheer drop off to one side and a wall of rock on the other.

The terrain gradually changed to bare, rocky earth. The trail seemed to end at the base of a cliff, but the Durranis fighters continued their climb along a series of switchbacks that went straight up the side of the rocky wall.

It took Mahmud, Zahir, and two other men to carry the stretcher through the dizzying maze. The dog-tired men paused to catch a breath every three or four turns. The trail was treacherous, with unforgiving footing and loose rocks that broke away without warning. Each slide began with the rumble of cascading rocks and a shouted alarm that echoed between the rocky walls on either side. The men covered their heads with arms and rifle butts and dodged boulders the size of melons.

After an hour of backbreaking struggle the group carrying the stretcher finally reached the summit. Hamid and Zahir guided the stretcher into a cave tucked into the mountainside. The cave mouth was enormous. The massive main cavern extended for nearly forty meters, but abruptly narrowed at the rear. Its floor was strewn with rocks and boulders.

There was a smaller opening in the wall a few steps from the main cavern entrance. It led down a short incline into a connecting room. Mahmud directed the men carrying Ahmed, as they eased the stretcher through the passageway into a well-lit cavern. The chamber was nearly twenty meters across. There were two beds at the front of the cavern. Another doorway led off the back. The soft whine of a gas-powered generator came from the rear.

"Zahir, put him in that second bed."

The two men set the stretcher on the edge of the bed. Zahir and Hamid lifted Ahmed onto the bed and set the stretcher on end against the back wall.

A woman in a blue burqa stepped into the room from the back. She rushed to Mahmud, hugged him, and spoke in Pashtu.

"Father, I've been so worried."

She rubbed her hand across an angry bruise and blackened eye on the left side of his face.

"Are you hurt?"

"No, Shakiba. Thanks to this man, they are only bruises. His name is Ahmed Jan. He is Tajik. Allah sent him from out of the darkness to save our lives. He rescued Zahir and six other men from certain death. He has a gash in the top of his head and both legs are broken. Care for him."

Shakiba examined the laceration across Ahmed's head and the displaced fractures in each of his upper legs. She started a large bore intravenous line and began hydrating Ahmed with lactated ringers. She opened an ampule of morphine, injected a dose into the line, and opened the IV so the painkiller could run into his vein. She cut away Ahmed's pants with a pair of bandage scissors.

"Zahir and Hamid," Shakiba ordered, "I need each of you to take one of his arms and pull when I tell you."

The two men stepped to the head of the bed and took hold of Ahmed's upper arms.

"Okay. We'll set the right leg first."

Shakiba hooked a belt across Ahmed's waist and locked the ends on either side of the bed frame. She fastened a line with a padded loop around Ahmed's right ankle and passed the rope over a pulley on an elevated rail at the end of the bed. Mahmud lifted a heavy metal weight off the ground. Shakiba fastened the other end of the rope to a ring on the weight. Mahmud gradually released the weight and Ahmed's right leg extended up into the air. Mahmud stepped to the head of the bed.

"Pull!" Shakiba yelled.

Zahir and Hamid pulled on Ahmed's upper arms, as Mahmud pushed down on his torso. Shakiba steadied and manipulated the leg. Ahmed grimaced involuntarily with pain. The upper leg began to straighten, as the men tugged at Ahmed's torso. A loud snap echoed through the chamber. The men eased up and Shakiba stepped around to the foot of the bed.

"Okay, relax for a moment while I set up the other weight."

Mahmud helped her remove the weight from the right leg and replace it with a smaller one. Shakiba tied the larger weight to the left ankle and they repeated the maneuver. When they were done, both legs were straight and held in the air by traction.

Mahmud turned to Zahir and Hamid.

"Let's hike up to the lookout station overlooking the trail to make sure the Taliban did not follow. Shakiba will take care of the Tajik."

The three men headed out through the passageway into the main cavern.

Shakiba added a Mannitol drip to ease pressure on Ahmed's brain. When the drip finished, she began intravenous antibiotics.

Shakiba turned her attention to the gash across the top of Ahmed's head. It extended down to the skull and across the crown. She poured antiseptic soap into a basin and diluted it with sterile water from an IV bag. She knelt on the floor beside Ahmed and cleaned the wound free of debris. She shaved the surrounding area with a razor. Finally, she closed the wound with two layers of sutures and applied topical antibiotic with a bandage.

Shakiba cut off the remainder of Ahmed's clothes and cleaned his body with soapy water. He was covered with bruises. She lifted his twisted left hand and ran her fingers across his scarred palm. She peered through the silk mesh in her burqa at Ahmed's weathered face.

"Do you search for trouble, Ahmed Jan, or does trouble just find you?"

Shakiba spent the next two hours putting casts on Ahmed's legs. Finally, she dressed the Tajik in a hospital gown.

She stood at the foot of the bed and regarded the stranger.

"I've done all I can, Ahmed Jan. Now Allah will decide."

CHAPTER FIFTY-FOUR

Shakiba looked up from her clipboard, as her father ducked through the entryway into the cavern. He nodded toward Ahmed.

"How's the Tajik?"

"His vital signs have stabilized, Father. I'm certain he has a brain injury. He's also at risk of pulmonary embolism because of the leg fractures. All I can do now is give him intravenous fluids and nutrition. He may wake up or he may not. Only time will tell."

"Shakiba, I have bad news. We must leave the cave. The lookout spotted a Taliban patrol on the switchbacks early this morning. They retreated, but it's only a matter of time before they return in force. We should've never crossed the Ghilzai land. I blame myself for this."

Shakiba dropped her hands to her side.

"The Tajik will never survive the trip to the valley. He's not stable, Father."

"Shakiba, we have no choice. There aren't enough supplies for the men and the winter snow will come soon. We must leave today."

"Only tribal members can go to the compound. Father, this is your own law."

Mahmud frowned regretfully and nodded his head.

"I know this, my little songbird. We must leave the Tajik here."

Shakiba glowered at Mahmud through her burqa in shocked disbelief.

"Then why did you bring him here, Father? You said yourself this man rescued you and Zahir from certain death. Have you no honor? How can you abandon him now?"

"We have no choice, Shakiba. I ordered the men to prepare to leave."

Shakiba looked down at Ahmed. He was breathing easily.

"Then I will stay here with him."

"No, Shakiba, I will not allow it."

"Father, I do not seek your permission. I am not your little girl anymore. The supplies are sufficient for me to hold out here with the Tajik until you return. I'll be safer here than in the valley. I'd rather die here than risk being forced to return to al-Zawar."

Mahmud stood contemplating. Finally he nodded and took Shakiba's hand. He sighed.

"As you wish, Shakiba. We'll conceal the entrance to this chamber with rocks. If the snow comes early we cannot return until the spring."

"I know this, Father. I will stay."

Mahmud squeezed Shakiba's hand.

"My little songbird, you have your mother's stubbornness and your grandfather's courage. Turn off the generator when we leave so the Taliban cannot hear the motor if they search the main cave. Use only one light in the infirmary. The batteries should last for two or three days. Then you must turn the generator back on. Come, I will show you how to operate the system."

Mahmud could not see her tears flowing beneath the burqa.

"I love you, Father," she sniffled, as she embraced him.

Shakiba heard the grating of boulders in the main cavern, as Mahmud supervised the efforts to camouflage the entryway. They used rollers and brute force to inch a boulder the size of a car over the entrance to the infirmary complex. When they finished, there was no sign of the passageway into the infirmary. Shakiba heard the thud of one last stone and then there was silence.

Shakiba waited nearly an hour before shutting down the generator and ventilation system. She turned off all the lights in the complex except for a single naked bulb in the ceiling of the infirmary. When the task was completed, she sat down on the side of the empty bed across from Ahmed.

"It's just you and me now, Mr. Ahmed Jan."

Shakiba adjusted the flow rate on the intravenous drip. She stepped through the doorway in the rear of the infirmary and into a long narrow passageway. There was a meter-wide fissure in the rock wall that diverged off to the right a few steps along the passageway. She ducked through the opening into a darkened room and felt for a string hanging down from the ceiling.

A naked bulb flashed on and illuminated the small grotto. There was a small bed positioned against one wall. The bed was covered with a wool blanket.

Another blanket was folded on the end. There was a small chest of drawers against the opposite wall. A small CD player was sitting on top of the chest. It was as close to luxury as one got in the caves of the Hindu Kush.

Shakiba pulled the burqa over her head. Beneath it she was wearing traditional baggy red trousers with a loose, long-sleeved tunic. She opened one of the drawers in the chest, placed the burqa in on top of a stack of garments, and closed the drawer. Stepping to the opposite corner of the room, she pressed her hand against the side of the water heater. It was still warm.

A small metal bathtub was resting against the bottom of the chest of drawers. Shakiba turned it upright and slid it to the middle of the room. She stretched a hose from the water heater into the bottom of the tub and opened the tap. Water began to flow. Shakiba removed her dress and trousers and set them on the bed.

She stepped into the tub and knelt down. The warm water felt good against her skin. She leaned out and fetched a plastic bottle filled with golden liquid off the rocky floor and a cotton cloth from the bedpost. She used the concentrate to bathe her skin and shampoo her hair. She rinsed the soap from her hair and leaned back against the edge of the bathtub, and she closed her eyes. The warmth was intoxicating.

Suddenly, a distant rumbling vibrated through the rock walls surrounding her. Another followed a few moments later.

Shakiba stood up in the bathtub and toweled herself off. She put her trousers and dress back on, before turning the tub over. The bathwater spread across the ground, vanishing into cracks in the dirt-covered rocky floor.

Another series of rumblings resonated through the rocky chamber. The last was strong enough to sway the hanging light bulb and knock fragments of rock loose from the ceiling.

Shakiba dropped to her knees at the side of the bed.

"Allah, most gracious, most merciful, I commit my life to you. Protect my father and brother. Shield my people with your goodness."

Shakiba pulled herself to her feet and glanced at her watch. It was two in the afternoon.

She stooped beneath the overhang and took a step into the darkened hallway, before stopping abruptly and ducking back into the bedroom. She pulled the middle cabinet drawer open, fetched a fresh brown burqa, and slipped it over her head.

Ahmed's respiratory rate was slightly elevated. Otherwise, his vital signs were normal. Shakiba changed the intravenous bag and adjusted the flow rate. She checked the graduations on the catheter bag. His urine production was excellent. She rolled Ahmed slightly to his left and tucked a pillow beneath his back. She looked down at the comatose Tajik.

"I'm hungry, Mr. Jan. I'll be back after I fix a bite to eat."

Shakiba ducked back through the passageway and past the bedroom to a chamber in the rear of the complex. She flipped on a fluorescent ceiling light.

The enormous rock-walled cavern was many times the size of the infirmary. Bags of rice, flour, and other supplies were stacked against the back wall. Metal shelves containing stockpiles of canned chicken, tomatoes, corn, and other food were arranged on the left side of the back wall. Hundreds of five-liter water containers lined the sidewall. A line of fifty-gallon fuel drums was arranged next to a power generator in a front corner of the cavern. The generator was hooked up to a bank of batteries and a fifty-barrel fuel reservoir. There was a potbelly stove sitting in the middle of the room. It had been fashioned from a barrel. A metal pipe extended upward from the stove through a hole in the ceiling of the cave. A generator exhaust port connected to the same vent. Several cords of wood were stacked on the ground next to the stove.

In the rear of the storage room there was another passageway. It dead-ended in a narrow crevice that dropped off for more than a hundred meters. None of the Durranis had ever explored this chamber. It had served as a toilet since the cave complex was built.

Shakiba stepped to a rough wooden table just inside the door. She lit a propane camping stove with a striker and set a teapot on the burner. She measured green tea into a cup. Shakiba broke off a portion of naan from a fresh loaf and placed it on a plate with a heaping spoonful of rice from a large pot. When the teapot began to boil, she turned off the burner and filled the cup.

She sat down at a rickety wooden table in the center of the room and stirred the tea. Leaning back into the chair, she took a bite of rice and a sip from the cup. The distant rumblings had ceased. The cave complex was silent.

CHAPTER FIFTY-FIVE

S hakiba was startled awake by a muted burst of gunfire and barely audible shouting that seemed to reverberate from just outside the entry to the complex. She scurried from the bedroom into the infirmary.

It was impossible to make out who was shouting on the other side of the rocky barricade. Shakiba trembled in fear.

She sat motionless in the failing light. The light bulb hanging from the ceiling had become more of a faint glow than a source of illumination, as the reserve batteries had discharged. Shakiba didn't dare turn on the generator for fear the sound of the motor or the smell of the exhaust would disclose the secret complex to those lurking inside the main cavern. The batteries went completely dead a few hours later.

Voices resonated from the main cavern for several hours. Shakiba sat on the floor next to Ahmed's bed silently listening to the garbled sounds. No one attempted to move the great stone that sealed the entrance to the infirmary. The shouting in the main cavern ended as abruptly as it began.

For the next two days, Shakiba crept around the complex using only a small backup flashlight. It was nearly impossible for her to see through the mesh in the burqa in the dim light, so she finally removed it.

Tasks that were difficult under normal conditions were out of the question in the shadowy darkness. Even then, she only used the flashlight to care for Ahmed, prepare her meals, and eat. It was critical to conserve the power in the batteries. She tried to sleep the rest of the time. Sleep was the only way of checking the terror that lay just below the surface-the panic of being entombed in blackness so absolute that she couldn't see her hand in front of her face.

The oxygen level declined and the carbon dioxide level steadily rose. Shakiba began to feel light-headed and confused. Uncontrollable fits of yawning soon followed. Finally, she decided there was a simple choice. She could leave the generator off and gradually slip into a coma or she could turn it on and risk detection.

Shakiba used the faint beam of the failing flashlight to shuffle back through the darkened complex to the supply cavern. She made her way to the generator and yanked on the pull-cord. The motor sputtered briefly and then ground to a stop. She pulled the cord again. Once more it sputtered to a stop. She tugged the cord again. The motor sputtered for a moment, but then settled into a quiet drone.

The fluorescent light in the ceiling flickered several times and then shone brightly. Cool air streamed into the room from the ventilation unit bracketed to the ceiling. Shakiba stood below the unit and enjoyed the freshness of mountain air blowing on her face.

Shakiba ran the generator until the reserve batteries were completely recharged. It took two days. After that, the ventilator unit had to be turned on and off every few hours. It was November and the air outside was too cold to continuously run the system.

It took Shakiba several days to work out a schedule that maximized fuel conservation while maintaining a tolerable environment within the complex. Eight hours of running the generator during the day was followed by sixteen hours of battery power. The daily schedule was structured around running the generator. Shakiba ate one meal just after turning the generator on and another just before turning it off. An eight-hour generator run was also long enough to heat the water heater. She took a bath one day and washed the laundry the next.

Shakiba cared for Ahmed night and day for the next three weeks. She passed a tube through his mouth and used a large syringe to feed him a puréed mixture of mashed rice, beans, and vegetables. The Tajik's vital signs remained stable, but he showed no signs of regaining consciousness. She settled into a lonely routine of eating, reading the Quran, caring for the stranger, praying, and sleeping. She'd endured far worse hardship during her short life.

Shakiba was awakened from a deep sleep. She listened from her bed trying to discern what had aroused her. The complex was silent.

She rolled out of bed and brushed her hair back from her face. Shakiba picked up a pen off the dresser and crossed off November 1 on the calendar. She slipped on her blue burqa and ducked through the passageway into the infirmary.

Ahmed Jan picked his head up off the pillow and stared back at her for a moment. Then he dropped his head down on the pillow.

Shakiba rushed to his side. She touched his arm and spoke in fluent Dari.

"How do you feel, Mr. Jan? Can you understand me?"

Ahmed looked up at the mesh covering Shakiba's face with an expression of utter bewilderment. He looked down toward his legs and across the room toward the rear chamber.

"Where am I?" he slurred around the feeding tube.

"We're in a cave complex in the Hindu Kush north of Kandahar. You've been in a coma."

"Who are you?"

"My name is Shakiba. I'm Mahmud's daughter."

"What happened?"

"You don't remember?"

Ahmed looked up with a confused expression. He shook his head.

"You were wounded in a battle between my tribe members and the Taliban. Falling rocks hit you. You had a serious blow to the head and both of your legs were broken. Mahmud brought you here."

Ahmed tried to role onto his side. Shakiba pushed him back down with a gentle hand.

"No, Mr. Jan, you had displaced fractures of both femurs. You must remain in traction for four more weeks. You might displace them again if you get up now. There's no one here to help me set them this time. I'll take the casts off in four weeks. I promise, you can start standing up then. It'll be two months before you can walk again."

"Where are the others?"

"My father and brother left to get help. They should be back soon."

"How long have we been here?"

"Almost a month."

"A whole month?" Ahmed uttered with shock.

"You've been unconscious. I was beginning to think you'd never wake up."

"What's the date?"

"It's the first of November."

Ahmed stared up at her for a few moments and then glanced down at the casts on his legs.

"Who put these casts on my legs?"

"I did."

Ahmed glanced up at Shakiba's mesh with surprise.

"Are you a nurse?"

"No, Mr. Jan, I'm a doctor."

"You're a doctor?"

"Yes, I'm a surgeon."

Ahmed reached up and tugged at the tube in his mouth.

"Can you remove this tube?"

Shakiba leaned over Ahmed and unwound the tape. She pulled the feeding tube out of Ahmed's mouth. It triggered a fit of coughing.

"Can I have a glass of water?" he asked.

"I'll get you something to drink. I'll be right back."

Shakiba ducked into the passage and returned a few minutes later with a bottle of water and a small can.

"I brought you apple juice. I'll give you some rice tomorrow if you can keep this down."

Ahmed glanced down at the catheter tube running out from beneath the sheets toward the urine bag. He motioned.

"Who put that in?"

"I did."

Ahmed looked up. His expression betrayed a hint of embarrassment.

"Mr. Jan, I'm a doctor."

"Maybe it'd be easier to accept if you took off the burqa."

"My people are very strict believers in Purdah, Mr. Jan. Our Muslim faith holds that it is the moral obligation of women to live in seclusion, in submission, and with modesty. The rules have been relaxed so that women can attend school and work in professions like medicine and teaching, but the burqa remains an important part of our culture."

Shakiba pulled the top off the can of apple juice. Ahmed took one sip and then another. He peered up at the mesh on the burqa.

"Thank you for taking care of me. I too studied to be a physician. I had clinical training at the King Khalid National Guard Hospital in Jeddah. I dreamed of one day becoming a neurosurgeon. My father called me home when the Taliban attacked the Panjshir Valley. I never had the chance to go back and finish."

"One day you will, Mr. Jan. It's a longing that's not easily dismissed. You have great empathy for your fellow man."

Ahmed smiled. He reached out and gently squeezed Shakiba's hand.

"How do you know that?"

"You saved my father's life. How often does a Tajik risk his own life to save the life of a Pashtun?"

"I don't remember."

"You did that, Mr. Jan. The Taliban captured my father and brother. They were returning from Kandahar with a group from our tribe. Several of our men were killed. You killed a Taliban officer and helped my father, my brother, and the rest of the men escape. You don't remember?"

Ahmed gazed up at Shakiba's silk mesh. He shook his head.

"My father told me you came in the night to kill another Tajik who was guarding them. He said you knew this man by name."

Ahmed's puzzlement deepened.

"Did your father know this man's name?"

"He didn't say."

"Was it Mohammajon?"

"I don't know. What's the last thing you can remember?"

"I recall traveling to Pakistan by ship. I remember crossing the border into Afghanistan. I don't recall anything after that."

"Give it time. You had a serious head injury. Sometimes it takes a while for your memory to return completely. Especially short-term memory."

Ahmed nodded. He put his hand to his face and rubbed his eyes.

"Where did you learn to speak Dari?"

Shakiba didn't speak for a moment. She stepped over to the empty bed, gathered her burqa beneath her, and sat on the edge of the bare mattress.

"I learned Dari from the man who taught me to be a surgeon. I worked with him for seven years in the hospital in Kandahar. He was also Tajik. He taught me Dari and I taught him Pashtu."

"The Taliban let him practice in Kandahar?"

"For a while. They broke his hands when they caught him breaking their laws against treating women. The Taliban forced me to stop working shortly after that. He spoke out against the injustice and they killed him. They dragged him from the hospital and shot him on the lawn in front of the building."

Ahmed shook his head and looked away. He turned back and peered directly into the mesh over Shakiba's face.

"He taught you well."

"He was a great, great man."

Shakiba stood up from the edge of the bed.

"You rest now. I'm going to start the ventilation system. It's getting stuffy."

Ahmed glanced over to the right. His parka was lying on a box of intravenous bags against the wall.

"Could you hand me my parka? I want to get a comb from my pocket."

Shakiba picked up the coat and handed it to Ahmed. Ahmed watched until she'd walked across the infirmary and ducked into the rear passageway. He grasped the front panel of the parka between his hands. The cylinder was still buried in the insulation.

CHAPTER FIFTY-SIX

November 15, 2002

A hmed recovered slowly. Shakiba pampered him throughout the Ramadan season with traditional meals of early morning suhoor and early evening iftar. Technically, Ahmed was exempted from the Ramadan fast because of his depleted state, but in the cave it was always night-time anyway. They heard nary a sound in the outside cavern. It was as if they were the only ones left in Afghanistan.

Both of Ahmed's legs came out of traction during the second month. Even so, Shakiba forbade him from bearing weight. There would be a period of grad-ual rehabilitation progressing to weight bearing.

The two of them spent long hours chatting about every conceivable topic. They seemed to reserve the most spirited conversations for dinner. Shakiba prepared dishes of rice and canned vegetables with naan. She'd sit on the bed opposite Ahmed and they'd chat as he ate. One day they'd discuss medicine and the next they'd argue about the Quran. They both came to relish these conver-sations. A close friendship began to blossom. Little-by-little they learned to laugh again. Considering their situation, it was a blessed Ramadan season.

Shakiba ducked beneath the overhang into the infirmary wearing a light-brown burqa. She handed Ahmed a bowl and a glass of water.

"Peaches! What a treat! Where'd you find them?"

"I discovered a case on the top shelf in the store room. They were hidden behind several cases of corn. I lifted a case of corn down and there they were. Here, hold my bowl. I have a surprise for you."

Shakiba gathered her burqa and hurried away into the passageway. A few moments later, a beautiful soprano voice resounded from the back of the cave. The music was faint at first, and then grew louder. Shakiba reappeared through the doorway a moment later.

"Do you like Afghan music, Mr. Jan?"

"Please call me Ahmed. No one ever calls me Mr. Jan."

"Okay. Ahmed, do you like music?"

"It's beautiful. Who is it?"

"Her name is Fariba Mohammad. She wrote and sang songs about the history of the Durranis Pashtun. She was my best friend."

"I don't understand the words, but her voice is wonderful. Why haven't you played it before?"

Shakiba looked at Ahmed through her mesh.

"I haven't felt like music for a long time, Ahmed. The Taliban forbad singing or even listening to music. The religious police caught Fariba singing at a family gathering two years ago. She disappeared a few days later. We still don't know what happened to her."

There was a prolonged silence. Ahmed looked up at Shakiba.

"I have something I want to give you, Shakiba."

"What is it?"

"Hand me my backpack."

Shakiba fetched the backpack from the ground. Ahmed unfastened a pocket on the side and pulled out his worn book of poetry.

"Do you like poetry?"

"Yes, I love poetry. It was also banned by the Taliban."

"This is a book of poetry by the great Persian poet Hafez. It's my dearest possession. Commander Massoud gave it to me just before he was killed. I want you to have it."

Shakiba was speechless. She reached out and touched the book, but withdrew her hand.

"I cannot take it, Ahmed."

"I want you to have it, Shakiba. It's my small gift for what you've done for me. You could have left with your family, but you stayed here with me."

Shakiba stood in silence for a moment. Finally, she sat on the edge of the bed.

"I cannot take this Ahmed. But I will share the poetry with you. Will you read to me?"

Ahmed opened the book.

"This one is called *Wild Deer.* 'Where are you O wild deer? I have known you for a while, here. Both loners, both lost, both forsaken. The wild beast, for ambush, have all waken.' "

Ahmed read for nearly an hour. Finally, he closed the book and set it down on the bed. He looked up and smiled.

"It's beautiful, Ahmed. Thank you for sharing it with me. I'll read for you tomorrow."

Shakiba picked up the plates from the bed. She walked away toward the passageway.

"Shakiba," Ahmed called after her, "how long will the food in the store-room last?"

Shakiba stopped near the doorway and turned.

"I think there's enough food and water to last for four to six months. I'm more worried about having enough fuel to run the generator. I've been con-serving it from the very beginning, but I'm guessing we only have enough for about four more months."

"Surely your father will send help before then."

Shakiba peered at Ahmed through her silk screen. He couldn't see the look of despair on her face.

"Yes, I'm sure he will return before then. The snow probably came early this year. The trail up to the cave is very steep. It's even difficult when the weather is good, but it's impossible when the slope is covered with snow. He knows we're safe here. That's the reason my father built this complex. Hundreds of our people hid here for months during the last days of the Taliban."

"When does the snow melt?"

"It usually melts by late March, at least enough to make it up the trail."

Ahmed glanced at Shakiba.

"So you and I must spend several more months here alone? Is that why you confine me to the bed?"

Shakiba walked back across the room and busied herself with straighten-ing the medical supplies.

"Ahmed, does it make you sad to think of staying here so long? You know, without your family?"

"I don't have a family, Shakiba. I'm the only one who survived the war."

"A sweetheart then?"

"There is no sweetheart."

Neither spoke for a few moments. Shakiba continued to sort through the medical supplies. Ahmed finally broke the silence.

"Shakiba, can I ask you something?"

"You can ask me anything, Ahmed."

"Do you like to wear the burqa?"

Shakiba turned and looked toward him through the mesh.

"It's our custom for the women to wear burqas in public. It was our custom even before the Taliban."

"But we are not in public."

She did not answer. She turned and began to sort through instruments in a plastic case.

"Shakiba, it makes me sad to think of leaving here without ever seeing your face."

Shakiba stopped fiddling with the supplies. Ahmed watched in silence, as she stood motionless. Suddenly, she whirled around with a large pair of bandage scissors in her hand.

"It's time to take the casts off your legs. But you can't walk yet. You must follow my directions and only stand next to the bed for two more weeks."

Ahmed's face broke into a mischievous smile.

"Ahmed, you must promise me or I won't remove the casts. If you break the bone again, there will be no way to fix it."

"You'd have to shoot me like a horse."

"Ahmed, I'm not joking."

"Okay, okay, I promise."

Shakiba pressed his hospital robe down between his legs and propped his right leg up on a pillow. She sat beside him on the edge of the bed and began to cut through the plaster on the right cast. She held the scissors wide open to generate the force needed to cut through the plaster.

Ahmed watched her hands as she worked. She had long, delicate fingers and neatly contoured fingernails. The heel of Shakiba's hand brushed against the side of his leg. Her skin was smooth as silk. Ahmed felt something stir deep within him.

She finished removing one cast and repositioned the pillow to start in on the other. It took the better part of thirty minutes to finish cutting all the way through the plaster and break the cast apart. Shakiba lifted his leg and slid the cast off.

"Okay, that's it. Sit up now. I want you to scoot your legs off the bed."

Ahmed slid his legs over the side of the bed. Shakiba held out her hands. He took them and she pulled him to the sitting position. Ahmed felt light-headed from lying flat on his back for two months.

"Okay, now I'm going to help you stand up next to the bed. I don't want you to walk. Just stand there for two minutes. Sit down if you feel dizzy."

Shakiba pulled and Ahmed struggled to his feet. At first he bent over to maintain his balance. Then he slowly stood erect. He grinned.

"You did it!"

They laughed with glee for a few moments, as they absentmindedly held each other's hands. The laughter ended in an uncomfortable silence. Shakiba stared up at Ahmed's face through her burqa. He stared down toward her. He could barely make out the faint contour of her eyes behind the silk mesh.

"Shakiba, your eyes? What color are they?"

Suddenly, Shakiba felt awkward. She dropped Ahmed's hands.

"They're dark brown."

Ahmed smiled tenderly and nodded.

"I imagined they were brown. I imagine they're kind eyes."

Shakiba blushed beneath the burqa. She turned away and walked to the table in the corner of the room. She kept her back to Ahmed, as she slid the bandage scissors into a plastic container and put them back in the instrument box. She filled a basin with soapy water and placed it on the edge of the bed next to Ahmed. She handed him a towel.

"Sit down now, Ahmed. I want you to stand up and bear weight three or four times a day for the next five days. Please don't walk yet. As long as there's no pain, you can add a few seconds each time you stand up. We'll start taking a few steps when you're able to stand for ten minutes without pain. Use this towel to clean the dead skin from your legs. I'll bring your dinner in a while."

Ahmed watched in silence, as Shakiba walked to the back of the room and disappeared into the rear passageway.

CHAPTER FIFTY-SEVEN

December 4, 2002

A hmed rolled over on his side and half opened his eyes. An enchanting a capella ballad sung by a beautiful soprano voice drifted through the infirmary. He couldn't make out the words. It was like a dream.

He lay there listening for some time while the sweet music played. After a while, the familiar ballads of Fariba Mohammad began to echo through the room. Shakiba ducked from the passageway carrying a tray a few minutes later. She wore a light blue burqa.

"Ready for breakfast? I brought you fresh-baked naan with honey and peaches."

Ahmed scooted back against the pillow and took the tray.

"Thank you, it smells wonderful. I love your friend's singing. Her voice is among the most beautiful I've ever heard."

"This song is my favorite. I'll be right back. I have tea brewing."

Shakiba scurried away and returned a short time later carrying another wooden tray. She set the tray down on the bed and handed Ahmed his mug.

"This is Keemun tea from China. A friend of my father's brought it to me from China over a year ago. I'm afraid it's not as good without sugar. We're running low and I'm conserving what we have left."

Ahmed stopped chewing and glanced up from his tray with a wide-eyed look.

"We're running low on tea?" he garbled with a mouth full of naan.

"No, we have plenty of tea, both green and black, but we're running short on sugar."

Ahmed finished chewing and swallowed.

"Praise Allah, sugar I can live without, but tea never. My father used to say that every good conversation begins with tea. Even the Russians loved tea. I remember when I was a boy, I'd trade with some of the Russian soldiers in Taloqan. Some of them traded guns for tea. I'd give the weapons to my father and the Mujaheddin would use them to kill more Russians. This is very good tea."

"I enjoy mine better with sugar. There was an English nurse who worked at the hospital in Kandahar before the Taliban took it over. She used to say a man without a mustache is like a cup of tea without sugar."

"Did you like me better with a mustache?"

"No, I think you're more handsome without it. But Susan wasn't attracted to men without mustaches."

The music stopped. Shakiba stood up and walked toward the doorway.

"I'll be right back. There's something I want you to hear."

She disappeared into the passageway and scurried back a moment later. A cheerful tune of dueling lutes began to play. She sat down on the edge of the bed and waited for the first few bars to play.

"Do you like it?"

"Very much. It makes me want to get up and dance."

"First you must learn to walk. This is Aziz Herawi's *Memories of Heret*. It was my mother's favorite."

Ahmed took a sip of his tea and set the cup down on the edge of the bed.

"I never knew anyone who had such love for music. Did your friend Fariba Mohammad influence you?"

Shakiba hesitated for a moment.

"It was my mother who taught me to love music, Ahmed. She'd play the zither and sing when I was just a little girl. She encouraged me to sing along from the time I was two. She'd say 'Shakiba, music is baklava for the soul.' "

"Your mother was a musician?"

"No, not really. She just loved music. Our home was filled with singing and people playing every sort of instrument. She treasured all types of music — Afghan lute, sitar, harp, Pashtun folk music, and especially western classical music. She adored Mozart. Nothing touched my life more than music. To this day my father calls me his little songbird."

Shakiba went silent. She bowed her head. Her hands began to quiver and she clenched her fists.

"Then the Taliban came."

Shakiba began to sob quietly. Hidden by the burqa, a periodic sniffle was the only sign of her sorrow. Ahmed scooted his legs off the bed and reached out to touch her hand.

"They cannot hurt you any longer, Shakiba."

She began to weep uncontrollably, her head bobbing up and down with grief. Ahmed rested his hand on hers. After a few minutes, Shakiba regained her composure.

"I'm sorry. Even now they hurt me, Ahmed. The Taliban forbade us to sing or even listen to music. A neighbor told the mullah my mother was defying the laws against the playing of music. The religious police searched the house while father, Zahir, and I worked. They found her hidden box with records and music. They burned the house down with my mother, two little sisters, and baby brother still inside."

Ahmed shook his head.

"All in the name of Allah. How could they do these things? They are nothing but cowards. These barbarisms made me question my faith in Islam."

Shakiba took a deep breath and sighed. After a few moments, she lifted her head. Ahmed could make out the outline of her eyes through the mesh in her burqa.

"Ahmed, I've come to treasure your friendship. You are a kind and gentle man. There is something else I must tell you. I wanted to tell you before. I really did try, but I just couldn't. It's so horrible, I fear you will hate me."

Ahmed patted Shakiba's hand.

"I could not hate you, Shakiba."

"Ahmed, after the Taliban captured Kandahar, the Arabs soon followed. They were members of al-Qaida. One of the commanders noticed me at the hospital. He threatened my father. He said give me your daughter or I will kill your son. Still my father refused. They beat him senseless. The Arabs watched us everywhere we went. We tried to flee Kandahar and they beat my father again. I knew they'd eventually kill him. I finally convinced my father I wanted to marry the Arab. He consented and the marriage was arranged. I was forced to live in seclusion with all the windows in the house painted over. I rarely left the house and then only with my husband Mohammad al-Zawar."

Ahmed bowed his head and listened in silence.

"I hated al-Zawar for what he did to my family. He beat me for the most trivial offenses. He insulted me daily for not preparing his food just the way he liked it. He forced me to have relations with him. My life couldn't have been more horrible."

Shakiba stood up and walked to the provisions. She began to sort a box of surgical supplies.

"Then my son Mohammad was born. He was the light of my life. There was finally something to live for. My little boy brought back the joy that had been missing since the death of my mother. My husband's verbal abuse and beatings never ended, but I survived by keeping my thoughts on my son."

"Then came September 11, 2001. Al-Zawar was puffed with bravado for the first month. You should have seen him crowing like a rooster. Then the Americans came to Afghanistan and one northern city after another began to fall. I've never felt such happiness as when Kabul fell and the Americans began to bomb Kandahar. It was over in a matter of weeks. Al-Qaida fled Kandahar. Al-Zawar left during the middle of the night without saying a word."

Her voice cracked. She began to sob.

"He took my little Mohammad with him!"

Ahmed waited for Shakiba to regain her composure. She sighed.

"People danced in the streets. They did everything that had been forbidden the day before. They played music, danced, and took each other's pictures. Men shaved their beards and women wore scarves and painted their fingernails. As for me, I felt only despair. Each day without my son seemed like a month."

She sniffled and grew silent. Ahmed reached across and rested his hand on hers.

"I never saw him again. I don't know whether he's alive or dead. The other Pashtun call me 'the Arab wife.' The government calls me 'an al-Qaida wife.' The authorities threatened to arrest my father for selling his daughter to be an al-Qaida wife. Can you imagine?"

Shakiba sighed, as though a weight had been lifted from her shoulders.

"So you see, Ahmed, I am an unclean woman. I don't know if I'm married, widowed, or divorced. My life ended the day I was forced to marry the Arab al-Zawar."

Ahmed bowed his head. He lifted his hands to his face and rubbed his brow. Afghan lute music echoed from the passageway. He looked up with his eyes filled with tears.

"Shakiba, you saved my life. I will always cherish you. You can count on me for the help you need when we leave this place. I will always value your friendship."

He pulled his hand away and shifted in the bed.

"Shakiba, why did the members of your tribe leave Kandahar if the Taliban and al-Qaida are gone?"

"They aren't gone. They're regrouping in the South. The Americans slaughtered hundreds of them in the Tarin Kowt Valley six months ago. But many others are in Paktia Province between Khowst and the Pakistani border. Mullah Omar has been seen there. Father decided to prepare for the worst. The Americans abandoned us once, and he believes they'll do it again. That is why we prepared this cave complex and established a secure compound farther east. What else can we do?"

Shakiba stood up next to the bed.

"Well, now you know everything there is to know about me. I need to refill the fuel tank. It's time for you to do your exercises."

Shakiba brushed by Ahmed's knees and strode across the infirmary. She disappeared into the passageway and the music cut off a moment later.

Ahmed was emotionally drained. He felt weariness like that when he first awakened from the coma. He performed his standing exercise, but stopped after five minutes.

He sat in the bed with his back propped against a pillow for several hours. He heard nothing from the back room of the complex. Ahmed debated calling Shakiba, but decided she needed to be alone.

Shakiba ducked through the doorway wearing a dark blue burqa. She carried a tray of food with a wooden staff tucked beneath her arm.

"Hi Ahmed. Are you hungry for lunch? I brought you tea and canned pears with naan."

She sat the tray down on the edge of Ahmed's bed and leaned the staff against the mattress.

"Thank you. It looks delicious. I love pears."

"I found this staff in the storeroom. I thought you could use it to begin taking a few steps."

"Shakiba, I—"

Shakiba shook her head beneath the burqa and Ahmed stopped in mid-sentence.

"You don't have to say anything, Ahmed. I shouldn't have troubled you with these things. It's not your burden to bear."

"Comforting you will never burden me, Shakiba."

Shakiba sat on the edge of the bed opposite Ahmed and watched as he hungrily ate the naan and pears.

"These are wonderful. Thank you."

"Do you know what today is?"

Ahmed looked up at her with a puzzled expression.

"No, should I?"

"Allah will forgive you. You've been isolated in this place for so long. It is Eid-ul-Fitr."

"The last day of Ramadan? I've completely lost track of time."

He took one last bite and handed her the tray.

"Ahmed, Ramadan is a time to prosper by going without and a time to grow stronger by enduring weakness. Our month of sacrifice is over. I have a special gift for you."

Ahmed smiled. His face glowed with the enthusiasm of a child.

"What is it?"

"I'll be right back."

Shakiba darted off into the passageway. She reappeared a few seconds later carrying a wooden box with detailed carving on the outside. She sat on the edge of the bed and placed the box next to her. Ahmed watched, as Shakiba grasped the front corners and opened the top.

"A chess set! I can't believe it. The last time I played was with Commander Massoud."

"I found it this morning in a cabinet in the storeroom. My father taught me to play when I was a young girl. I'm not that good, but do you want to play?"

"Of course. You take the white."

Shakiba took the board out and set it on the mattress next to Ahmed. She poured out the pieces and the two of them set the board for play. Soon they were engaged in a spirited game. Ahmed was on the attack, but Shakiba ably defended. Ahmed soon realized he was in an inferior position. Shakiba slipped from the room, as he rubbed his chin and pondered his predicament. Classical piano began to echo through the cavern.

Ahmed looked up and smiled when Shakiba re-emerged from the passageway. She sat down and he advanced his knight.

"That's an interesting play."

Shakiba advanced her bishop next to Ahmed's king. Ahmed pondered the new position for a moment and then looked up.

"I think you're what the Americans call a 'ringer' ."

Shakiba chuckled.

"You let me win to make me feel better."

"No, I did not."

"Yes, you did."

She reached out and squeezed his hand.

"You're a kind and generous man, Ahmed Jan."

CHAPTER FIFTY-EIGHT

A hmed tucked the pillow behind his head and stared at the rocky ceiling above his bed. The chamber echoed with the same unforgettable soprano voice he'd heard two days before. The unseen siren sang a velvety a capella ballad that time and again soared to ethereal highs. It made the hair on the nape of his neck stand up. He listened for some time to the graceful Pashtu vocalist, before he sat up and struggled to his feet beside the bed.

Ahmed stood still for a few moments. Then he reached out and grasped the wooden staff leaning against the wall behind the bed. He steadied himself and then slid his right foot forward along the dusty ground. He pulled his left foot even. After resting a moment, he took another step. Ahmed used the staff to support his weight and took one deliberate step after another until he reached the passageway in the back of the infirmary.

The beautiful ballad drove him on. He stopped for a moment to catch his breath and rest muscles that were weakened from disuse, before ducking beneath the overhang.

There was a light on in a doorway to the right. Several more halting steps brought him to the threshold. He stepped over a rock that protruded from the ground. He took one more step and looked up into the room.

Ahmed caught his breath. Several tall candles were burning against the back wall of the small cavern. The shimmering light cast mystical shadows from objects around the room and created glimmers in crystals in the rocky ceiling. A metal bathtub was sitting in the middle of the room overflowing with bubbles that reflected thousands of sparkles from the flickering candles. A woman was standing in the tub with her back to the door. He listened with awe, as she sang yet another celestial high. Her raven hair was on top of her head and held in place with a comb. Her figure was perfection, with creamy skin and an alluring back with prominent dimples. Utterly mesmerized, he watched in silence, as she swabbed a washcloth across her back.

Her voice trailed off in a vibrato finale and Ahmed lost his grip on the wooden staff. He lunged to catch it, but it was too late. It fell to the rocky floor with a resounding crack.

She cringed and spun around, drawing her arms up to cover her breasts. Her shocked expression melted to timidity. The flickering light in the grotto glistened off the bubbly foam that streaked down her naked body. She stared back at him without speaking.

Her eyes were smoky brown. She had high cheekbones. Her lips were full and red. Her delicate arms and shoulders framed a curvaceous figure. She was a ravishing beauty.

For Ahmed, the inescapable realization was oddly slow in coming.

"Shakiba?"

Shakiba returned his gaze, but said nothing.

Ahmed flushed with embarrassment. He bowed his head and turned. Without picking up the staff, he shuffled back through the passageway. He made his way across the infirmary and rolled onto the bed. He clutched the pillow to his chest and lay there bemused.

Ahmed felt a gentle hand grasp his arm. He glanced back over his shoulder. Shakiba was standing behind him. She wore a sheer yellow and orange robe made from exquisite Oriental fabric. Her long black hair fell across one eye and cascaded down her back. She leaned over and kissed him.

Ahmed sat up and wrapped his arms around her. Shakiba, in turn, pulled him toward her. He brushed the hair back from her eyes and kissed her tenderly on the forehead. She trailed kisses across his cheek to his earlobe. Ahmed moaned softly.

Shakiba stood up from the bed and pulled Ahmed's shirt over his head. She stooped to one knee and pulled his trousers down to his ankles. Slipping his feet through the trouser legs, she dropped the pants on the bed.

Shakiba stood next to the bed and let the robe drop off her shoulders to the ground. Her breasts rose and fell with each breath. She knelt on the bed with her knees straddling Ahmed's legs and pressed her breasts against his chest. She lingered in his arms for a moment and then raised her head to kiss him on the lips.

Ahmed closed his eyes and breathed in the intoxicating fragrance that surrounded him. He ran his fingertips up her belly and cupped her breasts gently in his hands. Their tongues entwined in a lover's duel. Little by little, their ardor grew.

Ahmed and Shakiba lay in each other's arms. Shakiba took a deep breath.

"I love you, Ahmed Jan," she whispered softly.

He sighed.

"I love you too. I love you with all my heart, Shakiba. Allah is truly forgiving and merciful."

Ahmed traced his index finger across each of Shakiba's eyebrows, down her delicate nose, and across her chin. He kissed her lightly on the lips. She smiled and took his hand in hers.

"So what happens now?"

Ahmed propped his head up on his arm.

"I guess that depends."

"On what?"

"On you. Will you be mine?"

Shakiba closed her eyes and smiled. She stroked Ahmed's chest with her fingernails and opened her eyes. Her eyes overflowed with tears of joy.

"With you I've known the simple joys I've yearned for all my life. Ahmed Jan, I am yours."

Ahmed kissed her tenderly on the lips. He sighed.

"When I was a teenager, I was in love with a girl who lived in the village. I'd lie awake at night and think about her face and the way she'd smile when she caught me staring at her in school. We exchanged secret looks and smiles for years. When she turned sixteen her father arranged for her to marry a man from a wealthy Konduz family. It broke my heart. I wasn't interested in any other woman for years. I really don't think I ever got over her. My mother told me, 'Ahmed, someday there will be a love so true, that even this will pale by comparison.' "

Ahmed ran his fingers through Shakiba's hair. She half-closed her eyes and enjoyed the warmth of his hand against her skin.

"You know what?"

Shakiba opened her eyes wide.

"What?"

"Mother was right."

She smiled warmly and cuddled against his chest. He combed a strand of hair behind her delicate ear.

"Can I ask you something?"

"You can ask me anything, Ahmed."

"Where did you learn to sing so beautifully?"

Shakiba stared off in the distance for a moment without speaking. Her thoughts drifted to another time and another place.

"I sang children's songs with my mother as a young girl. As I got older, she encouraged me to sing all the time. I remember singing at family gatherings when I was only ten years old. Then Fariba Mohammad's family moved to Kandahar when I was fourteen. Her mother sang professionally as a young woman. They taught me to use my voice as an instrument."

"I've never heard such a beautiful voice. Why didn't you share it with me?" She peered lovingly into his eyes.

"Ahmed, I stopped singing three years ago when mother was killed. There was nothing to sing for after that."

Shakiba brushed her fingertips across Ahmed's face and kissed him on the lips.

"Until now, my love."

CHAPTER FIFTY-NINE

January 15, 2003

L ittle by little, Ahmed recovered the strength in his legs. At times his knees ached, but he managed to fight through the tightness with exercise and stretching. The discomfort ebbed over time, until he finally felt like himself again.

Life in the cave underwent a remarkable transformation. The young lovers packed away the instruments, medications, and other supplies in the infirmary and changed it into a roomy bedroom suite. They converted the small grotto into a getaway where they traded massages on the bed and shared leisurely baths in the candlelight. The cavern in the back became their primary living space. It served as a kitchen, dining room, living room, and storeroom. It was the room where they ate meals, played chess, and sipped cups of tea during long conversations next to the potbelly stove. The complex echoed with music from the time they got up in the morning to the time they turned out the lights to sleep.

Shakiba folded her burqas and packed them away. She spent most days in tunic dresses, but at times she never got out of her robe. Ahmed was limited to the garments he brought with him in his backpack: two pair of loose-fitting white trousers, two shirts, and the parka.

Shakiba and Ahmed cherished the simple things their Spartan life had to offer. The young lovers held hands and kissed for hours on end. If they wanted to spend the entire day snuggling in bed, there was absolutely nothing to dictate otherwise. They giggled at nothing and frequently laughed until they cried. The refuge, austere as it might be, was also void of the irritating interruptions that plague normal everyday life. It was perpetual springtime.

Shakiba turned off the burner and poured the boiling water into two cups with black tea. Ahmed sauntered in behind her. He wrapped his hands around her waist and kissed her on the back of the neck.

"Have I ever told you how beautiful you are?"

Shakiba leaned her head back and kissed him on the cheek.

"Let's see, I believe you have. I'd say at least three times today."

"Really? It must be that perfume you're wearing."

She smiled.

"Would you like tea?"

"Sure. I also want to avenge last night's humiliating defeat on the chessboard. I thought of a new strategy."

Shakiba bowed deeply with mock trepidation.

"I feel your power, oh great chess master of Taloqan. Sure I'll play, as long as the loser makes dinner."

"For the next week?"

"Even better."

Ahmed fetched the board and game pieces from the top of a stack of unopened cases of food. He set the board on the table and sorted the pieces. Shakiba set the teacups on the table and advanced her queen's pawn two squares before she even sat down. Ahmed advanced his king's pawn and the game was on.

Shakiba took on her typical defensive posture. Ahmed formulated an aggressive attack. They traded moves in silence for the better part of an hour. Ahmed traded his knight for Shakiba's rook and then took her black bishop. Shakiba countered by advancing her queen. Ahmed castled to safety. Shakiba took a sip of her tea and stared at the board.

"Shakiba, I think it's time to start thinking about what we're going to do when we leave this place."

She glanced up from the board.

"What do you want to do, Ahmed?"

"I've been thinking about it. I want to leave Afghanistan. I want to live in a safe place where a Tajik man and Pashtun woman can live in peace. Somewhere we can raise a family."

Shakiba moved her black bishop two squares.

"Ahmed, I'm willing to go anywhere with you, but shouldn't we think about getting married before we plan a family?"

He glanced up with a smile and then looked back down at the game.

"Yeah, I was thinking we should," he muttered, as he concentrated on his next move.

Shakiba grinned with amusement. She reached across the board and lifted his chin.

"Ahmed, are you asking me to marry you?"

Ahmed looked down at the board and moved his queen all the way across the board from left to right.

"Don't you think we should?" he asked.

Shakiba dropped her hands down on the table. Her expression was one of astonishment. She snickered sarcastically.

"Ahmed, you're so romantic!"

She moved her queen diagonally to a square next to Ahmed's king.

"Checkmate!"

Ahmed stared at the board for a few moments and then looked up with a bemused smile.

"Okay. I'll throw something together for dinner. Do you have anything special to wear?"

Shakiba smiled.

"I think I may have something."

"Go enjoy yourself. Put on that classical music you like so much and take a long warm bath. I'll come and get you when it's ready."

Shakiba stood up and kissed him on the cheek.

"See you in a while. Let me know if you need any help."

She strolled across the room, looked back, and smiled, before ducking out through the doorway.

Ahmed put the last touches on dinner and set the table. He poured two large glasses of water. Finally, he stood back and surveyed the room. It was as perfect as he could make it.

Shakiba was standing before the small makeup mirror on the chest-of-drawers when he stepped into the candlelit grotto. She smiled at him in the mirror and turned around to face him.

An emerald-green blouse with long sleeves exposed her midriff. It was detailed with embroidery across her bosom and down the arms to the cuffs. The skirt and shawl were a matching gold and emerald-green print with delicately beaded borders. Her hair was piled on the top of her head. She was breathtaking.

Ahmed shook his head with admiration. He held her hands.

"Shakiba, you are always full of surprises!" he exclaimed. "Where did you get this beautiful dress?"

"So you approve?"

"Approve? You are a vision of loveliness."

"It was my mother's. Father gave it to her for their twentieth wedding anniversary. Even before the Taliban, she could never wear it in public. She wore it for my father at a private anniversary dinner for just the two of them. She gave it to me when I turned eighteen. I hid it here in the cave when the Taliban first took over the country. It's the only keepsake of hers I have."

"It's dazzling. I only wish I had something fitting to wear."

Shakiba smiled and kissed him on the cheek.

"You are handsome the way you are. How's the dinner coming?"

"I think it came out pretty good. I have a surprise for you. Close your eyes and I'll tell you when to open them."

Shakiba giggled and squeezed her eyes shut. Ahmed guided her slowly through the passageway and into the back cavern. He took her to the center of the room, let go of her hand, and stepped away.

"Okay. Open your eyes."

Shakiba gasped. The room was decorated with more than two hundred flickering candlesticks. They were sitting on the table, the storage racks, tables along the side of the room, and even on the floor. The dining room table alone had more than a dozen candles. The flames set the cavern aglow with shimmers that reflected off the walls and ceiling.

"Oh Ahmed!" Shakiba exclaimed, as she whirled around. "It's wonderful!"

Ahmed took her hands into his and stood facing her.

"I only wish I could have done more to make this an evening you'll always remember. We don't have a holy man to perform the Nikah, so I must do it. Allah is our witness. Shakiba, will you marry me?"

Shakiba's face glowed with happiness.

"Yes, Ahmed. There is nothing that could make me happier than spending my life with you. You are my friend and you are my lover."

"Then before Allah, I take you for my wife. I pray our life together will be blessed and we will bring forth many children who will obey the words of the prophet and serve Allah."

Ahmed removed a golden chain from around his neck. He undid the clasp, slid off a golden band, refastened the chain, and put it back around his neck. He slipped the golden band onto Shakiba's ring finger. It fit perfectly.

"This was my mother's ring."

He fetched a small package wrapped in plain packing paper from the table.

"This is my gift, the mahr that Allah commanded every husband to give his wife."

Shakiba took the package and opened it. It was the worn book of poetry by Hafez.

Shakiba was speechless with joy. Tears welled in her eyes and ran down her face. She wrapped her arms around Ahmed and held him. Ahmed kissed her on the forehead, wiped the tears from her cheeks, and gave her a lingering kiss on the lips.

Ahmed took Shakiba by the hand and showed her to the table. He pulled out a chair and motioned to Shakiba. She gathered her dress and sat down.

"This simple ceremony lacks many of the traditions you dreamed about, Shakiba, but we will have the traditional wedding feast. I've prepared Afghani *qabili pilau.*"

"*Qabili pilau?* How could you do this?"

"Our old family recipe was passed down for several generations. I found several cans of chicken, along with canned carrots, raisins, and rice. I found a few spices in the box by the stove. Not all of them, but I think it's pretty good."

Ahmed served two plates. He slid one in front of Shakiba and another across the table from her. He picked up a spoonful, smiled with glee, and held the spoon across the table for her.

"I love you, my little songbird."

Shakiba smiled joyfully. She opened her mouth, chewed for a moment, and grinned.

"Umm, it's wonderful, Ahmed! Really, it's as good as I've ever tasted."

Ahmed pampered Shakiba all through the evening. He followed the main course with a medley of canned fruit. They played traditional Afghani lute music and danced and sang until the early morning hours. Finally, he blew out all the candles, picked Shakiba up in his arms, and carried her off to bed. They made love and fell asleep in each other's arms. It was truly a wedding night to cherish for a lifetime.

Living as husband and wife dramatically changed life in the cave complex. Ahmed and Shakiba grew steadily closer day by day. Most of their waking hours were spent doing what was necessary to enhance their existence.

Ahmed took over responsibility for fueling the generator and keeping it running. He refined the schedule for the ventilation system to further improve conservation. He estimated there was sufficient fuel to last at most a couple more months. Ahmed also took on the heavy work of carrying supplies to the kitchen and maintaining a tally of the stores that were plentiful and those that were running short.

Shakiba prepared the meals and did the best she could to make the cave a home. She washed the dishes, mended clothes, and helped with rationing food supplies. Ahmed chipped in with the cooking, especially when the occasion called for *qabili pilau*.

In a peculiar way, it was an ideal existence. There were no distractions. No family members to stir up trouble between the newlyweds. No anxiety about the outside world. They spent countless hours playing chess, listening to music, and talking about their hopes and dreams. Saturday nights became a special night for singing. It was a treat both of them looked forward to with anticipation. In short, they focused on staying alive and enjoying each other, one hour at a time, one day at a time.

CHAPTER SIXTY

February 17, 2003, Langley, Virginia

Stone Waverly picked up a magazine from an end table in the waiting room outside the CIA director's private office. Mrs. Pendleton, the director's secretary, was sitting behind the reception desk typing on a computer. She was a pleasant, matronly-looking woman with her hair pulled up in a bun. Her glasses hung from her neck by a gold chain. She reminded Stone of his grandmother.

The phone rang and Mrs. Pendleton picked it up. After a few words she hung up.

"The director will be with you in a few minutes, Mr. Waverly."

Stone nodded without speaking. The butterflies in his stomach began to flutter anew and perspiration beaded on his brow. He wiped his forehead with his sleeve, took a deep breath, and exhaled loudly to release the tension. The last time Stone remembered feeling this much anxiety was during interviews for his first position at the CIA.

The door to the director's door opened. Stone's eyes widened with surprise, as Deputy Director Richards shuffled out the door and closed it quietly behind him. His tie was askew and a white handkerchief was hanging out of the back pocket of his wrinkled pants. He looked even more disheveled than usual. It was the first time Stone had ever seen him without a cigar in his mouth.

Richards looked up toward Stone. The two men locked eyes for a moment. Richards didn't acknowledge him. He turned toward the door and strode out past the receptionist without speaking.

The phone rang a moment later. Mrs. Pendleton answered.

"Yes, sir."

She hung up the phone and walked around the desk.

"The director will see you now, Mr. Waverly."

Mrs. Pendleton winked and gave him a little smile.

"Don't worry, sir. Everything's going to be fine."

Mrs. Pendleton headed toward the door and Stone fell in line behind her. She opened the door and held it for him to pass. The director was sitting behind his desk scanning a report. He didn't look up. Mrs. Pendleton motioned toward a chair in front of the desk and Stone sat down. She stepped back outside and gave Stone a slight smile as she pulled the door closed.

The director looked surprisingly young. His close-cropped hair was jet black, with no hint of gray. He wore a red print tie that complemented a nicely tailored charcoal suit. He looked more like an executive from a Fortune 500 company than the director of the CIA.

The director continued to read through the document, shuffling from one page to the next. Finally, he shook his head and closed the folder. He placed the report down on the desk and looked up over the top of his glasses.

"Thank you for coming, Mr. Waverly. This report you sent me sends a chill down my spine every time I read it."

"It's been weighing on my mind for several months now, sir."

"You must have realized this would really piss a lot of people off here at the agency? You violated the unwritten rules that have guided this organization for decades."

"Yes, sir, I did. But I decided I'd rather leave the company than live with something like this on my conscience for the rest of my life."

The director nodded and folded his hands on top of his desk.

"Well, Mr. Waverly, I appreciate what you've done. Your report was the first inkling I had that we didn't find all of the Armageddon vector during the operation in Vancouver. I knew the Tajik and American got away, but I was never informed about the cell phone call from Bombay or the freighter that left Vancouver for Karachi."

"I'm sorry, sir," Stone replied apprehensively. "I should've made sure you got the information sooner. Mr. Richards told me he'd take care of it."

The director nodded and waved his hand.

"You did the right thing, Mr. Waverly. If you can't trust your superiors to do what's right, well then, we're all in big trouble, aren't we? I asked Mr. Richards for his resignation. He gave it to me a few minutes ago."

"That wasn't my intention, sir."

"Mr. Richards put the president and the country at risk of being seen as an accomplice to genocide. That's flat out unacceptable. He knew it."

"I just hate to see his career tarnished this way."

"Don't be too concerned about Mr. Richards. He's had a long and distinguished career here at the agency. It was time for him to step down anyway. He'll be treated with dignity."

The director held up the report.

"But we still have a problem, don't we?"

"Yes, sir, we do."

"Mr. Waverly, I think we must assume that the Tajik Ahmed Jan arrived in Karachi with the vector and that he's either hiding in Pakistan or already found his way into Afghanistan. That's what I'll tell the president this afternoon. This virus has the potential to wipe out half the population of central Asia."

The director stood up from his desk and walked to the window. He gazed out at the well-manicured grounds surrounding the main building of the CIA headquarters. Thousands of daffodils were in bloom along the main entrance. The director turned, stepped back across to his desk, and sat in the chair.

"Mr. Waverly, it's been four months since Jan arrived in Karachi and there's been nothing to suggest he released the vector. That's the only thing we've got going for us. You've been on Jan's tail for over a year now. What's he up to?"

Stone shook his head.

"I don't know, sir. Ahmed Jan hasn't used his cell phone since early October. If he's headed for Afghanistan, there's no way he can avoid traveling through Pashtun country. He could be dead or in prison somewhere. Maybe the ampule broke on his way to Karachi and he just gave up. Maybe he released it and for some reason there were no infections. It's even possible he released it in some isolated area in the tribal provinces of Pakistan and it just hasn't been reported to the central authorities yet. It's puzzling sir."

"Well, Mr. Waverly, the president will want solid information. You know as much about Pakistan and Afghanistan as anyone here at the CIA. I'd like you to go find out what happened. Can you do that?"

"Yes, sir, I'll do what I can."

"There are more than four hundred agency operatives in Afghanistan and another two hundred in Pakistan. Blake Jenson is our man working with the Special Forces at the Bagram Airbase just outside of Kandahar. I want you to leave immediately for the aircraft carrier *John F. Kennedy* on station in the Arabian Sea. One of our helicopters will take you in from there. Your instructions are to find Ahmed Jan and the rest of the vector. All of our resources are at your disposal."

"I'll do my best, sir."

"Let me know the minute you find him."

"I will, sir."

"Did you hear we picked up Khalid Shaikh Mohammed in Rawalpindi?"

"Yes, sir, I did. He's the biggest al-Qaida fish yet. Congratulations. The president must be pleased about catching the mastermind of the 9/11 attacks."

"Yes, he's feeling much better about our efforts. We're not going to make an announcement to the world for two weeks. That will give us time to track down other al-Qaida in Afghanistan and elsewhere using the computer files we found with him. When we do make the announcement, we'll make it appear we just found Shaikh Mohammed that day so the terrorists will think they have a little time. So keep the information about his capture top secret when you get to Afghanistan."

The director stood up behind his desk and stepped around to the door. He opened it and turned around to offer his hand. Stone took it.

"Good luck Mr. Waverly. Take care."

"I will, sir."

CHAPTER SIXTY-ONE

S tone stared out the cockpit window as the C-2 transport plane turned to
line up with the aircraft carrier for touchdown. The pilot peered through
the rain-drenched windshield and eased into his descent toward the deck
below. To Stone's eye, it seemed like they were aiming to land on a postage
stamp floating in a vast sea churning with whitecaps.

The flight deck steadily rose to meet the plane until the C-2 touched
down with a jarring screech. They decelerated from over one hundred miles per
hour to a standstill in an instant.

The door opened and one of the crew hustled Stone down a ladder to the
flight deck. Another crewmember hauled his bag out behind him. An officer
was waiting on the windy deck, as Stone stepped off the last rung. He held his
cap on with one hand and pointed to the far end of the flight deck with the
other.

"Sir, the helicopter's waiting for you," he yelled above the whining turbo-
prop engines. "It's headed for the Bagram Airbase in Kandahar."

They scurried across the deck beneath the spinning rotor and into the
open door on the giant Chinook helicopter. One of the crew offered Stone a
hand and hoisted him up into the aircraft, while another crewman took his bag.
Stone barely found a seat before the rotors on the big bird began to accelerate
and the lumbering helicopter lifted off the deck. The aircraft dipped to the
north and angled off across the water. A gunner manning a fifty caliber machine
gun leaned over and shouted, "Welcome aboard, sir. You better buckle up. It's
going to be a rough ride."

Stone signaled his understanding and snapped on the harness. The helicopter tossed and turned as it skimmed across the water. Then the ride got

smoother for a few seconds. Stone leaned back into his seat and glanced out the window. Without warning, the floor seemed to collapse beneath them. Stone thought the turbulence would rip the chopper apart. He gripped the arms of the seat and held on for dear life as he tried to suppress a rising wave of nausea.

The soldier sitting in the next seat glanced in his direction and grinned. He handed Stone a paper bag. Stone buried his face in the bag and retched uncontrollably.

It took nearly twenty minutes for the helicopter to make land. Straight away the flight smoothed out and Stone began to relax. He folded up his bag and set it on the floor. The soldier next to him leaned over and bellowed to be heard above the aircraft engines.

"You CIA?"

Stone nodded.

"Well, you might as well get comfortable. It'll take us another two hours to get there. We're over Pakistan now. In another hour and a half we'll cross into Afghanistan. You should move to one of those seats up front before we get there so you won't get hit by shell casings ejected from the machine gun."

Stone nodded. He unbuckled his harness and shuffled to one of the forward seats. He buckled himself in and leaned his head back into the seat. The rhythmic whine of the engines was like a sedative. He soon drifted off to sleep.

It seemed like only a few minutes passed before he was jarred awake by the helicopter touching down. Stone glanced out the window at the surrounding barren and featureless terrain. The engines decelerated rapidly and the rotors spun to a stop. One of the crewmembers pulled the door open and jumped down to the ground. He zipped his parka against the cold, as the wind gusted through his hair.

"Welcome to the Kandahar Resort and Spa, sir. Don't forget your bag."

The man helped Stone down to the ground and one of the other crewmen handed him his duffle bag. He pointed.

"The CIA command center is over there."

Stone turned and spotted a middle-aged balding man in civilian clothes headed across the clearing from a cluster of single-story prefabricated wood buildings. He waved enthusiastically toward Stone and thrust out his hand with a smile.

"Mr. Waverly, welcome to Bagram Airbase. I'm Blake Jenson. It's a pleasure to finally meet you. You're a legend here in southern Afghanistan. How was your trip?"

"Rough as hell. Call me Stone."

Jenson shook his head and sighed.

"That's par for the course. I dread those damn helicopter transfers off the carrier. I passed up my last leave just to avoid flying out of here during a storm. Let me take your bag. We're in those buildings over there. A good stiff drink usually helps. I've got a bottle of Johnny Walker Blue from home. Feel like a drink?"

"No, I think I'll pass. Thanks for the offer though."

Stone followed Jenson across the rutted clearing to a doorway in the first building. He opened the door and stepped inside. Jenson closed the door behind them.

Several tables filled with all sorts of electronic equipment lined the walls. Stone recognized some of it as an advanced communication system, but the rest was unfamiliar. Two men were sitting at consoles. Three others were hunched over a table sorting through a pile of documents.

Jenson set Stone's bag on the floor and walked over to the table.

"Stone, this is Jackson, Peters, and Bates. That's Wilson over at the first console and Hood in the back."

The three men at the table stood up and shook Stone's hand. Wilson and Hood nodded from their stations. Jenson directed Stone to another table at the front of the room. He handed Stone a bottle of water and sat in the seat next to him.

"You must be beat."

"Yeah, I'm running on auto-pilot. I haven't slept much the past thirty-six hours."

"Well, let me brief you on a few things and then I'll take you back to the living quarters. I received a coded briefing from Langley yesterday. I know about the vector. Damnedest thing I ever heard. How long have you been looking for this Tajik Ahmed Jan?"

"I've been tracking Jan for over a year now. I helped him and his conspirators escape from Pakistan in January 2002 and I've been one step behind that son-of-a-bitch ever since. I've tracked him from Southern Asia to Europe to North America and back to Asia."

Jenson slid a folder across the table in front of Stone. Stone picked up the file and opened it.

"What's this?"

"It's a summary of a report we took from an informant. A taxi driver named Awar told a couple of other drivers about a Tajik he picked up at the Cheman border crossing last October. Several local taxi drivers are on the CIA payroll. We get information from them about al-Qaida and Taliban all the time. One of them contacted me last October. Not much to it really. The Tajik asked the driver to take him to a long-distance calling service in Kandahar. When the fellow came out of the service, he spotted a group of Pashtun loading trucks at a warehouse across the street. He forced the driver to follow the truck into the mountains north of Kandahar at gunpoint."

"Was it a robbery?"

"No, he paid the guy. The Tajik got out of the taxi in the middle of Taliban country and just walked off into the night. He must be some crazy son-of-a-bitch. When I got the message last night I pulled this file. Look at the last few sentences."

Stone read out loud.

"The Tajik told the taxi driver his name was Ahmed. The driver took him to make a phone call at a telephone service. While he was there, he spotted a man working with some Pashtun loading a truck with supplies. The Tajik said the man was a traitor named Mohammajon."

Stone bolted upright in his chair.

"Shit! It was Jan. No doubt about it. Mohammajon was one of the other Tajiks involved in this mess from the beginning. He came back to Afghanistan last year."

Stone looked up from the report.

"When can I talk to this taxi driver, Blake?"

"I tried to track him down yesterday. No one's seen him for at least two months. That warehouse across from the Internet café was shut down last month. It was a front used to supply Taliban forces holed up in caves north of the city."

"Damn. So what do we do now?"

"There's not much we can do. I sent out a priority message to our operatives throughout Afghanistan. I told them we're offering a hundred thousand-dollar reward for information about a Tajik named Ahmed who came to the area in October. All we can do is wait and hope for a break."

Stone rested his elbows on the table and ran his hands through his hair. He sighed.

"Damn it, Blake. I'm never going to find this guy. He's either dead or already released the virus. Maybe both. What's our strength here?"

"We've got several attack helicopters, eight Chinook transport helicopters, and close to a hundred armed CIA operatives. Seventy-five or eighty Special Forces are also at our disposal, along with several hundred Pashtun Mujaheddin loyal to the interim government. We also have access to British and Australian Special Forces. But it's a piss in the ocean. There's a lot of territory out there. Jan could be anywhere by now."

Stone sighed loudly, shook his head, and pushed himself up from the chair.

"Damn, I'm tired."

"I'll take you to the living quarters. We'll start getting our shit together after you get some rest. If that Tajik's still alive, we'll find him."

CHAPTER SIXTY-TWO

February 19, 2003

S hakiba cried out in terror and bolted upright in the bed. Hyperventilating, she sobbed uncontrollably.

"Father, oh Father!"

Ahmed sat up and wrapped his arms around her.

"Shakiba, everything's all right. It's a nightmare, my darling. It's only a nightmare."

Shakiba, still sobbing, pressed her head against Ahmed's chest and clung to his side.

"They aren't coming for us, Ahmed! They aren't coming!"

Ahmed brushed Shakiba's hair from her eyes and kissed her tenderly on the forehead.

"Shakiba, it was a dream. It was just a dream."

"It was more than a dream, Ahmed. Father came to me in white flowing robes. He told me he could not return."

"It was just a dream, darling."

"No, Ahmed. Father would have come for us by now. We only have fuel to run the generator for two weeks, maybe three at the most. We already ran out of wheat and there's less than a bag of rice left. There's no hope. This will be our tomb."

Ahmed hugged her tenderly. He stared across the infirmary at the passage to the outside of the cave, as she gradually regained her composure.

Ahmed got out of bed a few minutes later. He stepped across the room into the entryway and placed his hand on the rock covering the passage. He turned around and gazed across the shadowy, candle-lit infirmary toward Shakiba.

"There's always hope, Shakiba. With Allah's help, we'll move this rock."

"Ahmed, it took many men to move that boulder just two meters. It's hopeless."

"We will move it Shakiba. We will move it one pebble at a time. Come, help me turn on the generator."

Ahmed grabbed a candle and the two of them ducked through the passageway to the rear cavern. Ahmed started the generator and Shakiba turned on the lights in the storeroom. Ahmed turned slowly and scanned the room. His eyes fell on one of the empty barrels sitting next to the fuel reservoir. He strode across the room and tipped it over on its side. Ahmed grasped it with a hand at each end and lifted it against his chest.

"Shakiba, turn on the ventilation system."

"What are you going to do?"

"I want to try something."

Ahmed carried the barrel through the doorway toward the infirmary. As Shakiba activated the ventilation system, a resounding, hollow toll echoed from the infirmary. Another clang reverberated through the cavern a moment later.

Shakiba ducked back through the passageway and into the infirmary. Ahmed was standing at the entryway holding the barrel with both hands. He swung it in a wide vertical arc and pounded the steel edge against the underside of the boulder. Several fragments of rock ricocheted back into the room. Dusty debris rose in the air like a cloud. Ahmed repeated the maneuver over and over again, swinging the barrel in a low arc and crashing it against the stone in the entryway. He set the barrel down after more than a dozen blows and rubbed at his deformed left hand.

"This will take time, but it will work. You must have faith."

Shakiba shook her head.

"Ahmed, my husband, the hunger plays with your mind. It'll take forever to break through that stone to the outside cave."

"We can't give up now. Think of all we've been through and all we have to live for. This is our only hope, Shakiba. Let's further ration the fuel and supplies and pray Allah gives us strength."

Shakiba glanced around the room at the beds and the boxes of medical supplies. She sighed.

"Okay, let's move everything from this room. It'll be covered with dust and debris if we leave it here. Help me move the beds."

The two of them broke down the bed closest to the entryway. They carried the pieces into the rear cavern and reassembled it on one side of the chamber. Shakiba picked up a box of medical supplies and carried it toward the passage-way. Ahmed bent over and lifted the mattress off the second bed.

"Shakiba, there's something hidden here."

Ahmed wrestled the mattress away from the bed and leaned it against the wall. He stooped over a shallow wooden box that was lying on the ground within the bed frame and lifted the lid.

"Look! Look what I found!"

He hoisted a Kalashnikov rifle into the air.

"There's a case of ammunition in this box. You see, Shakiba, we ask Allah's help and He provides for our needs."

Little-by- little, they cleared the infirmary of everything useful. They only left the bed frame and a few empty boxes behind.

Ahmed wrapped a cloth around his twisted left hand. He picked up the barrel and swung it against the boulder that blocked the entryway. He regrasped the barrel and pounded the stone again.

For days on end Ahmed used the barrels as crude tools to break away fragments of the stone. He quickly learned that the sharp edges of the barrel rims made the most effective chisels. The force of the blow was directed to a smaller spot on the rock when the edge collided with the stone. The steel edge of each barrel gradually turned under, as Ahmed repeatedly pounded it against the obstruction. He'd rotate the barrel every ten to fifteen blows so a new edge was exposed. Once one end of a barrel was flattened, he'd turn it around and use the other. When both ends were flattened, he discarded the barrel in the storage room and grabbed another.

Ahmed and Shakiba settled into a tedious routine. They slept on the bed in the back cavern. Upon awakening they shared tea and a ration of food. Rice was the mainstay. It was all they had left, except for a few cans of vegetables and fruit. Every few days they'd include some canned vegetable or fruit. Then that ran out too.

After breakfast Ahmed worked for several hours pounding barrels against the stone. When he was too exhausted to deliver another blow, he'd eat a light lunch and rest while Shakiba cleared the gravel away from the entryway. When she was done, Ahmed resumed pounding at the boulder until he was spent. He slept while Shakiba cleared the new debris and prepared dinner. Then the two of them would share a ration of rice before finally crawling into bed. Everyday was the same. They both shed weight, as the food reserves continued to decline and the portions dwindled.

The drudgery was all the worse because of the constant swirl of dust. The perpetual cloud got into everything. Shakiba eventually sacrificed the mattress on the second bed. She propped it against the doorway into the passageway to partially block the dust cloud from the rear of the compound. Despite these measures, and a nightly wet washcloth, the two of them were caked in dirt by the end of the week. They allowed themselves a Saturday night bath in a few centimeters of water until they opened the last case of five-liter containers. The wet washcloth had to suffice after that.

Progress was slow. After the first week, Ahmed had chiseled a rut that extended a little more than a half-meter deep into the boulder. It became increasingly more difficult to strike an effective blow against the stone because of the shape of the rut and the diameter of the barrels.

Shakiba had a revelation at the end of the second week of excavation. Each of the massive racks in the storeroom had been constructed in place using heavy steel bars to support stainless steel shelves. Shakiba pointed them out to Ahmed. She thought the bars might make good battering rams.

It took Ahmed nearly an hour to break the welds on one of the bars by banging a cast-iron skillet against each joint until it finally gave way. Ahmed lifted the heavy bar off the rocky floor and carried it into the front cave.

Ahmed positioned himself next to the blocked entryway. He held the bar to his side with both hands and swung it in a sweeping upward arc so the end pounded against the boulder. Broken rock showered down around him. He swung again and more rock cascaded around his feet. Time after time, he pounded the bar against the stone until his muscles ached and he could lift the bar no more. Ahmed dropped the bar to the ground, stumbled to the rear cavern, and collapsed on the bed with exhaustion.

Still, the bars made perfect battering rams for breaking away rocky fragments from the deepening gutter. Progress increased three-fold. However, there was no way to guess the thickness of the stone that sealed the cavernous tomb.

Ahmed pounded the metal bar against the granite stone day after day, as the once seemingly limitless food supplies dwindled to less than a quarter bag of rice. Both Shakiba and Ahmed got progressively weaker as they further rationed the little that was left. Still, they found the strength to continue on.

Shakiba brushed a strand of wet hair away from her eyes with her fingertips. She held her once-smooth hands out before her. The skin on her palms was rough and lined with deep cuts that never seemed to heal. She sighed loudly and painstakingly scooped the last few grains of rice from the bottom of the pan with a spoon. She sprinkled them on top of a small rice mound and carried the plate to the table.

Ahmed was sitting at the table with his head propped up on his arms. Shakiba slid the plate of rice in front of him and sat across the table. Ahmed lifted his teacup and took a sip.

"Tea's just not the same without sugar."

Ahmed picked up his spoon and scooped up some rice. He lifted the spoon toward his mouth, but suddenly stopped.

"Where's your plate, Shakiba?"

"This is all that's left, Ahmed. You eat it."

Ahmed shook his head.

"No, Shakiba, we will share."

"Ahmed, maintaining your strength is our only hope. Please, eat the rice."

Ahmed held the spoon out toward Shakiba. His hand trembled with weakness and his voice quivered with emotion.

"No, my love, I will not. Not unless you take this bite first."

Shakiba didn't move. Her stomach churned with hunger. She bit her lower lip and stared into Ahmed's sunken eyes. She shook her head. Ahmed pressed the spoon against her lips.

"My darling, imagine this is delicious *qabili pilau.* It's our wedding night. One last bite and then a song of joy."

She parted her lips slightly and Ahmed slid the spoon into her mouth. He carefully scraped the spoon across her upper lip. Shakiba chewed and swallowed, as she stared into his eyes. A single tear tracked across her cheek. She reached across the table and took Ahmed's hand.

"Allah is great, my love. He blesses me still."

They alternated bites until the plate was bare. Ahmed pushed the plate away. Shakiba reached out grasped Ahmed's hands and stared lovingly into his eyes.

"Ahmed, my wonderful and loving husband, I've found the true meaning of contentment here with you. Life cannot offer more than this. I pray Allah grants me only one more wish. May I take my last breath in your arms and lie here with you for eternity."

Ahmed brushed the tears from her cheek.

"Shakiba, my beautiful songbird, all else is meaningless compared to the love that burns in my heart for you."

Shakiba smiled and reached down into the pocket of her dress. She pulled out a white plastic bottle and set it on the table.

"These are sedative pills. It's time, my love."

Ahmed stared down at the bottle. He grasped it with trembling fingers and cupped it in his palm, before raising his gaze to meet hers.

"Shakiba, perhaps tomorrow will be our last. Maybe you and I will walk hand-in-hand in paradise the next day, or the day after that. But, for now I will pray Allah grants us one more miracle. I am weak, but you are my strength."

Ahmed stood up from the table and staggered through the passageway toward the front room. Renewed pounding echoed through the cavern a moment later. Shakiba shuffled through the doorway to the infirmary. She crouched against the wall on the opposite side of the room. She had no more strength to give.

Ahmed struggled to lift the bar and crash it against the stone. Each pitiful thrust was feebler than the one before. Finally, he was depleted. He stood the bar on end and rested it against the cavern wall. He bent at the waist and held onto the bar with both hands to steady himself. He gasped for air.

Several minutes passed before Ahmed recovered to the point he could lift his head to glance at Shakiba. She was sitting with her arms folded over her knees. Her eyes were closed.

Suddenly, a bolt of rage swelled within him. He grasped the bar with both hands and lifted it over his shoulder like a spear.

"Allah, why do you toy with us? Ahhh!"

In one powerful and synchronized motion, he hurled the bar like a javelin toward the malevolent stone.

Ahmed stared down into the crevice. Only half a meter of rod protruded from the stone. It took a moment for him to grasp what had happened.

"Shakiba! Shakiba look! Our miracle!"

Shakiba crawled across the ground on her hands and knees. She watched, as he grasped the end of the bar and withdrew it back into the cavern. It fell to the ground with a clanging ring. There was a five-centimeter hole punched in the middle of the crevice.

"Allah is great!" Ahmed called out, with his arms spread wide.

Ahmed lifted the bar again and thrust the end against the stone. A melon-sized chunk of rock tumbled to the ground.

Ahmed's strength was renewed. Time after time, he lifted the pole and hurled it headlong against the stone. He stopped for a brief rest, only to renew the assault a few minutes later. Progress was slow, but within an hour he'd expanded the hole to several times its original size. He tried to slip his head into the void. The hole was still too small.

CHAPTER SIXTY-THREE

March 12, 2003

B lake Jenson and Stone Waverly sat at a table in the CIA command center. They scanned across a detail topographic map of the area surrounding Kandahar. It extended from the Pakistani tribal provinces in the South to the Hindu Kush range north of the city.

More than fifty pushpins were scattered across the map. Almost all of them were green, but a few white ones were scattered over the mountains north of the city. Jenson set a memo down on the table, pulled out a white pin, and replaced it with a green one.

"It doesn't look good, Stone. We haven't heard from these operatives in the North. I'm guessing we'll have all the reports in by the end of the week."

Stone scooted his chair back and stood up from the table. He stepped to a side table and jerked a bottle of water from a rack.

"Hell of a deal. The son-of-a-bitch is probably sipping tea in some café in Mazar-e-Sharif."

"You've done everything you can, Stone. Don't be so hard on yourself."

"We had him! We had the SOB! We would've polished this off long ago if it weren't for Richards. He's back home nibbling on shrimp cocktail at some retirement banquet, while we're here eating MREs."

Peters trotted to the table from the back of the command center. He held out a sheet of paper.

"Blake, I think we might have something here. It's from Ed Savage's unit."

Jenson held up the paper and read it aloud, as Peters and Waverly listened.

"In contact with remnants of clan of Durranis Pashtun in complex at coordinates 32.452 and 66.982. Several clan members captured by Taliban in early October. Rescued by sole Tajik named Ahmed. Tajik seriously wounded in subsequent battle. Last known hiding in cave complex ten kilometers to west of current position. Likely dead. In route with guide. Beacon activated, frequency red 174.4."

"Son-of-a-bitch," Stone blurted, as he pressed in behind Jenson's chair. "Now the Tajik's rescuing Pashtun. No doubt about it, this guy's a freakin' lunatic. Where does that put them on the map?"

Jenson pulled out one of the white pushpins and replaced it with a red one.

"Right about there. Ten kilometers to the west would put the caves somewhere near here," he said, as he stuck in another red pin a short distance from the first. "That's some really rough country. It will probably take them three to four hours to get there. Let's see. The message was transmitted at oh-nine-forty hours."

"What's our plan?" Stone queried, as he glanced at his watch.

"It's ten hundred hours now. That gives us just enough time to organize a patrol, get them into the helicopters, and meet up with Savage by fourteen hundred hours. Unfortunately, all of our operatives are off in Khost."

Jenson handed the memo back to Peters.

"Peters, tell the pilots to get two Chinooks and two Apaches ready! We need to lift off by eleven thirty hours. Brief Captain Connor on the message. Ask him to get fifty of his Delta guys together. They need to be fully armed with night vision gear. Tell them its still damned cold at the target area."

"Yes, sir. Right away, sir."

"Then call air command and give them the coordinates. Tell Harper we need a Warthog over the area by thirteen hundred hours."

"I'll take care of it, sir."

Peters scurried off toward the opposite end of the command center. Jenson watched him disappear through the open door. He turned to Stone.

"You want to come along?"

"Are you serious? Just try to keep me away!"

"You'll need to wear a bullet-proof vest."

"You got two?"

Blake chuckled and shook his head.

"Let's get your gear ready."

The landing pad was abuzz with activity by twelve thirty hours.

Crewmembers were stowing ammunition and supplies in two Chinook transport helicopters. Mechanics and other ground personnel were swarming over three attack helicopters and both transports. American soldiers in camouflage battle gear filed into one of the giant Chinooks. A group of Afghan Mujaheddin were climbing into the other. Jenson and Waverly strode up to Lieutenant Anton wearing heavy camouflage parkas."

"How's it going, Bill? Where's Captain Connor?"

"He's got the flu, but we're just about ready. Shouldn't be more than ten minutes. We couldn't rustle up more than thirty from A-group. The rest of them are off on that operation near Khost. I don't expect them back until tomorrow."

"Do you think that's enough men, Bill?"

"We have sixty Mujaheddin coming with us. They're good soldiers. This outfit's been fighting beside us ever since operation Anaconda. We've also got three Apaches coming along. I spoke with air command. They're sending two Warthogs. They'll be over the area before we are. That's enough to handle anything they can throw at us."

"I guess it'll have to be. Bill, this is Special Agent Stone Waverly. He's in charge of the CIA operation."

"How's it going, Waverly?"

"Fine. Good to meet you. Lieutenant, we're looking for a Tajik man who may be carrying a dangerous biological weapon. It's possible he's hidden it somewhere in these caves. This is a targeted vector that's unlikely to infect Americans, but it could be deadly to any Pashtun. Are the Mujaheddin equipped for biological warfare?"

"Yes, sir. They all are."

"That's good. Now this vector could be anywhere. It's very important for me to take this man alive. We may never find the vector if we kill him. Do you understand?"

"Yes, sir. I'll pass the word to the men not to use deadly force unless absolutely necessary. You two better travel with me in the lead transport."

The lieutenant strode away toward the Chinook.

"Damn," Jenson muttered, just loud enough for Stone to hear.

"What's wrong, Blake?"

"Nothing. It'll be fine. The lieutenant's just one card shy of a full deck."

"Great," Stone murmured with a shake of his head.

Waverly and Jenson jumped up into the giant bird. All of the soldiers were already strapped into their seats. Two gunners manning fifty-caliber machine guns were at their positions.

The two CIA operatives ducked into seats near the front and buckled their harnesses. Lieutenant Anton vaulted through the door and slid it shut behind him. He banged his fist against the fuselage, as he leapt into one of the seats.

"Okay. Let's go, Mac."

The engines whined and the rotors began to spin. The helicopter lifted off the landing pad and banked toward the North. It only took a couple of minutes to reach cruising altitude. Lieutenant Anton pulled down a microphone and hollered over the PA system.

"Men, we'll be arriving at the target area in thirty minutes. This is Mr. Jenson and Mr. Waverly from the CIA. They have reason to believe there's a Tajik carrying a biological weapon where we're heading. Now, as I understand it, this vector was specially designed to infect Pashtun, but not Americans or Tajiks. Is that right, Mr. Waverly?"

Stone nodded.

"I conferred with the Pashtun commander. His men will play a supporting role on this mission. First, we'll locate the caves. Then the Mujaheddin will guard our rear while we secure the caves. It's very important we take this guy alive. There will be absolutely no deadly force. Use stun grenades if you're threatened. Do you understand?"

"Yes sir!" the men barked in unison.

"Good. Now sit back and enjoy the ride. Turn on your communicators as soon as we land. Our first objective will be to secure the area around the landing site when we set down."

Jenson monitored his hand-held GPS the entire flight. There was a green blip on the screen identified by longitudinal and latitudinal coordinates. The blip got closer and closer to the center, as the chopper flew further north. Blake pushed a button labeled zoom, and the graphic zoomed in to show greater detail. The blip moved a little farther from the center of the screen. Blake called out the destination coordinates to the pilot.

"Five minutes to touchdown," the pilot bellowed over the PA.

Lieutenant Anton pulled down his microphone.

"Okay, men, activate your communicators the moment we hit the ground. Remember, hold your fire until you hear my orders."

Jenson fetched a hand-held communicator from his belt, turned it on, and held it up to his ear.

"Stargazer, this is Mother Goose. Can you read me?"

Jenson listened for a moment.

"Yes stargazer, I hear you loud and clear. Anything going on down there?"

He listened and nodded.

"Okay. Hold your position, stargazer. Find a clearing and secure the perimeter. You should hear our rotors in two to three minutes. Mother Goose out."

Blake reattached the communicator to his belt.

"Everything's quiet. They're at 32.410-66.885 near the bottom of a steep climb up to the caves. Savage says it's too steep and exposed to bring the choppers in at the top. We'll have to hike up."

The lieutenant nodded and sat back in his seat. He lifted his rifle and checked the safety.

"Thirty seconds," the pilot called over the PA.

Stone looked out the window. Suddenly, the side of the mountain jumped into view. The chopper spun in a sweeping descent. It set down hard in a wide clearing and one of the gunners threw the door open. Lieutenant Anton jumped to the ground.

"Move it!" he shouted above the engines.

Within seconds, all of the Delta Force troops filed out behind him and dispersed in all directions away from the helicopter.

"Hedges, monitor red 174.4," Jenson yelled to the pilot. "Don't wander off too far."

The pilot nodded and signaled with his hand. Jenson jumped down to the ground and Waverly followed. They ran behind Lieutenant Anton toward a formation of rocks thirty meters from the helicopter. Stone shielded his eyes from the sun as he ran, glancing skyward at two Apache helicopters circling above them. He looked back just as the Chinooks lifted off the ground.

Lieutenant Anton and Blake Jenson were looking at a map with a man dressed in a camouflage parka and pants. A middle-aged Afghani was standing with them. He was wearing a turban and white chupan over a jacket and trousers. Jenson looked up.

"Stone, this is Ed Savage. He sent the message about the Tajik. This is his guide, Mohammed."

Stone nodded.

"Good work, Ed. What have you got for us?"

Savage pointed toward a steep slope in front of them.

"The caves are at the top of those switchbacks. It looks like a tough climb with a lot of exposure."

Stone scanned up the switchbacks. Most of the snow was gone. Just a few mounds were visible.

"At least it's dry. This is the best weather we've had since I arrived in Afghanistan."

The lieutenant held up his hand for silence and turned to listen to his communicator.

"The area's secure. No sign of the enemy. I ordered the Delta unit up the switchbacks with a Mujaheddin patrol. Let's go."

The men jumped down from the rocky perch and headed for the trail. More than fifty men started up the steep incline advancing from one switchback to the next. One group provided cover as another ran for higher ground. Several of the Mujaheddin were in the lead. Stone followed Anton to the first turn.

After the first few switchbacks, the grade suddenly steepened. Waverly and Stone lagged behind with the lieutenant, huffing and puffing.

Stone caught up with the lieutenant about a third of the way up the cliff. He held Anton back for a moment until he could catch his breath.

"Lieutenant," he puffed, "the Pashtun must not approach the caves."

"Don't worry, Waverly. They'll stop shy of the top. I made that clear to their commander."

Blake Jenson stepped up behind Stone and patted him on the back.

"Relax, Stone, everything's under control. If Ahmed Jan is up there, we'll find him."

Stone nodded his head and managed a weary smile.

Ahmed bent over and thrust the end of the bar against the rock. The expanding hole in the boulder was more than thirty centimeters across. He dropped the rod and ducked his head into the tunnel. He pressed forward as far as he could, before pulling his head out.

"I can almost squeeze my shoulders through. Just a little more."

"Ahmed, let me move more rock out of the way."

Shakiba knelt to her hands and knees. She dragged rocky debris back into the cavern and cleared it off to the side. She scooted out of the way, as Ahmed lifted the bar. He repeatedly hammered the end against the inside of the tunnel. He stopped to briefly catch his breath, before starting in again. A large chunk of rock gave way on the third blow. It rolled back into the infirmary.

"Praise Allah. That should do it."

Ahmed bent down and struggled to lift the heavy rock out of the tunnel. He stooped down on all fours and squeezed his head and torso into the tunnel. It was still tight, but he slipped through to the other side.

It was much colder outside the cavern. As Ahmed scrambled to his feet, the foul odor of rotting flesh enveloped him. He pinched his nostrils.

Three decaying bodies were lying against the wall a few meters from the tunnel. The facial features were decomposed beyond recognition, but Ahmed flashed back to the brown Chitrali hat Shakiba's father wore the first night.

"Shakiba, stay there until I make sure it's safe. Pass me the Kalashnikov and my parka."

Shakiba shoved the parka out first. The rifle followed a few moments later.

"Where are you going, Ahmed? Please don't leave me!"

"I'll be right back. Let me make sure it's safe before you come out."

Ahmed slipped on the parka and headed for the light at the mouth of the cave. Rifle in hand, he stumbled outside into the bright sunlight. He shielded his eyes against the brilliant rays, but reveled in their warmth.

It was below freezing, but there was only a wisp of wind. A sensation of intense liberation and revitalization sweep over him. They were free after more than four months of confinement. He dropped the rifle. spread his arms before the sun, and shouted.

"There is but one God and Mohammed is his prophet."

Ahmed heard the distant whine of an engine. It sounded like a helicopter. He shielded his eyes to search the sky, but couldn't make out the source. His eyes tracked down to the ridge toward the east. The adjacent peak soared more than a thousand meters above him. He scanned down the trail from the cave entrance to the three switchbacks at the top of the slope. All was quiet.

Ahmed ducked back into the cave. He bent down before the tunnel.

"Shakiba, are you there?"

"Yes, Ahmed! I'm so excited! I can barely control myself. Can I come out?"

"Gather the things you want to carry out and put them in my backpack. Wait for me to call you."

"Okay. I want to take a few clothes, Fariba Mohammad's CD, and the book of poetry. What's it like?"

"It's so beautiful! The sun is shining, but it's cold. Bring your coat. Pass me a towel."

Shakiba tossed the towel through the tunnel. Ahmed tied the towel across his nose and mouth and plodded toward the first corpse. He leaned the Kalashnikov against the wall of the cave, picked up the Chitrali cap, and tossed it onto the first torso. He grabbed both ankles. The body was frozen stiff.

Ahmed dragged the corpse out of the cave along the muddy trail that led to the lookout post. He dropped Mahmud's legs at the edge of the cliff and rolled the corpse over the edge. The body tumbled through the air for five- or six-hundred meters before landing in a snowy crevice far below.

Ahmed pulled the towel from his face, leaned over with his hands on his knees, and gasped for air. It took him several minutes to catch his breath. Finally, he turned and slogged back along the trail toward the cave entrance.

Stone, head down, followed the switchback around a bend and headed up yet another steep incline. He looked up and froze in his tracks. Several soldiers were crouched behind a boulder looking up toward a ridge a couple hundred meters above them. A few Mujaheddin were with them. Stone rushed ahead to Blake Jenson's position behind an earthen knoll and knelt beside him on the ground. Blake had his binoculars trained on the ridge. Stone shielded his eyes and peered into the distance. A lone figure was trudging along the ridgeline. Blake held out the binoculars.

"Take a look," he whispered.

Stone lifted the binoculars up to his eyes. It was a man with an aquiline nose clutching a cloth in his hand. Stone zoomed in on his face. It was the Tajik. He was emaciated, but it was unquestionably Ahmed Jan.

"It's him, Blake," he whispered.

Stone zoomed out and scanned along the ridge to the cave. He peered at the mouth of the cave for a moment and scanned back along the ridgeline. A rifle shot rang out at the instant Ahmed Jan came back into his view. The Tajik clutched his chest, dropped to his knees, and collapsed face down on the ground.

"God damn it!" Stone bellowed. "Who did that?"

Lieutenant Anton jerked the Kalashnikov away from one of the Mujaheddin a few meters ahead of them and tossed it away. Stone pulled himself to his feet and sprinted up the trail.

"Son-of-a-bitch, Anton! What the hell are you doing? I told you not to shoot him!"

The lieutenant threw up his hands in exasperation.

"I ordered them not to shoot. This meathead claims he pulled the trigger by accident."

Stone was beside himself with anger.

"Get them the hell out of here! I only want you to use Delta troops from this point on. Shit! Damn it! I knew it!"

Blake Jenson jogged up behind them.

"Stone, there's nothing we can do about it now. Let's get the hell up there."

Ahmed pulled himself along the ground toward the cave entrance. Moaning with pain and hyperventilating, he pressed his palm against his right breast to stem the bleeding. He managed to struggle to his feet and stagger into the cave. He knelt to the ground, wormed his body through the tunnel, and rolled into the infirmary.

Shakiba was cinching down the last clasp on the backpack. She looked up and caught sight of the blood soaking through Ahmed's parka. She screamed and rushed to his side, her hands clutched to her face.

"Oh Allah! Ahmed! Oh my Ahmed!" she cried with anguish.

Ahmed's face was pale and sweat beaded on his forehead. His breathing was shallow and labored. He grimaced and opened his eyes. Shakiba knelt beside him and cradled his head in her arms.

"No, Allah, no! Please! Not like this! Not after all we've been through! Oh, Ahmed."

Ahmed looked up and tried to speak. He could only muster a weak groan.

"Ahmed, let me help you to the back."

Shakiba rolled Ahmed over on his stomach and helped him to his knees. He stood up and draped his arm over her shoulders. They stumbled through the passageway into the back storeroom.

Shakiba led Ahmed to the bed and helped him onto his back. She covered his body with a blanket and scurried to the boxes of medical supplies on the other side of the cavern. She fetched a bottle of saline and a large bore intravenous needle, before dashing back to the bed.

Shakiba tossed the supplies on the edge of the bed and unzipped Ahmed's bloody parka. She helped him pull his arm from the sleeve. Attaching the line to the bag of saline, she opened the valve to fill the tubing. She tore open an alcohol pad, wiped his forearm, and tied a rubber tourniquet around his upper arm. She jerked the cover off the needle.

Tears flowed from her eyes. She passed the needle beneath the skin until a trickle of blood flowed back into the needle. She inserted the catheter, withdrew the needle, hooked the tubing to the catheter, and let the saline flow wide open. She taped the catheter to his arm.

Ahmed moaned. He opened his eyes and whispered.

"Please, Shakiba, bring me some water."

Shakiba stumbled frantically to the table and filled a plastic cup from a two-liter bottle. She rushed back to the bed, crouched to her knees, and lifted Ahmed's head. He took a few sips and dropped his head back on the pillow. He looked up at her, lifted his quivering hand to her cheek, and struggled to smile.

"I love you, my little songbird."

"Oh Ahmed, I love you too."

Shakiba clutched his head to her bosom and sobbed hysterically. She kissed Ahmed on the forehead and held him close.

"Please don't leave me! Please!" she cried.

Ahmed gurgled and raised his hand to cough. Shakiba pulled his hand away. Bloody foam oozed from his mouth. She wiped his mouth with the corner of the blanket. Ahmed stared up at her and opened his mouth to speak. He stared into Shakiba's eyes and struggled to murmur in a barely audible whisper.

"My desired one, I will await you in paradise."

He closed his eyes, took one more halting breath, and was still.

Shakiba tore at her hair and screamed with unbridled anguish. Mumbling incoherently, she struggled to her knees and crawled to the table. She seized the bottle of barbiturates and tipped out a handful of white capsules. She stuffed the pills in her mouth and gulped them down. She raised the jug of water to her lips and took a drink. She poured another handful of pills into her hand, stuffed them into her mouth, and drank again.

Shakiba dropped the bottle to the ground. Pills scattered across the rocky floor around her knees. She crawled back to the bed and knelt over to kiss Ahmed on the lips. She rolled beside him on the bed, wrapped his arm around her, and closed her eyes.

It took the Delta troops close to half an hour to reach the top of the switchbacks. Lieutenant Anton pointed at one of the men with night vision goggles and then to the cave entrance. It was thirty meters across a barren strip of rocks to the mouth. He pointed to another A-teamer, motioned toward the cave, and thrust his arm against his chest. Anton leaned over and whispered to Stone.

"This'll be a non-lethal stun grenade."

The soldier rose up, took careful aim with a grenade launcher, and pulled the trigger. A bright flash lit up the cave entrance a moment later. The two Delta fighters, machine guns at the ready, sprang from their cover and sprinted across the clearing into the cave. Four other men darted in behind them.

There was an eerie silence for nearly five minutes. The only sound was the intermittent whistle of the wind against the mountain ridge. Stone took a deep breath and glanced over his shoulder at Blake Jenson. Jenson stared back.

Suddenly, one of the A-teamers appeared in the mouth of the cave and signaled the lieutenant. Anton and the CIA operatives darted across the clearing to the mouth of the cave.

"What's the situation, Thomas?" Anton queried.

"We found two dead men in the cave, sir. From the looks of it, they've been there a long time. There are signs of recent excavation outside a narrow tunnel. We're not sure where that goes, but there's light inside. We shouted down the hole, but got no response. Come on, I'll show you."

The cavern was illuminated with battery-powered lanterns set up by the Special Forces. Waverly and Anton scurried up to the tunnel. Anton got down on his hands and knees.

"Turn out the lights."

The soldiers complied and he peered into the hole."

"All I see is a bunch of rubble. Turn the lanterns back on."

Anton leaned over to Stone and whispered.

"I'm going to toss in stun grenades down the hole and send a man inside."

"Let me try something first."

Stone knelt beside the tunnel, cupped his hands around his mouth, and shouted in broken Dari.

"Ahmed Jan, Stone Waverly CIA. Come out for medicine."

He shouted again, but his cries were met with silence. After a few moments, he nodded toward the lieutenant.

The lieutenant motioned to one of the soldiers and then at the cave. The man dropped his backpack and pulled a nine-millimeter semiautomatic pistol from his belt. He knelt beside the tunnel. Anton signaled another soldier. The A-teamer jerked two grenades from his belt, pulled the pins, and lobbed one after the other through the tunnel. A pair of muffled explosions followed a moment later. The soldier wriggled down the tunnel in a heartbeat.

"All clear, Lieutenant," the soldier yelled from the infirmary a few moments later.

The lieutenant dropped his backpack to the ground and bent to his knees. He ducked head first into the tunnel and snaked through to the other side. Waverly and Jenson dropped their packs and followed behind him.

The cavern was filled with rocky debris. A filthy mattress was leaning against one wall. The room was illuminated by a single light bulb. The hum of a generator could be heard coming from the back.

Anton ducked through the passageway, followed by Waverly and Jenson. On the right was a smaller cave with a bed, dresser, and bathtub. There was an electric hot water heater in the corner. Waverly and Jenson followed him into the little grotto. Anton peered under the bed and turned back toward the CIA operatives.

"I can't imagine living in here. It must've been hell."

The three of them stepped back into the passageway and moved toward the rear cavern. One of the soldiers approached them from the back. He pointed to the bed.

"They're both dead. There's a chamber with a deep crevice in the back corner. They've been using it as a head. Otherwise, this is it."

Waverly and Jenson stepped over to the bed and peered down. Ahmed Jan was lying on his back with his eyes open. Blood was pooled on the ground beneath the bed. A young woman was draped across him. She was holding a small, worn, black book in her hand.

Stone rolled the woman over on her side and cleared the hair from her face. Blake Jenson stepped up beside him.

"God, she's beautiful."

"I'll be damned," Stone muttered, "she looks Pashtun."

"I was thinking that myself. I wonder how she died?"

"I'm guessing she killed herself with these pills," Anton called out. "I can't read the label, but there are a bunch of them here on the floor."

Stone picked up the black book and thumbed through a few pages. He handed it to Jenson.

"It looks like a book of poetry written in Dari."

"Stone, if she's Pashtun, Jan must not have released the vector in this cave."

Stone nodded. He pondered for a moment and then whirled toward Anton.

"Lieutenant, can you get Savage's Pashtun guide in here? Make sure he wears a biohazard suit. I want to see if he recognizes this woman. We also need a couple more men to help search this place."

"Sure, I'll take care of it."

Anton walked out through the passageway tunnel. Stone scanned around the cavern.

"This is unbelievable. Look at the generator and that mountain of empty fuel barrels. There must be a thousand empty food cans in that pile over in the back. Whew, the stench is unbearable."

"I wonder how many more of these complexes are scattered around the mountains in Afghanistan. No wonder we haven't found bin Laden and his henchmen."

Stone looked down at the two bodies. He shook his head.

"Damn it! I can't believe they killed him. We were so close!"

Anton stepped through the passageway with two more Delta soldiers and the Pashtun guide dressed in an brown suit. His face was visible through the head panel. Blake Jenson uttered a few words in Pashtu. The man stepped toward the end of the bed and looked down. He grimaced, turned to Jenson, and muttered in Pashtu.

"He thinks she's a woman named Shakiba. She's the clan leader's daughter. He's not sure, because all the women in the clan wear burqas. She stayed behind to care for the Tajik. He heard she's beautiful."

"Okay, tell him he better leave. We're not sure it's safe in here."

Blake Jenson said a few more words to the Pashtun guide and the man retreated through the passageway.

Stone opened the breast pocket on his parka and pulled out a black case. He unsnapped the lid and pulled out a glass ampule. He held it up.

"This is what we're looking for, men. It's a glass ampule. We believe there is another one that looks like this, containing a yellowish-white powder. There may be black writing on the side. The powder should be harmless to anyone who isn't Pashtun, but be careful not to break it anyway. You two men search the front room. There's not much in there, but sift through the rocks with your hands. Lieutenant, you search through that small grotto in the middle."

"No problem, Stone."

"Okay. The rest of you stay in here with us. Go through everything. Jenson and I will search the bodies. You men sift through the rest. Search every empty can and sack. Look inside all the barrels. Just start at one end of the room and go through everything systematically."

The CIA operatives and soldiers went through the cave complex with a fine-toothed comb. It took close to three hours. Stone and Blake didn't find a trace of the ampule on the bodies. They found a few bloodstained papers written in Arabic in a plastic bag in Ahmed Jan's pocket. That was it.

Stone lifted up a rice sack and turned it inside out. He drew the bottom seam between his thumb and index finger. It was empty. He tossed it on a pile with the others he'd searched and picked up another.

"Stone," Jenson barked, "I found something here in the stove."

Waverly struggled to his feet and strode across the cavern. Jenson was on his knees in front of the potbelly stove holding out his hand. His face and arms were caked in soot.

Waverly squatted beside Jenson and peered down at the ash-covered glass ampule lying in his palm. There was a crack along one end and the tip was missing. Smudged black marks were visible on the outside of the vial. A plug of black debris was wedged in the unbroken end. Stone took a deep breath and shook his head.

"I'll be damned!" he sighed. "He just threw the damn thing in the fire."

"From the looks of it, this stove hasn't been used for quite a while. The ashes are cold as ice."

Stone stood up and pulled a plastic bag from his pocket. He opened it wide so Jenson could drop the ampule inside. He sealed the adhesive strip.

Stone fetched a small metal container from his pocket and unscrewed the cap. He rolled up the plastic bag, tucked it inside the cylinder, and screwed the top back on. He stuck it in his pocket.

A bewildered expression lingered on Jenson's face. He shook his head.

"It doesn't make any sense, Stone. The Tajik could have released the vector in Kandahar or even in Pakistan. I don't get it."

Stone turned and gazed down at the Tajik lying on the bed next to the young woman. He carefully folded the woman's hand into Ahmed's and set the book of poetry on the bed between them. Finally, he picked up a blanket and spread it across the bodies.

"You know, Blake, it's perfectly clear to me what happened here."

Stone turned toward Anton.

"Lieutenant, do you have high explosive charges to seal this cave?"

"Yes, sir. The men outside are carrying enough C4 to blow the top off this mountain."

"Leave these two the way they are and seal the mouth of this complex so it can never be opened. Can you do that?"

"Yes, sir. No problem."

Stone patted Blake on the shoulder.

"Come on. Let's go."

The two men strode through the passageway toward the infirmary. Stone squeezed back through the opening into the main cavern with Jenson right behind him. They made their way out the mouth of the cave into the bright sunlight. Stone took a deep breath and scanned the vista below.

"You got any of that Johnny Walker Blue left back at the base, Blake?"

Blake grinned and patted Stone on the back.

"I think there may be a couple shots left."

"Good. I'll give the director a call and then join you in a drink while I wait for transport back to the aircraft carrier."

EPILOGUE

Five years later

F atima took a sip of iced tea and set it back on the picnic table. She glanced across the table at Mustafa and smiled. He was wearing a pair of reading glasses and thumbing through the Sunday edition of the *Santa Fe New Mexican*. The glasses gave him the look of a scholar.

She shielded her eyes against the bright summer sun and scanned across the small one-story stucco rambler they called home. Fatima took a deep breath and sighed contentedly. She reached across and patted Mustafa on the arm.

"What's that you're reading, darling?"

"This American game baseball makes no sense to me. I watched it for a while on the television last night. Look at this picture."

He held the newspaper for Fatima.

"This player wears a special padded outfit with a wire mask. His job is to squat down and let the other player throw balls at him as hard as he can. This third guy tries to hit the ball with a long club before it hits the fellow in the mask. If the man hits the ball, he runs around in a circle while the other players throw the ball at him. It's a strange game."

"Mustafa, can I ask you something?"

Mustafa set the paper down on the table.

"What is it, Fatima?"

"Do you miss Afghanistan?"

Mustafa took a sip of iced tea and leaned back in his chair. He looked out over the small front yard. Two small boys were playing in a sandbox at the front of the sandy lot. The smaller boy was shoveling sand with a plastic shovel while the older boy held a bucket.

"I guess there are some things I miss about my country. I miss the rugged beauty of the soaring mountains. I miss a good game of Buzkashi."

He swelled with pride and patted Fatima on the back of the hand.

"Did I ever tell you? I was one of the finest Buzkashi horsemen in all of the North. Once I carried the carcass around the marker to the scoring circle myself. That was a great honor for one so young. Then the Taliban banned the game."

Mustafa took another sip of tea as he watched the children.

"I don't miss the blood feuds and fighting and killing. I don't miss those things at all. Here our sons live in peace. They'll have opportunities in this country they'd never have in Afghanistan."

Mustafa set his glass down and leaned back in his lawn chair. His thoughts drifted back to another time and another place.

They sat in silence for several minutes, each engrossed in private thoughts. Suddenly, Fatima sat up in her chair and reached out to grasp Mustafa's arm.

"Mustafa, I want to become an American citizen."

Mustafa looked up with surprise. He crossed his arms across his chest and thought for a moment.

"An American citizen," he repeated.

"Would you support me in this, Mustafa?"

Mustafa glanced across the yard. The younger boy had climbed out of the sand box. He was crawling toward the street.

"Nadir, grab your brother!" Mustafa shouted.

The older boy jumped out of the sandbox. He grabbed his brother's arm and pulled him away from the curb.

Mustafa and Fatima walked out to meet them. Fatima lifted the toddler into her arms, patted him on the head, and headed back toward the porch. Mustafa picked up Nadir with one arm and wrapped his other arm around Fatima. On the pourch, Mustafa pulled the screen door open and followed Fatima into the house.

"Nadir, guess what Mommy and Daddy are going to do?"

The little boy gazed up at Mustafa with big brown eyes.

"Give me a present?"

Mustafa smiled down at Nadir and then at Fatima.

"Well yes, in a way, I guess we are going to give you a present. We're all going to become Americans, just like your little brother Ahmed."

First impressions rarely hold true.
The wise discount them.

STEVEN E. WILSON, is a cornea and refractive surgeon and scientist with an international reputation and has been published in more than two hundred medical and scientific publications. *Winter in Kandahar* is his first published work of fiction.

Originally from Whittier, California, the author was educated at California State University, Fullerton (B.A. Biology, 1974) and the University of California at Irvine (MS Molecular Biology and Biochemistry, 1977). He received his M.D. degree from University of California at San Diego in 1984, took his residency in ophthalmology at the Mayo Clinic in Rochester, and his fellowship in Cornea and Refractive Surgery at the LSU Eye Center in New Orleans. Dr. Wilson served on the faculties at the University of Texas Southwestern (1990–1995) and the Cleveland Clinic Foundation (1995–1998) and was Professor and Chair of Ophthalmology at the University of Washington (1998–2003). He is currently Director of Corneal Research and Staff in corneal surgery and refractive surgery at the Cole Eye Institute of the Cleveland Clinic Foundation.

Steven Wilson is currently at work on a new novel, *Ascent from Darkness*.

If you have enjoyed *Winter in Kandahar,*
please consider leaving a review at Amazon.com.

We invite you to visit Hailey-Grey-Books.com
for background information on this book
and other titles from Hailey-Grey Books.